VIEW OF GALLIPOLIS FROM CEMETERY HILL LOOKING EASTWARD, OCTOBER, 1890.

OHIO

Archæological and Historical

PUBLICATIONS.

Volume III.

WILDSIDE PRESS

INDEX.

	PAGE
Annual Meeting, Fifth, Proceedings of	236
Annual Meeting, Sixth, Proceedings of	261
Bradbury Horace R. Address of	26
Brush Dr. E. C., Address of	241
Burnham Major John and His Company	40
Campbell Governor James E., Address of	161
Centennial Anniversary, Proceedings of	1
Century and its Lessons, The	27
Davis Rev. J. M., Address of	164
Dawes E. C., Address of	40
Divine Workmanship, Rejoicing in, Sermon	227
Educational Lessons of the Hour	168
Farrar Wm. M., Address of	276
Fort Ancient, Description of	313
French Settlement and Settlers of Gallipolis	45
Gladden Rev. Washington, Sermon of	178
Graham A. A., Paper by	300
Jones J. V., Address of	175
Judiciary, Laws and Bar of Ohio	141
Lasher Rev. George W., Sermon of	227
Marshall R. D., Address of	172
Methodist Success, Philosophy of, Sermon	196
Methodism in Gallipolis, History of	206
Migrations and their Lessons, Sermon	178
Military Posts, Forts and Battlefields in Ohio	300
Moncure Rev. John, Sermon of	221
Moore Rev. David H., Sermon of	196
Moorehead Warren K., Paper by	313
Moravian Massacre, The	276
Morrison Prof. N. J., Address of	27
Muskingum Valley, Pioneer Physicians of	241
Ohio Arch. and Hist. Society Act of Incorporation	319
Synopsis of By-Laws	320
Board of Trustees	320
Officers of	321
Honorary Members	322
Corresponding Members	322
Life Members	322
Active Members	323
Annual Meetings	241–276

PAGE

Ohio, Description of, in 1788...................... 82
Pioneer Physicians, Muskingum Valley............. 241
Presbyterians of Ohio, Sermon...................... 211
Remember the Days of Old, Sermon................. 221
Relic Room, Gallipolis, Articles in................. 19
Reports Secretary 266
   Treasurer 270
   Trustees 269
Rio Grande College, History of.................... 164
Ryan Daniel J., Address of........................ 109
Secretary, Report of.............................. 266
Scioto Company and its Purchase.................. 109
Scovil Rev. S. F., Sermon of...................... 211
Thompson, Rev. H. A., Address of................. 168
Treasurer, Report of.............................. 270
Trustees, Report of............................... 269
Trustees, Meeting of.............................. 236–269
Vance John L., Address of......................... 45
Watson David K., Address of...................... 141

ILLUSTRATIONS.

Barlow Joel Portrait.....................Facing page 115
Cabins built 1791 by Maj. John Burnham...... page 42
Gallipolis, View of, 1890.................... Frontispiece
Gallipolis, Public Square, Centennial Day....Facing page 17
Gallipolis, Public Square, 1790..............Facing page 40
Gallipolis, Public Square, 1846..............Facing page 40
Gallipolis, Plat of, 1791 .... page 61
Monument, Gnadenhutten..................Facing page 279
Portrait, Joel Barlow.......................Facing page 115
Portrait, Samuel F. Vinton..................Facing page 141
Rio Grande College.........................Facing page 164
Vinton, Samuel F., Portrait.................Facing page 141

MAPS.

Fort Ancient................................. page 312
Gallipolis, Map of, 1791..................... page 61
Military Posts, Forts and Battlefields in Ohio..Facing page 306
Ohio Company's Proposed Purchase.......... page 117
Ohio and Scioto Companies Purchases........ page 121
Scioto Company, (French map)............. page 124

PREFACE.

THE present volume is the third issued by this Society. The first and second were issued in pamphlet form, quarterly, but many members expressing a preference for the publication in bound (annual) form, this volume is so issued. Should this form seem best, it will be continued.

Some delay has been experienced owing to serious illness on the part of three of those whose papers are among the best in the volume. This has necessarily delayed the publication several months beyond the regular time of issue, a delay which could not be avoided.

In addition to the anniversary exercises in connection with the Centennial of the settlement of Gallipolis, the volume contains the proceedings of the Society for two years, and several papers prepared for the annual meetings of these years, as well as the Act of Incorporation, a synopsis of the By-Laws, and a complete list of the members from the organization of the Society until the present time. The Society has been in existence five years, and few societies can show so good a growth and better results. The volumes now issued are sufficient evidence of the work already done, and of that before us. The next volume will contain a full history of the boundary questions between Virginia and Ohio, together with a full discussion of the claims of Virginia to the territory north of the Ohio River. It is also intended to include in this volume a discussion of the boundaries between Ohio and Indiana and between

Ohio and Michigan. This volume has been in contemplation for some time, and it may be expected next.

The publications of this Society now consist of volumes one, two and three, issued during the years 1886–1887, 1888–1889 and 1890–1891. These volumes are not for sale, but are sent free to members. Each volume may be obtained by the payment of the annual membership fee—$5.00. Life membership is $50.00, entitling to all publications, and such membership are exempt from all dues.

The State is now indebted to the Ohio Archæological and Historical Society, for three valuable historical volumes, and if the Society had done nothing else its existence is more than justified.

A. A. GRAHAM, *Secretary*,

Columbus, Ohio.

PREFATORY NOTE.

The first edition of this volume, published in 1891, having been exhausted, in response to continued demands for copies of the same, the Legislature of Ohio of '93–94 appropriated the sum of five hundred dollars to be used by the Society in defraying the expense of republication. The original edition was published under the direction of Mr. A. A. Graham, at that time Secretary of the Society, and is now reprinted as it first appeared, without alteration.

Mr. Graham tendered his resignation as Secretary, to the Trustees of the Society, in the fall of 1894, which was accepted and the subscriber hereto was then elected to fill the vacancy.

It should be stated, also, that at the annual meeting of the Socie held February, 1895, a new constitution was adopted by which the annual membership fee was reduced from five to three dollars, and the life membership fee from fifty to twenty-five dollars.

The new constitution will appear in full in volume IV, which will be published during the present year (1895).

E. O. RANDALL,

Secretary.

Columbus, Ohio, April, 1895.

PROCEEDINGS

OF THE

CENTENNIAL ANNIVERSARY

OF THE CITY OF

GALLIPOLIS, OHIO.

October 16, 17, 18 and 19, 1890.

PRELIMINARY ARRANGEMENTS.

As early as April, 1890, the citizens of Gallipolis, through their Board of Trade, took action to secure a proper celebration of the approaching centennial of the city's settlement. On April 22, 1890, at a meeting of the Board of Trade, the following named gentlemen were elected an Executive Committee of arrangements:

John L. Vance, Chairman; C. Fred Henking, W. B. Shober, H. R. Bradbury, Joseph Mullineux, J. A. McClurg, Geo. House, J. C. Hutsinpiller, C. W. Henking, Dr. J. Eakins, B. F. Barlow, P. A. Sanns, J. C. Priestley, B. T. Enos, E. L. Menager, C. D. Kerr, J. M. Kerr, S. A. Dunbar, A. W. Kerns, W. Kling, A. Ufermann, Charles Regnier.

The organization of the Committee was completed by the selection of the following named gentlemen to the positions stated:

Vice-Chairman — B. F. Barlow.
Secretary — H. R. Bradbury.
Treasurer — C. W. Henking.

The meetings of the Committee were held at the Auditor's office, the use of which was tendered by A. W. Kerns.

The Committee at its first meeting, tendered an invitation to the General Assembly of Ohio to be present at the Centennial, which invitation was presented to the House of Representatives by Hon. J. Eakins, a member of the House from Gallia County. The invitation was accepted by the General Assembly, and arrangements made by the members of that body to attend.

On the evening of April 28th the Executive Committee met and appointed a Sub-Committee to confer with the Ohio Archæological and Historical Society in regard to the Centennial celebration: Hon. J. Eakins, Wm. B. Shober, C. F. Henking, J. A. McClurg, H. R. Bradbury, Jos. Mullineux, and John L. Vance.

Messrs. B. F. Barlow, William Kling, A. W. Kerns, J. M. Kerr and B. T. Enos were also appointed a committee to suggest names and duties of sub-committees.

The first named committee went to Columbus, May 12th, and the next day met the Executive Committee of the Archæological and Historical Society, and after a conference, a committee consisting of H. R. Bradbury, Jon. L. Vance, C. F. Henking, F. C. Sessions, and A. A. Graham was appointed to prepare a programme for the Centennial. This committee met in Gallipolis, Saturday, June 7th, and arranged a provisional programme, and assigned to John L. Vance and A. A. Graham the duty to arrange the details necessary to its completion, and authorized them to make such alterations and additions as might be necessary for the final programme.

Steps were now taken by the Society and the Gallipolis committee to secure in permanent form the papers, addresses and proceedings of the Centennial in volume third of the Historical Society's publications. The Secretary of the Society was authorized to prepare a circular setting forth the proposed contents of the volume, and to secure a subscription thereto from the people of Gallipolis. In pursuance of this action, the following circular was prepared and submitted to a meeting of the Board of Trade of Gallipolis the evening of Friday, June 20th, and a subscription of 150 copies of the publication secured. The circular is as follows:

THE OHIO ARCHÆOLOGICAL AND HISTORICAL SOCIETY. CIR-
CULAR OF INFORMATION NO. 2, 1890. THE
PUBLICATIONS FOR 1890.

The Centennial of the Settlement of Gallipolis, Ohio, will
occur October 19th, next. It will then be one hundred years
since the colony of French emigrants landed on the northern
bank of "La Belle River."

This settlement, the only one of its kind in Ohio, bears no
little impress on our history, and merits more than merely a Centennial celebration. Its history contains not only the location of
the colony, and the founding of a town, but also carries with it
many questions of national interest. Made about the opening
of the French Revolution, when the attention of all Europe was
drawn to the questions of civil and religious liberty; and when
the minds of men were easily turned to any solution of the problems then agitating mankind, there clusters about this settlement
many interesting and instructive questions in our early annals.
The scheme of locating a foreign colony upon land in an American wilderness, obtained from the Government through organized
land companies was watched by many, not only in Europe, but
also in America. It was not merely local interest; the attention
of nations was drawn thither.

The history of this colony, the formation of the Ohio and
Scioto Land Companies, both more or less interested in its success, and the relation each bore to the other, with a concise history of their transactions so far as they relate to this colony, will
appear in this volume. Original maps, plats, drawings and documents will be used to illustrate the text. The "French Grant"
will be carefully and fully described, and such plats and maps, as
will elucidate the text, will be used.

The story of the French emigrants will be faithfully given,
and as far as possible a complete list of the first settlers will be
printed. Plats and plans, views and portraits, as far as can be
obtained, will be used to illustrate the work.

The volume will therefore not be merely an account of the
exercises commemorative of the Centennial. It will be a history

of the colony, and a careful digest of the questions pertinent thereto.

The work when published will be somewhat similar to that issued in 1888, *i. e.*, "The Marietta Centennial of April 7th," save that this will be a bound volume, and will be the Society's publication for 1890. Like all publications of the Society, the volume is not for general circulation. Members of the Society will be supplied, and additional copies will be printed only for exchanges, societies, and for those who request them.

Several thousand copies of this circular were issued and sent liberally to all parts of the country, and through the Board of Trade at Gallipolis, were freely distributed there.

On August 19th, the Board of Trade appointed the following committees on detail work:

ADVERTISING.

P. T. Wall, Chairman; I. F. Chapman, Theo. N. Wilson, Chas. D. Kerr, S. A. McClurg.

AMUSEMENTS.

Thos. R. Hayward, Chairman; J. Will Clendinen, N. R. Canaday, P. T. Wall, A. L. Roadarmour, C. B. Hanson, Geo. D. McIntyre, C. H. Small, H. C. Johnston, Jas. W. Gardner.

ATHLETICS.

Arthur Williams, Chairman; Henry Neal, Fred Kling.

BADGES.

Ralph C. Jones, Chairman; C. C. Olmstead, Frank Moore.

DECORATIONS.

O. M. Henking, Chairman; Chas. W. Uhrig, C. H. McCormick, Dr. F. A. Cromley, Ed. W. Vanden, Ross Williams, A. R. Weaver, Frank Ulsamer, W. B. Fuller, B. Frank Barlow, A. A. Lyon, J. C. Staats, C. F. Hudlin, C. A. Smith, C. M. Adams, Samuel T. Cook, S. D. Cowden, J. Will Clendinen, Chas.

Gentry, Jas. H. Sanns, S. A. Rathburn, Charles Johnston, Aaron Frank.

DRINKING WATER.

C. W. Ernsting, Chairman; E. T. Moore, J. H. Frank, Fred H. Kerr, E. Lincoln Neal, John Pepple, B. L. Gardner, A. Moch, J. M. Smith, Frank Bell, Jos. Ziegler, G. W. Cox, Paul Dober, Dr. J. R. Safford, Geo. W. Alexander, E. L. Menager, J. C. Shepard, C. J. Schreck, J. S. Billups, Henry House, Chas. F. Jenny, Alvin Brown.

ENTERTAINMENT.

John C. Hutsinpiller, Chairman; J. H. Schaaf, Charles Stuart, S. F. Crane, C. H. D. Summer, Henry Gilman, W. G. Fuller, A. J. Greene, Dr. John Sanns, Henry R. Bell, Henry Beall.

FIREWORKS.

E. E. Gatewood, Chairman; Thomas R. Hayward, J. A. Blazer, A. B. Williams, C. Fred Henking, Geo. N. Bolles, M. S. Hern.

GROUNDS AND SUPPLIES.

Geo. House, Chairman; Jos. F. Martin, A. F. Lasley, John Lupton, James H. McClurg, W. H. Billings, W. R. White.

HORSES AND CARRIAGES.

W. C. Hayward, Chairman; James G. Priestley, Frank Hutsinpiller, Geo. Wetherholt, Charles C. Baker.

HOTELS, BOARDING HOUSES, ETC.

W. H. Hutchinson, Chairman; J. C. Morris, Creuzet Vance, Frank Ulsamer, J. W. Gardner, J. L. Hayward, Chas. Jenny, John C. Graham, Amos Troth, A. A. Lyon, Ed. Gills, Chris. C. Mack.

INTELLIGENCE.

John C. Vanden, Chairman; A. F. Moore, Chas. Mack, C. W. Bird, Frank J. Donnally.

LIGHT.

Jas. A. McClurg, Chairman; C. W. Henking, C. D. Kerr, B. T. Enos, F. W. Dages, S. Witham, Chas. Stockhoff.

MUSIC—INSTRUMENTAL.

James H. Sanns, Chairman; Geo. D. McBride, L. B. Shaw.

MUSIC—VOCAL.

Jas. M. Neal, Chairman; D. W. Jones, Gus Mack, Dr. Jas. T. Hanson, J. E. Matthews, John R. McCormick, E. S. Aleshire, G. A. Roedell, F. O. Fowler, Wm. Mullinuex, T. P. Williams, F. M. Snead.

MILITARY DISPLAY.

C. H. McCormick, Chairman; Silas Pritchett, E. S. Aleshire, A. G. Beall, D. W. Jones, Geo. D. McBride, H. R. Bradbury, Chas. Weihe.

PRESS.

William Nash, Chairman; D. W. Jones, John L. Vance, jr., H. LeClercq Ford, J. E. Robinson, J. D. Olmsted.

PROGRAMME.

F. C. Sessions, Chairman; A. A. Graham, John L. Vance, H. R. Bradbury, Jehu Eakins.

RAILROAD AND RIVER TRANSPORTATION.

W. B. Shober, Chairman; John R. McCormick, H. W. Ellis, S. M. Cherrington, P. A. Sanns, John Nevius, Miles H. Brown, W. A. Barrows, S. Silverman, F. J. Donnally, Geo. W. Bay.

RECEPTION.

John M. Alexander, Chairman; Geo. House, James Mullineux, W. H. McCormick, C. D. Maxon, P. A. Sanns, W. C. Hayward, James Harper, A. Ufermann, Dr. E. W. Parker, G. B. Little, Dr. H. C. Brown, D. B. Hebard, Frank Cromley,

James Gatewood, Alexander Vance, Wm. C. Miller, M. C. Barlow, John L. Kuhn, R. D. Neal, D. S. Ford, H. N. Ford, C. Doepping, H. H. McGonagle, Joseph Mullineux, S. R. Bush, C. A. Clendinen, Charles Mack, Dr. P. Gardner, Albert Mossman, Daniel Calohan, Eliza Smith, E. Betz, C. C. Welbert, C. D. Bailey, John Dages, James Vanden.

SABBATH PROGRAMME.

Rev. P. A. Baker, Chairman; Rev. John Moncure, Rev. C. A. McManis, Rev. R. H. Coulter, Rev. Father Oeink, W. L. Robinson, H. N. Ford, A. J. Greene, W. G. Bradley, Jos. F. Hund.

SANITARY.

William Kling, Chairman; A. Henking, J. C. Priestley, Dr. James Johnson, C. A. Hill.

SCHOOLS.

T. W. Karr, Chairman; D. B. Hebard, Dr. John Sanns, Dr. E. G. Alcorn, A. L. Roadarmour.

STEAMBOAT EXCURSION.

S. A. Dunbar, Chairman; R. L. Hamilton, John W. Holloway, Chas. Regnier, John Damron, M. V. Nelson.

TENTS AND AMPHITHEATRE.

A. W. Kerns, Chairman; Jas. Mullineux, Jr., S. F. Neal, P. B. Pritchett.

TO FORM TOWNSHIP COMMITTEES.

I. F. Chapman, Chairman; W. T. Minturn, A. W. Kerns, V. H. Switzer. W. R. White.

LADIES' RECEPTION COMMITTEE.

The following ladies were appointed a Committee to prepare a suitable reception for the Governors, their Staff officers, State officers, members of the Legislature, and other distinguished guests:

Mrs. C. Fred. Henking,	Mrs. J. E. Robinson,
Mrs. H. R. Bradbury,	Mrs. W. B. Shober,
Mrs. B. F. Barlow,	Mrs. P. A. Sanns,
Mrs. W. G. Brading,	Mrs. Sam'l Silverman,
Mrs. Josephine Cadot,	Mrs. J. H. Sanns,
Mrs. F. A. Cromley,	Mrs. J. C. Shephard,
Mrs. S. A. Dunbar,	Mrs. J. M. Smith,
Mrs. B. T. Enos,	Mrs. John L. Vance,
Mrs. W. B. Fuller,	Mrs. Mary A. Wood,
Mrs. J. C. Hutsinpiller,	Mrs. A. Uhrig,
Mrs. E. S. Aleshire,	Mrs. H. N. Ford,
Mrs. O. M. Henking,	Miss Mary Aleshire,
Mrs. W. H. Hutchinson,	Miss Hattie Beard,
Mrs. John T. Halliday,	Miss Belle Coffman,
Mrs. James Johnson,	Miss Blanche Cadot,
Mrs. D. W. Jones,	Miss Callie Deletombe,
Mrs. C. D. Kerr,	Miss Mary Graham,
Mrs. Genevieve Maxon,	Miss Kate McClurg,
Mrs. John Moncure,	Miss Kate McIntyre,
Mrs. J. C. Morris,	Miss Ida Nevius,
Mrs. Geo. D. McIntyre,	Miss Alice Pitrat,
Mrs. C. W. Ernsting,	Miss Annie Uhrig,
Mrs. A. W. Kerns,	Miss Marie Drouillard.

Each committee arranged all details necessary and by the middle of October everything was in readiness.

The Committee on Tents arranged for a large tent for the Auditorium with a seating capacity of 2,000. A stage was built in it on the parquet order with a seating capacity of 400. Near it were arranged a dozen tents for Committees' headquarters. The main tent was erected in the center of the Park next the river, where the reunion tent was spread in 1888. This gave a fine view up and down the river and was convenient to every one. The main tent was well lighted and comfortably seated.

Early in October, John L. Vance and A. A. Graham arranged the following programme, which, in the main, was carried out:

1790   1890

PROGRAMME

OF THE

CENTENNIAL ANNIVERSARY

OF THE

SETTLEMENT OF THE CITY

OF

GALLIPOLIS, OHIO,

BY THE

French, October 19, 1790.

October 16, 17, 18 and 19,

1890.

The following account of the reason of the settlement of this locality by the French emigrants was printed in the programme:

"On October 19, 1790, a party of French emigrants landed at the site of the present city of Gallipolis, Ohio. These emigrants were part of a number who had purchased land in the Ohio country from the Society of the Scioto in Paris. This Society had acquired the right of purchase in this part of America from Joel Barlow, agent of the Scioto Associates in America. They had contracted to buy from the United States a large tract of land in the Northwest Territory. Through the failure of the Society of the Scioto to meet its payments the Scioto Associates were unable to fulfill their obligations and the lands continued in possession of the American government. To satisfy the claims of the emigrants to whom the Society of the

Scioto had given deeds for lands in the 18 ranges of townships—
but which, upon the map furnished by Mr. Barlow, were located
at and adjacent to the site of Gallipolis—the Scioto Associates
contracted to buy from the Ohio Company the land represented
by its shares, which had been forfeited for non-payment—about
200,000 acres. This land they were permitted to locate in the
fourteenth, sixteenth and seventeenth ranges of townships, including the site of Gallipolis. Owing to the failure of the principal men among the Scioto Associates in the financial panic of
1792, they were unable to pay for this tract. This left the
French without titles to any of their purchases. The Ohio
Company was unable to complete the tract it had originally contracted for, but, by its settlement with Congress in 1792, it
acquired the title to the land in the 14 and 15 ranges of townships, including Gallipolis. In 1795, through the efforts of Jean
Gabriel Gewase, seconded by the leading men in the Ohio Company, a grant of 24,000 acres of land, in what is now Scioto
county, was made to the French emigrants. In the same
year the Ohio Company sold to them two fractional sections,
about 900 acres of land, including the town site of Gallipolis, at
$1.25 per acre. It also offered to each 'French settler at Galli-
polis,' one hundred acres of land from the donation tract granted
to it by Congress to be given to actual settlers.

FRIDAY MORNING, OCTOBER 17, IN THE AUDITORIUM.

MUSIC.

Address...................... Hon. H. R. BRADBURY, Mayor of Gallipolis
Address .... PROF. N. J. MORRISON, of Marietta
    On behalf of Ohio Historical Society — "A Century and Its Lessons."

MUSIC.

FRIDAY, 2 P. M.—AUDITORIUM.

MUSIC.

Address............... . ...Hon. D. K. WATSON
        "The Early Bar of the Ohio Valley."

SHORT ADDRESSES.

MUSIC.

FRIDAY EVENING — 7:30 O'CLOCK.

MUSIC.

Address....................HON. JAMES E. CAMPBELL, Governor of Ohio
Address................A. A. GRAHAM, Secretary Ohio Historical Society
"French Exploration and Occupation in America."
(Illustrated by the Stereopticon.)

This address was, by request of the audience, repeated Saturday evening. It was of such a nature it could not be prepared for publication.

SATURDAY, 10 A. M.—AUDITORIUM.

MUSIC.

Address ....COL. JOHN L. VANCE
"The French Settlement and Settlers of Gallipolis."

Owing to other duties this address could not be given, but it is printed in this volume. Short addresses were made by Rev. H. A. Thompson, Prof. J. M. Davis, Mr. R. D. Marshall, Mr. R. D. Jones, Judge R. A. Safford, Gen. C. H. Grosvenor, and others.

SATURDAY AFTERNOON — 2:00 O'CLOCK.

Excursion by Steamboats to points of interest on the Ohio and the Kanawha.

SATURDAY EVENING — 7:30 O'CLOCK.

MUSIC.

Address.............................. HON. DANIEL J. RYAN
"The Scioto Company and the French Grant."

CENTENNIAL DAY.

SUNDAY, OCTOBER 19, 1890.

10:00 A. M.— Services in all the Churches under charge of the City Pastors' Association; appropriate exercises.

In each church an historical sermon was given by the pastor, or by some one selected by him. A synopsis of these addresses appears in this volume.

SUNDAY AFTERNOON, 2:00 O'CLOCK — AUDITORIUM.

MUSIC BY AUDIENCE.

Historical Discourse......... ....REV. WASHINGTON GLADDEN, D. D.

MUSIC.

SUNDAY EVENING — 7:30 O'CLOCK.

Closing services in the Churches.

The programme at first provided for opening exercises Thursday evening, the sixteenth; but that day being very wet and disagreeable, and owing to an extra session of the General Assembly being called, but few persons could leave Columbus with the members of the Archæological and Historical Society. The train bearing the party was late, and did not reach Gallipolis till after nine o'clock in the evening. The opening exercises were, therefore, deferred until Friday morning, and the programme arranged accordingly. Members of the Assembly invited to take part, were detained at Columbus, and their places filled by others. The citizens of Gallipolis had made ample preparations, and when the guests arrived everything was in readiness. The following from the *Gallipolis Bulletin* of October 21st, is a very good account of the celebration:

Friday morning opened clear and beautiful. The clouds and rain had disappeared and the sun shone out, diffusing warmth and beauty. By 10 A. M. the large tent was filled. The meeting was called to order by Hon. H. R. Bradbury, City Mayor, who in the opening address extended a hearty welcome to all who came. At the close of his address and after music by the band, Rev. N. J. Morrison was introduced, and for an hour spoke on the topic assigned to Mr. Sessions. Mr. Sessions, the President of the Society, to whom had been assigned this address, was absent, in New York, on account of illness, and had secured Dr. Morrison to fill his place. The address was scholarly, eloquent, and filled with information. It was a timely and most excellent resume of the century just closed.

Following Dr. Morrison, Rev. J. M. Davis, President of Rio Grande College, gave a brief history of the educational institutions in Gallia County, especially of the college at Rio Grande.

Rev. H. A. Thompson, one of the Trustees of the State Historical Society, and for many years President of the Westerville College, spoke on the value of education, especially that given in the small colleges of the country, and in the academies.

The afternoon exercises were varied in character. Owing to the late arrival of the Governor's train, no attempt was made to gather the people until near 4 o'clock. Col. R. D. Marshall, of Dayton, was introduced by Secretary Graham, and about half an hour spoke on the general theme of the Centennials and the value of their influences on American life.

Following this address came a civic parade, in which Governors Campbell, of Ohio, and Fleming, of West Virginia, and their staffs, took part; also many civic societies. At the close of the parade the people gathered at the tent.

The audience was called to order by Col. John L. Vance, who introduced Hon. D. K. Watson, Attorney General of Ohio, who delivered an address on the "Early Bar of the Ohio Valley." At the conclusion of his address, Governor Fleming, of West Virginia, was introduced and spoke on the relation of Virginia to the Ohio Valley. Governor Campbell was then introduced. As it was getting late the Governor spoke but a few moments, deferring his speech until evening.

Assembling again in the evening, Governor Campbell resumed his remarks. They were largely relative to the value of proper centennial celebrations as educational in character and as agencies in impressing on the minds of the young the value of American institutions.

Mr. Graham was then introduced, and for an hour spoke on the "Early Exploration and Occupation of the French in America." The address was illustrated by a series of stereopticon views, showing the routes of the early explorers by sea and by land, also the various posts, stations and forts built in the Western valleys. Maps showing the possessions and territory claimed by the English and French in North America, especially in the Valleys of the St. Lawrence and Mississippi Rivers and their tributaries, were shown, and at the close of the address a series of pictures were shown illustrating life on the Ohio a century ago. These included pictures of Marietta, Belpre, Fort Harmar, the "floating mill" used in grinding grain, and views of Gallipolis as it appeared when the French landed, October 19, 1790, and also views of the city as it appears to-day. At its close, numerous requests were made for the repetition of the address the next evening. After music by the Parkins quartet the meeting adjourned to a reception in the

Elks' Hall, tendered the Governors, their staffs, and the visitors in the city.

Saturday morning the audience assembled at 10 o'clock and were addressed by Mr. J. V. Jones, of Fostoria, a resident of Gallipolis in 1832. His address related to the city as it was at that time and the people residing here.

He was followed by Judge W. H. Safford, of Chillicothe, a lineal descendant of Col. Robert Safford, one of the original party who, under Maj. Burnham and employed by the Ohio Company, cleared the ground and erected the cabins on the Square for the occupation of the French settlers.

Following this address, the visitors and guests in the city were taken on an excursion up the Ohio River on the steamer Bostona a short distance above Point Pleasant. In the afternoon a second excursion was taken on the same steamer, thereby accommodating those who could not go in the forenoon.

At 2 o'clock the meeting was called to order by Mayor Bradbury, who introduced Gen. Charles H. Grosvenor, who spoke on the Virginia claims to the Northwest Territory and on the capture of the British posts by Gen. George Rogers Clark, in 1788. At his request, Mr. Graham explained in detail the part taken by Gen. Clark and his men, and narrated the history of Clark's expedition.

Following this, Judge Safford gave an account of the finding of one of the lead plates buried at the mouth of the Kanawha by direction of the French commandant in Canada, as one of the means of establishing the claims of France to this territory. He also gave an account of the capture of Richard Garner and others for assisting runaway slaves in 1848. The case was ably argued by Samuel H. Vinton on the part of Ohio.

The people gathered in great numbers in the evening to witness a fine display of fireworks on the river's bank. After that, the tent was quickly filled and Mr. Graham repeated that portion of his illustrated address relating to the French settlements, posts and exploration in the Northwest Territory.

After this, Hon. Daniel J. Ryan, Secretary of State, delivered a timely address on the "Scioto Company and the French Grant," reviewing the entire history of the land transactions relative to this settlement by the French. This done, the Parkins quartet, which had furnished the music of the evening, sang a selection and the audience dispersed.

THE CENTENNIAL DAY.

Sunday was distinctively the Centennial Day, it being on the nineteenth day of October, 1790, when the French emigrants arrived on the site of where Gallipolis now stands. The city was full of visitors, as during the other days of the celebration, and there was a deep interest manifested to hear the subject of the happenings of a hundred years considered from religious standpoints, which is the most beautiful and significant of any.

Centennial services were conducted in most of the city churches. The programmes which had been arranged for the occasion by the Pastors' Union were of the most attractive character, and will be long remembered by the appreciative congregations. A brief synopsis of these services is appended:

BAPTIST CHURCH.

The congregation was given a treat here which was much appreciated. Rev. Mr. McMannis, the pastor, had secured the services of Rev. Dr Lasher, editor of the *Journal and Messenger*, the organ of the Baptist church in Ohio, and published in Cincinnati. His sermon, like all the others, was on the practical lessons of the century, looking at the matter particularly in reference to the denomination to which he belonged.

METHODIST CHURCH.

An elaborate musical programme was most ably rendered, the Parkins Brothers being among the singers. The bass solo by Mr. Matthews was also one of the enjoyable characteristics of the service. Rev. David Moore, D. D., editor of the *Western Christian Advocate*, preached the sermon. The historical features were directed to the consideration of the history of Methodism, and the wonders which it has accomplished, as a medium for making the country better.

PRESBYTERIAN CHURCH.

The music was under the supervision of Professor J. M. Neal. Rev. Sylvester Scovill, the President of Wooster College, was the preacher, and the wisdom of selecting him was clearly demonstrated by the excellent address of more than an hour to which the large congregation listened. Presbyterianism in its different stages in Ohio, during the century, was the instructive and useful topic of his discourse, and the feeling of gratitude was no doubt paramount in the minds of his hearers, for the blessings which it has given our country in the way of a preached Gospel and a Godly example.

EPISCOPAL CHURCH.

In the services here the rector was assisted by Rev. D. I. Edwards, of the diocese of Newark, N. J. The music was of an appropriate character, Mrs. Moncure presiding at the organ, and a solo, by Miss Nora Kerr, gladdening the hearts of the congregation. The sermon, by the rector, Rev. Moncure, was like the others, on the teachings of the century. These were briefly considered from a secular standpoint, and more elaborately from that of the church, particularly the Protestant Episcopal church, the organization, difficulties and success of which were recounted, as they applied to the Nation, State and City, and the mercies of God, as illustrated by His blessings upon its endeavors gratefully mentioned.

ST. LOUIS CHURCH.

The day was appropriately observed by the Roman Catholic churchmen. First mass was celebrated at 7:30 A. M. and High mass at 10 A. M. Bishop Watterson, of the Diocese of Columbus, was present at both services. In the afternoon he confirmed a large class. The Centennial services were held in the evening, when the Bishop preached an interesting and instructive sermon on the events of the past century. The musical part of the services was good.

Public Square and Tent, Centennial Day, October, 19, 1890.

OPERA HOUSE SERVICES.

In the afternoon service was held at Betz Opera House, when the Rev. Washington Gladden, D. D., of Columbus, de-livered the Centennial address. A large audience was in attend-ance, and many members of the Legislature, with their ladies, occupied seats upon the stage. The following is the order of service observed:

Music by the choir.

Prayer by President Davis, of Rio Grande College.

Music by Parkins' Quartet.

Sermon by Dr. Gladden.

Music by the choir.

Benediction by Rev. Dr. Moore.

Dr. Gladden's sermon was closely listened to, and will long be remembered by those present. His text was: "By faith Abraham, when he was called to go out into a place which he should after receive for an inheritance, obeyed; and he went out not knowing whither he went."—Hebrews, xi.-8. The sermon is given in full in this volume.

Sunday evening the visiting clergy, who filled the pulpits in the morning, preached to appreciative congregations, and thus closed the exercises commemorative of the settlement of this city.

THE GRAND PARADE.

The delay in the arrival of trains, made a corresponding delay in the formation and start of the parade.

It was fully three o'clock before the formation was completed by Chairman McCormick and Marshal W. P. Small. The organization was as follows:

1. Gates Second Regiment Band, West Virginia N. G.

2. Governor Fleming and Staff—General Oxley, Colonels MacCorkle, Hagan, Bowyer, Gallaher and White.

3. Governor Campbell and Staff—Generals Hawkins, Vance, Groesbeck and Hart; Colonels Courtright, McKinney, Denver, Wilkins, Dill, Hinman, Spangler, Kinnane, Bresler,

with Sergeant Fred Steube, carrying the banner, and Chairman Hayward in advance.

4. Porter Band.
5. Grand Army Posts and other veterans.
6. Company Ohio National Guard from Middleport.
7. Ben Hur Division, U. R. K. P., of Gallipolis.
8. Patriarchs Militant Band, of Columbus.
9. Grand Canton Ohio, No. 1, of Columbus.
10. Canton Fidelity, No. 1, of Huntington, W. Va.
11. Canton Sanns, of Gallipolis.
12. Canda Hose Company, of Huntington.
13. Gallipolis Fire Department.
14. Citizens in carriages.

The parade formed on Third and Court streets, with right resting on Second, and the line of march was up Second to Olive; Olive to Third; Third to Grape; Grape to Second; Second to State, where the parade was dismissed.

The pupils of the Union Schools were drawn up in line on Third street, between State and Locust, and reviewed the parade amid great enthusiasm. At Court, the Governors and their Staffs left the procession and took up a position on Second, just above Court, and the parade passed in review before them. While this was being done the schools marched down Second. They were headed by President Alcorn, Supt. Mohler and Prof. Karr, and each school accompanied by its teacher. When Court street was reached a halt was made and the pupils faced Second street, and sang "America" with profound effect. At the conclusion of the song, three rousing cheers were given for Governors Campbell and Fleming.

THE RECEPTION.

The Reception at the Elks' Hall on Friday evening was continued until a very late hour, and was a brilliant affair. Mrs. Jas. E. Robinson, the Chairman, and the ladies of the Committee having the matter in charge, are to be congratulated upon the great success that attended their efforts. The refreshments were elegantly prepared and served with skill. The music was furnished by the Logan Orchestra. Governor Campbell and Staff, Governor Fleming and Staff, Governor Marquis, Mr. C. C. Waite, Colonel R. D. Marshall, General D. K. Watson, and many others of our distinguished visitors were present, together with the ladies accompanying them.

During the progress of the banquet, in answer to calls, short responses were made by Governor Campbell, Governor Fleming, Mr. Waite, Governor Marquis, Colonel R. D. Marshall, General D. K. Watson, and General Morton L. Hawkins.

A CENTENNIAL RELIC ROOM.

The Committee in charge of the display of relics, secured a room in which were arranged all articles illustrating the life of the century. The following shows the list of those who furnished articles and the articles displayed, as given in the *Bulletin :*

S. C. Maguet, dish and plate used for 60 years; salt cellar used for 64 years; brass candlestick brought with the first French settlers.

Wm. Waddell, shoe hammer given to grandfather in 1796; ginseng hoe over 100 years old; leather wallet, once the property of Nathan Waddell; small spinning wheel 150 years old.

Mrs. Lewis Maguet, quilt made during the Revolutionary War from clothing worn at that time; chair, 70 years old, used by Major J. P. R. Bureau, Dr. E. Naret and Hon. S. F. Vinton; saddlebags, 70 years old, used by Hon. S. F. Vinton.

Mrs. J. E. Robinson, tea-cups and saucers, 85 years old; stew-pots 75 years old; picture of husband taken when he was 3 years old, by Thomas Wilkinson; picture of J. C. Robinson, Principal of Gallia Academy in '43-4, taken 1833; picture of Mrs. Elizabeth Dickerson, the first col-ored female child born in Gallipolis, now 67 years old.

Mrs. Guthrie, brass badge of Tippecanoe; towel, woven and spun by herself and 75 years old.

Mrs. Mary Coulson, tin plate 150 years old, used by the sixth generation.

Mrs. Mary J. Hebard, old Cincinnati papers, of date of 1822-5.

Mrs. R. C. Smithers, shawl belonging to her mother, 70 years old, and prayer-book printed in 1782.

Wm. Preston, trunk brought from France, over 100 years old; tea-kettle and pot, same.

Miss Titia Jones, Cadmus, book printed in 1702.

Miss Maggie Northup, large collection of books, among the first printed.

A. A. Wade, Gallipolis *Journals* of the early part of the present century.

Dr. J. R. Safford, beautiful crayon

picture of his grandfather, Col. Robt. Safford, who cut down the first tree on the present site of Gallipolis, executed by Miss Lily Calohan from an old daguerreotye; the Colonel's horse-pistol, candlestick, powder horn, sword, sleeve-buttons worn by him and 150 years old; pair of candle snuffers.

Gus Vollborn, tablecloth 267 years old.

Hon. H. R. Howard, Pt. Pleasant, 2 bound books of newspapers (daily) subscribed for by the Sebrill family in 1800 and 1807.

A. C. Safford, wolf trap presented to Col. Robt. Safford by Daniel Boone, his bosom friend; holster, shaving-case, old papers, books, gun, pistol, histories, bullet pouch, horn, and silver watch owned by Col. Safford.

Lydia Safford, tea-pot, water urn, tallow pot, candle moulds, candlesticks, owned by Col. Robt. Safford.

M. L. Muzio, marble mortar, 100 years old; Italian flag and coins (½ cent U. S. 1826 and silver piece of 1773, and French coin of 1810.)

Jas. Moats, spurs worn during the Revolutionary War; block of wood out of Libby Prison building.

Reuben Aleshire, jr., canteen picked up at battle of Point Pleasant during the late war; R. Aleshire, sr.'s flatboat pilot license; Luther Shepard's commission as Major of battalion, signed by Jos. McLain, Secretary of War.

Mrs. J. C. Cadot, vinegar bottle over 100 years old, candlestick 95 years old.

C. M. Whitmer, collection of rare Indian relics, 50 spears, pipe, medal, and 10 old coins.

John Irion, Bible owned by the celebrated Ann Bailey, and used 135 years.

Mrs. R. T. Carter, old Gallia Free Press of 1825.

Mrs. E. J. Miles, fruit dish 100 years old.

Lena Wood, Bible of 1828, excellent state of preservation.

Frank Donnally, snuff box, warming pan and fire tongs about 100 years old, brought from France by Jos. W. Devacht's father; saw, chest of silversmith's tools, etc., trunk of French books, 11 account books, among first kept in the city.

Capt. Polsley, pieces of wood caught in the river after the Johnstown flood.

Mrs. John Atkinson, Japanese broom; silver spoons 85 years old.

Mrs. M. Reynolds, sugar bowl brought from France 200 years ago.

Mrs. A. W. Buskirk, Portsmouth, cane carried by Jos. Devacht, sr., 100 years old; parasol carried by Mrs. Devacht, sr., 100 years old.

Jas. Beall, an interesting case of Indian relics.

Mrs. O. M. Henking, cradle 80 years old.

Mrs. M. L. Shepard, piece of log-wood used in old times; picture of Marie Louise LeClercq, the first white child born in Gallipolis; candlesticks 100 years old.

W. C. Hayard, Bible over 100 years old; marriage certificate and license of Henry Whitman and Sophie Tilley, his mother's sister; a letter written to Elijah Hayward, jr., by Solomon Hayward, dated Alexandria, Va., Oct. 11, 1806, while on his way here from Massachusetts.

Miss S. E. Rodgers, spoon 60

years old kettle 85 years old; handkerchief 50 years old.

Mrs. John S. Mills, reel 99 years old.

Miss Lily Calohan, pitcher, over 50 years old; waffle irons 60 years old; picture 77 years old.

Mrs. L. A. Hern, plate, book and saucer 100 years old; sugar bowl brought from Scotland, over 100 years old; calico 53 years old.

Dr. John Sanns, song and music written by Calvin Shephard in 1800; the contract for the building of the first Methodist Church, with signers; the muster and pay roll of Brig. Gen. Tupper; account book of 1805.

Lilian Stewart, vest, coverlet, veil, box, and cuff buttons, bowl, steelyards of great age.

Ella B. Smeltzer, andirons 100 years old.

J. H. Hannan, Colonial and Brazilian money.

C. H. McCormick, kettle made by his grandfather in 1801; his hunting bag, flax hackle, rocking chair 90 years old; bread oven, tea kettle and iron kettle over 65 years old.

Mrs. Frank Barlow, pitcher from Switzerland, plate, linen sheets made in 1804; flax hackle, waffle irons, wood cards, skillet, andirons and crane of centennial years.

H. W. McGath, cuff buttons 250 years old; spectacles of 1800; clasp and book of 100 years.

Mrs. Scheneberger, ink-stand over 100 years old; book over 200 years old; nut cracker and cup from Paris 75 years old.

Miss Jennie Myers, a table of 100 years old made from one of the first trees cut on the square in Gallipo-

lis (poplar and maple); basket over 100 years old.

T. R. Hayward, spinning wheel 75 years old; sample of fancy work over 100 years old.

Ernest Shober, papers over 100 years old.

W. T. Minturn, Third Year of Commonwealth; picture of Burke, and one of Washington; the Indian Chief Cornstalk's pipe.

P. T. Wall, axe used by Col. Safford to cut down the first tree.

H. U. Maxon, dress skirt from Scotland in 1870.

Mrs. A. H. Alexander, bread bag 75 years old, knit bag 75 years old.

Mrs. Cavin, picture and ink stand from France.

Mrs. Chas. Hern, old picture.

Allen Reifsnyder, moccasins 100 years old.

Miss M. J. Rodgers, book of 1678 and 1646.

Claude Parker, gun brought from England in 1789.

Mrs. H. N. Ford, two pictures in brass frames brought from France; the Lord's prayer in French; picture of Mary Bobin Menager; Sabots, belonging to A. LeClercq; two cut glass tumblers belonging to R. LeClercq and to R. Doszedardski; box of chips with which the French settlers played the game of Boston; old commissions in frames; old papers of the Scioto Co.'s land deeds; Postmaster's commission; certificate of naturalization of Frances LeClercq; appointment of treasurer in Gallia county in 1804; deed for land signed by President James Monroe; certificate of first commission of Rosalie LeClercq; needle book of Marie C.

Marret; scent bottle of same; sugar bowl decorated by one of the first colonists in Gallipolis; candle snuffers and tray; spelling book of 1817; almanac of 1829; book of French poems belonging to Dr. Doszedardski.

Mrs. Julius Pitrat, picture of Peter Menager, born Oct. 22d, 1793; first Wheeler & Wilson sewing machine brought to Gallipolis, bought by Mr. Menager in 1845, a great curiosity, turns with a crank; picture of Christ, by Claude Miller in 1636.

Jas. W. Gardner, three pictures of Public Square, Second and Front streets, during the war; records; tax duplicate of Gallia county in 1804; original specifications of Gallia county court house, Dec. 29, 1806, Commissioners of county being Orasha Strong, Chas. Buck, Chas. Mills; assessors return of personal property in Harrison township in 1820, Vernon Northup, lister; commissioners journal from July, 1804, to July, 1807.

E. Deletombe, family relics brought from France in 1820; pair of silver candlesticks, brass candlesticks, cut glass tumbler, cut glass vinaigrette, pair gold ear-rings, 100 years old; diamond ring in box of straw; Mosaic, dating back five generations; meerschaum pipe 125 years old; ivory dominoes over 100 years old; pen portrait of Voltaire; lady's portrait, painted on ivory; amber beads; embroidered fichu; white shawls; Tambour embroidery; Tambour working cotton and stilletto; silver bodkins and knitting sheath; sandal wood needle case set with turquoise; ivory needle case; fine clocked hose; mouseline-delaine

shawl in colors; velvet reticule; beaded purse; porcelain pen stand; cut glass ink bottle and blotting sand; E. Deletombe's miscellaneous family relics—souvenirs of the Mexican war of 1847; lady's fan-kid—fancy painting steel sticks; child's toy cupboard made of glass; pack of Mexican playing cards; cannon ball from Mexican battlefield; pair of painted china vases; shell jewel box from Cologne, Germany; silk jewel box with mirror from Germany; cut glass vinaigrette over 50 years old; lady's shell comb 65 years old; toy chair over 50 years old; paper weights of agate from Turkey; of onyx from Mexico; of marble from the Hartz mountains; glass stylographic pen 50 years old; sea biscuit brought to America in 1810 by Mrs. Deletombe's father, G. Steinman; pack of playing cards made for use during the rebellion with flags, shields, etc., to replace the original designs; California flowers pressed in 1849; sandal wood from the Sandwich Islands; horn of buffalo killed on the Public Square; tomahawk found on Gallipolis Island in 1879; amber beads used 60 years; silver spoon used 85 years; incense 68 years old; lava and ornaments made of it, from Mt. Vesuvius; spun glass from Vienna, Austria; a leaf of the silver fir from the Southern coast of Africa; pieces of the flag staff erected after the defeat of St. Clair at Ft. Recovery; amethyst from the Black Hills; button worn in the war of 1812; Harrison badge of 1840; fac simile of a $1,000 bill, the first ever owned by E. Deletombe, and executed by the late Chas. Henking with a pen; picture of the Star

House of Hiram Fisher on Public Square built in 1844, and from which Dr. Maxon fell and killed himself in 1851; bottle of vinegar, over 40 years old, made by Francois E. Deletombe's father; portrait of Dr. Saugrain, one of the first settlers; of Mrs. Elise Marie Kennesly, living in St. Louis, 91 years old; photo of the old Deletombe house that stood 77 years at the corner of Fourth and Court streets, and built in 1810; picture on parchment presented with a medal to August Loyn (uncle of E. Deletombe) for his faithful services in the Bureau of Correspondence of the National Guard of Paris, dated Jan. 4. 1817; deed of land in the French Grant to one J. Pignolet, one of the first settlers; marriage certificate of Francois Deletombe and Natalie Loyn, dated Oct. 19, 1808, parents of E. Deletombe; baptismal certificates of Francois Deletombe and other members of his family, the earliest of which is dated Jan. 2, 1804; carrier's address of the Lancaster Gazette and Enquirer, printed on white satin, and dated 1838; apron and shoes 80 years old; dress brought from Mexico in 1847.

Mrs. Elise M. Kennesly, St. Louis, a sketch in pamphlet form in 1827 of her father, Dr. Saugrain, a photo of the monument of Dr. Saugrain's great-grandfatder standing in the cemetery of Pere-la-Chaise, Paris.

J. L. Hayward, Gen. E. W. Lupper's sash; his own bady cap at 4 months; wedding coat of Leonard Beck, 60 years old, made by the father of J. L. Hayward; gourd bottle made in 1820.

Mrs. Priestly, dish 65 years old.

Mrs. Ella Gordon, a smoothing iron 120 years old, and a tea pot 147 years old.

Mrs. H. N. Hayward, lace shawl about 100 years old; winding-sheet, brought from Scotland in 1802, it is 18 feet long and 6 feet wide; a baby dress in which herself and three sisters were christened; a beautiful fan belonging to Miss Isabel Rodgers, 70 years old; a coverlet brought from Scotland in 1802.

John Lupton, bottle of wine made by Rosina LcClercq in 1830.

Mrs. Fannie Miles, platter and tablecloth 50 years old, woven by Mrs. Rodgers.

Malbry Hern, a Masonic apron framed by Solomon Hayward over 70 years ago, and which is 125 years old.

G. D. McBride, a French picture with translation of great age, and of Rio College.

Mrs. E. Westlake, plate 250 years old.

Robt. Gates, picture of Gen. Geo. House.

Mrs. H. H. Jones, wooden tray 120 years old, and glass dish 112 years old.

Henry House, sword captured at Kickapoo Bottom.

Henry Beall, a silver spoon used in the Revolutionary War, and a paper trunk of valuable papers, belonging to Col. Strickler.

Mrs. Sam Silverman, a Jewish Bible picture of great age; knife and fork 200 years old; a Hebrew Bible printed in 1840; cup made in 1713; sheet 300 years old.

Thos. Arrington, a cane 63 years old, used by his father.

John Alexander, bottle of stream

tin and lot of quartz from Black Hills; saber captured by himself in deadly conflict at Blacksburg, Va., and given to Capt. Alexander by special order of Col. Turley.

Mrs. Judge Thomas, a platter 100 years old.

James Mullineaux, Sen., Bible printed in 1772.

James H. Sanns, a bottle of water taken from the center of the Park in flood of 1884.

Mrs. G. S. Stevenson, a sugar bowl 200 years old; tin sugar bucket over 100 years old.

Capt. W. V. Martin, a book that is Centennial on border warfare.

Mrs. S. Rodgers, a silk bag 125 years old; needle book 100 years old; great-grandmother's belt worn at her wedding in one of the Block Houses at Harmar, and nearly 200 years old.

Mr. Ed Gills and Miss Clara Heaton, old relics, consisting of key to first Gallipolis Jail, belonging to Claude Pritchett; pair scissors 111 years old, belonging to Mrs. Marie McConnell; petrified russet apple 125 years old, belonging to Miss Heaton; gold key with heart, belonging to Mrs. Adelaide Maguet, one of the original settlers, who died in 1889, eighteen days short of 100 years old, her picture, and many other relics, belonging to the family.

Mrs. S. F. Neal, copy of the Ulster County (N. Y.) *Gazette*, containing complete account of circumstances, death and obituary address of President George Washington, dated January 4th, 1800; also a Postal Guide, showing the number of Postoffices in the U. S. in 1811, to be only 2400.

F. E. Duduit, Portsmouth, razors, solid silver spoons, brought from Paris by his father.

Marion Beall, Indian relics, fine collection.

Picture of Mrs. Adelaide Maguet, who came here when 5 years old, and died just short of 100 years.

Miss Mary Johnson, skillet 100 years old.

A. E. Jones, plate, 95 years old.

Mrs. L. A. Stanley, teapot, glass cane, box specimens, the teapot made in England and 70 years old.

Mrs. Sallie Smith, kettle belonging to Extra Billy Smith, of great age.

A. J. Green, whip made of hoof and horn of deer in 1848.

Jonas McCarty, flat iron used in the Revolutionary War.

Alex Beatty, Portsmouth, candlestick brought to America in 1790.

Jos. Walter, cartridge box used in battle of Waterloo; tomahawk 100 years old, and Indian relics.

David Irwin, newspaper of 1828.

L. M. Shepard, cane belonging to Col. Robert Safford; scissors presented to Col. Safford by Col. Tupper in 1795; bellows from Quebec by Col. Robert Safford.

Mrs. Hudson Maddy, cup and saucer 100 years old.

Miss Blanche Cadot, marriage certificate of her great-grandmother; lock that was on first fort in Gallipolis.

Jas. Thomas, Charity, O., cash box 273 years old.

Ralph C. Jones, cane carried by Col. Safford and made from first tree cut on the site of Gallipolis.

H. U. Maxon, waiter of dishes 75 years old; bag very old.

Mrs. Lalla Moncure, bottle of water from River Jordan.

John Morrison, Indian relics and used at Andersonville.

John Nealon, apron 100 years old.

Jas. L. Clark, sabre of the Revolutionary war.

Jos. Walter, five-dollar bill of the old Gallipolis bank.

Mrs. S. Brosius, samples embroidery (2 pieces), painting in velvet, very old, no date.

Bevery Grant, pewter spoons, and novels of 1780.

C. H. D. Summers, male and female buffalo horns, captured in Montana by Harry and Fred Summers.

Mrs. C. Knapp, beads 100 years old.

Mrs. A. McCormick, bellows, seaweed, French letter, handkerchief, picture. All these things belonged to the Warth family and are very old.

Ellis Swisher, wolf-trap over 100 years old.

Mack Sprague, sign, auction, 200 years old; mortar, made in England in 1725; books, 1828.

Mrs. C. C. Row, Portsmouth, silver snuff box made in France, and brought fom there 100 years ago.

Mrs. F. M. Womeldorff, hackle and flax made and brought from Ireland over 86 years ago by her grandmother.

Mrs. Isabel Rodgers, copper kettle 70 years old, and old papers.

Mrs. Alex Vance, pan and andirons belonging to General E. W. Tupper, and Bible 139 years old.

Mrs. Madeline Langley, John Peter Roman Bureau's wedding tie of white satin, cigar case, beads, French picture (Virgin Mary), handsome snuff box with the Constitution of the United States on lid, pearl needle case, shell box, coin, spoon and various articles of age belonging to Madeline Francis Charlotte Bureau; watch-seal, breastpin and cane belonging to J. P. R. Bureau; needle case and reticule belonging to Margaret Hughes Bureau.

Mrs. Mary Johnson, skillet 100 years old.

Ella Olmstead, steelyards 150 years old, and clock made of different materials.

J. L. W. Evans, tomahawk, about 200 years old.

Mrs. Emma Lang, German and English Bible and table-cloth, all 100 years old.

Miss Lily Heisner, sand-box, needle-book and turquoise necklace used during the Revolutionary War; night-cap 58 years old, owned by Mrs. Charles Creuzet.

J. M. Davis, Nehemiah and Parmelia Atwood's pictures, the founders and endowers of Rio Grande College.

Flora Jackson, book of poetry of 1810; Wm. Diamond, author, beautiful book.

Hattie Miles, Chinese idols from Foo-Chin, China.

S. R. Davis, ancient coin found in West Virginia.

OPENING ADDRESS BY HON. HORACE R. BRADBURY, MAYOR OF
GALLIPOLIS.

Fellow-Citizens, Ladies and Gentlemen:

As the official head of this city, representing the people of
Gallipolis, in their behalf and in behalf of the Executive Committee, by whom this Centennial celebration has been projected
and managed thus far, and while welcoming other distinguished
guests, it becomes my pleasant duty to extend an especial welcome to the members of the Historical Society of this State.

Gentlemen and ladies of the State Historical Society, I
therefore extend to you the sincere and cordial greetings of the
citizens of Gallipolis, and I assure you that our people are united
in extending this welcome, and we, one and all, hope that your
stay among us may be pleasant and your labors profitable.

When, one hundred years ago, a handful of settlers, voyaging down the beautiful river which flows at our feet, rounded-to
their primitive vessels and landed at this spot, no such welcome
as this was extended to them. The place whereon we stand was
a part of the wilderness extending northwardly to the great
lakes, and the only welcome they received was that extended by
the savage wild beasts and still more savage wild men who
roamed therein unchallenged.

These pioneers left civilization and its comforts and con-
veniences behind them; they found before them untamed natives,
requiring infinite and exhausting labor to subdue. What hopes
animated, what fears and doubts depressed them?

But it is no part of my duty to recount the trials of these
men — how they succeeded or where they failed — this is the duty
of other and abler minds. They will tell you how the wilderness
was subdued, how the forests gave way before the sturdy blows
of the pioneers, and how cities and towns arose and flourished,
and smiling farms made glad the waste places; how our beloved
State arose from humble beginnings, her destinies guided by the
worthy sons of noble sires, to shine the bright particular stars,
in the glorious galaxy of States evolved from the great Northwest Territory; all this and much more will pertain to the duties

of the distinguished gentlemen whom we have assembled here to greet.

This city of ours has in time sent forth her sons and daughters, who, with willing hands and strong hearts, have engaged in founding other cities and States, thus following the noble example set by their ancestors. Many of these sons and daughters have returned in response to invitations cordially extended; and I desire to say to them, as well as the strangers within our gates, we extend a thousand hearty, cordial welcomes to you all.

This gavel, which I hold in my hand, and with which this assembly was called to order, is of some historic interest; the wood of which it is made is a portion of a log taken from one of the first cabins built for the French emigrants at Gallipolis. This wood is emblematical of the trials, suffering and hardships endured by our forefathers in making possible the great advance in the arts and sciences made by their descendants, this advance being fully represented by the beautiful silver binding of the gavel and the inscription thereon.

Again, I bid you all thrice welcome.

At the conclusion of this address, a selection of music was given by the band, after which Mayor Bradbury introduced Dr. N. J. Morrison, of Marietta College, who spoke on the topic "A Century and its Lessons."

THE CENTURY AND ITS LESSONS.

Each century of human history is marked by a train of peculiar events, characterized by its own peculiar spirit, gives birth to its own family offspring of ideas, and bequeaths to after-ages a heritage of peculiar and instructive lessons.

Thus the philosophic historian characterizes one century as an age of intellectual and political decadence and another as an age of intellectual and political renaisance; this century as a period of Augustan brilliancy in Letters and that as a period of Invention and Discovery.

And so we call the Eleventh Century of our era the "Age of the Crusades," when a wave of religious and martial fanaticism swept from West to East over all Europe and culminated in overwhelming the Moslem power in the Land of the Cross, and crowning Baldwin, Count of Flanders, as Christian King of Jerusalem, just as the Clock of Time was striking the morning hour of the year 1100.

The Thirteenth Century is distinguished in European history from all precedent and subsequent ages, by the development and perfection of that matchless form of Christian Architecture, known as the Gothic Cathedral. York Minster, Westminster Abbey and Salisbury Cathedral in England; the Notre Dame of Paris, and the Cathedral of Rheims in France, and the Cathedrals of Strasbourg and Cologne in Germany, each a specimen of "poetry crystalized into stone," are illustrious examples of the almost inspired skill of the church-builders of the Thirteenth Century.

The Sixteenth Century, introduced in 1492-98 by the Columbian discovery of the New World, is marked throughout by the influence of the most tremendous intellectual awakening and intellectual *commotion* which the world has yet experienced. This was the period of Copernicus, Tycho Brahe and Galileo in Astronomy, and of the resulting revolution in men's ideas about the system of the universe. Then also the Art of Painting reached its perfection in the works of the three great masters, Michael Angelo, Leonardo da Vinci, and Ranzio. It was the Elizabethan era of Literature and Philosophy in England. It was also the era of Luther, Calvin, Knox and Loyola, and the great religious revolutions and counter-revolutions, which these historic names signify.

This Nineteenth Century has *its* stream of characteristic events, moved by its own forces, along its own channels, toward its own predetermined end. We call this the "Age of the People,"—meaning that mankind have at last reached that stage in their toilsome progress, when the bonds of hereditary authority and prescriptive privilege are broken, and men are moving forward into the full enjoyment of an equality in personal liberty, equality in civil rights, and equality in opportunity.

Properly regarded, the present century begins with the last ten years of the Eighteenth Century. In that decade, events of such momentous importance took place in one quarter of the world, as to give permanent impulse, character and direction to the course of civilization since. It was then that Democracy burst its Mediæval fetters and marched forth from the prison-house of ages, as a strong man armed, upon the stage of human affairs to rule the world.

The French Revolution of 1789 set in motion political and social forces which have dominated and given character to the course of human events during the century since. It will aid us in estimating the influence of these forces and in rightly inter-preting the "Lessons of the Century," if we briefly recapitulate the causes of the Revolution. These are commonly ascribed by historians to the tyranny and reckless extravagance of the reign-ing Bourbon monarchy; the iniquitous privileges and corruption of the nobility and clergy; the unspeakable misery of the mass of the people; and the revolutionary spirit of contemporary French philosophy and literature.

The French king held in his own despotic power the pro-perty, liberty and life of every subject, enacting the spirit of that arrogant phrase of Louis XIV, "I am the State." He imprisoned without trial and without preferring charges; gov-erned without cabinet or legislature,— the royal edicts were laws; imposed taxes according to the royal whim, or at the beck of a corrupt courtier, that were spoliation and confiscation on the property of the hapless people;—and the revenues thus obtained were squandered in extravagances and debaucheries that would shame a Turkish Sultan. One writer declares that "Louis XV probably spent more money on his harem than on any depart-ment of the French Government."

In 1790 the nobility of France comprised one quarter million of souls in a population of 25,000,000 in the nation. They were mainly the "Rubbish of Mediæval Feudalism," living in idleness and dissipation at the Court, and pensioners on the royal bounty. Though numerically scarcely one one-hundreth part of the French people, they monopolized more than one-fifth of all the land. They were the "absentee" landlords of the time, exact-ing exorbitant rents from the poor tenants of their estates with remorseless rigor. And yet, though thus supported from the public revenue and holding vast territories of the richest land, they were practically exempt from the burden of public taxation.

The French clergy constituted a decayed feudal hierarchy, enormously wealthy; the higher stations, filled with scions from the nobility, "Patrician Prelates," often of the most dissolute morals, of whom the famous Talleyrand, at once secular Prince and Primate of the Gallican Church, is an instructive example; the clergy holding title to one-third of all the lands of France, and receiving stipends from the public exchequer, yet privileged with exemption from the public burthens.

On the other hand, the "plain, common people," the mass of the French nation, oppressed and despoiled through many generations by King and Court and Clergy, were reduced to a condition of suffering penury. As the great Fenelon wrote in an appeal to the King, "France is simply a great hospital, full of woe and empty of bread." They were helots,—without influence in the State, without power or hope of redress for their wrongs, their only " Use to the State to pay feudal duties to the lords, tithes to the priest and imposts to the king."

To these primary causes of the impending catastrophe of the kingdom of Louis XVI, must be added the great influence on the opinions of Frenchmen, during the last half of the Eighteenth Century, of the philosophical writings of Voltaire, Rousseau and the Encyclopaedists generally. Their philosophy was sceptical, iconoclastic, subversive of the existing order. They assailed with undiscriminating ardor the abuses which had barnacled on existing institutions and the institutions themselves. Religion, the State, society itself, in their view, needed not reformation merely but an overturning. To restore the lost purity and happiness of mankind, society must return to the state of nature. They entered upon a crusade for the recovery of Human Rights.

By the winter of 1787, the financial disorders of the kingdom reached a crisis,—there was a deficiency of 140,000,000 francs. The King called an assembly of the Notables, who had not been previously summoned since the days of Henry of Navarre, in the Sixteenth Century. But, unwilling to tax themselves, or to surrender for the general good any of their immunities and prerogatives, they adjourned without accomplishing anything. As a last resort, Louis XVIth resolved to convoke the States General, comprising representatives of the three orders of the State, the Nobility, the Clergy and the Commons. This body, representing the French Nation at large, had not before been invited to take part in the government for 175 years. During all this period the King and his Court had governed France alone.

The States General met at the Palace in Versailles, May 5th, 1789, and consisted of 1200 members, of whom a majority were from the commons, the lesser half being divided about equally between the nobility and the clergy. The King had consented that the "Third Estate," as the commons were called, should outnumber the aristocratic deputies, presuming on the continuance of the ancient usage of the States General, according to which voting was by the orders. But the Third Estate, perceiving that they would be outvoted and powerless, and feeling that they were backed by the public sentiment of the nation, demanded that individuals, and not orders, should be counted in the deliberations and decisions of the States General.

For five weeks the contest went on between the orders in the States General when finally the Third Estate declared themselves the National Assembly, and invited the two orders to join them in their deliberations, giving them clearly to understand that if they declined, the commons would proceed to transact public business without them.

The King, in anger at this revolutionary proceeding, promptly prorogued the Assembly and closed the doors of the Palace against the deputies. Undismayed, the Commons met in tennis court of the Palace, and there bound themselves by a solemn oath never to separate until they had given a constitution to France. Shut out from the Palace the deputies found places of meeting in the churches, where they were soon joined by a great part of the clerical deputies, and a little later by many nobles. On the 17th day of June, 1789, the States General became in reality the National Assembly, its President, in welcoming the adhesion of the other orders, exclaiming, "This day will be illustrious in our annals; it renders the family complete.''

Meanwhile events of startling moment are maturing. The King masses troops around Versailles to overawe the National Assembly. The rumor reaches Paris that he intends to disperse the assembly by force of arms. The capital is in a ferment. Leading men from the various wards of the city come together and constitute themselves a Provisional Committee to protect the city's interest and direct its government,—thereby creating the germ, out of which speedily grew the Paris Commune of such portentous power and tendency. The National Guard, so famous in the after wars of the Republic and the Empire, is organized and, with Lafayette at its head, placed under the direction of the Commune. Rumor flies among the people that the guns of the old Bastile, that grim mediæval prison-house of tyranny, are being trained on the city. "To the Bastile!" wildly shout the excited multitude. And quickly a vast, armed, infuriated mob have surrounded the fortress, battered in the doors, slain the defenders, liberated the imprisoned, razed its towers and walls to the ground. The fourteenth of July, 1789, has sounded. Paris is in the hands of an armed mob.

When the report of this outbreak in the Capital reaches the King, he cries out: "What, a rebellion?" "No, Sire," "but revolution."

When the news of this great event reaches the National Assembly a scene transpires, the like of which the world has never witnessed in any deliberative body. The privileged orders realize that it is all over with their exclusive privileges. Rising in the tribune, prominent members of the nobility declare their willingness to renounce all exemptions. A contagious enthusiasm of generosity seizes the members. Nobles and prelates crowd to the tribune to emulate this patriotic example. Everybody is eager to make sacrifices for the common good. The members embrace each other in transports of joy, and sing the *Te Deum* in celebration of the advent among men of peace, equality and good-will.

The revolution moves on with quickening pace. The Parisian mob, led by frenzied Amazons, stream out of the city to

Versailles, encamp about the Royal Palace for the night, and in the morning assault and sack the Palace, and compel the King, the Royal Family and the National Assembly to march back with them to Paris. And thus is made "the joyous entry of October 6th, 1789," famous in the annals of the Revolution.

From this time the Paris Commune controls in public affairs, holding the King hostage in the Tuilleries, and dictating legislation to the National Assembly. The Assembly votes to curtail the Royal prerogative, to confiscate the accumulated wealth of the Church, to abolish the religious orders, and to give universal suffrage to the people, meanwhile busying itself with the task of framing a free Constitution for France.

Presently the Constitution, providing for the continuance of the Monarchy, limited by a National Legislature, for an independent judiciary, for local self-government throughout the realm, for the election of all civil officers by the people, for the abolition of rank and privilege and the installation of equality among citizens, for a free press and absolute freedom of religion, is offered to the Nation for solemn ratification. On the 14th day of July, 1790, in the Champs de Mars, "in the presence of half a million Frenchmen," the Abbe Talleyrand as representative of the National Church; Lafayette as Commander of the National Guard, the President of the National Assembly, and the King, in succession take oath to maintain this Constitution; the Queen also holding up the infant Crown Prince before the eyes of the people, and pledging his future fidelity to that instrument.

Such solemn approval of the new civil institutions of France by the several national powers, seemed, at first, to mark the inauguration of a millenial era of political freedom and brotherhood; the spirit of the transcendant motto of the Revolution, "Liberty, Equality, Fraternity," seemed about to be realized.

But the King, tiring of his confinement in the Tuilleries, secretly leaves Paris and attempts to fly from France; is caught at the frontier, brought back, incarcerated, cited to trial as a conspirator against the public safety, condemned, beheaded. The Republic is proclaimed; the massacres of the "Bloody Reign of Terror" follow. The hapless Mary Antoinette is brought to the guillotine, pathetically crying out to the tribunal

which had condemned her: "I was a Queen, but you took away
my crown; a wife, and you killed my husband; a mother, and
you robbed me of my children; my blood alone remains—take
it, but do not make me suffer long!"

The historical sequel is familiar—the Directory, the Consul-
ate the Empire, the prolonged struggle with embattled Europe,
until Waterloo, and then the restored Bourbons under Louis
XVIII.

I have tarried thus long in the presence of these great
events, because they have so largely dominated and shaped the
course of human affairs since. The motto of the Revolution,
"Liberty, Equality, Fraternity," embodies the political ideal of
humanity, and toward the attainment of that ideal have the
struggles of humanity since been directed. The political
progress of the century is but the progressive realization in
society of this ideal.

Thus the Revolution gave the *coup de grace* to feudalism in
all its forms; ecclesiastical, vassal and lord, military service, land
tenure and prerogative by inheritance.

The "divine right of kings" received mortal hurt by the
same stroke that slew its twin offspring of the Middle Ages —
Feudalism. Monarchy has never recovered from the rude shock
given it by the fall of Louis XVI. Throughout Christendom —
save Russia—wherever sceptered monarchy still lags "super-
fluous" on the world's stage, kings have learned that they reign,
if at all, only as "citizen" kings deriving authority from the
consent of the governed. Since the days when the holy alliance
of Austria, Russia and Prussia was formed on the downfall of
Napoleon, to prop up the tottering thrones of Europe, half the
nations of the world have thrown off the trammels of monarchy
and become republics; and the other half only await favorable
opportunity to follow their example.

The nineteenth century is an era of revolution. Not a
country of Europe or America has, since the day of Waterloo,
remained unshaken. Scarcely had the holy alliance replaced the
expelled Bourbons on their forfeited thrones, when the people
of Italy, of Spain and Spanish America rose in revolt. In 1830
another revolutionary wave swept over Europe, lifting the

"citizen" king to the throne of France and inaugurating a new kingdom in Belgium of the most liberal tendencies. In 1848 again all Europe trembled in the throes of civil convulsions. The boundaries of States were changed, kindred peoples arbitrarily separated coalesced, and political institutions were generally liberalized. Hungary sought national autonomy, and gained political equipoise with her rival and late enemy in the dual Empire of Austria-Hungary.

Many of the uprisings of the people during this period have indeed aborted and been suppressed in blood; and yet, plainly the aggregate result of all these revolutions and revolts of nearly a century is the vindication of human rights and the advancement of human freedom.

The hundred years that expire to-day have been a century of emancipation. At its dawning, the echo of the Marseillaise, sung by the conquering legions of Republican France, heard across the seas, roused the black slaves in the French West Indies to strike for freedom. The eloquent pleadings of Granville Sharp, Wilberforce and Brougham in Parliament, finally impelled the British government, in 1833, to break the shackles of every slave on British soil, decreeing England's eternal reprobation of the "wild and guilty phantasy that man can hold property in man." In 1861 Alexander of Russia put his seal to a state paper of transcendent human importance, by which 46,-000,000 Russian serfs, slaves of the soil, have attained to freedom. By the fortunate issue of our own terrible civil war, invoked by human selfishness to perpetuate American slavery, 4,000,000 human chattels on our soil have been transformed into free men, endowed with full citizenship. And lately, by the great act of the enlightened ruler of Brazil, African slavery in that country has ceased to exist, and vanished, finally, from the soil of the American continent.

The present century has been made illustrious by the renaissance and rehabilitation of ancient nationalities. In the third decade, the public life and literature of England and America thrilled with the heroic story of the Greeks striking for freedom from Turkish despotism, and for the restoration of the commonwealth of Pericles and Epaminondas. Italy, since the

days of Charlemagne, the victim of internal dissensions and the
sport of Transalpine greed, combining her previously dissevered
members into one body, has again become a nation, under one
political constitution, from the Alps to Sicily—independent,
free, progressive. And the historic people of the German
States, boasting one language and one noble literature, but
for centuries broken into an unstable chaos of political frag-
ments, feeble, discordant, often belligerent, and always the easy
prey of harpy nations around, led by the "Man of Blood and
Iron," have recently coalesced in the gigantic Military Empire
of revived and united Germany.

No feature of the Nineteenth Century is more striking than
the development of Parliamentary government. When the Great
Revolution opened Parliamentary rule existed only among Eng-
lish-speaking peoples in Great Britain and America. The irresponsible despots of France had not consulted the people in
legislation for two hundred years. But now, at a century from
the storming of the Bastile, Russia, alone, of all Christian powers, is ruled without the intervention of a legislature chosen by
the people and for the people.

And as the people have thus, by their representatives, acquired authority and the functions of government, in like proportion has legislation been ameliorated and fitted to conserve
the rights and the interests of the people. Formerly laws were
promulgated by the *classes* for themselves; now the *masses* control in statute-making, or are coming to control. In America
and in Western Europe men are now substantially equal before
the law. A century ago the judges of England concurred in
this dictum of one of them—"There is no regenerating a felon
in this life; and for his sake, as well as for the sake of society, I
think it better to hang!" They *did* "hang" for nearly every
offense known to English law. Contrast the spirit of this horrible maxim of jurists *then* with the humane spirit of the laws
and the humane practice of the Courts of England and America
to-day.

The present is *par excellence* the age of discovery in science
and of invention in the useful arts. The eloquent panegyric of
Macaulay on Science, as applied to the arts in promoting human

welfare, is justified, and more than justified by the facts about us: "Science has lengthened life; it has mitigated pain; it has extinguished diseases; it has increased the fertility of the soil; it has given new securities to the mariner; it has furnished new arms to the warrior; it has spanned great rivers and estuaries with bridges of form unknown to our fathers; it has guided the thunderbolt innocuously from heaven to earth; it has lighted up the night with the splendor of the day; it has extended the range of the human vision; it has multiplied the power of the human muscles; it has annihilated distance; it has facilitated intercourse, correspondence, all friendly offices, all dispatch of business; it has enabled man to descend to the depths of the sea, to soar into the air, to penetrate securely into the noxious recesses of the earth, to traverse the land in cars which whirl along without horses, to cross the ocean in ships which run ten knots an hour against the wind." And all these achievements of science, and others since Macaulay still more wonderful, have accrued to the benefit and glory of mankind since the Great Revolution.

Consider a few familiar contrasts between then and now: There were then no locomotives, no railroads, no steam ships, no telegraphs, telephones, or phonographs; no power printing press, no stereotype, no electrotype; no hard rubber with its ten thousand admirable utilities; no known utility of the then tameless power of frictional electricity, which now swiftly draws our carriages by day, and lights up with the splendor of the sun our streets and houses by night; no photography; no spectroscope to analyze the beams of the sun and the far off twinkle of the fixed stars, and no microscope to reveal to human ken the infinitude of organized beings which float unseen by us in the air we breathe and swim in the water that we drink; no agricultural machines for the farm. It took Washington eight days to journey from Mt. Vernon to New York to be inaugurated First President. Our present Chief Magistrate makes the same journey to celebrate the Centennial of Washington's inauguration in less than eight hours. The French immigrants, whom we honor to-day, were longer in making their toilsome journey from Alexandria to this place, than Miss Bisland lately required to travel round the globe.

I should seem wanting in due honor for the profession to whose service I have given my life, if, in this hasty resume of some of "the lessons of the century," I should accord no place to the progress of education.

In the year 1809, when, by the Peace of Tilsit between Napoleon and Alexander with his allies, Prussia was left dismembered, stripped of half her territory, her military power broken, her exchequer bankrupt, her people beggared by devastating war and disheartened, two of her statesmen, William Von Humboldt and Baron Stein, set themselves to the great task of national regeneration and recovery; and they began their work of rebuilding Prussia at the point where skillful architects of States must always base the foundations of their edifices — *in the education of the people.* They founded the University of Berlin, at the moment of the lowest ebb in the life of the nation, which has now grown into the dignity of the most powerful University known to history. They reorganized the whole system of public instruction and provided that every Prussian child not only *might* but actually *should attain* to a fair education. And to their plan instituted in the crisis of Prussia, publicists tell us Prussia owes her remarkable advance among modern nations, her invincible military prowess, her primacy in founding and directing the destiny of the German Empire.

The liberalizing of the political institutions of Western Europe has been accompanied with widespread revival in public education. Provision for the education of all the children of the State is now an accepted maxim of government in all enlightened nations. And in America how the galaxy of colleges, starting with Harvard, has spread as a zone of living light across the broad firmament of the continent. And how the institution of the common schools, offspring of Puritan parentage, at first slowly following the New England emigrant in his march to the Pacific, has lately, by the overthrow of its deadly enemy, slavery, hastened southward and captured the country. And to-day every State, from ocean to ocean, and from the lakes to the gulf, wills that every child within its bounds shall enjoy the blessings of education.

And with this progress of the nations during the last hundred years in respect to larger freedom, better legislation, more general and improved education, in discovery in science, in invention, in the arts, what advancement in national and individual wealth! The Golden Era has dawned, if by that is meant an age of accumulated and accumulating wealth. How the comforts and elegancies of life have multiplied, and how widely are they distributed. Men generally live far more rationally, as if endowed with a more than animal nature, than ever before. This is a grand age—a privilege to live in and be a part of it. We may not produce statues that can rival the work of Phidias; we may have no painter that can limn like Raphael; the age builds no gothic cathedrals to vie with Milan and Cologne. We do better than all this—we dedicate our highest powers to the production of agencies by which the higher well-being of the average man may be promoted. Our works of art are the cotton gin, the locomotive, the power press, bridges for commerce across the straits of the seas, tunnels under the Alps, canals to connect oceans, great laboratories and museums of science, and school houses for the people.

The motto which inspired whatever good inhered in the Revolution, and which has so far moulded human thought and action since, "Liberty, Equality and Fraternity," approaches its full realization in human society. The average man has all the freedom he needs. On the whole the equality of men is pretty fairly attained, certainly before the law, and largely in respect to opportunity. Much progress also is making in the attainment of the spirit of fraternity among men. To the full realization of the spirit of brotherhood, and so of applied Christianity in the world, is the summons for to-day—is the task of the coming age.

MAJOR JOHN BURNHAM AND HIS COMPANY,

Mr. Barlow had written Colonel Duer early in December, 1789, that huts must be built on land opposite the mouth of the Great Kanawha to accommodate at least one hundred persons. The cost of these huts was to be paid by the agent of the immigrants upon their arrival. In March, 1790, General Rufus Putnam, as agent for the Trustees for the Scioto Associates, employed John Burnham of Essex, Massachusetts, to enlist in New England a company of fifty young men who were expert woodmen and who would submit to military discipline. They were to be employed for six months and were to build the huts on the site selected for the city of Gallipolis, to assist in clearing the lands adjacent, to act as hunters when required and to keep such guard as might be necessary. There was peace along the border, but it was an "Indian peace," and the frontier was infested by marauders, white, red and black. No better leader for such a party than John Burnham could have been found. He had served as an officer of the line through the war of the Revolution and was present at every important battle from Bunker Hill to Yorktown. The company he commanded in the eighth Massachusetts regimiment was, in 1782, complimented in general orders by General Washington himself for its "soldier-like and military appearance." He quickly enlisted the company and on the twenty-ninth of May, 1790, reported to Gen. Putnam at Wellsburg, on the Ohio river with thirty-six men. Of the fifty whose services had been engaged ten had not yot joined and four had deserted. The following is the roll, omitting the names of the deserters:

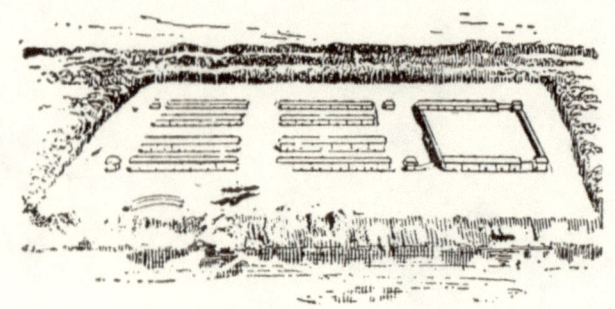

CABINS BUILT BY MAJ. JOHN BURNHAM, ON SITE OF PUBLIC SQUARE, 1790.

PUBLIC SQUARE OF GALLIPOLIS IN 1846.

"SUBSISTENCE ROLL FOR A COMPANY OF MEN ENGAGED IN THE SERVICE
OF THE SCIOTO COMPANY TO MAKE A NEW SETTLEMENT ON THE
BANKS OF OHIO FROM THE TIME THEY LEFT THEIR SEV-
ERAL HOMES 'TILL THEY ARRIVED AT YOUHIOGY.

Men's Names.	No. Days.	Places of Residence.	Pay Day.	Whole Amount of Pay.	Casualities.
				Cts.	
William Potter.........	31	Ipswich.........	26	$ 8 06	
Isaac Choate......	31	Leicester.......	26	8 06	
Nathan Page...........	31	Danvers.........	26	8 06	
Jacob Proctor	31	Danvers.........	26	8 06	
Elijah Bodell...........	31	Mathuen	26	8 06	
Ichabud Olivant.........	34	Ipswich........	26	8 84	
Abraham Dodge........	34	Ipswich........	26	8 84	
Aaron Brown..........	34	Ipswich........	26	8 84	
Thomas Silk..........	34	Ipswich.	26	8 84	
John Andrews.....	34	Ipswich........	26	8 84	
Roger Sergeant.........	34	Ipswich.........	26	8 84	
John Moors...........	34	Cape Ann.......	26	8 84	
John Hart....	31	Wenham... ...	26	8 06	⎧ Detained
Phineas Richardson.....	39	Leicester........	26	10 14	⎨ by sickn'ss
Reuben Rice......... .	26	Keen............	26	6 76	⎩ on road.
Ebenezer Randol........	26	Putna..........	26	6 76	
Zacheus Goldsmith......	29	Andover.	26	7 54	
Isaac Dempsie.........	29	Danvers.........	26	7 54	
Samuel Thomas........	29	Danvers.........	26	7 54	
Jonathan Sheldon.......	31	Danvers.........	26	8 06	
Michael Carroll....... .	31	Danvers.........	26	8 06	
Gideon Batchelor.	31	Danvers.........	26	8 06	
Nathaniel Brown.......	31	Ipswich.........	26	8 06	
Benjamin Potter.........	31	Ipswich.........	26	8 06	
Robert Safford...... ...	20	Woodstock, Vt..	26	5 20	
Samuel Lewis.........	20	Newburgh.......	26	5 20	
William Dunlap........	24	Newburgh.......	26	6 24	
James Dorsey..........	26	Danvers.........	26	6 76	
Frederick Palmer.......	26	West Springfield.	26	6 76	
Ithamer Shaw.........	26	West Springfield.	26	6 76	
Daniel Maynard........	26	New Marlboro...	26	6 76	
Joseph Smith.... ...	26	West Springfield.	26	6 76	
David Butler............	26	Suffield	26	6 76	
William Bridge.........	29	Rutland	26	7 54	
John Miles......	29	Rutland	26	7 54	
Asaph Pimuy...........	29	Simsbury	26	7 80	Not joined.
Aaron Pimuy...........	29	Simsbury.......	26	7 80	Not joined.
Asa Bullard............	31	West Springfield.	26	8 06	
Jonathan Pimuy..	31	Simesbury	26	8 80	Not joined.
Melancton Foster......	31	Simesbury	26	8 80	Not joined.
Thaddeus Humphrey....	31	Simesbury	26	8 80	Not joined.
Josephus Lee.....	31	Southwick	26	1 56	Not joined.
Silas Fowler......... ..	31	Southwick	26	1 56	Not joined.
Gamaliel Ingraham....	31	Southwick	26	1 56	Not joined.
Luther Freman.........	31	Colchester.......	26	1 68	Not joined.
Joseph Thompson......	31	Colchester.......	26	1 70	Not joined.

"WELLS BURG, May 29, 1790.

"I hereby certifie that the within Subsistance roll is just and true and that the moneys paid to Deserters, sick, left sick on the way or not joined I will endevor to recover, and if recovered or any part thereof I will repay the same to Rufus Putnam or his ordor.

JOHN BURNHAM."

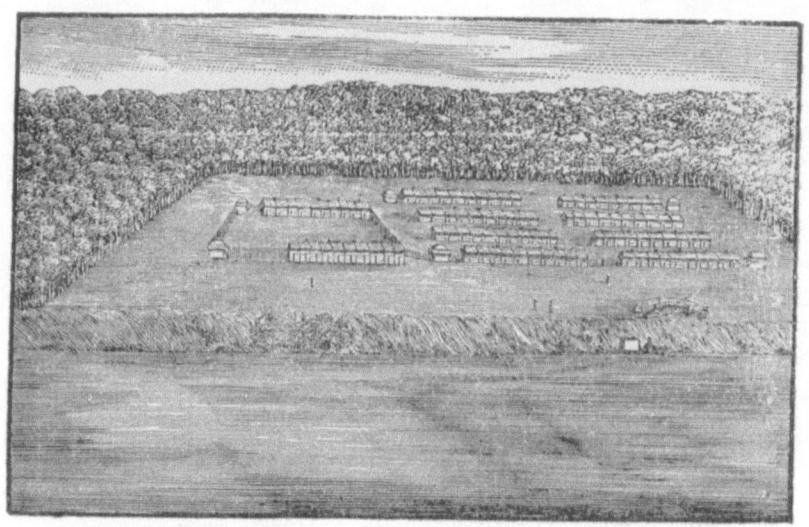

CABINS BUILT BY MAJ. JOHN BURNHAM ON THE PUBLIC SQUARE, GAL-
LIPOLIS, IN THE SUMMER OF 1790.

From Wellsburg the party proceeded by water to Marietta, where General Putnam gave to Major Burnham the following letter of instructions:

"MARIETTA, June 4th, 1790.

"Dear Sir:

"You will please to proceed with the people engaged in the service of the trustees of the Scioto proprietors, in consequence of my letters to you of the —— day of March last, to a place on the Ohio [river] next Chickamaga creek, which will be marked out and shown to you by Col. [R. J.] Meigs, [Sr.,] where you will begin your operations and prosecute the business

in the best manner you can for the interest of your employers
and safety to yourself and people. The object is to erect four
block [houses] and a number of low huts, agreeably to the plan
which you will have with you, and clear the lands. Your own
knowledge of hut building, the block house of round logs which
you have will have an opportunity to observe at Belleprie,
together with the plan so clearly explained, renders it unnecessary to be very particular; however, you will remember that I
don't expect you will lay any floors except for your own convenience, nor put in any sleeper or joyce for the lower floors;
plank for the doors must be split and hewed and the doors hung
with wooden hinges; as I don't expect you will obtain any stone
for the backs of your chimneys, they must be made of clay first,
moulded into tile and dried in manner you will be shown an
example at Belleprie.

When Col. Meigs has assigned the spot and set the stakes
for the center of the four block houses, you will first clear a spot
(which will be pointed out) and throw up a work, which must
be as near the place marked on the plan as you can find a convenient or the best landing, where you will erect a temporary or
stone house and a cover to keep you men dry till the block
houses are completed, which should be your next object and
after that proceed to building huts. In clearing the lands, whatever timber is useful for your building, should be cut and selected for the purpose as you go along and the rest cleared and
burned entirely off. Your clearing must be in one continued
body and extended up and down the river equally from your
work as well as from the river. Supply yourself and party with
whatever you find necessary and reasonable and take care that
the provisions are used with economy. I wish you to inform
yourself with respect to a supply of beef at Kanawha and let me
know by Col. Meigs what may be depended on that I may, if
necessary, send you beef from some other quarter.

You will pay no wages to the carpenters, Smith Brown and
son, nor to John Gardiner, as the carpenters will be paid by
myself or Col. Meigs and I am bound for Gardiner for more
than three months full pay. The pay of your men must commence on their arrival at Youghioganee, deducting four days for

their passage to Muskingum. If anything more should occur which it may be necessary to communicate to you, I will endeavor to inform you by letter.

Wishing you a prosperous voyage and successful campaign, I am, with the most perfect sentiment of esteem,

Your humble servant,

RUFUS PUTNAM."

The party reached its destination on the 8th of June. In November, at the expiration of the six months' term for which the men were engaged, most of them re-entered the service of the Scioto Associates, under Captain Isaac Guion, who had succeeded General Putnam in charge of their affairs in the West. Two, Isaac Choate and Asa Bullard, joined the party that established the settlement at Big Bottom. In the attack by the Indians upon that post, on the second of January 1791, Choate was captured and Bullard escaped. Major Burnham returned to his home in New England, after a long delay in securing a settlement of his accounts. The total cost to the Scioto Associates of Burnham's party during his command of it was $3,243.02.

E. C. DAWES.

THE FRENCH SETTLEMENT AND SETTLERS OF GALLIPOLIS.

Preceding addresses and other papers have given the story of the Scioto Company, under whose auspices the French settlers came to America. I shall not attempt to repeat any part of this history, but begin my narrative with the sailing of the first party of emigrants to their new homes in the unknown West, which had been described to them in such glowing terms by those who had induced them to come. In February, 1790, six hundred emigrants set sail from Havre de Grace. Five ships had been chartered to take them to Alexandria, Va., probably the nearest port to their new homes. Their experiences then were inauspicious as an omen in regard to the future. In these days of rapid transit, when a voyage across the ocean represents a not unpleasant journey of a few days' duration, we cannot imagine what it must have been when, on account of stormy seas and contrary winds, the traveler was compelled to spend weeks, and even months, on the great deep. Yet such experiences as the latter were common once, and they were felt by the Franch emigrants. A desolate feeling must have been theirs then. Behind them was stormy France, its peace that was, having been swept from it, with little hope of its return in the near future; about them the stormy waves of old ocean threatening to engulf them, and thus violently end their new-born hopes. Before them—what? A fair land they believed, but an uncertainty; they had only man's representation upon which to base their hopes, and man is more than liable to misrepresent facts when he has a purpose to gain thereby. The future only could reveal that which they so ardently desired to know, and they awaited its developments, which, with their characteristic, sunny disposition, we believe they did as contentedly as was possible with men. At length, after a voyage of about three months' duration, they arrived at the town of Alexandria, about seventy-five miles up the river Potomac. Here they encountered circumstances which both cheered and depressed them. They were gladdened by a cordial reception on the part of the people to whom a Frenchman was a welcome visitor in view of the recent benefits conferred upon the country by the assistance of the French Government in the war with the British. The emigrant, no doubt, felt as if his fond hopes were about to be realized, as, with his land titles in his pocket, he landed on these hospitable shores. But he was destined to be bitterly disappointed, for it was not long before he knew that difficulties had arisen, which threatened the complete frustration of his plans. The Scioto Company, from which he had made his purchase, had forfeited its title to the lands, having failed to make the payments according to contract with the government, and consequently their dealings with it were null and void. Furthermore, the lands which they thought they had purchased, had been purchased from the government by another corporation, known as the Ohio Company, and contrary to representation, their prospective homes were far away in the Western land, in a wilderness infested by hostile bands of Indians. A pitiable condition, truly, and one which called forth the sympathy of their new-made friends. They were literally strangers in a strange land, and their own country, for which they would naturally yearn under such circumstances, unsafe as a retreat from the dangers which there presented themselves.

Their sad condition soon became noised abroad, and reached the ears of those in authority, and ere long a movement was inaugurated, in which President Washington was interested, to compel the Scioto Company to reimburse them the money of which they had been defrauded. As might have been expected, these negotiations occupied much time, and sorely tried the patience of the forlorn emigrants, insomuch that some gave up in despair, and sought other homes, some going to New York and Philadelphia, some settling in Alexandria, and a few returning to France. At length an agreement was entered into with Colonel Duer, the Company's agent at New York, whereby, as far as the means under his control would permit, the emigrants should be transported to the West, and established on the Ohio River at a point opposite the mouth of the Big Kanawha, where they expected their town to be located, erect suitable block houses for defence against the attacks of Indians, and survey and lay out a town to be divided among them in proportion to cash paid in Paris by each individual on their lands. 'A written agreement to this effect was made, and with such a compromise, which was more perhaps than they had dared to hope for, the emigrants abandoned all claims upon the lands for which they held deeds. The second stage journey was now about to begin. Wagons and supplies were obtained, and the travelers departed. This journey was far more perilous, no doubt, than the long and stormy passage across the Atlantic. The dangers by the way-side consisted of attacks from the Indians, sickness and fatigue. In addition to these, progress was slow in consequence of the almost impassable condition of the roads, and the insufficiency of the supplies provided for their maintenance. Their route was through the Valley of Virginia, near the town of Winchester; thence in a north-westerly direction via Brownsville, Pennsylvania, and to the Ohio. The traveler of the present day, when he speeds through this section of the country, and views it from the window of his Pullman car, can form but little idea of the trials and privations of that long jonrney. Think of a number people, including women and little children, finding a way over those high mountains, and across swollen streams, meagerly supplied with food, and harassed at all times by fear of the ever-vigilant savage, and you may fancy the experience of these emigrants. The Scioto Company had contracted with General Rufus Putnam to erect buildings and furnish the settlers with provisions for a year, and he sent Major Burnham down from Fort Harmar on the Muskingum River with forty men for that purpose. The first town, under the name of Fair Haven, had been laid out by the Company opposite the mouth of the Kanawha, was intended as the point for the location of the French settlers, but as the ground was considered low there, and liable to overflow, Major Burnham and his party wisely proceeded to a point four miles below, where the high banks could well withstand the rising waters, as has been since proved to the satisfaction of the residents. The locating party arrived here June 8th, 1790, and immediately began the work of preparation for the settlers, who would make a home here in the wilderness. This was no doubt a most arduous undertaking, but determined energy made itself felt, and soon there were evidences that order would emerge from chaos. Trees, brush, and other debris made

way for the houses, which formed the new town. On what is
now the Public Square were erected eighty log cabins, twenty
in a row. At each of the corners were block-houses two stories
in height. In front of the cabins, close by the river bank, was
a small log breast-work. Above the cabins, on the square, were
two other parallel rows of cabins, which, with a high stockade
fence, and block-houses at each of the upper corners, formed a
sufficient fortification in times of danger. These upper cabins
were a story and a half in height, built of hewn logs, and
furnished in better style than those below, being intended for
the wealthier class, and those appointed to manage and superin-
tend the interests of the colony. Such was the home which the
emigrant found for his reception, when, weary and travel-worn,
he at length reached his final destination. He had journeyed
far by sea and land, and dreamed bright dreams, and was it all
for this? A few log cabins with a background of forest, in
which was the home of the sworn enemy of the white race.

France is a country no larger in extent than one of the
average-sized states of the Union, and at this time its population was about twenty-five millions. Think of five hundred
people from this thickly populated place, and composed entirely
of those ignorant of what would be required of them in a new
land — physicians, lawyers, jewelers and other artisans, a few
mechanics, servants to the exiled nobility, and many with no
trade or profession — suddenly placed in a wilderness of this
kind, and infested by wild beasts and murderous bands of
Indians. They were as inexperienced in pioneer life as children.
The hardy natures of such rugged characters as Daniel Boone,
or any one of those who preceded the march of progress, could
readily combat the difficulties which were likely to present themselves. They knew what to expect in frontier life, and it was
even with a sense of enjoyment perhaps, that they engaged in
the work of preparing the way for the settler. Our French
emigrants, however, could not view the prospects without
consternation and conjecture as to the many difficulties which
would arise in their work of making the best of a bad bargain.
The solution of the problem was with them, and as subsequent
events proved, many of them rose bravely to the occasion.

There are some people whose strength and grandeur of character would never be known save by means of severe tests. Heart trials most frequently prove to be blessings in disguise, on account of the way in which they represent the true worth of a man's character. The pure metal cannot be obtained save through the medium of the smelting furnace. Thus it was with the French settlers at Gallipolis, for they not only determined to remain, but made a success of what appeared a hopeless cause. At an early meeting of the settlers, the town was named Gallipolis (City of the Gauls—French). The work of making their new home attractive was long and arduous, this latter being the natural result of the inexperience of the settlers. Everything that they did had to be learned, and with as many hard knocks as a school-boy experiences with his Latin verbs, but indomitable perseverance gave its usual testimony, in that the lesson was learned. Quoting the words of one who has written on this subject: "A description of early attempts to adapt themselves to circumstances, would be amusing, but doubtless was no joke to them."

A number were seriously wounded, and some lost their lives in learning to fell trees. Having no knowledge of the use of the axe, some two or three would tackle a monster of the forest, girdling the tree, and giving the death blow at the heart; as can readily be seen, the tree would oftentimes slip from the stump upon the workmen, or more frequently they (or the admiring group who were watching the process) not being able to tell the direction in which the tree would fall, would be crushed to the ground under the heavy branches. A short experience of this kind sharpened their wits, and by placing strong men at the ends of the two ropes, the other end being fastened to the tree, they found that they could guide it in its fall, and this operation thereafter became less dangerous.

It will be seen from such incidents as this that, although the settlers were enterprising, courageous, and willing to work, and mainly very intelligent, as a class, they were obliged to suffer by practical experience before they were able to adapt themselves to the new mode of living, or make much substantial progress in rendering their situation comfortable, as we must all suffer, when we are learning a new principle in life. We must always learn effectually, by means of experience, but experience is quite frequently a stern and merciless teacher.

An account of this settlement, by an eye witness, will not, we believe, be uninteresting here. The letter of Monsieur Mentelle to the *American Pioneer*, a magazine published in Cincinnati, in the April number, 1843, among other matters contains the following: "I did not arrive till nearly all the colonists were there. I descended the river in 1791, in flat boats loaded with troops, commanded by General St. Clair, destined for an expedition against the Indians. Some of my countrymen joined that expedition, among others was Count Malartie, a captain of the French Guard of Louis XVI." Concerning the settlement at Gallipolis, he said among other things: "Notwithstanding the great difficulties, the difference of tempers, education and professions, the inhabitants lived in harmony. The Americans and hunters employed by the Company, performed the first labors of clearing the township which was divided into lots. Although the French were willing to work, yet the clearing of the American wilderness and its heavy timber was far more than they could perform. To migrate from the eastern States to the 'far west' is painful enough now-a-days, but how much more so must it be for a citizen of a large European town! Even the farmer of the old countries would find it very hard, if not impossible, to clear land in the wilderness." The hunters, who supplied the colonists with fresh meat, "were paid by the colonists, to prepare their garden ground, which was to receive seeds brought from France; few of the colonists knew how to make a garden, but they were guided by books on that subject, likewise brought from France. The colony began to improve in its appearance and comfort. The fresh provisions were supplied by the Company's hunters, the others came from the magazines." These represented some of the bright features of the early life of the colonists, and all seemed working well, and no doubt lively hopes were excited in their breasts that the difficulties of their hitherto trying position were lessening, but again they were called upon to face disappointment. At this time it became apparent that the Scioto Company could not obtain for them any further remuneration for the impositions that had been practiced upon them. The Company had fulfilled nearly all their engagements for the first six months, after which they ceased their supply of provisions to the colonists, and it was given as a reason, that one or two of their agents who had received the funds in France for the purchased land, had run off with the money to England, and the Company were defrauded of the whole, without having purchased or gained title to any of the tract which they had sold to the deceived colonists.

An unusually severe winter had set in, and the rigor of climate was added to other trials and difficulties. The Ohio had frozen over, so that flat boats could not come down with flour from above; the hunters no longer had meat to sell. The people were destitute of almost everything except a scanty supply of vegetables, and almost a famine was produced in the settlement. The money and clothes they had brought with them were nearly gone; they knew not to whom to go to get their lands (for they did not even own their homes), and their condition became such as to excite despair. Looking back upon them through the lapse of years, our minds are filled with sympathetic thoughts, and the fact that these difficulties were successfully combated kindles within us a feeling of admiration and pride. The Pilgrim Fathers, who landed "on wild New England's shore," and whose hardihood and determination have sounded their praises down the ages, deserve little less laudation in the pages of history than the settlers of our town, who have left, as a rich heritage, to those who have lived after them, the testimony of the unconquerable nature of brave perseverance. Following this condition of affairs, the fear of the Indians disturbed their peace of mind. "When," says Mentelle (speaking of some months previous of the expeditions of Generals St. Clair and Wayne), "many of the troops stopped at Gallipolis, the Indians who, no doubt, came there in the night, at last saw the regulars going morning and evening round the town in order to ascertain if there were any Indian traces, attacked them, killing and wounding several—a soldier, besides other wounds, was tomahawked, but recovered. A French colonist, who had tried to raise cane some distance from town, seeing an Indian rising from behind some brushwood against a tree, shot him in the shoulder. The Indian, hearing an American patrol, must have thought that the Frenchman made a part of it, and sometime afterward a Frenchman was killed, and a man and woman made prisoners as they were going to collect ashes to make soap, at some distance from town. After this, although the Indians committed depredations on the Americans on both sides of the river, the French had suffered only by the loss of some cattle carried away, until the murder of the man referred to. As the severe winter advanced, "the dangers from the Indians augmented every day. Kanawha had been visited by one of these sad events, that few of the present generation can realize, otherwise than by comparing it to a romantic tale with ghosts. A Captain Vonbever had gone to make sugar at a little distance from and opposite to Kanawha. He had his negro man with him, intending to make sugar and raise corn, but staid to make sugar only. The camp was fronting the river and in sight of Kanawha. They had not been there long when the negro saw an Indian running after him. He warned his master, who was not far from the house, and they both entered it at the same time and secured the door. The Indian, thinking they had no arms, and whose intention it was to carry off the negro, turned back as soon as he saw them in the house, and was shot by the negro with a gun that was loaded with buck-shot. The alarm spread to Kanawha; the inhabitants came in their canoes, thinking that there might be more Indians, but on their landing they saw only the body of a single one, which, after having stripped of what he had, they threw into the river; the corpse floated down and was carried by the stream on the shore of Gallipolis the next day, as if to confirm the rumor which they had heard that morning, and as a warning to themselves. Captain Vonbever had let his beard grow, and had sworn to leave it so until he should have taken a complete revenge of the Indians, who had killed one of his children.

The expedition against the Indians by General St. Clair having met with signal defeat, the Indians were encouraged to greater depredations in the Western land, but fortunately for our colonists they were directed principally against Americans. The hostile tribes imagined that the French settlers were from Canada, and with the French at that place they were on terms of friendship. Immediately after St. Clair's defeat, Colonel Sproat, of Marietta, appointed four spies for Gallipolis, one of whom was Monsieur Mentelle from whom we quoted a moment ago. These were released after the treaty of Greenville in 1795. Honorable Rufus Putnam, at Marietta, was the acknowledged head of all the settlements in Washington county, which then embraced a territory now covered by nearly forty counties, and to him an application was made and steps were taken to organize a defensive force. By his orders, Colonel Ebenezer Sproat appointed Captain Dr. Francis Hebecourt, a man of distinguished qualifications, to take command. A Frenchman named Malden was appointed Lieutenant, and C. R. Menager, Ensign. A company of ninety colonists offered their services, who were divided into squads of ten, and on each succeeding day one squad, or patrol company, was to start out in the morning to act in conjunction with the scouts or spies, whose duty it was to return every night and report the presence or absence of Indians. In this way a defense was kept up until General Wayne defeated the Indians at the battle of "Fallen Timbers," on the Maumee Rapids, five miles above Perrysburg, Ohio, August 20th, 1794, and made the treaty of peace at Greenville in 1795 with all the Western tribes. After peace was declared, a free intercourse took place between them and the colonists from Massachusetts and other New England states at Marietta and Belpre, and with settlements at Point Pleasant and Charleston, Virginia. Thus, in an alternate atmosphere of hopes and fears, the colonists passed the first years of their lives in the New World. They were, perhaps, becoming accustomed to the changed conditions of their existence. Even in the far away western wilderness, they were recognizing home ties, and pleasant associations were being formed which endeared this wild country to them. France, with its attractions, had passed out of their lives; such represented but features of the past, and would be to them but fond recollections of what had been. There was one great difficulty which had to be surmounted, however, before they could reso-

lutely face life in this country. The titles to their homes had
never been perfected; indeed, there was every reason to suppose
that they were living on land which belonged to other people.
Although it had been sold to them by the Scioto Company,
which had transported them thither, the fact remained that the
Ohio Company still held the titles to it, inasmuch as that corporation had bought and paid for it, and there had been no just or
legal transfer of it to other parties, it was but rational that the
owners should be demanding their rights   This dilemma which
they had known that they must face, when it reached its climax,
brought with it its disheartening influences; indeed, so great
must have been the discouragements that the disruption of all
the new ties must have been threatened,   A letter from Mr.
B. J. D. Le Ture, a Gallipolis merchant, who had removed to
Cincinnati for business purposes, and which is now in the
possession of Maj. E. C. Dawes, of Cincinnati, throws some
light on the situation at this time.   It is written under date of
July 6th, 1792, and is addressed to Mr. John Matthews at
Gallipolis. Mr. Le Ture says: ''The situation of the colony
alarms me much. I cannot think so many people will be sacri-
ficed to a few speculators. Should anything turn up that would
oblige me to go to the settlement, I believe it will be in my
power to advise them on the methods they are to take in order
to have justice done them.'' Some of the colonists became disheartened and went off and settled elsewhere with the means
that remained to them, and resumed their trades in more populous parts of the country. Others led a half savage life, common among pioneers, as hunters for skins; and affairs, for a
time, wore a gloomy aspect. The more determined ones, however, who appear to have represented the rank and file of the
colony resolved upon a course of action, which, if successful,
would give them homes which they so ardently craved. Six
years had now passed since they had sailed from Havre de
Grace, and an enumeration showed that but three hundred of
them were left. These, in general assembly, resolved to make a
memorial of their grievances and send it to Congress. The
memorial claimed no right from that body, but was a detail of
their wrongs and sufferings, together with an appeal to the

generosity of the government, and they did not appeal in vain. Monsieur Jean G. Gervais started with the petition, and at Philadelphia met with a lawyer, M. Duponceau, through whose aid he obtained from Congress a grant of twenty-four thousand acres of land, known as the ''French Grant,'' and located opposite the Little Sandy, for the people who still remained in Gallipolis. The act annexed the condition of settling on the lands for three years before the deed of gift would be given. M. Gervais received four thousand acres of this land for his services in the matter, according to previous agreement. Each inhabitant had thus a tract of two hundred and seventeen and a half acres of land; but before the surveys and other arrangements could be made, some time was necessary during which those who had reclaimed the wilderness and improved Gallipolis, being reluctant to lose all their labor, and finding that a company, owning the lands at Marietta, had met to divide lands, which they had purchased in a common stock, the colonists sent a deputation with a proposal to sell to them the tract where Gallipolis is situated, and to be paid in proportion to what was improved, which was accepted. When at last the distribution of the French grant was achieved, some sold their share, others went to settle on it, while many sent tenants, and either remained at Gallipolis or went elsewhere. Colonel Robert Safford, so familiarly known as one of the number of Major Burnham's band, who felled the first tree on the site of what was afterward Gallipolis, was present at the drawing of these lots, and has thus related the circumstances: ''General Putnam appointed Mr. Martin to survey the grant, and after this was done and the lots numbered, Messrs. Manmey, Putnam and Talmadge appointed a day when all who were to get land were to meet in the public square. The day came and all assembled. The names of those having an interest were written upon square pieces of paper, and as many like pieces were numbered. The papers were placed in two small boxes, two clerks were appointed and two disinterested men were selected, to each of whom one of the boxes was given. When all was ready, the boxes were shaken and then opened. Colonel Safford was selected to draw out the papers which were numbered. As he drew out one and announced the number the clerk took it down, then from the other box a name was drawn which, being announced, was taken down as the owner of the number just drawn. They proceeded thus until the whole number were distributed."

After a long time, as it appeared to the settler, some of the hopes which had encouraged him, were realized, in that the French grant had been obtained and Gallipolis had become the property of its citizens. True, there were not many left, comparatively speaking, to enjoy the homes which had been won in so laborious and perilous a manner, but there was deep satisfaction, no doubt, in realizing, that although the fierce battle had been fought, the victory was won.

Now, having described the inauguration and accomplishment of this enterprise of establishing a colony and building a town on the banks of the Ohio, we will turn our attention, for a brief period, to the topography of 'Gallipolis, in the first stages of its growth. We have before us a map of the town and surrounding country as they were in earlier days. It represents the plan of the lots drawn by the inhabitants of Gallipolis January 20, 1791, and the outlines of the city are very accurate, and easily recognized by those acquainted with it now. A more interesting document than this, and which we have been fortunate enough to secure, is a list of the town lots of Gallipolis with their original disposition. The original of this was probably made in Paris, when the anticipative colonist was about to depart to his new home, or it may have been made after the first stages of his long and weary journey had been completed, when, after having been tortured by apprehension, the order had come for him to move on to possess the land, just before he left Alexandria, Virginia. We append this list, thinking it peculiarly interesting in this connection.

A numeral list of the town lots of Gallipolis, with their original disposition:

Claude Morrell	1	Jean B. Parmentier	46
Jean B. Laurent.	2	Francis Valten	47
Charles Vaux Maret	3	Laurent Bergnen	48
Maguet, son.	4	Jean B. Duchallard	49
Colinet	5	Nicholas Petit.	50
Etienne Chandivert	6	Antoine Porquier	51
Mad. Clavet	7	Etienne Willermy	52
Jean B. Cherrin	8	Francis Quartel	53
Pierre A. L. Huillier	9	Benjamin Armand.	54
Francis Picard	10	Jean M. Guillot	55
Minguey, father	11	Charles Soudry	56
Pierre Louis LeClerc	12	Catherine Avelin	57
Claude Bana	13	Matthieu Berthelot	58
Claude J. Naudet.	14	Peter Lecke	59
Marchand	15	Jacques Renouard	60
Winant Devacht	16	Antoine Vibert	61
Jean M. Hammer	17	Jean B. Ginat	62
Jean Buzenet	18	Sigisbert Chevraux	63
Nicholas Vissinier	19	Pierre Lafellard	64
Sald	20	Gervais	65
Grouet	21	Lemoyne, younger	66
Humbert Pamar	22	Jean C. Belliere	67
Guillaume Duduit	23	Droz	68
Jean G. Vallot	24	Joseph Dupont	69
Louis Victor Vonschritz	25	Jean Louis Vonschritz	70
Michaud	26	Francis Dutiel	71
Jean B. Ancil	27	Alexander Frere	72
Michel Cranzat	28	Claude DuBois	73
Pierre Chandivert.	29	Jean B. Ferard	74
Nicholas Thevenin	30	Jean P. Laperouse	75
D'Hebecourt	31	Nicholas Hedouin	76
Retained 30th Dec	32	Michel Mazure	77
" "	33	Pierre M. Richards	78
" "	34	Colat	79
Saugrain	35	Petit	80
"	36	Coupin	81
Pierre Magnier	37	"	82
D'Hebecourt	38	Laforge retained	83
Jos. Dazet	39		84
Frederick Bergeret	40	Jean Louis Imbert	85
Jacques Petit Jean	41	Jean Courtier	86
Jean G. Petit	42	Pierre Matry	87
Francis Darveux	43	Joseph Goiyon	88
Alexander Roussell	44	Alex. Chevalier	89
Jean B. Quetee	45	Claude Dupligny	90

Jean Louis Colat 91
    Minguey, son 92
Louis DelaBouye 93
Cesar Maufelit 94
Pierre Chabot.................. 95
    Taillem 96
Pierre L. Guibert. 97
Pierre A. Laforge........ 98
Claude Berthelot. ∴ 99
Antoine Duc........ 100
Jean F. Grand Jean. 101
Michel Chanterelle 102
Jean Pellison 103
Jean B. Anthiaume............ 104
    Lemonye, elder 105
    Louis Roublot 106
Antoine Saugrain 107
Thoncy Dehafosse............. 108
Marin Dupont...... 109
Petit Jean.................. . 110
Antoine Prieur............... 111
Augustin LeClerc 112
Leclerc and .... ⎫ 113
    Genet .... ⎭ 114
    Petit Jean 115
    Gervais................... 116
Sigismund D'Ilmee.... 117
Jean L. Violette............... 118
Madam LaCaisse 119
    D. Petit............. 120
Jean Pierre Ginet............. 121
Louis P. LeClerc 122
Francis L'Anguette............ 123
Pierre Serre...... 124
Louis A. Viment 125
Jean Autran ......⌐....... ... 126
Pierre Duteil.................. 127
Maximin Lefort................ 128
Minguet DeViguement 129
Francois Bourgougnat......... 130
Louis Berthe 131
Louis Maldant 132
Antrox Noel 133
Nicholas Quelet............... 134
    Valton.................... 135

Philip Aug. Pithon 136
John Rowe 137
    Mennessier 138
    DeHibecour.............. 139
    do   140
Firmin Bremiere ?............. 141
Brice DuCloz.......... 142
    Valton.................. 143
Claude Coupin 144
Pierre Maguet 145
Jean Desnoyers 146
Pierre Bidon 147
Claude Cadot................ 148
Pierre Thomas 149
    Malcher 150
Remy Cuif.................. 151
Claude Menager.............. 152
    De Hibecour 153
    do   154
    do   155
    do   156
    Menager..... 157
    Bastede...... ····· ... 158
    LeClar.................. 159
Etienne Allrien 160
Jacques Auger 161
Pierre Ferard 162
Marie Dallier............. .. 163
Michel Chillard 164
    Menager.................. 165
    do......... 166
Doctor Petit 167
Berthelot Senior.............. 168
    Gervais.................. 169
    DeLaBaume............... 170
    do   171
Louis Vialett... 172
Francois P. Malcher.......... 173
Francois Durand 174
I. Guion Caille............. 175
Antoine Jacquemin 176
Francois Patin 177
Joseph Damervalle........ ... 178
Antoine Charpentier........... 179
Jean Louis Devanne.......... 180

Jean Rouilly	181	Jean A. Foulon	193
Julien Pradel	182	Hullier	194
Simen Batterelle	183	do	195
Jean Aug. Pingard	184	DeHebecourt	196
Mouvel	185	Rouby	197
George Chalot	186	Emille Lefeve	198
Jean Regnier	187	Nicholas Hingston	199
Antoine Rouby	188	Pierre F. Perot	200
Cesar Baredot	189	Francois Valot	235
Jacquemin	190	Francois Carteron	236
Eloy Frere	191	Prioux Aiglemont	234
Abel Sarazin	192		

Whether this plan was followed, we are unable to say, but are inclined to the opinion that it was not, in view of the complications arising from subsequent events. We have access also to the account of the price and distribution of the lots of Gallipolis, which were written about five years after the settlers landed here. This also we think is right to give in full: "Gallipolis, this the 14th day of December, 1795. P. Bureau and J. M. Berthelot have published and given notice, that Monday next they will render account to the French inhabitants of their mission as agents to treat with the Ohio Company. To-day, Monday, the assembled inhabitants, after having agreed to purchase the land of the Ohio Company, have proceeded to choose by secret ballot, commissioners to examine the rights of pre-emption of the inhabitants to the city lots, and of four acres of cultivated land, and also to fix the price of city lots and of the four acres according to what they were worth before they were occupied. Whereupon the inhabitants have unanimously named for commissioners: Marin Duport, Mathieu Berthelot, Jean Parmentier, Christopher Etienne, Francis DeVacht, Jean Baptiste, Le Tailleur, Jean Pierre, Roman Bureau. To-day, Monday, 6 o'clock P. M. The commissioners have unanimously appointed Marin Duport moderator, and Christopher Etienne secretary, of the committee. It has also been resolved that Anselm Tupper, surveyor, be chosen for any operations of surveying that may be found necessary. *Resolved*, That Mr. Tupper, accompanied by Mr. Bureau, shall go to examine the line which separates the lands proposed to be bought from the reserved lands, and from

those belonging to the Ohio Company, in order to proceed immediately to such operations as they shall judge to be proper.
[These reserved lands were those set apart for educational and
religious purposes, being sections 16 and 29.]   It has been resolved that the public be warned by notices to repair to the
house of Messrs. Saugrain and Bureau. in order to make known
their rights and claims to the property of Gallipolis.   Signed Le
Tailleur, Parmentier, M. Berthelot, J. G. DeVacht, M. Duport,
P. Bureau

December 16.   The committee, after having been occupied
the entire day in receiving the claims of proprietors, have resolved to give new notice to those who have not yet presented
their claims to come to-morrow, in order to finish the work.

December 16.   *Resolved*, That this plan shall hereafter be
placed before the eyes of the people as the only one which appears proper, in order to conciliate the different interests of the
proprietors considering the position of the different pieces of
land, in order that those persons who have few lots, and of
which the situation is not advantageous, be not overcharged.

PLAN.

The banks of the river and the commons not having been
surveyed, and never having been regarded as property, we have
thought it right that they be placed at a price proportioned to
their importance by reason of their position.   Lots on the bank
of the river and of the square (Public Square), being a source
of wealth by reason of their position, we have thought that they
should be placed at a price higher than the others.   The lots on
the banks of the river more remote have been placed at a price
lower than the preceding, but higher than those which are remote from the river.   The lands which remain to be divided,
being for the greater part mountainous or hilly, have been, in
consequence, placed at a low price.   Then follows the designa-
tion of the lots, and prices attached, after which the following
resolutions:

Resolved, For the public good, and for the interests of the
inhabitants, the streets and Public Square shall remain free,
without being closed on the bank of the river by any building,
or being sold.

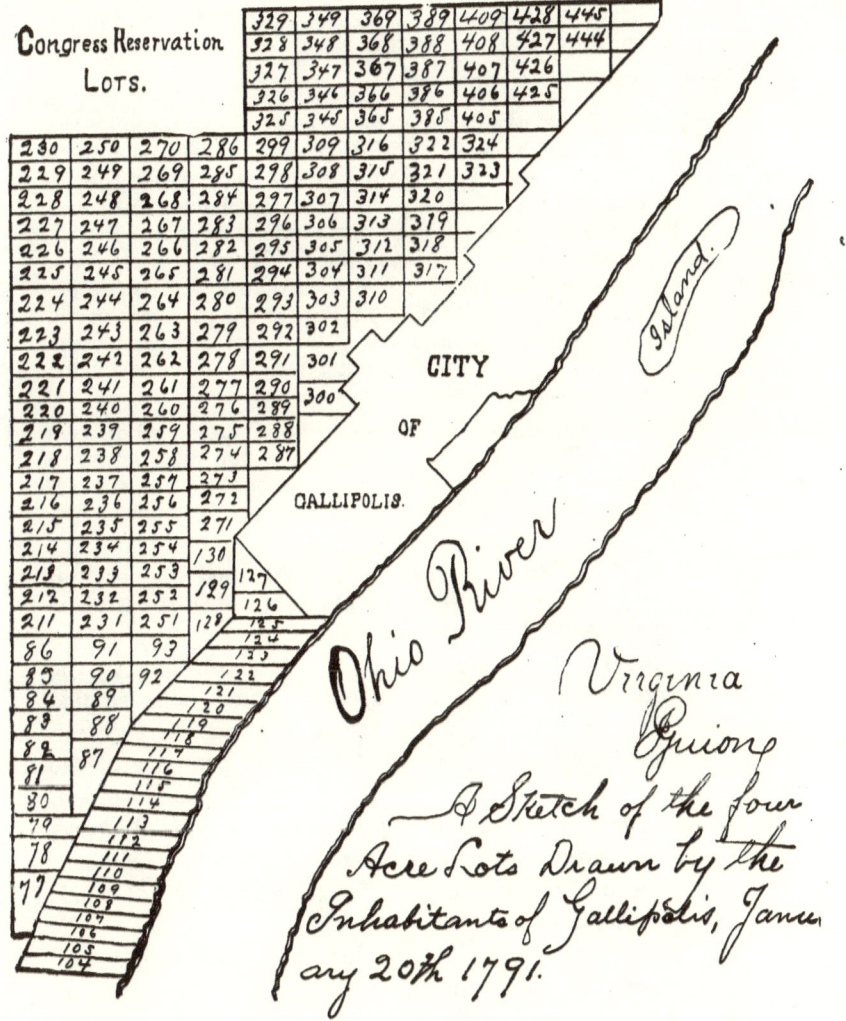

(61)

Resolved, That the public be notified to meet to-morrow to receive the report of the work of the committee.

Resolved, That the banks of the river shall remain open, facing each street, that lines shall be drawn in the direction of the streets, without trespassing thereon.

Plans accepted, Etienne, sec.

December 17, *Resolved,* That the secretary be ordered by the committee to go the house of DHebercourt, to request him to declare if it is his intention to join himself with us for the acquisition of our property, as his partner Dr. Petit has done; and to say to him that the execution of the plan adopted by the inhabitants requires a positive answer. Etienne, sec. Mr. DHebercourt has replied that he is disposed to agree to the acquisition of the lands of Gallipolis, paying for his property seven shillings, six-pence per acre, and that he will not conform to the plan adopted until he has taken such steps as he believes his interests require. Etienne, sec.

Resolved, That Messrs. Berthelot and Duport, whom we have appointed collectors, go to the houses of the inhabitants to receive the sums set down on the list made between us, according to the plan agreed on by the inhabitants, December 17th, 1795.

Resolved, That Mr. Duport is by us appointed cashier, and in this capacity the money remain in his hands until the time of payment for the lands.

December 19, 1795. According to the resolutions of the committee on the 16th of this month, agreed to by the assembled inhabitants, reserved lots near the square, divided into eighteen equal portions, have been drawn by lot, in the presence of the assembled inhabitants, and fell to Messrs. Vandenbemben, Chandiver father, Chandiver son, Vonschriltz, Gervais, Ferrare, jr., La Cour, Davoux, Villerain, Muqui, Quarleron, Michau, Brunier, Bureau, Lafillard, child of Vonschriltz, sr., Francis Valodin, and Pierre Richou.

Dec. 22d. By virtue of the resolution of the committee of the 18th, Messrs. Marin, Duport and Mathieu Berthelot have engaged in receiving the sums to be given by each proprietor, which sums have amounted to £194 5s. 6d. in money, and orders to Mr. Sproat for the appointment of spies, of which sum the money amounted to £91 3s. 2d. Bills on different persons,

£ 203. Orders of spies on current appointment, £ 553, which sums form a total of £ 1042 2s. 8d.

Resolved, That Messrs. Mathieu, Berthelot, Roman Bureau, and Marin Duport, De Vacht, and Jean Le Tailleur, go to Marietta in the name of the committee of the inhabitants of Gallipolis, to conclude with the . Ohio Company the acquisition of the two squares (of land) indicated in the plan which has been given us by the agents of the Ohio Company.   ETIENNE, Sec.

                                                PARMENTIER.

Of the manner of life of the early settlers in Gallipolis, our sources of information are meagre, but sufficient to give us a tolerably accurate idea of the state of affairs. The French, like other nations of Southern Europe, possess a cheerful disposition, but being also excitable, this is characterized very often by extreme degrees of elation or depression. They have winning manners and are warmly hospitable, and are remarkable for their thrift and ingenuity. That these traits were marked among the early settlers we think is proved by what has already been said, as well as what we have learned from the early historian.

Quite a flood of light is thrown upon this branch of our subject by the account given by John Heckewelder of his visit to Gallipolis, in company with General Putnam, when making a journey from the upper waters of the Ohio to the Wabash River in the interest of the government in Indian affairs, in the year 1792. He says: "We rode to the French settlement of Gallipolis, situated on the north bank of the Ohio, between three and four miles from the Kanawha. Here we spent the whole of the following day in visiting the skilled workmen and the gardens laid out in European style. The most interesting shops of the workmen were those of goldsmiths and watchmakers. They showed us work on watches, compasses and sundials finer than any I had ever beheld. Next in interest were the sculptors and stonecutters. These latter had two finished mantels, most artistically carved. General Putnam at once purchased one of them for twelve guineas, the other was intended for a rich Dutch gentleman who has built a two-story house here, fifty feet long. The upper part of a mantel was lying there, ordered by a Spanish gentleman in New Orleans, which,

because of the fine workmanship upon it, was to cost twenty or
twenty-two guineas. The worker in glass seemed to be a born
artist. He made us a thermometer, a barometer, a glass tobacco
pipe, a small bottle (which would contain about a thimble full),
and a most diminutive stopper, and a number of works of art
besides. He also manufactured precious medicine, nitric acid,
etc. As we were on a journey, and were in daily need of light
and fire, he presented us with a glass full of dry stuff, which
burns as soon as a match is applied. This stuff, he told us, was
manufactured from bones. Concerning the fine gardens, I must
add the following: that in them were to be found the most beautiful flowers, artichokes, and almond trees, and besides many
vineyards and some rice fields. At a distance of about one hundred steps from the Ohio, there is a round hill, which probably
dates its origin from the former inhabitants of this land, as also
the remarkable fortifications and buildings to be found in this
country. The hill, about thirty feet high, has been improved as
a beautiful pleasure garden, with a pretty summer house on top.
The town of Gallipolis consists of one hundred and fifty dwellings. The inhabitants number between three and four hundred. A detachment of from fifty to sixty men of the regular
army is stationed here for protection. Besides a few Virginia
spies or scouts are kept and paid by the government. The
militia are also willing to serve for remuneration. The Chicke-
mage Creek flows back of the town, and below it empties into
the Ohio. Fine boats are also manufactured in this town; our
vessel is one of them. At noon we dined with the most prominent French gentleman of the place, at the home of the judge
and doctor, Mr. Petit."

On his return from Vincennes, on the Wabash, Mr. Heckewelder speaks of again stopping at Gallipolis, and alludes feel-
ingly to the troubles through which the people were passing,
owing to the complications in the matter of their land titles, a
very clear but concise account of which he gives, together with
the whole transaction with the agents of the Scioto Company.
From this it will be seen that our settlers were not people who
would remain inactive or slothful even when surrounded by
many and great difficulties, but worked faithfully to make their

new homes attractive, and their works have, through the years
which have since elapsed, borne testimony to their earnestness
of purpose.

A much fuller account of life among our settlers is given in
a work entitled "Recollections of Persons and Places in the
West," by H. M. Brackenridge. Mr. Brackenridge was born
at the village of Fort Pitt, on the site of what is now the
city of Pittsburg. At a very early age he was sent by
his father to the village of St. Genevieve in Louisiana for
the purpose of making him acquainted with the French language. This distance of fifteen hundred miles, which lay between him and his home, was traveled by means of a flat boat.
After spending several years at the village of St. Genevieve, and
acquiring the language, he departed in company with a gentleman sent for him to return to Fort Pitt. On account of the inclemency of the weather to which he was exposed, owing to the
scanty accommodations afforded by the flat boat, as well perhaps
as climatic causes, he was taken quite sick with fever and ague
shortly after the arrival at Louisville, where, it seems that a stop
of some days was made. After the journey had been further
prosecuted, he grew no better, and on the arrival at Gallipolis
he was taken to a house in the village and left there. The
exact date of this is not given, but from the dates previously
mentioned it appears to have been some time previous to 1795.
The account of his sojourn here can best be given in his own
words:

"Behold me once more in port, and domiciliated at the
house or inn of Monsieur, or rather Doctor, Saugrain, a cheerful, sprightly little Frenchman, four feet six, English measure,
and a chemist, natural philosopher, and physician, both in the
English and French signification of the word. I was delighted
with my present liberation from the irksome thralldom of the
canoe, and with the possession of the free use of my limbs.
After wrapping my blanket round me, which was my only bed-
ding, I threw myself into a corner for a couple of hours, during
the continuance of the fever and ague, and then rose up re-
freshed, with the lightness of spirits which I possessed in an
unusual degree. I ran out of the house and along the bank,

where I met a boy about my own size. I laid hold of him in mirth, but he, mistaking my vivacity, gave me a sound beating. The next day the doctor tried his skill upon me, or rather upon my ague, and pretty much on the plan of another celebrated physician, whether on the principle of the *solviente universal*, I do not so well know, but certain it is, he repeated the very words recorded by Gil Blas : '*Bebe agua, hijo mio, bebe agua in abundancia'*— drink water, my son, drink plenty of water. But the ague was not to be shaken off so easily ; it still continued to visit me daily, as usual, all that winter and part of the next spring. I was but poorly clad, and was without hat or shoes, but gradually became accustomed to do without them; like the Indian, I might in time have become all face. My guardian left no money, perhaps he had none to leave; Mr. Saugrain had none to spare; besides as this was the period when the French Revolution was at its height, *sans culottism* was popular with those who favored the breaking up of social economy. Dr. Saugrain, however, and many others in Gallipolis were not of that party, they were royalists, who bitterly lamented the condition of their native country. Gallipolis, with the exception of a few straggling log houses, of which that of Dr. S. was one, consisted of two long rows of barracks built of logs, and partitioned off into rooms of sixteen or twenty feet wide, with what is called a cabin roof and wooden chimneys. At one end there was a larger room than the rest, which served as a council chamber and ball room. This singular village was settled by people from Paris and Lyons, chiefly artisans and artists, peculiarly unfitted to sit down in the wilderness and clear away forests. Their former employments had only been calculated to administer to the luxury of high polished and wealthy societies. There were carvers and guilders to the King, coach-makers, frizeurs and peruke-makers, and a variety of others, who might have found employment in our larger towns, but who were entirely out of their place in the wilds of Ohio. Their means by this time had been exhausted, and they were beginning to suffer from the want of the comforts and even the necessaries of life. The country back from the river was still a wilderness, and the Gallipolitans did not pretend to cultivate anything more than small

garden spots, depending for their supply of provisions on the
boats, which now began to descend the river; but they had to
pay in cash, and that was become scarce. They still assembled
at the ball room twice a week; it was evident, however, that
they felt disappointment, and were no longer happy. The pre-
dilections of the best of them being on the side of the Bourbons,
the horrors of the Revolution, even in their remote position,
mingled with their private misfortunes, which had, at this time,
nearly reached their acme, in consequence of the discovery that
they had no title to their lands, having been cruelly deceived by those from whom they had purchased. It is
well known that Congress generously made them a grant
of twenty thousand acres, from which, however, but few of
them derived any advantage. As the Ohio was now more frequented, the house was occasionally resorted to, and especially
by persons looking out for land to purchase. The doctor had a
small apartment, which contained his chemical apparatus, and I
used to sit by him, as often as I could, watching the curious
operations of his blow-pipe and crucible. I loved the cheerful
little man, and he became very fond of me in turn. Many of
my countrymen used to come and stare at his doings, which
they were half inclined to think had too near a resemblance to
the black art. The doctor's little phosphoric matches ignited
spontaneously when the glass tube was broken, and from which
he derived some emolument, was thought by some to be rather
beyond mere human power. His barometers, and thermome-
ters, with the scale neatly painted with the pen, and the frames
richly carved, were objects of wonder, and some of them are
probably still extant in the West. But what astonished some of
our visitors was a large peach in a glass bottle, the neck of
which could only admit a common cork. This was accomplished
by tying the bottle to the limb of the tree, with the peach when
young inserted into it. His swans, which swam round basins
of water, amused me more than any of the wonders exhibited
by the wonderful man. The doctor was a great favorite with
the Americans, as well for his vivacity and sweetness of temper
which nothing could sour, as on account of a circumstance
which gave him high claims to the esteem of the backwoods-

men. He had shown himself, notwithstanding his small stature and great good nature, a very hero in combat with the Indians. He had descended the Ohio, in company with two French philosophers, who were believers in the primitive innocence of and goodness of the children of the forest. They could not be persuaded that any danger was to be apprehended from the Indians; as they had no intention to injure that people, they supposed, of course, that no harm could be meditated on their part. Dr. Saugrain was not altogether so well convinced of their good intentions, and accordingly kept his pistols loaded. Near the mouth of Big Sandy, a canoe with a party of warriors approached the boat; the philosophers invited them on board by signs, when they came rather too willingly. The first thing they did on entering the boat was to salute the two philosophers with the tomahawk; and they would have treated the doctor in the same way, but that he used his pistols with good effect; killed two of the savages and then leaped into the water, diving like a dipper at the flash of the guns of the others, and succeeded in swimming to the shore, with several severe wounds, whose scars were conspicuous.

"The doctor was married to an amiable young woman, but not possessing as much vivacity as himself. As Madame Saugrain had no maid to assist in household work, her brother, a boy of my age, and myself, were her principal helps in the kitchen. I used to go in the morning about two miles for a little milk, sometimes on the frozen ground, barefoot. I tried a pair of sabots, or wooden shoes, but was unable to make any use of them, although they had been made by the carver to the king."

Speaking of his other occupations, Mr. Brackenridge says: "In the spring and summer a good deal of my time was passed in the garden weeding the beds. It was while thus engaged that he formed an association which is interesting, as it bears somewhat on the future history of Gallipolis. He formed the acquaintance," he says, "of a young lady of eighteen or twenty, on the other side of the palings," who was often occupied as he was. "Our friendship," says he, "which was purely Platonic, commenced with the story of Blue Beard, recounted by her, and with the novelty and pathos of which I was much interested.

"Connected with this young lady there is an incident which I feel pleasure in relating. One day while standing alone on the bank of the river, I saw a man who had gone in to bathe and had got beyond his depth without being able to swim. He began to struggle for life, and in a few seconds would have sunk to rise no more. I shot down the bank like an arrow, leaped into a canoe, which, fortunately, happened to be close by, pushed the end of it to him, and as he rose, perhaps for the last time, he seized it with a deadly, convulsive grasp, and held so firmly that the skin afterward came off the parts of his arms which pressed against the wood. I screamed for help; several persons came and took him out perfectly insensible. He afterward married the young lady, and they raised a numerous and respectable family. One of his daughters married a young lawyer, who now represents that district in Congress. Thus at eight years of age I earned the civic crown by saving the life of a human being. I say this incident is interesting, and you will agree with me when I tell you the young lawyer referred to was Hon. Samuel F. Vinton, whom we recognize as one of the prominent figures, both in our State and Nation.

"Continuing his narrative in reference to the life in Gallipolis at that time, Mr. Brackenridge says that toward the latter part of the summer, the inhabitants suffered severely from sickness and want of provisions. The situation was truly wretched. The swamps in the rear, now exposed by the clearing between it and the river, became the cause of a frightful epidemic from which few escaped, and many became its victims. He, himself, had recovered from the ague, and was among the few exempted from the disease; but the family with whom he lived, as well as the rest, suffered much from absolute hunger. To show the extremity of the distress, he says that on one occasion, the brother of Madame Saugrain and himself pushed a light canoe to an island above the town where they pulled some corn and took it to a flouring mill, and excepting some of the raw grains, they had had nothing to eat since the day before, until they carried home the mela and made some bread, but had neither

milk nor meat. "I have learned," said he, "to be thankful
when I had a sufficiency of wholesome food, however plain, and
was blessed with health; and I could put up with humble fare
without a murmur, although accustomed to luxuries, when
I have seen those, who had never experienced absolute starvation, turn up their noses at that which was very little worse
than the best they have ever known, such are the uses of
adversity?"

It has not been our privilege to learn the internal state
of affairs in the colony during the years which immediately
succeeded this interesting narrative, but from what can be
learned through old inhabitants, some of whom were acquainted
with the early colonists, and most of whom have gone to their
reward, we feel assured that the thrift and enterprise of these
early days was but an index of what was to come after. After
the colonists had been safely established in their new homes, and
knew that in the future they would be free from the harassing
influence of litigation in consequence of defective land titles,
and had learned some of the secrets of border life, insomuch
that the prospective attacks from the Indians lost much of their
terror, being better acquainted as they were with the modes of
defence, their minds being less harassed, they were the better
able to enter heartily in the work which was before them, of
making the wilderness blossom as the rose.

We are persuaded that these years, which represented the
lull after the storm, were years of peace and contentment, and
consequently could, in after years, be regarded by those who
passed through them with pleasant remembrance. We are often
told that the good works which live after the performers have
gone, are the most powerful witnesses as to their faithfulness,
inasmuch as they not only benefit their day and generation, but
bespeak the earnestness of purpose, as well the kindly dispo-
position of the performers.

There are not many institutions among us which were
identified with the far off time indicated by our subject, but
there are those which indirectly sprung from the efforts of that
time and in which the characters and desires of the citizens are
so clearly portrayed, that we are forced to acknowledge that they

being dead yet speak. The influence of the French settlers has been felt through the many intervening years, and though our town has changed its population to a great degree, and American blood is flowing in the veins of many of our people, we cannot but think that the happy disposition of La Belle France is ever cropping out, and the pleasure-loving hearts of long ago are calling to us across the ages, and that the name Gallipolis is still appropriate when applied to our town, for in love, sympathy, and gratitude, as well as by the nearer ties of blood, we are the inhabitants of the city of the French.

Among the institutions which bring us into a close relationship with the earlier years of our town's history, there is one which we feel illustrates, to a certain degree, what has been said in regard to the works of its early inhabitants. A time honored and much appreciated institution we consider in the Gallia Academy. True it is, that this was not founded until about twenty years after the settlers arrived here, but the names of those who inaugurated it as an Educational medium are to be found among those who braved the difficulties identified with the settlement. This is among the oldest institutions of learning in the State, and at it "not only nearly all of the older residents of Gallipolis and Gallia county received their education, but many who afterward became men of great prominence, throughout the country, here took the first step in learning which led them on to fame."

A short account of its organization may not be inappropriate in this connection. A meeting was held February 8, 1810, for the purpose of taking into consideration the expediency of erecting in Gallipolis, an institution to be appropriated to the instruction of the youth, and such other purposes as may be deemed of public utility. Robert Saffort was chosen chairman and Nathaniel Gates secretary. A series of resolutions, embodying these principles, was passed at this meeting, and a subscription started which was circulated with satisfactory results. Among the subscribers are to be noted the names of some of the oldest and most honored citizens, many of whom are to be seen among the lot holders of Gallipolis of colonial

days. In due time, a lot was purchased, and a commodious.
building erected thereon, and the work of refining the mind, by
means of education, received an impetus which showed that the
builders of the Gallia Academy had done wisely and well.
From its portals have passed many who, as we say, have won
for themselves fame in after years; men whom the country delighted to honor, as well as those, who, in the more quiet walks
of life, have met the requirements of good and upright citizenship, and who were representatives of that class which compose
the rank and file of those who labored for the sure and steady
advancement of our country, and which has made it the grandest the sun shines upon. This venerable institution, could it
speak, could bear greater testimony to the admirable traits of
our forefathers than any ever yet recorded by the pen of the
historian.

As we pause in the spirit of meditation over the shifting
scenes which rise before us in a consideration of the early ages
of the French colony here, as well as the intervening years
which separate us from that distant date, we can find food for
much instructive thought, and we draw our lessons principally
from those who witnessed the early dawn of civilization in this
then far away Western wilderness.

The first trait of character which claims our admiration
was the earnestness of purpose which marked the lives of the
pioneers. 'Tis true, as we have shown, everything seemed
bright and promising when, in accordance with the representations of the land agents, they resolved to cast their lots in the
new and attractive land across the seas, but when subsequent
events changed the rosy dreams to a dark reality, and they
realized that they must face life in its most responsible and for-
bidding aspects, it required the strongest natures to remain un-
moved. No wonder it is that our record tells us that some of
them were not equal to the emergency, and went to seek satisfaction in life in more congenial atmospheres, some finding it in
the populous sections of our own country; and some, acknowledging themselves completely defeated, returned to France.
With the principal part of them, however, it was otherwise.
They had not left home and old associations, and come to this

distant land to fail. Although they had been grievously disappointed, they would accomplish that which they came to perform, a home where they would be unmolested by political storms or persecution. The mountains were high, the valleys deep, and the distance great which separated them from the homes of their adoption, but nothing was impossible in the face of that earnestness, which marked their progress. This disposition is the material of which heroes are made. The biographies of the good, the true, and the powerful tell us of exactly the same spirit as this, and which was the medium by which success crowned their efforts, and the world greatly was blessed.

Every inventor has to face the difficulties arising from an incredulous world. Every discoverer has to encounter opposition which would make those who are less determined quail and desist. Every person who embarks upon an undertaking which has as its object the upbuilding of truth has to run the gauntlet, so to speak, of the furious opposition such as the powers of darkness only can command. Yet all of these workers, as their titles indicate, have been successful, nothing has baffled them, because they made up their minds to succeed, and succeed they did, not merely to their own satisfaction but to that of their fellow beings, who have been benefited by their efforts.

It was no idle sentiment which prompted them to action, but an inborn determination founded upon a deep-set principle that "whatever is worth doing is worth doing well." Whenever such a spirit animates man, we know that there is no such word as failure in his vocabulary. This feature in man's character has made him the truly wonderful being that he has proved himself, and were it omitted, the history of the human race, instead of being as it is now, one of the most absorbingly interesting subjects which could claim the attention of the thinking mind, would not be worth the reading, and man who was made as the Bible tells us, but little lower than the angels, and crowned with glory and "honor," would long since have fallen from his high estate, and his life be as devoid of interest as that of the beasts that perish. This is but reasonable, for it indicates that when man is in earnest in what he does, his heart is given to his work. How marked is this, we say, among the great ones of our world. Think of such a man as Napoleon Bonaparte, when he was entering upon a great campaign, which would involve the destinies of Europe. Could the thoughtful one have been able to read his mind at such a momentous time, what mighty plans and calculations would be these; what wonderful lines of battle, what anticipative thoughts when through the mists of the future he could see success and glory; or take one nearer home, General Washington, so appropriately known as the Father of his Country. Think what daring plans he must have formulated, by which he expected to be borne to success. He, who, with a small army of half-fed and half-clothed men, dared to stand up before the mightiest nation of the world and defy it. We might, if we were privileged to read his thoughts, see some such words as these: "My country must and shall be free, and my hand shall be the instrument to give her great assistance." The horrors of cold winter and starvation were not sufficient to cause him to desist in what many of his contemporaries, no doubt, considered a mad venture, for he made up his mind to succeed, and saw no such probability as defeat in his pathway.

We might take examples from other departments of work, and read the thoughts of a great writer, who, by his pen, has resolved to make the world better, and as his after-works testify they bear the stamp of earnestness, yes and such earnestness as will unquestionably bear the stamp of Divine approval. The great feature of this earnestness, is the utter absence from the mind of anything which savors of failure. That is not anticipated as a possible contingency, and it rarely comes. Do you think that any of those just mentioned anticipated failure when they gave their hearts to the work? Not only are we convinced to the contrary, but it is our firm conviction that if such had been the case the downfalls of most of them would now be among the many wrecks which strew the sands of time. Looking, therefore, at our French colonists in this light, we see them in their true grandeur of character as we perhaps have never viewed them before. Instead of the weary and disheartened band, worn out with the cares and discouragements of the hour, and ready to faint by the way-side, we see the fire of determination kindled by deep-set earnestness flash from their eyes. The

little rows of rough cabins in the forest, the back-ground of
seemingly impenetrable wilds, and before them the winding
river, which, to many, would seem to be murmuring the fare-
wells to departed hopes, but represent to them the life which is
before them, and the grand medium through which they shall
attain success, so that at the conclusion of their mortal existence, it shall be said of them what we emphatically say to-day:
"They lived not in vain."

The early history of our country is ever presenting scenes
such as these, and how often are we constrained to go back
through the past years and sympathize with our forefathers, and
consider that our lines have, as compared with theirs, "fallen
in pleasant places;" but yet there are other thoughts in this connection that should fill the mind. In consideration of the work
which was given these and its mighty significance, as it bore
upon the events of the future, and the earnestness of purpose
with which it was prosecuted, and its great aim accomplished,
were not their blessings which arise from the fact that they were
the promotors of such a mighty work, as great, yes far greater
than those benefits which accrue to many now-a-days? It were
a privilege, indeed, to live as they lived, and to be moved as they
to do with all their might that which their hands found to do, in
laying the foundation for future success in a great land.

Another trait of character which was the natural outcome of that just considered, and which shone brightly
among our colonists, was bravery. As we have remarked
they had much to tax their patience, and many things from
which human nature would shrink in fear and trembling, but
if fear entered their hearts it was promptly banished. The
blood which flowed in their veins was near akin to that which
flowed in the veins of those heroes, whose warlike valor, soon
after our town was settled, filled the minds of the all-great people with wonder and admiration. These people showed by their
lives that there was a strong bond of union between them and
such men as the great Napoleon, the hero of France, and of
those fearless and determined men who followed him through
the smoke and carnage of his many battles to victory and re-
nown. We know how invaluable this virtue of bravery is as an

element of character. Faint hearts and wavering actions are not such as characterize true men, and only the true man is the successful man. We have not with the meagre resources at our command, been able to recount many of their deeds which bear upon this point, but, from those recited and personal associations with their descendants, we feel at liberty to pay them this tribute, and after the lapse of a hundred years, such convictions of their true worth, in this respect, come to us as to make their memory grateful to us, who are reaping the fruits of what they planted.

There is one trait of character, however, which we feel constrained to emphasize, and which was peculiarly apparent among them. This bears a close relationship, in its turn, to those just considered. It was the love of country that actuated them, whether that country was in the sunny fields and populous cities of beautiful France, or among the wilds of Ohio. Wherever their home was, there was also their heart. This love of country, too, is a virtue indispensable with true people. There is no more unfavorable sign in an individual or community of people than that of a rebellious spirit toward their government, unless, of course, such is thoroughly corrupt, and deserves the censure they are so willing to bestow. When in our reading we see histories of those, who cheerfully left all the dearest objects of life, to take up arms in defense of the land they love, our hearts are filled in a manner inexpressible by the grandeur of character manifested. In the fierce battle which was waged in the siege of Quebec, the world witnessed a double tragedy, and yet scenes of grandeur in the deaths of the two leaders of the opposing forces. General Wolfe, the English general, being mortally wounded, as his eyes were about to close upon this world forever, being told that victory had perched upon his country's banner, said: "I die happy." The Marquis De Montcalm, who commanded the French defensive force, and who was also wounded unto death, expressed himself as glad to die in that he would not be obliged to see Quebec surrendered. Those were brave expressions, and the men who uttered them were great men; gallant sons of worthy lands, for a land must be worthy which has such representatives. The love of country is a fixed principle in the minds of those who love great things, and to the true man his country can make no unreasonable request when she calls upon him to defend her from her enemies, and make her name to be glorious in this great world.

There is an old and familiar Latin maxim, which stirs within us those feelings which are of an ennobling character; it is *dulce et decorum est pro patria mori* — it is sweet and honorable to die for one's country. There is also a great principle embodied in another somewhat similar to it, and which is: 'tis sweet and honorable to *live* for one's country. To die for a principle, indicates that having been brought to a stop, as it were, in the discharge of our duties for it, on account of the difficulties which would impede our progress in our careers of duty, we give our lives to the cause of surmounting those difficulties. It is therefore the bright ending of a conscientious course; an ending produced because it is beyond our power to do more. To *live* for one's native land, or the land of one's adoption, however, indicates a determination to use every opportunity for its advancement; to face the future with that bravery characteristic of a noble nature, and acknowledge no difficulty of sufficient moment to baffle you in what you know to be right.

In the case of dying for one's country, the work is finished, and, like the bright sunset, the grand life closes in this world. When we live for our country, the work is about us, the opportunities thicken around us; our hands are the instruments that can do it, and the responsibilities of our position are great.

One point in this connection needs to be emphasized, that unless we live for our country, the chances are not very favorable for our dying for it. There are, perhaps, instances in which men died for the love of country without having given their lives to the same cause, but such instances are extremely rare.

Now, we love the memory of our early settlers, because they both lived and died for this, the home of their adoption. We would dwell particularly on the former of these, as we believe you will think it meet and proper in view of the life of privation which marked the first years of the history of Gallipolis, and to which we have called your attention.

'Tis not natural to suppose that when they came from their

far-away habitations, and met with the discouraging reception in
America, that they should love the latter place; and the idea that
it was to furnish them their future homes, must at first have been
even repugnant to them, but after having cast their lots here,
and witnessed the returns of their self-denying labors, they began
to love this rough land, and as the years passed away, and home
ties were formed, that love increased and strengthened, until they
became thoroughly domiciled, and then the hearts, which had
once yearned for the beauties and attractions of La Belle France,
awakened, as it were, to the consciousness that their France was
with them.

It is home where the heart is, and their hearts were not
across the seas, but here on the banks of the beautiful river.
They lived, I say, for this home; all of their refined tastes were
called into requisition to make it beautiful. A reference to this
fact, we have already seen in the interesting narrative of Mr.
Heckewelder. In after years, however, we have cause to know
that what he saw in those pioneer days was but an indication of
what would be. The expression, ''the wilderness blossoms like
the rose,'' which we have used, was most appropriate, concerning
the results of their labors, for the wild bluff on the river side became in due time the site of a fair town, inhabited by useful and
contented people.

The town was honored by visits of two distinguished visitors
in its early days. In 1824, General Lafayette, who had assisted
our land so materially in former years, made Gallipolis a visit,
and we cannot but believe that when he left, he was convinced
that his countrymen had proved true to their nature in upholding
the interest of their homes and governments wherever they
might be. Louis Philippe, (then the exiled Duke of Orleans),
stopped here once on his way to New Orleans, and his homeless
feeling and longing after the joys of native land must have been
intensified when he witnessed the thrifty contentment of these,
his brothers, in the home of their choice.

Thus they lived, and thus they died, and when we consider
that death was the culmination of lives given to their country,
we feel additional gratitude for their memory, and should be inspired to renewed endeavors in furthering the interests of our

town and county. We would do honor to their memory, we would in sacred thought, traverse the years which separate us from them, and we would thank them for this example which they have bequeathed to us and the many others who have and will come after them, being filled with the conviction that the love of home and country, such as was exemplified in them is one of the great secrets of a successful community.

Another instructive point presents itself for consideration as a closing thought, in connection with the work which they did, and should commend itself to us, as do all of the others hitherto mentioned: The thorough character of the undertaking upon which they engaged and which they perfected. There is only one way in which a thing can be done right, and that is by beginning at the very root of the matter. We must find a good foundation upon which to build, and then make our edifice of the strong and abiding materials. The Bible tells of two men who built houses, one with a good foundation and one with an indifferent one. ''The rain descended and the floods came, and the winds blew, and beat upon the former and it fell not, for it was founded upon a rock,'' while the same forces acting upon the latter caused its ruin. ''It fell, and great was the fall thereof.'' The same principle applies in every undertaking, whether it is great or seemingly insignificant, and we feel certain, from what history tells of the past, and what we see about us, that our settlers were moved by it in the performance of their duties here. The reasons why we feel certain of this are to be seen in the development of our town during the years which made up the century, and the result of the works of the hundred years. The improvements at first were not rapid, as might naturally be supposed in view of the difficulties of the settler, but the flying years brought wonderful changes.

Let us hear what Mr. Brackenridge has to say in regard to the town as he saw it in after years: ''As we passed Point Pleasant, and the little island below it, Gallipolis, which I looked for with anxious feelings, hove in sight. I thought of the French inhabitants—I thought of my friend Saugrain, and I recalled in the liveliest colors the incidents of that portion of my life which was passed here. A year is a long period of time; every day is

crowded with new and striking events. I hastened to the spot
where I expected to find the abode (of Dr. Saugrain), the little
log house, tavern, laboratory and garden of the Doctor—but
they had vanished like the palace of Aladdin. I took a hasty
glance at the new town as I returned to the boat. I saw brick
houses, painted frames, fanciful enclosures, ornamental trees!
Even the pond, which had carried away a third of the French
population by its malaria, had disappeared, and a pretty green
had usurped its place, with a neat brick Court House in the
midst of it."   .

Looking at the place to-day, we see a substantial and prosperous town. True, there are many in our great State which
are much larger, and regarded by outsiders as far more important; but the basis upon which we stand as a town, is a firm
and solid one, which showed that its beginning was marked by
faithful efforts. We would remark, however, and we do so with
sadness of heart, that the French population of Gallipolis de-
creased with rapidity during the years which marked its early
history, and it was American hands which prosecuted the work
here for many years, and made our town more successful, as was
evidenced by its different stages of prosperous development.
Mr. Brackenridge, in his description of the second visit to Gallipolis, expresses great disappointment that the French were
nearly all gone. We cannot forget, however, that it was the
French hands that laid the foundation, and the French mind
which planned the building in its earliest stages, so that to the
French rather than to the American is due the prosperity of
after years.

Memories of the past are freighted with their lessons, and
filled with joys and sorrows. It is pleasant to recall the events
which have passed away, on account of the many pleasant characters with which they bring us into close association. The very
difficulties which were encountered by the pioneers have a
charm for us, as we view them by the light of a hundred years.
When soldiers have passed through the wars successfully, or
sailors have endured the perils of the sea, it is a peculiar joy to
them to sit by some bright fireside and go over their perilous
adventures with one another, and the greater the dangers that

once were, and the more trying the sufferings, the greater pleasure they appear to derive from their naratives. Thus when our town looks back over her history and beholds what she was, and what she might have been but for the brave and determined efforts of her faithful inhabitants, there is a peculiar charm attached even to her hardships, inasmuch as she knows that they were successfully faced. Thankful are we for the works done for us by those of the century gone, and we can utter no more fervent wish than that our memory may be as sacred to those who shall stand upon this ground, when the morning of another hundred years shall dawn upon Gallipolis.

JOHN L. VANCE.

CONTEMPORARY DESCRIPTION OF OHIO IN 1788.

In 1888, Mr. John H. James, of Urbana, Ohio, whose collection of historical works is hardly excelled, published a translation of a French pamphlet used by Mr. Barlow and his associates in Paris, when engaged in the sale of lands in the Ohio country. "The pamphlet," says Mr. James, in his introduction, "was published in French and English; the French copy being a translation of the English copy, first published in Salem, Massachusetts, in 1787. The French edition was published in Paris in 1789, the year of the breaking out of the French Revolution. It was one of the means employed by Joel Barlow and the agents of the Scioto Company to promote the emigration from France, which resulted in the settlement of the French at Gallipolis in 1790."

"The French copy from which I make the translation," continued Mr. James, "is dingy with age, and formerly belonged to one of the early settlers at Gallipolis, whose name, with the date, 1805, is inscribed on the cover."

The title page of the pamphlet is as follows:

"A Description of the Soil, Productions, etc., of that Portion of the United States Situated between Pennsylvania and the Rivers Ohio and Scioto and Lake Erie."

Mr. James, in his introduction, says of the authorship of the pamphlet, that "it was published anonymously, but was written by Mr. Manasseh Cutler," and "that while its tints are sufficiently *couleur de rose*, and some of its statements * * * appear extravagant in the light of our present knowledge, yet it must be remembered that one hundred years ago Ohio was a comparatively unknown region, concerning which all intending settlers were enthusiastic; and a comparison with other contemporary authorities shows that it represents very fairly the state of information existing concerning the Western country."

The extravagant statements in the pamphlet, it will be noticed, are acceded to by Mr. Thomas Hutchins, the geographer of the United States, and by others who had visited the country.

The following is Mr. James' translation of the French edition of the pamphlet, with foot notes added by him:

MR. JAMES' TRANSLATION OF THE FRENCH EDITION OF OHIO.

The great river Ohio is formed by the confluence of the Monongahela and the Allegheny in Pennsylvania. It flows from about 290 miles west of the city of Philadelphia, and about 20 miles west of the western boundry of Pennsylvania. In following the ordinary route the 290 miles are increased to 320, and the windings of the Ohio increase the 20 miles to about 42.

These two sources of the Ohio are both great navigable rivers; the first flows from the southeast, and there is, between it and the navigable waters of the Potomac, in Virginia, a portage of only about 30 miles;[1] the latter opens a passage to the northeast, and rises not far from the source of the Susquehanna.

The State of Pennsylvania has already adopted the plan of opening a navigation from the Allegheny River to Philadelphia by way of the Susquehanna and the Delaware. In following this route there will be only a transit by land, or portage of 24 miles.[2]

At the junction of these two rivers, or at the source of the Ohio, we find Fort Pitt, which gives its name to the city of Pittsburgh, a flourishing settlement in the vicinity of the fortress. From this city the Ohio pursues its way to the southwest for 1188 miles (including the windings of the river) and empties into the Mississippi, after traversing for this prodigious distance a most fertile and agreeable country, and having increased its waters by those of several other navigable rivers: the Muskingum, the Hockhocking, the Scioto, the Miami, and the Wabash from the northwest; the Kanawha, the Kentucky, the Buffaloe,[3] the Shawnee,[4] and the Cherokee[5] from the southwest; all these rivers, navigable for a distance of from 100 to 900 miles, fall into the Ohio, and it is this river that furnishes a great part of those united waters which flow into the ocean through the bed of the Mississippi.

The Ohio, from Pennsylvania to the Mississippi, sepa-

rates the State of Virginia from other domains of the
United States, or in other words from the territory not
comprised within the limits of any particular State. This
territory extends westward to the Mississippi, and north
to the frontiers of the United States. Commencing at the
meridian which forms the western boundary of Pennsylvania
they have laid off a space sufficient for seven ranges[6] of *municipalities* (townships). As a north and south line extends along
the Ohio in a very oblique direction, the western boundary of
the seventh range strikes the Ohio nine miles above the
Muskingum, which is the first large river which empties into the
Ohio. Their junction is 172 miles below Fort Pitt, following the
winding of Ohio, but in a straight line little more than 90 miles.

The Muskingum is a river which flows slowly, and has
banks high enough to prevent all inundation. It is 250 yards
wide at the place where it enters the Ohio, and is navigable for
large vessels and bateaux as far as Tree Legs, and for small boats
to the lake at its source. From thence by means of a transit by
land of about one mile,[7] communication is opened with Lake
Erie by means of the Cuyahoga, which is a river of great value,
navigable through its whole length, without any cataracts to
obstruct its course. The passage from Lake Erie to the Hudson,
through the State of New York, is well known. The longest
transit by land on this route is that which is caused by the falls
of Niagara, which interrupts the communication between Lakes
Erie and Ontario. After that, one passes by the River Oswego,
Oneida Lake, Woods Creek (the bay of the woods), and by
means of a short portage, enters the Mohawk; another portage
occasioned by the cataract near the confluence of the Mohawk,
and the Hudson brings the voyager to Albany.

The Hockhocking is somewhat like the Muskingum, but not
so large. It is navigable for large vessels for about seventy
miles, and much further for small ones. On the banks of this
much frequented river are inexhaustible quarries of building
stone, great beds of iron ore, and some rich mines of lead. We
find also, very frequently in the neighborhood of this river, coal
mines and salt springs, which abound in this Western country.
The salt which is obtained from these springs furnishes a never-

failing abundance of this article of prime necessity.[8] Beds of clay, both white and blue, of an excellent quality, are met with also throughout this region. This clay is adapted for the manufacture of glass, of pottery, and all kinds of brick. Armenian[9] clay, and several other useful deposits, have also been discovered along the different branches of this river.

The Scioto is a river longer than either of those of which we have thus far spoken, and furnishes a navigation much more considerable. For an extent of two hundred miles large vessels can navigate it. Then there is a passage to be made by land of four miles only to the Sandusky, a river also navigable, which enters into Lake Erie.[10] It is by the Sandusky and Scioto that they pass generally in going from Canada to the Mississippi. This route is one of the most considerable and most frequented found in any country. By it are united some of the most extensive territories, and when we consider the rapidity with which settlements are made in the Western part of Canada, upon Lake Erie, and in Kentucky, we may predict that there will be an immense commerce between these people.[11] It is certain that the lands which border upon, and which lie near these rivers, will be of the greatest value from their situation alone, and quite apart from their natural fertility. There can be no doubt that the flour, wheat, hemp, etc., exported from the extensive regions surrounding Lakes Huron and Ontario would have an easier transit by means of Lake Erie and the neighboring rivers than by any other route. The merchant who shall in future inhabit the banks of the Ohio will be able to pay more for these commodities than the merchant of Quebec, by reason of these advantages, because they can be transported from the former of these countries to Florida and the West India Islands with much less expense and risk, and at a much lower rate of insurance than from the latter. In fact, the transportation of these productions of the soil, the expenses upon the Ohio included, would not amount to a fourth part of what it would cost from Quebec, and it will be still cheaper than it is by way of Lake Oneida.

The Scioto has a gentle current, which is interrupted by no cataracts. Sometimes in the spring it overflows its banks, which

are covered by vast fields of rice, which nature here produces
spontaneously.[12] For the rest, we find in abundance in the
country which borders upon this river, salt springs, coal mines,
deposits of white and blue clay and of free stone.

The general expressions of admiration which are commonly made use of in speaking of the natural fertility of
the countries watered by these western rivers of the United
States render difficult the description one would wish to make,
unless one takes particular pains to mark on the map the places
which merit especial attention, or unless he gives an exact
description of the territory in general without regard to the risk
he runs of being charged with exaggeration. But upon this
point we are able to say that we have with us the unanimous
opinion of geographers, of surveyors and of all those travelers
who have collected precise information concerning the characteristics of the country, and who have observed with the most scru-
pulous exactitude all the remarkable objects which nature there
displays. They all agree that no part of the territory belonging
to the United States combines in itself so many advantages,
whether of salubrity, fertility or variety of productions, as that
which extends from the Muskingum to the Scioto and the Great
Miami.[13]

[a] Colonel Gordon speaking of his travels through a country
much more extensive in which this is included and of which it
is indubitably the most beautiful part, makes the following observations: "The country along the Ohio is extremely agreeable,
filled with great plains of the richest soil and exceedingly salubrious. One remark of this kind suffices for all that region bounded
by the western slope of the Allegheny Mountains and extending
to the southwest a distance of five hundred miles down the Ohio,
thence to the north as far as the source of the rivers that empty
into the Ohio, and thence eastward along the hills which separate the lakes from the river Ohio as far as French creek. I
can, from the perfect knowledge which I have of it, affirm that
the country which I have just described is the most salubrious,

a. An English Engineer during the war of 1755-63.

the most agreeable, the most advantageous, the most fertile land which is known to any people of Europe, whatsoever."

The lands which are watered by the different rivers emptying into the Ohio, of which we have just spoken, are, since the time of Col. Gordon, better known, and can be described with more precision and in a manner which ought to inspire confidence.

They are remarkable for their variety of soil from which results everything which can contribute to the advantages due to their local position and which promise the success and the riches which ought to burst forth among every agricultural and manufacturing people.

The great level plains which one meets with here and which form natural prairies, have a circumference of from twenty to fifty miles, they are found interspersed almost everywhere along the rivers. These plains have a soil as rich as can be imagined and which with very little labor can be devoted to any species of cultivation which one wishes to give it. They say that in many of these prairies one can cultivate an acre of land per day and prepare it for the plough. There is no undergrowth on them and the trees which grow very high and become very large[a] only need to be deprived of their bark in order to become fit for use.

The kinds of timber fit for the purposes of the joiner which grow most abundantly in this country and the most useful of trees which are found here are the sugar-maple, the sycamore, black and white mulberry, and black and white walnut, the chestnut, oaks of every kind, the cherry tree, beech tree, the elm, the cucumber tree, ironwood, the ash tree, the aspen, the sassafras, the wild apple tree, and a great number of other trees of which it is impossible to express the names in French.

General Parsons has measured a black walnut near the Muskingum, of which the circumference, five feet above the ground, was twenty-two feet. A sycamore measured in the same way had a circumference of forty-four feet. One finds on the heights white and black oaks as well as the chestnut, and nearly all the trees we have just named, which grow there, very large and to a

---

a. Large and high trees are an indication of rich soil.

proportionate height. One finds both on the hills and on the plains a great quantity of grapes growing wild, and of which the inhabitants make a red wine, which suffices for their own consumption. They have tried the experiment of pressing these grapes at the settlement of [b]Saint Vincent,[14] and the result is a wine which, by keeping a little while, becomes preferable to the many wines of Europe. Cotton of an excellent quality is also a product of the country.

The sugar-maple is of great value to a region situated as this is in the interior of the country. It furnishes enough sugar for the use of a large number of people, and for this purpose a small number of trees are usually kept by each family. A maple tree will produce about ten pounds of sugar per year, and it is produced with little difficulty. The sap of the tree flows in the months of February and March; it becomes crystalized after being boiled, and the sugar is equal in flavor and whiteness to the best Muscavado.

All parts of this country are abundantly supplied with excellent springs, and one finds everywhere both small and large creeks, on which mills may be established.[15] These brooks, useful for so many purposes, have the appearance of being disposed by the hand of art in such a manner as to contribute toward procuring every advantage which can make life desirable.

There is a very little bad land in this territory, and no marsh. There are plenty of hills; their position is agreeable, and they are not high enough to interfere with their cultivation. Their soil is deep, rich, covered with trees of good growth, and adapted to the cultivation of wheat, rye, indigo, tobacco, etc.

The communication between this territory and the ocean is principally by the four following routes:

First: The route by the Scioto and Muskingum to Lake Erie, and thence by the River Hudson we have already described.

Second: The passage by the Ohio and Monongahela to the transit by land already mentioned, which leads to navigable

---

b. A French settlement made some fifty years ago on the Wabash river to the westward of the Scioto.

waters of the Potomac. This land transit is about thirty miles, but it will very probably be diminished in a little while, by means of the plan which is actually in contemplation for opening a communication between these rivers.

Third: The Great Kanawha, which empties into the Ohio toward the confines of Virginia, between the Hocking and Scioto, affords a very ready navigation toward the Southeast, and requires but a short portage to reach the navigable waters of the James River in Virginia. This communication, useful to the settlements between the Muskingum and Scioto, will very probably be the most frequented for the exports of the manufactures of the country,[16] and still more for the importation of foreign goods, because they can be carried more cheaply from the Chesapeake to the Ohio, than they now are from Philadelphia to Carlisle and the other counties situated in the lower parts of Pennsylvania.

Fourth: But above all, it is upon the Ohio and Mississippi that there can be transported a great number of things necessary for the markets of Florida and the West Indies, such as wheat, flour, beef, bacon, timber for joinery and ship-building, etc, that they will be more frequented than any river upon the earth. The distance from the Scioto to the Mississippi is eight hundred miles, thence to the ocean nine hundred; all this journey can be easily made in fifteen days, and the voyage in reascending these rivers is not so difficult as one would suppose. Experience has demonstrated that one can make great use of sails on the Ohio.[17]

Here again is a fortunate circumstance: it is that the Ohio Company[a] is on the point of establishing its settlements, and it is making them in a manner alike, systematic and judicious. Its operations will serve as a useful model for all the settlements which will be found in the future in the United States. Add to this that this new colony is established so near the western boundary of Pennsylvania as to appear to be only a continuation of the older settlements, by reason of which there will no longer be reason to fear that these unsettled regions may be occupied

---

a. At this moment the establishments of this company are commenced and are very flourishing.

by the savages, as has too frequently happened in situations very far removed from the seat of government.[18]

The intention of Congress, and that of the inhabitants, is that these settlements shall be made in a regular manner; that they shall follow the course of the Ohio, and that they shall commence by occupying the northern part of the country toward Lake Erie.[19] And it is hoped that not many years will probably elapse until the whole country above the Miami will be raised in value to such a point that the advantages which travelers have celebrated will be seen in their true light, and it will be admitted that they spoke nothing but the truth when they called this country the garden of the universe, the center of wealth, a place destined to be the heart of a great Empire.

The following reflections will not escape either the philosopher or the statesman, who shall see this delightful part of the United States settled upon a wise system and in a well ordered manner:

1.   The labor of the agriculturists will here be rewarded by productions as useful as, and more varied than in any part of America; the advantages which are generally found divided in any other climate are here united; and all the advantages which other parts of the United States present, are here combined in the highest perfection.   In all parts the soil is deep, rich, producing in abundance wheat, rye, corn, buckwheat, barley, oats, flax, hemp, tobacco, indigo, the tree that furnishes the food for the silk worm, the grape-vine, cotton.   The tobacco is of a quality much superior to that of Virginia, and the crops of wheat are much more abundant here than in any other part of America. The ordinary crop of corn is from sixty to eighty English bushels per acre.[a]   The bottom lands are especially adapted to the production of all the commodities we have just enumerated. There where the vast plains, which are met with in this territory, are intersected with little brooks, the land is suitable for

---

a. General Parsons, one of the Commissioners for negotiating the Treaty of 1786 with the Indians, reports that Mr. Dawson, who has lived in this country ten years, has raised from eighty to one hundred bushels per acre. Last year he cultivated seven acres, on which his crop was six hundred bushels.

the culture of rice, and it grows here abundantly. Hops also are produced spontaneously in this territory, and there are also the same peaches, plums, pears, melons, and in general all the fruits which are produced in the temperate zone.

There is no country more abounding in game than this. The stag, fallow deer, elk, buffalo and bears fill the woods and are nourished on these great and beautiful plains, which are encountered in all parts of these countries, an unanswerable proof of the fertility of the soil; wild turkeys, geese, ducks, swans, teal, pheasants, partridges, and so forth, are here found in greater abundance than our domestic fowls in all the older settlements of America. The rivers are well stocked with fish of different kinds, and several of these fish are of an exquisite quality. In general they are. large, the cat-fish (*poisson-chat*) has an excellent flavor and weighs from twenty to.eighty pounds.

One will find here provisions for several years, and the borders of each one of these rivers will serve for a long time in place of a market. When inhabitants shall come here from all parts of the world nature will have provided for them, at least for one year, all they need, without the necessity of making any purchases.

2. There is no place more suitable from its situation and productions for the establishment of manufactures than this. The necessaries of life are abundant and cheap. The raw material for all things necessary for clothing and personal adornment are here found in quantities. Silk, flax and cotton bring a good price here; but these articles, being manufactured and being adapted for the different purposes of use and luxury, would still be cheap here by reason of the small amount of freight necessary to pay for their transportation. The United States,[20] and perhaps other countries besides, will be replaced, or superseded in the market, by the competition of the inhabitants of the interior parts of America.

The construction of vessels will be one of the most considerable branches of business on the Ohio River and its tributaries.[21] In the lowest stage of water in the Ohio we find a depth of four fathoms from the mouth of the Muskingum to its junction with the Mississippi. In only one part is it very rapid, and there the

navigation is interrupted for about one mile. Elsewhere throughout its whole extent the fall is not more than fifteen feet, and
the bed of the river, which has a breadth of two hundred and
fifty rods, has never less than five feet of water. In winter it
increases to thirty feet. The river can be ascended not only by
means of oars, but they readily surmont the current by means
of sails only. Geographers and others who have seen the
locality are of the opinion that if a canal[22] were dug at a little
less than half a mile south of the river, at a point where a low
prairie is found, the current could be avoided and navigation
thus be without interruption the whole year round.

Hemp, iron and ship timber are abundant and of good
quality here. During the highest stage of water, which is from
February to April, and frequently in October and November,
vessels can easily pass the rapids with their cargoes to the sea
even in the present condition of the river.

An English engineer, who has made a thorough examination of the western country, has communicated the following
observations to Lord Hillsborough in 1770. This nobleman
was the Secretary of State for the Department of America at
the time when we were colonists of Great Britain, and when our
country was regarded solely, as it could be made available for a
market for English fabrics:[23]

"No part of North America has less need of encouragement in order to furnish rigging for ships, and the raw material
destined to Europe, and to furnish to the West India Islands
building material, provisions, etc., than the Ohio country, and
that for the following reasons:

"1. The country is excellent, climate temperate; grapes
grow without cultivation; silk worms and mulberry trees abound
everywhere; hemp, hops and rice[24] grow wild in the valleys and
low lands; lead and iron abound in the hills; salt springs are
innumerable; and there is no country better adapted to the culture of tobacco, flax and cotton than that of the Ohio.

"2. The country is well watered by several navigable
rivers, which communicate with each other, and by means of
which, with a very short transport by land, the productions of
the Valley of the Ohio can even at this moment[25] be conveyed at

a much lower price to the seaport of Alexandria[26] on the River Potomac, where General Braddock landed his troops, than merchandise can be carried from Northampton to London.

"3.   The Ohio river is navigable at all seasons of the year for large boats,[27] and during the months of February, March and April it is possible to construct large vessels upon it and send them to the ocean loaded with hemp, iron, flax, silk, tobacco, cotton, potash, etc.

"4.   Flour, wheat, beef, planks for ship-building and other things not less useful can descend the Ohio to Western Florida and go thence to the West India Islands more cheaply and in better condition than the same merchandise can be sent from New York or Philadelphia to the same islands.

"5.   Hemp, tobacco, iron and similar bulky articles, can descend the Ohio to the ocean at least 50 per cent. cheaper than the same articles have ever been transported by land in Pennsylvania over a distance no greater than sixty miles, although the expense of carriage there is less than in any part of North America.

"6.   The freight for transporting goods manufactured in Europe from the sea-board to the Ohio, will not be so considerable as it now is, and always will be, to a great part of the counties of Pennsylvania, Virginia and Maryland.   When the farmers or merchants who dwell upon the Ohio set about providing for transportation they will build vessels of all kinds suited for commerce with the West India Islands and Europe, or, as they will have black walnut, cherry, oak, etc., sawed ready for foreign commerce, they will make of them rafts in the same manner as is practiced by those who live about the headwaters of the Delaware in Pennsylvania, on which they will put their hemp, their iron, their tobacco, etc., and with which they will go to New Orleans.

."The following observations should not be omitted: They manufacture a great quautity of flour in the region situated in the west of Pennsylvania, and they send it by land to Philadelphia, which costs a great deal, and thence they send it by sea to South Carolina and Eastern and Western Florida, where they grow little or no grain.   One may say that nature herself has

designed the Ohio to be the river by which the two Floridas may
be supplied with flour, and that not only for the consumption of
these two provinces, but still more for a considerable commerce
which they carry on in that article with Jamaica and the Spanish
settlements of Mexico. Quantities of mill-stones may be procured from the hills which border the Ohio, and the country
everywhere abounds with water-courses suited to the construction of mills of every kind. The passage from Philadelphia to
Pensacola is rarely made in less than a month, and they ordi-
narily pay fifty shillings a ton freight (a ton consists of sixteen
barrels) for transportation that far. Boats carrying from 500 to
1000 barrels of flour go in nearly the same time from Pittsburgh
to Pensacola as from Philadelphia to Pensacola, and at half the
expense. Merchants on the Ohio can furnish flour on better
terms than Philadelphia, and without running the risk of dam-
age by sea or the delays of transportation on that element; and
besides, without paying insurance, advantages which can not be
enjoyed in the case of goods shipped from Philadelphia to Pensacola. And let no one imagine that this is a supposition
merely; it is the constant experience. About the year 1746
there was a scarcity in New Orleans, and the French settlements on the banks of the Illinois, feeble in number as
they were, sent thither in one winter alone 800,000 weight
of flour."[28]   So that, in place of furnishing other nations with
raw materials, some company of manufacturers might be introduced and established in the countries, so attractive their situation,
under the direction of men thoroughly competent to the task.
Such an establishment would produce a considerable augmenta-
tion of population and wealth to these new settlements and would
set a useful example to other parts of the United States.

3.   The measures which have been taken by the act of
Congress, providing for the disposition of the lands west of the
Ohio as far down as the Scioto for the establishment and maintenance of schools, and of a University[29] shed an especial lustre
on these settlements and inspire the hope that by the particular
attention which has been given to education, the fields of science
will be extended, and that the means of acquiring useful knowledge will be placed on a more respectful footing in this country

than in any other part of the world. Without speaking of the advantages of discovering in this new country species hitherto unknown in natural history, botany and medical science, it cannot be questioned that in no other part of the habitable globe can there be found a spot where, in order to begin well, there will not be found much evil to extirpate, bad customs to combat, and ancient systems to reform. Here there is no rubbish to clear away before laying foundations. The first commencement of this settlement will be undertaken by persons inspired with the noblest settlements, versed in the most necessary branches of knowledge, acquainted with the world and with affairs,[30] as well as with every branch of science. If they shall be so fortunate as to have at first the means of founding on an advantageous plan these schools and this University, and of sustaining them in such a manner that the professors may be able to commence without delay the different labors to which they may be called, they will, in the infancy of the colony, have secured to themselves advantages which will be found nowhere else.

4. In the ordinance of Congress for the government of the territory northwest of the Ohio it is provided that when the territory shall have acquired a certain amount of population it may be divided into several States. The most eastern of these[31] (this is already provided for) is bounded by the Great Miami on the west, and by Pennsylvania on the east. The center of this State will be between the Scioto and the Hockhocking. The seat of government of one of these States will very probably be at the mouth of one of these two rivers. And if we may be permitted to forecast the future, we may imagine that when the United States of America, composed of an intelligent and renowned people, shall have greatly extended the boundaries of their dominions the general government will establish itself upon the banks of the Ohio. This country is at the centre of the whole Nation, it is a place the most convenient for all, the most agreeable and probably the most healthy.

It is undoubtedly of the greatest importance that the Congress shall soon fix the place of its residence; nevertheless, in the present state of the country it is possible, some may think it not expedient to fix it immovably. Take the chain of the

Allegheny Mountains from north to south, it is probable that twenty years will not elapse before there will be more of the inhabitants of the United States living on the banks of the Western than on the Eastern rivers. The Western people ought now to understand that the government is disposed to favor them as much as their brethren who inhabit the Eastern part of the country. It is even necessary that they should have this feeling in order that they may not cherish dreams of independence, that they may not seek for other alliances, and that they may not take steps with especial view to their own welfare.[32] As it is indisputable that it ought to be the principal object of the Legislature, and the one dearest to its heart to unite as great a number of people as possible, and render them happy under one government, every step which Congress may take toward this new constitution will have this object in view; and, we will hope, will promote the success of the plan, and cause it to be regarded as inviolably established. There is no doubt, whatever, that sooner or later the government will either reserve to itself or purchase a suitable site on which to build *the city of the confederation*,[33] which will be at the center of the whole country; and that it will make known its intentions in this regard as soon as circumstances, such as an equal population in the new State, etc., will permit.

Such a determination, taken in advance, will give the older States the power of carrying it into execution without causing any disturbance or dissatisfaction to any person, whilst it would inspire the new States with the hope of some day seeing the plan realized.

Extracts from letters of an American farmer, by M. S'John de Crevecoeur, French Consul to America. Second edition, Vol. 3, page 394.

The Ohio is the grand artery of that portion of America which lies beyond the mountains; it is the center in which meet all the waters which flow on one side from the Allegheny Mountains, and which descend on the other from the high lands in the vicinity of Lakes Erie and Michigan. It has been calculated that the region watered by all these streams, and comprised between Pittsburg and the Mississippi, contains a territory of at least 260 miles square, or 166,980,000* acres. It is, without doubt, the most fertile country, with the most varied soil, the best watered, and that which offers to agriculture and commerce the most abundant and ready resources of all those which Europeans have ever discovered and peopled.

It was on the tenth of April, at eight o'clock in the morning, that we abandoned ourselves to the current of the Ohio. * * * * This pleasant and tranquil navigation appeared to me like a delightful dream; each moment presented to me new perspectives, which were incessantly varied by the appearance of islands, points and bends of the river, constantly changing with the singular variety of shore, more or less wooded, from which the eye would, from time to time, wander to survey the great natural prairies which intersect them; constantly embellished by promontories of different heights, which seemed to disappear for a moment, and then gradually develop to the eye of the navigator bays and coves, of greater or less extent, formed by the creeks (little navigable rivers) and the brooks which fall into the Ohio. What majesty in the mouths of the great rivers before which we passed. Their waters seemed as vast and as deep as those of the river on which we were voyaging.

Never before had I felt so disposed to meditation and revery; involuntarily my imagination darted into the future, the remoteness of which gave me no trouble, because it appeared to be near. I saw in fancy these beautiful shores ornamented with handsome houses, covered with crops, the fields well cultivated; on the declivities of the hills exposed to the north I saw orchards planted, on the others vineyards, plantations of mulberries, acacias, etc. I saw also on the low lands the cotton plant and the sugar-maple, the sap of which has become an article of commerce. I grant indeed that all the shores did not appear to me equally adapted to cultivation, but the different masses of trees with which they will necessarily remain covered will add still more to the beauty and the variety of the landscape of the

* Evidently an erroneous calculation.

future. What an immense chain of plantations! What a great
career of activity, of industry, of culture and commerce is
offered to the Americans. I consider therefore the settlement
of the country watered by this great river as one of the greatest
enterprises ever presented to man. It will be the more glorious
because it will be legally acquired with the consent of the ancient proprietors and without the shedding of a drop of blood.[34]
It is destined to become the foundation of the power, wealth and
future glory of the United States.

Toward noon of the third day we cast anchor at the mouth
of the Muskingum, in two fathoms and a half of water. To
give you a faint idea of what I may call the anatomy of the
Ohio, I wish to tell you about this river to make you understand
the utility of all its branches.[35]

It empties into the Ohio 172 miles from Pittsburg and has a
width of 120 toises,[36] it is deep and navigable for large boats for
147 miles into the interior. Its freshets are moderate and it
never overflows its banks, which are elevated, without being
steep. One of its branches approaches at the same time the
principal of the sources of the Scioto, called the Seccaium and
the Sandusky River. This last falls, you are aware, into the
great bay of the same name at the farther end of Lake Erie. It
is near one of the principal branches of the Muskingum that the
great Indian village of Tuscarawas is built, whence a portage of
two miles only leads to the Cuyahoga River, deep and but
slightly rapid, the mouth of which on Lake Erie forms an excellent harbor for vessels of 200 tons. This place seems designed for the site of a city, and several persons of my acquaintance have already thought so.[37] All the voyagers and hunters
have spoken with admiration of the fertility of the hills and
valleys watered by the Muskingum,[38] as well as the excellent
springs, the salt wells, the mines of coal, particularly that of
Lamenchicola, of the free-stone, fullers-earth, etc., which they
find everywhere.

The next morning at day break we weighed anchor, and
after three days of quiet and pleasant navigation we came to
anchor opposite the Scioto, 218 miles from the Muskingum and
390 miles from Pittsburgh, for the purpose of receiving on board

Gen. Butler, who came to conclude some negotiations with the Shawnees. It is from him that I had the following details concerning this fine river, upon the banks of which he resided during the last five years of the war: The Scioto is almost as wide as the Ohio; its current is navigable for boats of medium size as far as the village of Seccaium, 111 miles from its mouth; it is at this village that the great portage to the Sandusky begins, which is but four miles. Judge of the importance of this communication, always much frequented by whites and Indians; the latter who have horses and wagons, transport merchandise at so much per hundred. This river waters a most extensive and fertile country, but rather flat. These vast plains, so well known as the Scioto bottoms, commence a few miles above the river Huskinkus and continue almost to Seccaium. They are watered by the fine creeks, Alaman,[89] Deer, Kispoks, etc., and by a great number of considerable brooks. Several of these plains are from twenty-five to thirty miles in circumference, and as if Nature had wished to render them still more useful to men, she has sprinkled them with hills and isolated mounds, on which she had planted the most beautiful trees. These plains are never overflowed, and their fertility is wonderful. If a poor man, who had nothing but his hands, should ask me, "Where shall I go to establish myself in order to live with the most ease, without the help of horses or oxen?" I would say to him, "Go to the banks of one of the creeks in the Scioto bottoms; all that you will have to do will be first to obtain permission from the Indians from the neighboring village (this permission is no longer necessary since the treaty with them); second, scratch the surface of the earth and deposit there your wheat, your corn, your potatoes, your beans, your cabbage, your tobacco, etc., and leave the rest to nature. In the meantime amuse yourself with fishing and the chase."

Every spring a prodigious number of storks come to visit these plains; they are at least six feet high, and more than seven feet from tip to tip of wings. I have never seen them come to feed that they were not surrounded by sentinels, who watch around them to announce the approach of enemies. Sometimes before their departure they assemble in great flocks, and the day being fixed, all rise, turning slowly, and preserving always the same order, they describe long spirals until they are out of sight.

Finally, on the tenth day after our departure from Pittsburgh, we cast anchor in front of Louisville, having made 750 miles in 22½ hours of navigation.

CERTIFICATE.

Having read, attentively, the pamphlet in which is given a description of the Western Territory of the Untied States, I, the undersigned, certify that the facts therein contained concerning the fertility of the soil, abundant productions and other advantages for the husbandman, are true and reliable, and that they correspond perfectly with the observations I have made during ten years which I have spent in that country.

[SIGNED]   THOMAS HUTCHINS,
                                      Geographer of U. S.

NOTES.

NOTE 1.—All the produce of the settlements about Fort Pitt can be brought to Alexandria, by the Youghiogany, in three hundred and four miles, whereof only thirty-one are land transportation; and by the Monongahela and Cheat Rivers in three hundred and sixty miles, twenty of which only are land carriage.— *Gen. Washington to Gov. Harrison, Oct. 10, 1784.*

NOTE 2.—Pennsylvania—although the Susquehanna is an unfriendly water, much impeded, it is said, with rocks and rapids, and nowhere communicating with those which lead to her capital,—has it in contemplation to open a communication between Toby's Creek, which empties into the Allegheny River 95 miles above Fort Pitt, and the west branch of the Susquehanna, and to cut a canal between the waters of the latter and the Schuylkill, the expense of which is easier to be conceived than estimated or described by me. A people, however, who are possessed of the spirit of commerce, who see and who will perceive its advantages, may achieve almost anything. In the meantime, and the uncertainty of these undertakings, they are smoothing the road and paving the ways for the trade of the western world.— *Gen. Washington to Gov. Harrison, Oct. 10, 1784.*

NOTE 3.—The Buffalo—Apparently the Green River.

Note 4.—The Shawnee—The Cumberland River was so called until it was given its present name by Dr. Walker, in 1747, in honor of the Duke of Cumberland.

Note 5.—The Cherokee—The Tennessee was formerly so-called.

Note 6.—Seven Ranges.

Note 7.—This old Indian portage, between the head waters of the Muskingum and those of the Cuyahoga, is within the present limits of Portage county, from which the county derives its name.

Note 8.—Salt Springs—"We have found several salt-licks within our surveys, and we are assured there is a salt spring about forty miles up the Muskingum, from which a quantity of salt for the supply of the country may be made. Some gentlemen at Fort Harmar doubt this information, and think a supply may be made at a spring on the branch of the Scioto." —*Pioneer History.*

So great was the scarcity and value of salt during the first ten years of the settlement—not less than six or eight dollars a bushel—that the Ohio Company, in their final division of their lands, passed the following resolution:

"Whereas, It is believed that the great 'salt springs' of the Scioto lie within the present purchase of the Ohio Company; therefore,

"*Resolved*, That the division of land to the proprietors is made upon the express condition and reserve that every salt spring now known, or that shall hereafter be found, within the lands that shall fall to the lot of any proprietor, be and are hereby reserved to the use of the company, with such quantity of land about them as the agents and proprietors shall think proper to assume for general purposes, not exceeding three thousand acres; the person on whose land they are found, to receive other lands of equal value." It so happened that the Scioto springs were situated a few miles west of the purchase and on the lands belonging to the United States. When Ohio became a State, these noted springs, with those on Salt Creek, in Muskingum county and at Delaware, were reserved by Congress for the use of the State, with large tracts of land adjoining to furnish fuel for ooiling the salt water. For many years these springs were leased to individuals, and became a source of revenue to Ohio.

Note 9.—Armenian Clay—A sort of Ochre.

Note 10.—The routes of navigation and portage referred to in the text, between the lakes and the Ohio River, by way of the Sandusky and Scioto, and of the Cuyahoga and Muskingum Rivers, and also that from Presqu' Isle (Erie, Pennsylvania,) by way of French Creek to the Ohio, seemed to have been discovered and used by the French at a subsequent period.

General Washington, in a letter written October 10, 1784, to Benjamin Harrison, then Governor of Virginia (Writings of Washington, Vol. IX, p. 58), in which he discusses at length the best mode of communication

between the tide water region of Virginia and the Northwestern territory,
by means of the Potomac and James Rivers, says: "It has long been my
decided opinion that the shortest, easiest and least expensive communication with the invaluable and extensive country back of us would be by one
or both of the rivers of this State, which have their sources in the
Apalachian Mountains. Nor am I singular in this opinion. Evans, in his
map and analysis of the Middle Colonies, which, considering the early
period at which they were given to the public, are done with amazing
exactness, and Hutchins* since, in his Typographical Description of the
Western Country, a good part of which is from actual surveys, are decidedly
of the same sentiments."

"The navigation of the Ohio," he continues, "being well known, they
will have less to do in the examination of it; but, nevertheless, let the
courses and distances be taken to the mouth of the Muskingum, and up
that river (notwithstanding it is in the ceded lands) to the carrying place
to the Cuyahoga; down the Cuyahoga to Lake Erie, and thence to Detroit.
Let them do the same with Big Beaver Creek, although part of it is in the
State of Pennsylvania; and also with the Scioto. In a word, let the waters
east and west of the Ohio, which invite our notice by their proximity, and
by the ease with which land transportation may be had between them and
the lakes on one side, and the Rivers Potomac and James on the other, be
explored, accurately delineated, and a correct and connected map of the
whole be presented to the public."

He estimated that if the improvements here indicated should be con-
structed, the distance from Detroit, "by which all the trade of the Northwestern part of the United Territory must pass" to the tide - waters of Virginia, could be made 176 miles less than to those of the Hudson at Albany.
"Upon the whole, the object in my estimation is of vast commercial and
political importance." * * * "*I consider Rumsey's discovery for working boats against the stream by mechanical powers principally as not
only a very fortunate invention for these States in general, but as one
of those circumstances which have combined to render the present time
favorable above all others for fixing, if we are disposed to avail ourselves of them, a large portion of the trade of the Western country in
the bosom of his State irrevocably.*" (Gov. Harrison replied to this letter
that he had submitted it to the Assembly, which would probably take
favorable action. The James River Improvement enterprise, in which, if I
mistake not, Washington was a large stockholder, was doubtless the
result.)

It must be remembered that ideas to what constitutes a navigable
stream have greatly changed in the course of a century. When transportation and travel were carried on upon our western waters by means of
flat - boats, broad - horns, keel - boats, and even bark canoes, which drew

---

* The Geographer of the United States.

only a few inches of water, and pushed their way up the rivers and their tributary creeks and bayous, and "wherever the ground was a little moist," many a stream figured as a navigable river which in these days of steamboats would hardly be regarded as a reliable mill stream.

NOTE 11.— General Washington, in speaking of this country in 1784, says that it will, so soon as matters are settled with the Indians, and the terms by which Congress means to dispose of the land found to be favorable are announced, be settled faster than any other ever was, or anyone would imagine."—*Writings, IX, p. 62.*

NOTE 12.— A plant called wild rice, on which numerous wild fowl feed, is found in the marshes bordering Lake Erie. A similar growth on the low bottoms of the rivers may have been mistaken by the early explorers for the rice of commerce.

NOTE 13.— "By the advice of Thomas Hutchins, Esq., Geographer of the United States, this tract (the Ohio Company's purchase) was located on the Ohio and Muskingum Rivers, he considered it the best part of the whole western country, and he had visited it from Pennsylvania to Illinois."

NOTE 14.— St. Vincents, or Post St. Vincents, or Post Vincennes, as it is variously called, on the site of Vincennes, Ind., was one of the early French settlements in the Valley of the Mississippi.

NOTE 15.— "The other mill I saw in the year 1797 on the Scioto River: It was built on two large dug-outs or canoes, with a wheel placed between them. This mill, after being moved up or down as the settlers at different stations needed its assistance in grinding corn, was tied to a tree in a rapid current, which, running against the wheel between the canoes, turned the stones above under a kind of umbrella made of bark. At a distance it had the appearance of a crane flying up the river. It made a sound, for want of grease, like the creaking of a wooden cart."—*American Pioneer, Vol. I, p. 59.*

NOTE 16.— "For my own part, I think it highly probable that upon the strictest scrutiny, if the falls of the Great Kanawha can be made navigable, or a short portage be had there, it will be found of equal importance and convenience to improve the navigation of both the James and the Potomac. The latter, I am fully persuaded, affords the nearest communication with the lakes; but the James River may be more convenient for all the settlers below the mouth of the Great Kanawha, and for some distance perhaps above and west of it."—*Washington to General Harrison, October 10, 1784.*

NOTE 17.— The reader of to-day who is whirled over the distance separating Cincinnati and Pittsburgh between breakfast and supper, will be interested in the following advertisement of a line of packet boats running up and down the Ohio between those places one hundred years ago, making the round trip in four weeks, and which were doubtless regarded as attaining the very acme of speed and safety in traveling. The advertisement is taken from the "Centinel of the North Western Territory," published at Cincinnati in 1793, five years after the first settlement of Ohio, and the first paper established north of the river:

OHIO
PACKET BOATS.

Two boats for the present will set out from Cincinnati for Pittsburgh and return to Cincinnati in the following manner, viz.:

First boat will leave Cincinnati this morning at 8 o'clock, and return to Cincinnati so as to be ready to sail again in four weeks from this date.

Second boat will leave Cincinnati on Saturday, the 30th inst., and return to Cincinnati in four weeks, as above.

And so regularly, each boat performing the voyage to and from Cincinnati to Pittsburgh once in every four weeks.

Two boats, in addition to the above, will shortly be completed and regulated in such a manner that one boat of the four will set out weekly from Cincinnati to Pittsburgh and return in like manner.

The proprietors of these boats having maturely considered the many inconveniences and dangers incident to the common method hitherto adopted of navigating the Ohio, and being influenced by a love of philanthropy and desire of being serviceable to the public, has taken great pains to render the accommodations on board the boats as agreeable and convenient as they could possibly be made.

No danger need be apprehended from the enemy, as every person on board will be under cover, made proof against rifle or musquet balls, and convenient port-holes for firing out of. Each of the boats are armed with six pieces, carrying a pound ball; also a number of good muskets and amply supplied with plenty of ammunition, strongly manned with choice hands, and the masters of approved knowledge.

A separate cabin from that designed for the men is partitioned off in each boat for accommodating ladies on their passage.   *   *   *

Passengers will be supplied with provisions and liquors of all kinds, of the first quality, at the most reasonable rates possible.   *   *   *

NOTE 18.—One of the controlling considerations in the selection of a site for the settlement by the Ohio Company at the mouth of the Muskingum was that it might be under the protection of Fort Harmar.

NOTE 19.—The plan originally proposed by Congress for the survey and sale of the first seven ranges west of Pennsylvania contemplated that the ranges should extend northward to Lake Erie, but the subsequent arrangements with the State of Connecticut recognized her claim to the soil (but not the jurisdiction which was reserved to the United States) all in that portion of Ohio north of the 41st parallel of latitude, and east of a north and south line drawn at a distance of 120 miles west of the Pennsylvania line, and forming what is known as the Connecticut Western Reserve.

NOTE 20.— The expression "United States" seems to be used as referring to the older settled states of the Atlantic sea-board.

Note 21.—Ships on the Ohio—In 1799, Louis Anastasius Tarascon, a French merchant of Philadelphia, sent two of his clerks, Charles Brugiere and James Berthond, to examine the course of the Ohio and Mississippi Rivers from Pittsburgh to New Orleans, and ascertain the practicability of sending ships ready rigged to the West Indies and Europe. They reported favorably, and Mr. Tarascon, associating them and his brother with him as partners, immediately established in Pittsburgh a large wholesale and retail store and warehouse, a ship yard, a rigging and sail loft, an anchor-smith's shop, a block manufactory, and, in short, everything necessary to complete vessels for sea. The first year, 1801, they built the schooner Amity, of 120 tons, and the ship Pittsburgh, of 250, and sent the former, loaded with flour, to St. Thomas, and the other, also with flour, to Phila-delphia, from whence they sent them to Bordeaux, and brought back wine, brandy and other French goods, part of which they sent to Pittsburgh in wagons, at a carriage of from six to eight cents per pound. In 1802 they built the brig Nanino, of 250 tons; in 1803, the ship Louisiana, of 300 tons, and in 1804, the ship Western Trader, of 400 tons."—*American Pioneer, Vol. I., p. 307.*

"As soon as ship-building commenced at Marietta, in 1800, the farmers along the borders of the Ohio and Muskingum Rivers turned their atten-tion to the cultivation of hemp in addition to their other crops. In a few years sufficient was raised not only to furnish cordage to the ships of the West, but large quantities were worked up in the various rope walks and sent as freight in the vessels to the Atlantic cities.

"By the year 1805 no less than two ships, seven brigs and three schoon-ers had been built and rigged by the citizens of Marietta. Captain Jona-than Devoll ranked amongst the earliest of Ohio shipwrights. After the Indian war he settled on a farm five miles above Marietta, on the fertile bottoms of the Muskingum. Here he built a 'floating mill' for making flour, and in 1801 a ship of 230 tons, called the Muskingum, and the brig Eliza Greene, of 150 tons."—*Ibid, Vol. I, p. 90.*

Note 22.—A plan since carried out by the construction of the Louis-ville and Portland canal.

Note 23.—Since preparing the translation of the report to Lord Hills-borough, I have met with the original document in English. It will be found in Volume II, page 6, of the "Olden Times," a periodical published at Pittsburgh in 1846 and 1847.

This report to Lord Hillsborough appears to have been made when he was considering the petitions of Thomas Walpole and others to the king for the privilege of making a purchase of land and founding a colony on the south side of the Ohio River, which petition had been referred to the Board of Commissioners of Trade and Plantations, of which he was presi-dent, for report. See a very interesting article by Professor Hinsdale on the western land policy of the British Government, in the *Ohio Archæo-logical and Historical Quarterly* for December, 1887.

NOTE 24.—The English version has "rye" where the French has "riz"—rice.

NOTE 25.—In the English original are here inserted the words "in the year 1772."

NOTE 26.—"The new settlement at the mouth of the Muskingum attracted the attention of the House of Burgesses in Virginia, and an appropriation of money was made to survey a route for a road from Alexandria on the Potomac to the Ohio River opposite Marietta. The commissioners found a very feasible course, and the estimated distance only three hundred miles. A road was cut out, and for many years before the building of the National Turnpike from the Cumberland to the Ohio, merchandise was brought in wagons to the stores in Marietta from the Port of Alexandria."—*Pioneer History, p. 245.*

NOTE 27.—The English version here says, "like the west country barges, rowed by only four or five men."

NOTE 28.—The settlements in Illinois were the earliest made by the French in the Mississippi Valley; that at Kaskaskia dating back to the seventeenth century.

Vivier, writing from Illinois, in 1750, says: "We have here whites, negroes and Indians, to say nothing of cross-breeds. There are five French villages, and three villages of the natives, within a space of twenty-one leagues, situated between the Mississippi and another river called the Karkadiad (Kaskaskia). In the five French villages are perhaps eleven hundred whites, three hundred blacks, and some sixty red slaves, or savages. The three Illinois towns do not contain more than eight hundred souls all told. Most of the French till the soil; they raise wheat, cattle, pigs and horses, and live like princes. Three times as much is produced as can be consumed, and great quantities of grain and flour are sent to New Orleans."

Twenty years later one man is said to have furnished the king's stores from his crop 86,000 pounds of flour.

NOTE 29.—At the time of the sale by Congress of public lands to the Ohio Company, two townships of land (each six miles square) were reserved for the benefit of a university, and section number 16 (being a lot a mile square and containing 640 acres) in each township sold, was at the same time reserved for the support of the schools in said townships. Another section (number 29), was in the same manner reserved for the support of religion.

Note 30.—"The colony at Marietta, like those of some of the ancient Greeks, enrolled many men of highly cultivated minds and exalted intellects; several of them claimed the halls of old Cambridge as their alma mater. The army of the Revolution furnished a number of officers who had distinguished themselves for their good conduct, as well as for their bravery."—*American Pioneer, Vol. I, p. 85.*

NOTE 31.— Ohio.

NOTE 32.— The apprehensions here expressed were not wholly ground-less. The ties of Union among the states were probably at their weakest in 1787. The articles of confederation which, under the stress of a common danger had carried the State through the war, had since its close proved wholly insufficient to reconcile their conflicting interests and serve the purpose of a Federal Government.

NOTE 33.— This was written in 1787. At that time the Continental Congress was sitting in New York, and a convention which framed the Constitution of the United States was in session in Philadelphia. As the result of the convention's labors was not published until the autumn of 1787, it is probable that the clause of the Constitution giving Congress exclusive jurisdiction over such districts not exceeding ten miles square, as may by cession of particular States and the acceptance of Congress become the seat of Government of the United States, was not known to the writer of the pamphlet. At all events the site of the future Capital was wholly undetermined.

NOTE 34.— The Ordinance of 1787 provided that, "the utmost good faith shall always be observed toward the Indians; their lands and property shall never be taken from them without their consent, and in their property, rights and liberty they never shall be invaded or disturbed, unless in just and lawful wars authorized by Congress,; but laws founded in justice and humanity shall from time to time be made for preventing wrongs being done to them and for preserving peace and friendship with them."

NOTE 35. The valley of the Muskingum and of its chief tributary, the Tuscarawas, (both of which at that day were known as the Muskingum,) was not only the scene of the Christian Mission in Ohio — that of the Moravian Brethren. Fifteen years before the settlement of Marietta these Christians had penetrated the wilderness as far as the Tuscarawas, and within the next few years had established upon its banks several villages of Indian converts — Schœnbrun, Gnadenhutten and Salem. Schœnbrun had two streets, laid out in the form of a T. On the transverse street, about the middle of it and opposite the main street, which ran from east to west, and was both long and broad, stood the church. * * * * At the northwest corner of the main street was the school house. The bottom, from the foot of the bluff to the river, was converted into cornfields. The town contained more than sixty houses of squared timber, besides huts and lodges.— *Life of Zeisberger — page 380.*

NOTE 36.— Toise — An old French measure equal to about six feet, in use, so far as I know, only in Detroit. Long since superseded in France, I found it a few years ago surviving in that ancient and conservative city, in daily business transactions.

NOTE 37.— The site of the present city of Cleveland. "From an early day the leading Virginia statesmen regarded the mouth of the Cuyahoga

as an important commercial position. George Washington in his journey
to the French forts, Venango and Le Boeuf, in 1753, obtained information
which led him to consider it as the point of divergence of the future commerce of the lakes meeting the ocean; Virginia being then regarded as
the State through which this trade must pass to the Atlantic. Mr. Jefferson, in his "Notes" upon that State, points out the channel through which
it will move to the ocean. He considers the Cuyahoga and Mahoning as
navigable, and separated only by a short portage to be overcome by a canal.
Once in the Ohio, produce, in his opinion, might ascend its branches and
descend the Potomac to the sea."— *Charles Whittlesey in American
Pioneer, Vol. 2, p. 24.*

Note 38.— The Following Description of the Muskingum Valley
    in its Primeval Condition is from the Life of Zeisberger.

He (Zeisberger) was now in the valley which was to be the scene of
his greatest works and severest trials. Blooming like the rose, with its
farms, its rich meadows and gorgeous orchards, it was in his day, although
a wilderness, no less a land of plenty, and abounded in everything that
makes the hunting grounds of the Indians attractive. It extended a distance of nearly eighty miles, enclosed on both sides by hills, at the foot
of which lay wide plains, terminating abruptly in bluffs, or sloping gently
to the lower bottoms through which the river flowed. These plains, that
now form the fruitful fields of the "second bottoms," as they are called,
were then wooded with the oak and hickory, the ash, the chestnut, and the
maple, which interlocked their branches, but stood comparatively free
from the undergrowth of other forests. The river bottoms were far
wilder. Here grew walnut trees and gigantic sycamores, whose colossal
trunks even now astonish the traveler; bushy cedars, luxuriant horse-
chestnut and honey-locusts, cased in their armor of thorns. Between
these, clustered laurel bushes, with their rich tribute of flowers, or were
coiled the thick mazes of the vine, from which more fragrant tendrils
twined themselves into the nearest boughs, while here and there a lofty
spruce tree lifted its evergreen crown high above the groves. These forests
were generous to their children. They gave them the elm bark to make
canoes, the rind of the birch for medicine, and every variety of game for
food. The soil was even more liberal. It produced strawberries, black-
berries, raspberries, gooseberries, black currants and cranberries; nourished the plum, the cherry, the mulberry, the papaw and the crabtree, and
yielded wild potatoes, parsnips and beans, Nor was the river chary of its
gifts, but teemed with fish of unusual size and excellent flavor.

Note 39.— Alaman — Paint Creek.

[The pamphlet from which the foregoing description and
notes is taken is now out of print and quite rare. A few copies
may yet be had of A. H. Smythe, the publisher, Columbus, O.]

THE SCIOTO COMPANY AND ITS PURCHASE.

The history of the founding of Gallipolis, now turning in its career into its second century, is one of the most interesting and at the same time one of the saddest studies in American annals.   It is the story of a disappointing and impracticable scheme; and were it not for the fact that the blood of its founders, mingling with the American stock of their day and generation, has given strength, versatility and industry to the people of Southern Ohio, the influence of the early settlers of Gallipolis would be scarcely noticeable in the history of the State. Understand me, that I do not underrate the probity or the genius of your fathers, but their influence by reason of the historical failure of the settlement, has been in the lines of private and domestic life, rather than in shaping public affairs or influencing the destiny of the State. A careful study of the elements which made up the emigration from France one hundred years ago and which resulted in the settlement whose centennial we now celebrate, will readily develop the fact that it was an entirely different stock from that which landed at Marietta or which settled in the Western Reserve or which located in Cincinnati and its surrounding settlements. The hardihood of the pioneers who came into the territory of the Northwest from New England, Pennsylvania and Virginia, was a capital stock in all their enterprises which the more delicate and impractical French never possessed. The men and women who came from Paris and Lyons in 1790, under the flattering representations presented to them by the leaders of American emigration in France, were of good families, well educated and brilliant, and adapted by their previous occupations, methods of living and their surroundings to any other life then possible in the world, rather than that of pioneers on the banks of the Ohio. But I do not propose at this time to go into any discussion in relation to the social conditions of the French settlers of Gallipolis until we arrive at a better understanding of how and under what circumstances the emigration was accomplished, and to what end I desire to set forth, as clearly and as extensively as is necessary in an historical address of this nature, the different events leading up to the foundation of Gallipolis. Under what circumstances and by what authority were these people brought from a foreign land, and, under a system of emigration entirely foreign to American ways at that time, made one of the foundation stones in the structure of the great commonwealth of Ohio? In the settlement of the territory of the Northwest, this instance of Gallipolis is the only one where the pioneers were brought from an alien clime. How this was done, why, and the results of this interesting historical event in our State are worthy indeed of remembrance, and deserve the careful investigation of the student of history; and if to-day I go into historical details I justify it on the ground that we are here for truth and facts rather than rhetoric or eloquence. The evolution of the settlement of the great territory of the Northwest, and the opening out to emigration of the great broad acres of the Ohio Valley, were not only required to attain development of the country for the future, but it was absolutely necessary for the maintenance of the government at that time. For a better understanding of the Centennial which we to-day celebrate, let me review as concisely as I can the methods[1] [see Appendix No. 1] and the results of the distribution of the public lands here one hundred years ago.

The close of the War of the Revolution left an army of men, the defenders of the country, impoverished. They had given their best blood to establish a nation in which they could live as freemen, but that country could not repay them for their services. Its wealth lay not in gold or silver or precious stones, but in an unknown quantity—its western lands.

The formation of the Confederacy of the States was the first step toward a government, but that confederation, built almost entirely on the doctrine of state sovereignty, did not, and could not, long survive. It could enlist an army, but it could not pay it save by consent of the States. No national coin was then issued and a national treasury was then practically unknown.

The soldiers, looking in vain to a helpless government, remembered the promises made them by the "Resolves of Congress," which had, in the beginning of the struggle, in August and September, 1776, promised to each soldier a bounty in lands, an acre of which it did not then actually possess.

With the close of conflict came the settlement of these questions. Conservative opinions prevailed and by the cessions of the various States holding claims to the territory northwest of the Ohio river, beginning with New York in 1781, Congress became peacefully and quietly possessed of a vast domain of land, more than enough to supply all claims.

The derivation of a national revenue from the sales of public lands had long been a favorite idea with Congress. In fact, the idea prevailed long before an American government was anticipated. As early as February 2d, 1774, the Governor of the New York colony was instructed by Earl Dartmouth regarding "land sales" in the colony. Other colonial records show similar action regarding the disposition of the lands for the benefit of those holding title under kingly grants and charters, or for the benefit of the Crown. July 31st, 1782, the Congress of the Confederation took steps for the survey and disposition of the vacant lands, the "back country," for the "common benefit" and for support to the "public credit." A committee, representing every State, to whom the whole affair was referred, made report September 5th of the same year, "that it is their opinion that the western lands, if ceded to the United States, might contribute toward a fund for paying the debts of the States." On motion of Mr. Witherspoon the proposition was amended to read, "it would be an important fund for the discharge of the National debt."

Two years after, on April 5th, 1784, another grand committee reported that "Congress still considers vacant territory as a capital resource."

The subject came up in one form or another until settled by the cession by the States of all claims to the "back lands"—the western country. Immediately following the cessions made by Virginia, March 1st, 1784, and not awaiting final action by all the States claiming possessions in the territory (the cessions were New York, March 1st, 1781; Virginia, March 1st, 1784; Massachusetts, April 18th, 1785; Connecticut, September 14th, 1786), Congress on May 29th, 1785, passed an act providing for the

survey and sale of the lands therein. Its main provisions were
that a surveyor should be appointed from each State by Congress,
or a committee of the States, who shall serve under the Geographer of the United States. Under his direction these surveyors were to proceed to the territory and divide the same into
townships of six miles square by meridian and parallel lines
running due north and south. The first lines were to be established by the geographer to begin at a point on the north bank
of the Ohio river "which shall be found to be due north from
the western boundary of Pennsylvania, and from thence westward across the territory; and also a line to run north and south
from the same point;" the geographer to designate the "townships or fractional parts of townships by numbers progressing
from south to north, always beginning each range with number
one; the ranges to be numbered from east to west, the first range
extending from the Ohio river to Lake Erie to be numbered
one."

The townships were to be divided into lots one mile square,
six hundred and forty acres, each in the same direction as the
the external lines and numbered from one to thirty-six, beginning
at the south-east corner of the section, running northwardly;
each succeeding range of lots to begin with the number next to
that with which the preceding one concluded. As soon as seven
ranges should be surveyed, plats were to be sent to the Board of
Treasury, and so on with each seven ranges of townships
throughout the territory. The Secretary of War was authorized to take by lot one-seventh part of the surveyed ranges for
the Continental army until all bounties could be satisfied. The
remainder was to be drawn for by the thirteen States according
to the quotas in the last preceding requisition on all States. The
Board of the Treasury was then to transmit to the commissioners
of the loan in the States plats of the quota of each State, which
States could then proceed to sell the allotments. It was also
ordered in the act that the sale should be in the following
manner: "The township or fractional part of a township, No. 1,
in the first range shall be sold entire; and No. 2, in the same
range, shall be sold by lots, and thus, in alternate order, through
the whole of the first range. Township No. 1 in the second

range shall be sold by lots; and No. 2 in the same range, entire; and so, in alternate order through the entire range," each succeeding range alternating in townships and ranges as in the first two ranges.

There was also reserved to the government lots 9, 11, 26 and 29, and for the use of schools lot No. 16. In addition to these reservations others for various bounties, refugees etc., were also set aside by this same act of Congress for various objects specified in the act.

The method of surveys of public lands into well defined districts or townships on the meridian and parallel lines is worthy of note here. It is the New England idea as against the Southern or Virginia plan of "indiscriminate locations." Under this plan a small quit-rent, as it were, of two cents per acre was demanded of the crown or the proprietor, and anyone could lay out and survey a tract, suiting himself as to location and boundary, simply taking care not to overlap other claims made in like manner. As care was not always exercised in this particular, conflicting claims constantly arose, the disputes often extending to several generations. The Virginia Military District in Ohio is a good example of "indiscriminate locations," and it is worthy of remark that more litigation over land titles and boundaries has arisen in that section of Ohio than in all the remainder of the State.

The township system originated undoubtedly in New England. As early as June 17, 1732, the General Court of Massachusetts granted six miles square for a *township* to be laid out in a regular form by a surveyor and chainman under oath.

When the first "ordinance for disposing of the western lands" was reported, it required the townships to be ten miles square, each mile to be 6086 feet in length, thus dividing the township into one hundred lots of 850 acres each. This ordinance was not agreed to, and the next report, made April 26, 1785, proposed townships seven miles square, with sections of 640 acres each, forty-nine in a township. In this ordinance, one section, 16, was set aside for school purposes, and one, 29, for the support of religion. This latter provision was stricken out by seventeen votes against, to six for, the measure; the vote being by states. The question was argued further in Congress until May 20th, when the ordinance previously outlined was agreed upon and adopted. Under this act titles could be obtained only by entry in a government office of a tract surveyed and entered for sale. This method is substantially the New England idea, and for a system of distribution and ownership of lands, has no equal. It is now the system of the National Government in all public land surveys.

Western lands being now open to entry and settlement, the soldiers began again to press their claims on the attention of Congress. A petition signed by two hundred and twenty-eight officers in the Continental army was presented to that body. This petition set forth:

"That, by an solution of the Honorable Congress passed September 20th, 1776, and other subsequent resolves, the officers and soldiers engaged for the war * * * * * are entitled to receive certain grants of lands, according to their respective grades, to be procured for them at the expense of the United States.

"That your petitioners are informed that that tract of country bounded north on Lake Erie, east on Pennsylvania, south on the river Ohio, west on a line beginning at that part of the Ohio which lies twenty-four miles west of the river Scioto, thence running north on a meridian line till it intersects with the river Miami (Maumee) which falls into Lake Erie, thence down the middle of that river to the lake, is a tract of country not claimed as the property of, or in the jurisdiction of, any particular state in the Union.

"That this country is of sufficient extent, the land of such quality and situation, as may induce Congress to assign and mark it out as a tract of territory suitable to form a distinct government (or colony of the United States) in time to be admitted *one* of the Confederated States of the Union."

Shortly after this, General Rufus Putnam, in a letter to General Washington, dated June 16th, 1783, emphasizes the claims of the soldiers and urges upon the Commander-in-Chief the importance of their petition. The General forcibly points out the wisdom of planting such a colony in the western country. He adduces many weighty reasons for such a step, and solicits the aid of his superior officers and companions in arms. This aid is freely and earnestly given, "but at this time," writes General Washington in reply, "little can be expected until the conflicting claims of the states to the territory be quieted." This was done through the cessions by the states already mentioned and by the land ordinance of May 20th, 1785; they were, as fast as surveyed, thrown open to settlement. The claim of Connecticut comprised a large part of the tract of country in the boundaries outlined in the officers' petition to Congress, and, when the cession of that state was made, an extensive tract of country known as the "Connecticut Western Reserve" was set aside and the claims of the soldiers were satisfied elsewhere.

By the failure of Congress to satisfy the petition of the soldiers the idea of settlement in a colony in the western country was delayed, but not abandoned. A company, well known in history as the "Ohio Company of Associates, was organized March 3rd, 1786, to buy of Congress land in the "Ohio country," as it was commonly called. Payment was to be made in Continental specie certificates, worth then less one-fifth their face value. This company was organized by, and composed mainly of, the officers who had before petitioned Congress for lands to satisfy their claims. Gen. Rufus Putnam was the chief promoter of the enterprise. Generals Samuel Parsons and Benjamin Tupper, Rev. Manasseh Cutler, Winthrop Sargent, John Mills and others, were among those who subscribed to the shares of this company and became residents of the then western country.

Gen. Parsons was sent to New York to secure from Congress a tract of lands on the Ohio. He did not succeed, and Dr. Cutler was appointed by the directors of the company to negotiate for the proposed purchase. He reached New York early in July, 1787, and at once began negotiations for a purchase. The scheme was not entirely new and many members were opposed to any such measure. The State that had sent them owned large tracts of land which they were placing on the market, and any plan of such magnitude as proposed by the Ohio Company was, in the opinion of many delegates, detrimental to the pros-

pects of those States disposing of their lands. Still the scheme
presented a solution to the serious problem of raising money,
not only to redeem the country's promises to its defenders, but
also a revenue for future needs. This idea of a National
revenue from the sale of National lands had long engaged the
attention of Congress, and, when Dr. Cutler presented the plan
of the associates, though it met with some neglect and opposition, yet the time was opportune, and many friends came to its
support.

The intention of the Company was to purchase as much
land as one million dollars in continental certificates would buy.
Dr. Cutler on July 21st informed the members of the Congress
that if his offer was accepted he would extend the purchase to
the tenth township of the seventh range from the Ohio and to
the Scioto river inclusively, by which purchase some four million dollars of the public debt could be extinguished. This, and
the prospect of a compact organized settlement, able to defend
itself and containing within itself the germs of a new State,
gave impetus to the plan.

The offer of Dr. Cutler had a marked effect on the tardy
members in Congress. Two days after, July 23d, a resolution
was adopted which authorized the Board of Treasury [see
Appendix No. 2] to contract with any person or persons for a
grant of a tract of land bounded east by the seven ranges; south
by the Ohio; and north by a line drawn from the northwest corner of the tenth township in the seventh range due west to the
Scioto river; the same tract which Dr. Cutler proposed to purchase. In all, it contains about six million acres—more than
four times as much as the Ohio Company of Associates had proposed to purchase.

Coupled with the Ohio Company's offer was the require-
ment that a law should be passed for the government of the
territory. Certain principles were presented which the associates
desired incorporated and without which they did not care to
purchase. The act, which was secured largely through the
efforts of Dr. Cutler, is known in history as the "Ordinance of
1787." It became the fundamental law of the territory. Its
cardinal principles were, 1st.—The exclusion of slavery from

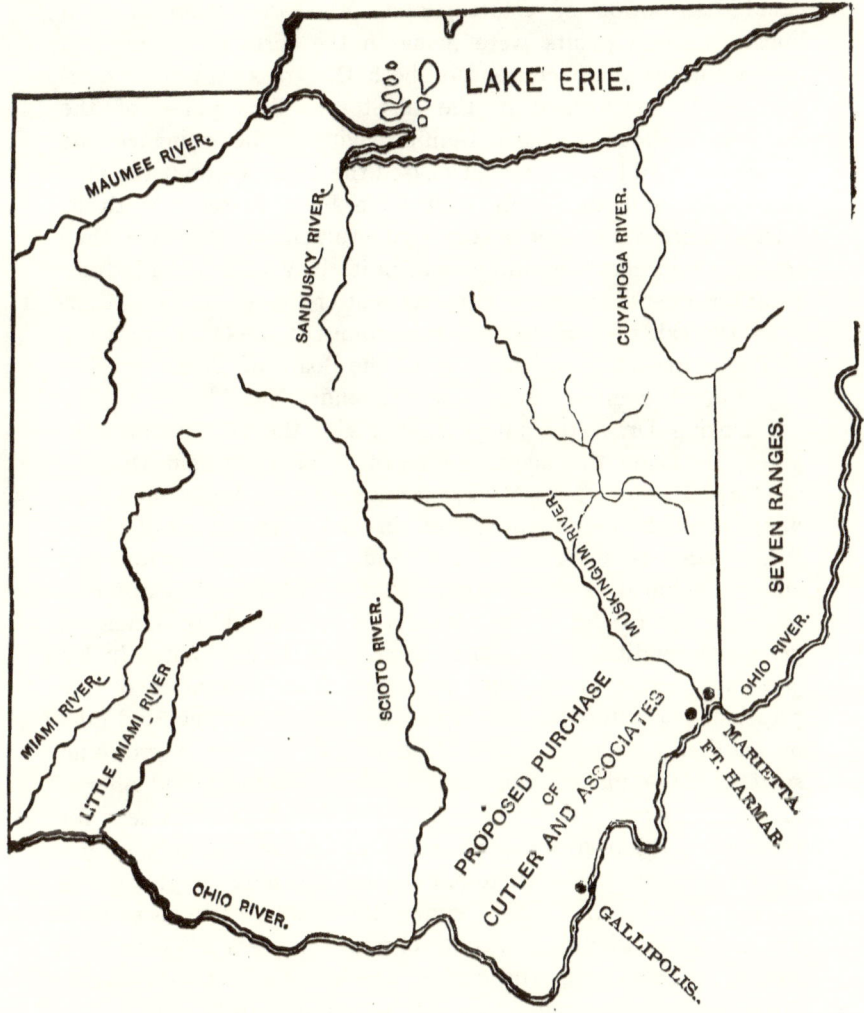

Map showing the proposed purchase of Manassah Cutler and Associates. The east boundary is the seven ranges, the south, the Ohio River;
the west, the Scioto; the north, the north line of the tenth township from
the Ohio River in the seven ranges.

the territory forever; 2nd.—Provision for universal education; 3rd.—Freedom in religious worship and opinion; 4th.—The equal distribution of estates; and, 5th.—Protection in civil liberty. These points were made in the form of a compact, irrevocable save by consent of both Congress and the States that might be formed in the territory. This phase of the negotiation should be borne in mind; without the ordinance, the associates would not have purchased the land; without the purchase, the ordinance could not have been passed. With it, settlers were assured of a stable government under which they could live in security, and which, in itself, would be an inducement for others to come. Three days after the resolution authorizing the sale of land in the Ohio country, the Ohio Company of Associates addressed a letter to the Board of Treasury offering to buy the entire tract. [See Appendix No. 3.]

During Dr. Cutler's negotiations with the Continental Congress, he made the acquaintance of Colonel William Duer, a wealthy citizen of New York, (secretary of the Board of Treasury), a man much interested in the proposed settlement. While matters were in doubt and when the Doctor had about concluded to abandon negotiations with Congress and buy of some one of the States, several of which offered lands on generous conditions, "Colonel Duer," Dr. Cutler writes in his journal, "came to me with proposals from a number of the principal characters in the city to extend our contract and take in another company, but that it should be kept a profound secret. He explained the plan they had concerted, and offered me generous conditions if I would accomplish the business for them. The plan struck me agreeably. Sargent insisted on my undertaking it, and both urged me not to think of giving the matter up so soon. I was convinced it was best for me to hold up the idea of giving up a contract with Congress and making a contract with some of the States, which I did in the strongest terms, and represented to the committee and to Duer and Sargent, the difficulties in the way and the improbability of closing a bargain when we were so far apart; and told them I conceived it not worth while to say anything further on the subject. This appeared to have the effect I wished. The committee were mortified and did not seem to know what to say, but still urged another attempt. I left them in this state, but afterward explained my views to Duer and Sargent, who fully approved my plan. Promised Duer to consider his proposals."

After noting incidents of an excursion in which many prominent actors in these affairs took part, the Doctor narrates further in his diary that " * * * I spent the evening closeted with Colonel Duer, and agreed to purchase more land if terms can be obtained for another company, which will probably forward the negotiations."

Several members of Congress called on the Doctor early the next day and expressed much anxiety about the contract, and assured him that Congress was more favorably inclined. Dr. Cutler was indifferent, and intimated he intended to abandon his efforts and leave. "At length," he says, "I told them that if Congress would accede to the terms I had proposed I would extend the purchase to the tenth township from the Ohio, and to the Scioto inclusively, by which Congress could pay near four millions of the national debt."

After further work on the part of Dr. Cutler and his associates, Congress passed an ordinance acceptable to the associates. The Doctor, under date of Friday, July 27th, writes, " * * * At half past three I was informed that Congress had passed an ordinance on the terms stated in our letter (of Tuesday, the 24th) without the least variation, and that the Board of Treasury was directed to close the contract. * * * By this ordinance we obtained the grant of near five million acres of land, amounting to three million and a half of dollars, one million and a half of acres for the Ohio Company, and the remainder for a private speculation, in which many of the prominet characters in America are concerned; without connecting this speculation, similar terms and advantages could not have been obtained for the Ohio company."

By the terms of this purchase, the Ohio Company's boundary was fixed by the seven ranges on the east, the Ohio river on the south, the west line of the seventeenth range (when surveyed) on the west, and on the north by a line drawn from that range to the seventh range, so as to include the required number of acres, allowances being made for the reservations (the sixteenth section in every township for schools, two townships for a University, salt springs, etc., and bad lands, estimated to be perhaps one-third of the whole). Had this been actually carried out, the north line of the Ohio Company's purchase would have been from near the north boundary of the fourth township in the seventh range westward to the Scioto river. Surrounding this on the west and north was the "private speculation" referred to in Dr. Cutler's journal. He states that some five million acres were obtained. In fact it was nearer six million. The "private speculation" lay between the north and west lines of the Ohio Company's purchase, and the north line of the tenth township of the seventh range, and the west line of the seventeenth range and the Scioto river,— in all about four million five hundred thousand acres.

The same day that Dr. Cutler and Winthrop Sargent contracted with the Board of Treasury for the Ohio Company's lands, they conveyed to Col. Duer one-half interest in this purchase, and also gave him full power to negotiate a loan or sale in Europe of the lands. Col. Duer advanced to the Ohio Company $143,000 in public securities to apply on its contracts in its first payments to Congress. The payments on the associates' purchase were to be half a million dollars when the contracts were executed, the remainder one month after the exterior line of the contracts had been surveyed by the Geographer or other proper officer of the United States. The payments in the "private speculation"— the remainder of the tract— were to be two-thirds of a dollar per acre in public securities in four semi-annual installments, the first falling due six months after the exterior line of the tract had been surveyed by the government.

Shortly after this transaction, Cutler and Sargent conveyed a little over three-fourths of their interest in about equal proportions to General Rufus Putnam, Benjamin Tupper, Samuel H. Parsons, Colonel Richard Platt, Royal Flint and Joel Barlow.

A company was at once formed for the disposal of these lands. It was named the Scioto Company; the President was Col. Duer; Richard Platt was Treasurer. The contract of sale between Cutler and Sargent for the Ohio Company and Col. Duer for the Scioto Company recites that "—— This day," October 29, 1787, "it is agreed between the said Manasseh Cutler and Winthrop Sargent for themselves and others, their associates, William Duer for himself and others, his associates, their heirs

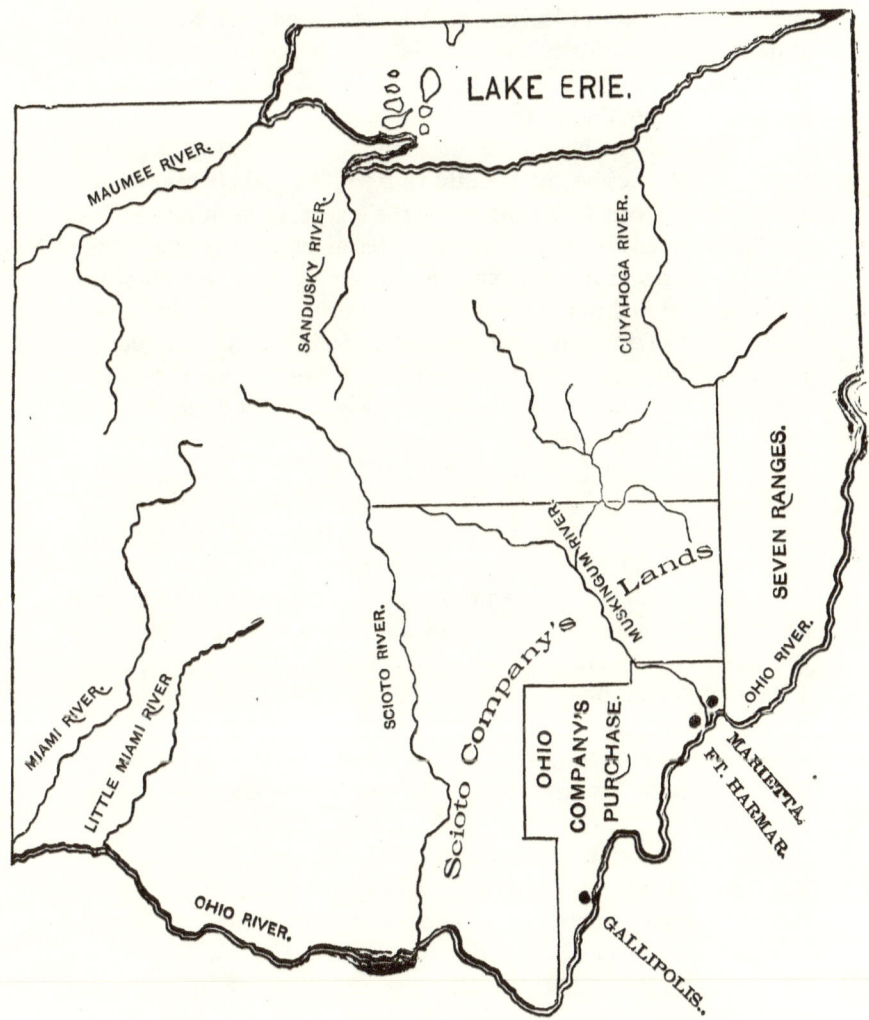

Map Showing Ohio and Scioto Companies' Boundaries.

and assigns, one equal moiety of the tract last described"
(i. e. that part bounded by the Scioto river on the west, the
north line of the tenth township in the seven ranges on the
north, and the Ohio Company's purchase and the Ohio river on
the south). Each party was equally interested in the disposal of
the lands, "either in Europe or America," and each was to share
equally in the profits or losses which "may accrue in attempting
to negotiate the sale or rentage of the same and in paying the
purchase money due to the United States.

" And it is further agreed upon and understood by the parties,
that . . . the tract be divided into thirty (30) equal shares or parts,
of which thirteen (13) shares are the property of William Duer
in which he may admit such associates as he may judge proper,
and (13) shares in like manner the property of the said Manasseh
Cutler and Winthrop Sargent. That the other four shares may
be disposed of in Europe at the discretion of an agent to be sent
there for the purpose of negotiating a sale or loan as above
mentioned, and if not so disposed of, to be equally divided among
the parties to this writing."

The contract further authorizes Col. Duer to negotiate a
loan upon or sell the lands in "Holland or such other parts of
Europe as may be found expedient, with power of appointing an
agent under him."

Looking about for the proper person to send abroad as their
agent, their choice fell upon Joel Barlow, a patriot and poet of
the Revolution. He had just published his famous poem, "The
Vision of Columbus," and was in the height of his literary
career. His capacity and education furnished sufficient passport
for his duties abroad. He had the confidence of his countrymen
at home, and his associates felt that he would be of great
advantage in representing their landed interests in France.
A modern historian has sneered at Barlow and his talents, and
has reflected upon the honesty of purpose of the originators of
the Scioto land purchase. The sneer and reflection are not
warranted by a close investigation of history. In May, 1788,
Barlow set out for France. He was a part owner by an assign-
ment from Colonel Duer of an interest in the Scioto contract,
and held at the same time the power of attorney from his

associates, to make the proper transfer of the title to purchasers. He was not successful at first. France was agitated by political dissensions, and it was nearly a year before the results of his efforts began to assume shape. In the summer of 1789, through the association and assistance of one William Playfair, an Englishman, he organized a society in Paris, known as the "Society of the Scioto," to which Mr. Barlow, acting for his associates and principals, sold three millions of acres of land lying west of the well-known Seventeenth Range of townships. This transfer of three millions of acres was made in November, 1789. It was provided that the payments were to begin in November, 1790, and to end April 30, 1794. The purchase price was $1.14 per acre. Associating with this company, and one of its members, was M. Jean Antoine Chais De Soisson.

The Society of the Scioto immediately proceeded to business. Mr. Barlow opened a land office at Paris and offered for sale the three million acres at a French crown per acre. The tract of land offered by Barlow fronted on the Ohio river. Its western boundary was the Scioto: its eastern, a line running North of the outlet of the Kanawha. On the plan of the tract a town was laid out and called Gallipolis, nearly opposite the mouth of the Kanawha. Maps of the surrounding country and of the Ohio were prepared and made ready for the inspection of the purchasers. The maps representing the country North of the Ohio river, the Ohio country, were highly colored and gave in outline the boundary of the Ohio company as well as the boundaries of the Scioto company and a plat of three million acres sold to Playfair and his associates in the Society of the Scioto.

The principal members of the Society or Company of the Scioto were M. Gouy de Arsy, M. Barond, St. Didier, Maheas, Guibert, Conquelon, Playfair, Barlow and Soisson. To this company Barlow contracted to transfer the rights of his principals to the entire Scioto tract save that part directly north of the Ohio Company's purchase, save so much of this part of the tract as might be necessary to complete the three million acres. The company was to make the deeds. In making this contract Barlow exhibited his powers of attorney, etc., thus apprising his associates in the Scioto Company fully of his authority. They

Copy of map* shown in France by the agents of the Scioto Company.
The original is in the French language, handsomely engraved and colored,
with the lands of the Scioto and Ohio Companies and the seven ranges
divided into townships six miles square. The Scioto Company tract was
divided into one hundred and forty-two townships and thirty-two fractional
townships. The north line of the Ohio Company's purchase is shown as
eight miles south of the Scioto purchase; the seven ranges as forty-eight
miles uorth; the north line of the Scioto purchase is supposed to be the
north boundary of the tenth township in the seven ranges.

* From Howe's History of Ohio.

could not claim ignorance of what authority they could hold under Barlow. The lands were to be located in equal tracts west of the seventeenth range, which was then supposed to be beyond the western boundary of the Ohio Company's purchase, hence no conflict of location could, it was presumed, occur. An agreement was drawn and properly signed, thus setting before all parties a full understanding of the rights and authority of each.

The Society appointed as attorneys to sell the lands, Playfair, Barlow and Soisson, and delegated to them "powers to resell all or part of 3,000,000 acres at the best price, terms or conditions of receiving the price thereof, or to assign it all or in part, and to discharge the Society with respect to the Suer Barlow, to give for this purpose every acquittance, consent, subrogation, and to disseize the Society of its rights of property over the objects of sale in favor of their purchasers, and generally to do for the ease and accomplishment of the said sale." * * *

Mr. Barlow agreed to put the Society in possession of the land in tracts less than the value of $500,000 each, thereby exceeding his authority from his principals in word, but had the money or securities been paid to the Treasury of the United States, nothing would have been amiss. As the French Society had examined fully Barlow's powers, and knew his authority, they could not plead ignorance, and acting with full knowledge, must be held accountable. Mr. Barlow did not send his principals a copy of the contract he had made, as he should have done, but he wrote to Colonel Duer, giving the fact of the sale, the price and terms and times of payments. He also urged that the west line of the seventeenth range be ascertained, and that the consent of the United States be obtained to the sale of the land in small tracts. Reference to the maps will show that the idea held by Barlow and his associates, was, that the west line of the seventeenth range would be at the mouth of the Kanawha, and on this supposition he made his sales, and he and his associates laid out a town—Gallipolis—ignorant of the fact that they were selling the lands of the Ohio Company, as the surveys, when made, showed their error, the seventeeth

range being further west than their supposition placed It. Sales.
were rapidly made, some purchasers paying in full, some par-
tially, securing the rest by mortgage.   Some made contracts for
lands, to be paid for at a future time.   The deeds were usually
signed by William Playfair and Jean Antoine Chais, "agents
and attorneys for the Society of the Scioto." To some, Barlow
added his approval.   One of these deeds is yet preserved in Gallipolis, and, as the last connecting link in the chain from the
government to the emigrant, is herewith given in full, the translation being made by Judge S. N. Owen, lately of the Ohio
Supreme Court.

This deed is from "William Playfair, engineer, Englishman,
and M. de Soissons, an attorney, Member of Parliament," to one
of the purchasers of an hundred acre tract of the land of the
Scioto Company:

" Before the undersigned, the King's Counsellors, notaries
of the 'Chatelet de Paris,' appeared M. William Playfair, engineer, Englishman, * * * and M. Jean Antoise Chais de
Soissons, attorney, Member of Parliament, * * * both cov-
enanting by these presents by virtue of the authority of the
Society organized under the name of the Scioto Company,
according to a title deed executed before M. Rameau and his
colleague, Notaries of Paris, August 3, 1789, for the purchase
made and evidenced by that deed by the said Society, of three
millions of English acres of land situated in North America between the Ohio and Scioto Rivers and more particularly designated by their boundaries, indicated in blue colors, by an engraved plat of the said three million acre tract of land, and
which was annexed to a memorandum of their purchase, received by M. Farmain, one of the undersigned Notaries, and his
colleague, November 3, 1789, containing the powers aforesaid;
who by virtue of the said powers have by these presents sold,
and promised to guaranty from every kind of eviction and
molestation, to M. Jean Baptiste Parmantier, citizen of Paris,
residing at number 359 St. Martin Street, Parish of St. Laurent,
purchaser, the entire depth and surface of one hundred contigu-
ous English acres of land, to be taken in a square form and by
straight lines from the above mentioned three million acres, in
the fourth municipality of the eighteenth rank of the said
municipalities or (at the choice of said purchaser) in the fifth
municipality of the same rank of the said municipalities; the
survey of which one hundred acre tract shall be made at the ex-

pense of the said Scioto Company, and along whichsoever shore
it shall please the said purchaser to select the said one hundred
acres, saving, however, such portions as may have been taken
by virtue of anterior sales by said Scioto Company, and also saving such portions as may be destined by the American Congress
for public buildings or public highways.

"Comprised in the present sale are the trees of every species
growing upon the tract of land by these presents sold.

"Wherefore the said Sirs Playfair and Chais hereby confer
upon the said purchaser, and subrogate to him, all the rights of
ownership, titles, claims, and rights of action of the said Society in and to the tract of land by these presents sold, yielding it
unto the profit of the said purchaser with all the rights therein
of said Society to the extent of the said quantity sold, and con-
senting that he place himself in full and peaceable possession
thereof when and as it shall seem to him good.

"The said purchaser and his successors to the ownership of
the land—the subject of this contract—shall enjoy the right to
transport each year to Europe or to the Islands of America, all
the big timber and the crops produced from the said land, paying only the freight and 'general average' according to the cus-
tom of, and as it shall be regulated by, the Captain 'bearer of
orders'—(*le Capitaine porteur d'orders*)—of the Scioto Company. The price of this sale and grant of right is agreed and
fixted at sixty pence per acre, which makes for the whole number of acres hereby sold a sum total of six thousand pence, upon
and in deduction of which sum the said purchaser has paid,
cash down, in legal tender, to M. Playfair, one of the said grant-
ors, who acknowledges it, three thousand pence for which this is
his receipt; and as to the residue of said purchase price, the
said purchaser binds himself to pay it to the said Scioto Company in two years from this day without interest, in guaranty of
which sum the land hereby sold shall remain, at the privilege of
said Company, expressly reserved, appropriated, obligated and
mortgaged, and without any appropriation derogatory thereto,
the said purchaser hereby thereunto appropriates, obligates and
mortgages all his property present and future.

"And in order the better to facilitate and secure the payment of the said sum of three thousand pence, the said purchaser has signed for the benefit of the said Scioto Company,
delivered the same to M. Playfair, who acknowledges the same,
his promissory note for said last named sum, payable also in two
years from this day, which promissory note once discharged
shall consequently acquit and discharge what remains due upon
the present contract; which said note shall be the only requisite

evidence of such payment by the said purchaser, who hereby acknowledges that the said Playfair and Chaise have communicated and remitted to him the substance of the deeds and powers which vested in them the right to make the present sale, for the execution of which the parties hereto have chosen their domicile in the establishment wherein are the offices of the said Scioto Company, Ninth Street of Petits-champs, No. 162, which place, however, we have chosen for the purpose of promising, contracting, obligating, relinquishing, etc.

Done and executed at Paris at the residence of M. W. Playfair, the 19th of January, 1790, P. M., and have signed this memorandum of contract.

Farmain, one of the undersigned Notaries,
(Not Legible.)   FARMAIN. [SEAL]"
[SEAL]
(Waxen Notarial Seal not Legible.)

These deeds were accepted without question by many. The desire for a change, the unsettled condition of France, the brilliant prospects held out to the emigrant, all combined to make the sales, once begun, an easy matter, and with little thought of the future, many prepared to go.

On the 8th of December, 1789, Mr. Barlow wrote Col. Duer that "everything was progressing well." On the 29th, that he expected to make the first payment, so that Col. Duer could pay Congress $500,000 when the first payment came due, and also that 500,000 acres would be concluded in January. The same date he authorized a draft on himself of 200,000 livres, "to be used in defraying the expenses of the first settlers." January 25th, 1790, he authorized another draft of 100,000 livres. "Don't fail," he wrote, " to put the people in possession of their lands. I pledge the faith of an honest man for the payment. If necessary, draw on me for a second 100,000 livres, at sight." By the middle of February, 1790, over 100,000 acres had been sold, and several hundred emigrants had sailed. Their first landing place, Alexandria, on the Potomac.

An examination of Barlow's letters discloses no reason for the failure to make the payment promised December 31, 1789, and the authority to draw for additional sums was evidence to Col. Duer, that if Barlow had not the money he had the securities.

Mr. Barlow's letter to Col. Duer showed that he had exceeded his authority by permitting the Society to give deeds, and that he erred in his calculations made from Thomas Hutchin's map in locating the western boundary of the seventeenth range as intersecting the Ohio River, opposite the mouth of the Big Kanawha. The survey, when made, located the line farther west, and hence the lands sold by Barlow and his associates were in the Ohio Company's purchase. This defect might have been remedied had Barlow met the drafts he authorized, as the Ohio Company was anxious not only to settle its own lands, but it was interested in the success of the Society of the Scioto, and was willing to do all it could to advance its interests. The connection between the Ohio Company and Col. Duer's control of the Scioto Company, caused some criticisms; but the prompt return of Dr. Cutler and his associates, and their concise statements regarding all the transaction, gave general satisfaction.

To meet the unexpected condition of affairs, Col. Duer, Royal Flint and Andrew Cragie united as "Trustees for the Scioto Associates." It was still supposed that Barlow held securities for all his sales, and as Dr. Cutler, neither for himself or for any of the Ohio Associates, was able to advance any money, they surrendered part of their interest, for which a power of attorney was given Col. Duer; the remainder to be exempt from assessments and to be indemnified from loss.

The Secretary of the United States Treasury had, in January, 1790, recommended to Congress a reduction in the price per acre of public lands, payable in certificates of indebtedness or in lawful money of a coin value. It became evident, however, that no action would be taken then. "On the 23d of April, Gen. Rufus Putnam and Manasseh Cutler, as directors of the Ohio Company and with its approval, made a contract of sale to Duer, Flint and Cragie, trustees for the proprietors of the Scioto lands, of the lands represented by the 148 forfeited shares to the Ohio Company for the non-payment, and located in a compact body, 196,544 acres fronting on the Ohio River between a point opposite the mouth of the Big Kanawha and the true line of the seventeenth range, the western boundary of the Ohio Company's purchase. The Scioto Associates also

released to the Ohio Company the right of pre-emption or purchase of that part of their lands lying immediately north of its
purchase. The contract was of great value to both companies.
It gave the Scioto Company control of every acre sold in France,
and enabled it to proceed upon a basis that, at that time, gave
assurance of solving the difficulties about its transactions.

Under instructions from Col. Duer, Gen. Putnam employed
Maj. John Burnham to enlist in New England a company of
men to build huts for the French emigrants, now ready to cross
the mountains. It is necessary to touch upon this part of the
history. It is fully told elsewhere, and gives in detail the work
of Maj. Burnham and his men. Neither is it necessary to recount here the history of these emigrants, nor to detail how
they found on reaching Alexandria that the deeds they held were
valueless, the country filled with Indians, and that there were
lands in plenty in Virginia. All these facts are told by Col.
Vance in his address and repetition is not necessary here. The
result of all this was that Col. Duer and his associates learned
through the misguided and wronged emigrants more fully of the
methods of the French Society in Paris and of their loose
methods of business. On the third of March, Mr. Barlow
wrote to Col. Duer that he had surrendered his contract with the
French Society, and was making the sales himself, though
under its name. M. Bourogne, Count De Barth's son, one of
the principal men in the colony of emigrants, and who had been
instrumental in securing a settlement with Col. Duer and associates satisfactory to the emigrants, and who had learned, when
in New York, of the efforts to secure a reduction in the price of
public lands, sailed for France in July, and there made a contract with Barlow, on behalf of himself, his father, M. Coquet,
Playfair and General Duvalette. This association was to assume
all obligations of the former French Company. It was to make
no payments until three months after the sale of each 300,000
acres; no limitations were to be made in location of lands. It
agreed to pay Barlow 50,000 livres for the American proprietors,
and authorized him to borrow on its credit 100,000 livres, also to
be advanced to the American proprietors. The whole transaction was a sharp move on the part of the new Company,

assuring itself a handsome profit, at the same time free from any risk. Mr. Barlow again appears to have implicitly trusted those with whom he dealt, despite the fact he had not been able to fulfill any of his promises' to Col. Duer, made "upon the promise of an honest man." Thus his final transaction only complicated matters more, and emphasized the fact that as a business man he was no success, and no match for the sharp and unscrupulous Englishman and his French associates. Had he followed his instructions, secured into his own hands the pro- ceeds of all sales, and promptly remitted them to the Scioto associates in America, all would have been well, and this melan choly chapter in Ohio's early annals would have never been written.

As soon as Col. Duer learned of this new contract, he sent Col. Benjamin Walker to France with "full powers of attorney to displace Barlow or to act as joint agent with him; directed him to refuse ratification of this last contract; examine fully into the accounts; obtain proceeds of sales; take entire charge of affairs if he deemed advisable, and endeavor to sell the con- tract as originally designed. Col. Duer wrote to Barlow that he, alone, was responsible to the French people to whom he had given or permitted to be given deals for the lands, and to the Scioto Associates, whose interests he had so shamefully mis- managed; upbraiding him in the severest terms for the manner in which he had conducted this business; for failure to give his principals definite information; and for permitting bills drawn on him that he had authorized, to be dishonored. Col. Duer was in a most embarrassing position by the non-payment of these drafts. He reminded Barlow of the pledges he had made 'on the faith of an honest man' for their payment, and urged him to make good the amount and save him (Duer) from ruin."*

When Colonel Walker reached France he found, as he sus- pected, that Playfair held the proceeds of all sales, and from him nothing, save a long letter of explanation, could be obtained, Finding nothing could be gained by persuasion, he placed the affairs of the Society in the hands of Colonel Rochefontaine.

---

* Life of Manasseh Cutler, page 516.

gave public notice that no sales from Playfair would be valid, and returned to America in April, 1791.

In the meantime, in October, 1790, one hundred years ago the first attachment of emigrants reached the new settlement prepared for them on the banks of the Ohio, and began their untried life on an American frontier. Colonel Duer, who now had the contract to supply the troops in the territory, opened a store in Gallipolis, placed Mr. John Matthews in charge, accepting in payment for the necessities of life whatever the colonists could give, even to deeds for their lots. By the next spring, however, they began to cultivate crops, chiefly the grape, and ere long Mr. Matthews was able to write Colonel Duer that a brighter prospect appeared.

But in April a financial panic came in New York. Colonel Duer failed, and was imprisoned for debt. Flint and Cragie also failed, and the notes given for the 148 forfeited shares of the Ohio Company were surrendered; the contract of sale conceded, and with it the only title the French emigrant could have. Col. Platt, Treasurer of the Ohio Company, went down in the general ruin, heavily indebted to the Company. On the 21st of April, 1792, Congress passed an act confirming the " Ohio Company's title to 750,000 acres'extending along the Ohio River from the west line of the seventh range to the west boundary of the fifteenth, including therein the site of Gallipolis. An additional grant of 214,285 acres was made to be paid for in bounty rights, and 100,000 acres were granted on the north to be held in trust to be deeded in tracts of 100 acres each to actual settlers. Both these grants were to adjoin the original 750,000 acre tract. The bill, as passed, made it impossible to give to the French settlers tracts of land at or near Gallipolis.

The failure of Colonel Duer and his associates threw the French settlers wholly upon their own resources. Mr. Peter S. Duponceau, a lawyer and Frenchman of eminence residing in Philadelphia, and who came to America in 1777, became interested in the fate of his countrymen, prepared a petition and presented it to Congress in 1794, asking the relief of the settlers. Some attempts were made to settle the matter, but nothing was, at that time, accomplished. In January, 1795, the donation tract of the Ohio Company was thrown open to settlers, and the French emigrants were invited to participate in its benefits. Not many did so; the majority who remained seeming to prefer to cling to the original settlement at Gallipolis in the hope that their titles would yet be perfected to them. Mr. Duponceau again pressed his petition to the attention of Congress, and in March, 1795, that body made a grant of 24,000 acres of land on the bank of the Ohio River, not far from the outlet of the Scioto, and each settler in Gallipolis, on November 1st, of that year, and over eighteen years of age, was entitled to a share in the distribution. Four thousand acres were given to M. Gervais, who had been instrumental in securing the services of Mr. Duponceau, and to whom much credit is due for the settlement of the problem. The remainder, 20,000 acres, was divided by General Rufus Putnam, appointed by the Secretary of the Treasury for that purpose, among ninety-two persons, each receiving 217 2-5 acres, settlement to be made on the land within five years. The tract was then and is still known as the " French Grant."

The directors of the Ohio Company met in December, 1795, to make a final disposition of their lands. The status of the French settlers in and about Gallipolis, and their condition, was fully and carefully considered. A committee of the Gallipolis settlers appeared before the meeting with a request that the French settlers be given the town site of Gallipolis. This the Ohio Company felt it could not do, but signified that an application to purchase at a nominal price would be acceptable, and after full consideration, agreed to sell to these settlers the two fractional sections on which Gallipolis was situated, containing 900 acres, with the improved land surrounding the town at the price of government land — one dollar and twenty-five cents per acre. This was donating all the improvements made by Major Burnham and his men, each received his land and a log cabin in which to live. This was all they could do, and was, all in all, a just solution of the long, difficult and unfortunate problem. The principal actors soon disappeared from view, lost in the absorbing events connected with the early settlements, the Indian wars, and the unsettled condition of the country at large.

DANIEL J. RYAN.

Note.— I am indebted largely to Maj. E. C. Dawes, of Cincinnati, who, in the life of Mannasseh Cutler, and in the *Magazine of American History*, has given exhaustive studies of this question. He generously placed his material at my disposal. I have also examined many private works, letters, documents, etc., and have aimed to give only a concise and simple narrative.

D. J. R.

Appendix No. 1.— (Ordinance of May 20th, 1785, 1. v. L. U. S. p. 563.)

"The surveyors, as they are respectively qualified, shall proceed to divide the said territory into townships of six miles square, by lines running due north and south, and others crossing these at right angles, as near as may be, unless where the boundaries of the late Indian purchases may render the same impracticable, and then they shall depart from this rule no farther than such particular circumstances may require. And each surveyor shall be allowed and paid at the rate of two dollars for every mile in length he shall run, including the wages of chain carriers, markers, and every other expense attending the same.

"The first line running north and south as aforesaid, shall begin on the river Ohio, at a point that shall be found to be due north from the western termination of a line which has been run as the southern boundary of the State of Pennsylvania, and the first line running east and west shall begin at the same point, and shall extend throughout the whole territory: Provided, That nothing herein shall be construed as fixing the western boundary of the State of Pennsylvania. The Geographer shall designate the townships or fractional parts of townships by numbers, progressively, from south to north; always beginning each range with No. 1; and the ranges shall be distinguished by their progressive numbers to the westward. The first range, extending from the Ohio to the Lake Erie, being marked No. 1. The geographer shall personally attend to the running of the first

east and west line; and shall take the latitude of the extremes
of the first north and south line, and of the mouths of the principal rivers.

" The lines shall be measured with a chain; shall be plainly
marked by chops on the trees, and exactly described on a plat;
whereon shall be noted by the surveyor, at their proper distances,
all mines, salt springs, salt licks, and mill seats that shall come
to his knowledge; and all water courses, mountains, and other
remarkable and permanent things, over or near which such lines
shall pass, and also the quality of the lands.

" The plats of the townships, respectively, shall be marked,
by subdivisions, into lots of one mile square, or 640 acres, in the
same direction as the external lines, and numbered from one to
thirty-six; always beginning the succeeding range of the lots
with the number next to that with which the preceding one concluded. And where, from the causes before mentioned, only a
fractional part of a township shall be surveyed, the lots pro-
tracted thereon shall bear the same numbers as if the township
had been entire. And the surveyors, in running the external
lines of the townships, shall, at the internal of every mile, mark
corners for the lots which are adjacent, always designating the
same in a different manner from those of the townships.

" The board of treasury shall transmit a copy of the original
plats, previously noting thereon the townships and fractional
parts of townships, which shall have fallen to the several States,
by the distribution aforesaid, to the commissioners of the loan
office of the several states, who, after giving notice of not less
than two nor more than six months, by causing advertisements
to be posted up at the court houses or other noted places in
every county, and to be inserted in one newspaper published in
the States of their residence, respectively, shall proceed to sell
the townships or fractional parts of townships at public vendue,
in the following manner, viz: The township or fractional part of
a township No. 1, in the first range, shall be sold entire; and
No. 2 in the same range, by lots; and thus in alternate order
through the whole of the first range. The township or fractional
part of a township No. 1, in the second range, shall be sold by
lots; and No. 2 in the same range, entire; and so, in alternate

order, through the whole of the second range; and the third range shall be sold in the same manner as the first, and the fourth in the same manner as the second; and thus, alternately, throughout all the ranges: Provided, That none of the lands within the said territory to be sold under the price of one dollar per acre, to be paid in specie or loan office certificates, reduced to specie value by the scale of depreciation, or certificates of liquidated debts of the United States, including interest, besides the expense of the survey and other charges thereon, which are hereby rated at thirty-six dollars the township, in specie or certificates as aforesaid, and so, in the same proportion, for a fractional part of a township or of a lot, to be paid at the time of sales, on failure of which payment the said lands shall again be offered for sale.

"There shall be reserved for the United States out of every township, the four lots, being numbered 8, 11, 26, 29, and out of every fractional part of a township, so many lots of the same numbers as shall be found thereon, for future sale. There shall be reserved the lot No. 16, of every township, for the maintenance of public schools within the said township; also, one-third part of all gold, silver, lead, and copper mines, to be sold, or otherwise disposed of, as Congress shall hereafter direct."

Appendix No. 2.—(In Congress, July 23rd, 1787, I. V. L. U. S. 573.)

The report of a committee, consisting of Mr. Carrington, Mr. King, Mr. Dane, Mr. Madison, and Mr. Benson amended to read as follows, viz:

"That the board of treasury be authorized and empowered to contract with any person or persons for a grant of a tract of land which shall be bounded by the Ohio, from the mouth of Scioto to the intersection of the western boundary of the seventh range of townships now surveying; thence, by the said boundary to the northern boundary of the tenth township from the Ohio; thence, by a due west line to Scioto; thence, by the Scioto to the beginning, upon the following terms, viz: The tract to be surveyed, and its contests ascertained, by the geographer or some other officer of the United States, who shall plainly mark the said east and west line, and shall render one complete plat to the board of treasury, and another to the purchaser or purchasers. The purchaser or purchasers, within seven years from the completion of this work, to lay off the whole tract, at their own expense, into townships and fractional parts of townships, and to divide the same into lots, according to the land ordinance of the 20th of May, 1785; complete returns whereof to be made to the treasury board. The lot No. 16, in each township or fractional part of a township, to be given perpetually for the purposes contained in the said ordinance. The lot No. 29, in each township or fractional part of a township, to be given perpetually for the purposes of religion. The lots Nos. 8, 11, and 26, in each township, or fractional part of a township, to be reserved for the future disposition of Congress. Not more than two complete townships to be given perpetually for the purposes off a University, to be laid of by the purchaser or purchasers, as near the center as may be, so that the same shall be of good land, to be applied to the intended object by the legislature of the State. The price to be not less than one dollar per acre for the contents of the said tract, excepting the reservations and gifts aforesaid, payable in specie, loan office certificates reduced to specie value, or certificates of liquidated debts of the United States, liable to a reduction by an allowance for bad land, and all incidental charges and circumstances whatever: Provided, That such allowance shall not exceed, in the whole, one-third of · a dollar per acre. And in making payment the principal only of the said certificates shall be admitted, and the board of treasury, for such interst as may be due on the certificate rendered in payment as aforesaid, prior to January 1, 1786, shall issue indents for interest to the possessors, which shall be receivable in payment as other indents for interests of the existing requisitions of Congress; and for such interest as may be due on the said certificates between that period and the period of payment, the said board shall issue indents, the payment of which to be provided for in future requisitions, or otherwise. Such of the purchasers as may possess rights for bounties of land to the late army, to be permitted to render the same in discharge of the contract, acre for acre: Provided, That the aggregate of such right shall not exceed one-seventh part of the land to be paid for: And provided also, That there shall be no future claim against the United States on account of the said rights. Not less than 500,000 dollars of the purchase money to be paid down upon closing of the contract, and the remainder upon the completion of the work to be performed by the geographer or other officer on the part of the United States. Good and sufficient security to be given by the purchaser or purchasers for the completion of the contract on his or their part. The grant to be made upon the full payment of the consideration money, and a right of entry and occupancy to be acquired immediately for so much of the tract as shall be agreed upon between the treasury and the purchasers.

"Ordered, That the above be referred to the board of treasury to take order."

Appendix No. 3.—The following is the letter referred to, of Cutler and Sargent, to the board of treasury, dated New York, July 26, 1787:

"We observe by the act of the 23d instant, that your honorable board is authorized to enter into a contract for the sale of a tract of land therein described, on certain conditions expressed in the act. As we suppose this measure has been adopted in consequence of proposals made by us in behalf of ourselves and associates, to a committee of Congress, we beg leave to inform you that we are ready to enter into a contract for the purchase of lands described in the act, provided you conceive yourself authorized to admit of the following conditions, which, in some degree, vary from the report of the committee, viz:

"The subordinate surveys shall be completed as mentioned in the act, unless the frequency of Indian irruptions may render the same impracticable without a heavy expense to the company.

"The mode of payment we propose is, half a million of dollars when the contract is executed; another half a million when the tract, as described, is surveyed by the proper officer of the United States, and the remainder in six equal payments, computed from the date of the first payment.

"The lands assigned for the establishment of a University to be nearly as possible in the center of the first million and a half of acres we shall pay for; for, to fix it in the center of the proposed purchase, might too long defer the establishment.

"When the second payment is made, the purchasers shall receive a deed for as great a quantity of land as a million dollars will pay for, at the price agreed on; after which we will agree not to receive any further deeds for any of the lands purchased, only at such periods, and on such conditions, as may be agreed on betwixt the board and the purchasers.

"As to the security, which the act says shall be good and sufficient, we are unable to determine what those terms may mean, in the contemplation of Congress, or of your honorable board; we shall, therefore, only observe that our private fortunes, and that of most of our associates, being embarked in the support of the purchase, it is not possible for us to offer any adequate security but that of the land itself, as is usual in great land purchases.

"We will agree so to regulate the contract that we shall never be entitled to a right of entry or occupancy, but on lands actually paid for, nor receive any deeds till our payments amount to a million of dollars, and then only in proportion to such payment. The advance we shall always be under, without any formal·deed, together with the improvements made on the lands, will, we presume, be ample security, even if it was not the interest as well as the disposition of the company to lay the foundation of their establishment on a sacred regard to the rights of property.

"If these terms are admitted, we shall be ready to conclude the contract."

By a resolution of 27th of July, 1787, it was "Ordered that the above letter from Manh. Cutler and Winthrop Sargent, to the board of treasury, containing proposals for the purchase of a tract of land described in the act of Congress of the 23d instant, be referred to the board of treasury to take order: Provided, That after the date of the second payment therein pro-

posed to be made, the residue shall be paid in six equal and half
yearly installments, until the whole thereof shall be completed,
and that the purchasers stipulate to pay interest on the sums
due from the completion of the survey to be performed by the
geographer."

SAMUEL F. VINTON.

THE EARLY JUDICIARY, EARLY LAWS AND BAR OF OHIO.

A proper study of the early judicial system and early laws of our State carries us to a period when, as a part of the great Northwest Territory, we were under control of the Federal Government.

On the 13th day of July, 1787, the Congress of the United States passed the ordinance for "The Government of the Territory of the United States, Northwest of the River Ohio." Relative to the judiciary, the ordinance provided, " There shall be appointed a Court to consist of three Judges, any two of whom to form a Court, who shall have a common law jurisdiction, and reside in the district, and have each therein a freehold estate in five hundred acres of land, while in the exercise of their offices, and their commissions shall continue in force during good behavior. The Governor and Judges, or a majority of them, shall adopt and publish in the district, such laws of the original States, criminal and civil, as may be necessary, and best suited to the circumstances of the district, and report them to Congress, from time to time, which laws shall be in force in the district until the organization of the General Assembly therein unless disapproved of by Congress; but afterward, the Legislature shall have authority to alter them as they shall see fit."

The ordinance conferred no authority on the Governor and Judges to make laws, but only to adopt and publish such of those in force in the original States, as might be necessary and suitable to the circumstances of the district. Acting under the provisions of the ordinance, Congress on the 16th day of October, 1787, just one hundred and three years ago yesterday, appointed Samuel H. Parsons, John Armstrong and James M. Varnum, Judges for the new territory. Judge Parsons was a native of Connecticut, and a graduate of Harvard University. He was admitted to the bar in 1759, and afterward served many years as a member of the Connecticut Legislature. His biography credits him with the distinction of having "originated the plan of forming the first Congress," which was the forerunner of the Continental Congress. He was a conspicuous figure in the Revolutionary war, attaining the rank of Major-General. He was also one of the military court which tried Major Andre on the charge of being a spy. At the close of the war he resumed the practice of his profession. In 1785 he was appointed by Congress a Commissioner to treat with the Miami Indians, and two years later, was appointed one of the Judges of the new territory.

Judge Armstrong resigned after a few months' service on the bench. He was born in Carlisle, Pennsylvania, and at the beginning of the Revolutionary war was a student at Princeton College, which he left to join the American Army. It is charged that while he was in the army he wrote the celebrated Newburg letters for the purpose of increasing the discontent already existing among the officers, and which had grown to such proportions that it required the personal efforts of General Washington to quell it. After resigning his judicial position, he retired to his farm, and for many years devoted himself to the pursuit of agriculture. He was subsequently United States Senator and Minister to France, and the author of several standard works.

Perhaps the most able and brilliant of the three Judges, who first presided over the courts of the Northwest Territory, was Judge Varnum. He was a native of Massachusetts and a graduate of Brown University, and like his associates on the bench, was a soldier of the Revolution. At the close of the war he resumed the practice of his profession and became the leading lawyer of his State. He was a member of the Continental Congress, and was recognized by that body as "a man of uncommon talents and most brilliant eloquence." There is a published oration which he delivered at Marietta on the 4th day July, 1788, while a member of the Territorial Court, which fully sustains his reputation as an orator, and shows him to have been of scholarly and historical attainments. No fact concerning the judicial history of the Northwest Territory is more clearly established, than that the Judges who constituted its first court, were men of classical education and recognized ability as lawyers, and thoroughly equipped for the discharge of their judicial duties.

Upon the resignation of Judge Armstrong, Congress appointed John Cleves Symmes his successor. He was a native of New York, served as a delegate in the Continental Congress, and was a distinguished Judge in New Jersey at the time of his appointment on the territorial bench. As the appointments which had been made by Congress, under the Articles of Confederation, expired upon the election of a president, Washington, after his election to that position, reappointed those persons who had previously been appointed by Congress. Consequently, Judges Parsons and Symmes were reappointed Territorial Judges. At the same time William Barton was appointed to the position made vacant by the death of Judge Varnum. Judge Barton declined the position, and George Turner was appointed to take his place. Shortly thereafter, Judge Parsons died, and Rufus Putnam, so well known in American history as General Rufus Putnam, was appointed his successor. He held the position for several years, and then resigned to accept the office of Surveyor General. He was succeeded on the bench by Joseph Gillman. In 1798, Judge Turner resigned and Return Jonathan Meigs was appointed his successor. He was a native of Connecticut, and a graduate of Yale College. His career was the most brilliant and eventful in the cluster of names which adorn the history of the Northwest territory. He afterward became a Supreme Judge of Ohio, Governor of the State, United States Judge in Michigan, a General in the war of 1812, a United States Senator and a member of the Cabinet of Presidents Madison and Monroe.

The Territorial Court, as organized under the provisions of the ordinance of 1787, lasted till 1799. While some of the acts adopted during this period were designed to meet the peculiar demands of those early times, many of them embodied the principles of a permanent and enduring judicial system.

The first law was passed by Governor St. Clair and Judges Parsons and Varnum, and was entitled, ''A law for regulating and establishing the militia in the Territory of the United States, Northwest of the River Ohio, published at the City of

Marietta on the 25th day of July, in the Thirteenth year of the
Independence of the United States, and of our Lord, 1788, by
His Excellency, Arthur St. Clair, Esquire, Governor and Commander-in-Chief, and by the Honorable Samuel Holden Parsons
and James Mitchel Varnum, Esquire, as Judges."

A difference of opinion arose between the Governor and
Judges concerning the extent of their powers in adopting laws,
the Governor maintaining that they could only adopt such laws
as were in force in some State; but the Judges out-voted the
Governor and the matter was subsequently referred to Congress,
which sustained the Governor's opinion. The second law which
was passed, provided for establishing county courts of Common
Pleas, and the power of single Judges to hear and determine
upon small debts and contracts, and for establishing the office of
Sheriff; and that there should be created in each county a Court
styled the General Quarter Sessions of the Peace, which was to
be held four times a year in each county. The act also provided
that a number of suitable persons, not exceeding five nor less
than three, should be appointed in each county and commissioned by the Governor under the seal of the territory, to hold
and keep a court of record, to be styled the County Court of
Common Pleas, and that said court should be held at two fixed
periods in each county in every year and at the same places
where the general courts of Quarter Sessions were held. This
law was promulgated on the 23rd of August, 1788, and the first
court in the Northwest territory was the Court of Common
Pleas, which commenced on the first Tuesday of September of
the same year. The following interesting account of the opening of this court, purports to have been given by one who witnessed the ceremony:

"On that memorable first Tuesday of September, the citizens, Governor St. Clair and other Territorial Officers and Military from Fort Harmar being assembled at the Point, a procession was formed, and, as became the occasion, with Colonel
Ebenezer Sproat, Sheriff, with drawn sword and wand of office
at the head, marched up a path which had been cut through the
forest, to the hall in the Northwest Block House of Campus
Martius, where the whole counter-marched, and the Judges,

Putnam and Tupper, took their seats on the high bench.
Prayer was fittingly offered by our friend, the Reverend Manasseh Cutler, who was on a visit to the new colony, after which
the commissions of the judges, clerk and sheriff were read, and
the opening proclaimed in deep tones by Colonel Sproat, in these
words: 'O, yes! a court is opened for the administration of
even-handed justice to the poor and the rich, to the guilty and
the innocent, without respect of persons; none to be punished
without trial by their peers, and then in pursuance of the laws
and evidence in the case.' This was the opening of the Court
of Common Pleas. The Indian Chiefs, who had been invited by
Governor St. Clair to attend the convention, were curious witnesses of this impressive scene."

On the second Tuesday of the same month was held the
first session of the Court of Quarter Sessions, of which Hildreth
says: "Court was held in the Southeast Block House occupied
by Colonel E. Batelle. It was opened with the usual proclamation of the sheriff, but not until the commission of the judges
had been read by the clerk. General Rufus Putnam and General
B. Tucker were appointed justices of the quorum, and Isaac
Pearce, Thomas Lord, R. G. Meigs, assistant justices. Meigs
was clerk. Paul Fearing was admitted as an attorney to plead
in all the courts in Washington county, being the first lawyer
ever admitted to practice in the Northwest Territory. He was
also appointed by the Court attorney for the United States in
Washington county. The Grand Jury consisted of the following person: William Stacy, Nathaniel Cushing, Nathaniel Goodale, Charles Knowles, Aselm Tupper, Jonathan Stone, Oliver
Rice, Ezra Lunt, John Matthews, George Ingersol, Jonathan
Devol, Samuel Stebbins, Jethro Putnam and Jabez True. William Stacy was made foreman. The charge to the jury was
given "with much dignity and propriety by Judge Putnam."
At one o'clock the Grand Jury retired and the Court adjourned
for thirty minutes. At half past one the Court again opened,
when the jurors entered and presented a written address to the
Court, which, after being read, was ordered to be kept on file.
Judge Putnam made a reply to the address. There being no

suits before the Court, it was adjourned without day. This closed the first Court of Quarter Sessions in the new territory."

One week after the publication of the law creating the Court of Quarter Sessions, the act establishing a Probate Court was promulgated. On the 6th of September, 1788, there was published "a law respecting crimes and punishments." It defined and provided the punishment for treason, murder, manslaughter, arson, burglary with theft, burglary with personal violence, burglary with homicide, robbery, riots and unlawful assemblies, perjury, suborhation of perjury, punishment for obstructing authority, receiving stolen goods, larceny, forgery, usurpation, assault and battery, and drunkenness, the penalty for the last offense being a fine in the sum of five dimes for the first offense, and for every succeeding offense the sum of one dollar, and "in either case upon the offender's neglecting or refusing to pay the fine, he was set in the stocks for the space of one hour."

The act also contained the following provisions concerning the use of improper and profane language:

"WHEREAS, Idle, vain and obscene conversation, profane cursing and swearing, and more especially the irreverently mentioning, calling upon or invoking the sacred and Supreme Being, by any of the divine characters in which He hath graciously consented to reveal His infinitely beneficent purposes to mankind, are repugnant to every moral sentiment, subversive of every civil obligation, inconsistent with the ornaments of polished life, and abhorrent to the principles of the most benevolent religion. It is expected, therefore, if crimes of this kind should exist, they will find no encouragement, countenance or approbation in this territory. It is strictly enjoined upon all officers and ministers of justice, upon parents and other heads of families, and upon others of every description, that they abstain from practices so vile and irrational; and that by example and precept, to the utmost of their power, they prevent the necessity of adopting and publishing laws, with penalties, upon this head. And it is hereby declared that government will consider as unworthy its confidence all those who may obstinately violate these injunctions."

And the following relative to the religious observance of the Sabbath:

"WHEREAS, Mankind in every stage of informed society, have consecrated certain portions of time to the particular culti-

vation of the social virtues, and the public adoration and worship of the common parent of the universe; and whereas, a
practice so rational in itself, and conformable to the divine pre-
cepts is greatly conducive to civilization and piety ; and whereas,
for the advancement of such important and interesting purposes, most of the Christian world have set apart the first day
of the week as a day of rest from common labor and pursuits, it
is, therefore, enjoined that all servile labor, works of necessity
and charity only excepted, be wholly abstained from on that
day.

Among other important acts which were adopted was one
directing the building and establishing of a court house, county
jail, pillory, whipping-post and stocks in every county.

Another, subjecting real estate to execution for debt.   In
Chase's Statutes appears this foot note: "These laws from
Chapter 37 to Chapter 74, inclusive, have been commonly known
to the profession as the 'Maxwell Code.'   They were adopted
and published in Cincinnati in 1795 by Governor St. Clair and
Judges Symmes and Turner."

Another was a law to prevent unnecessary delays in causes
after issue joined.   Still another, limiting the time of commencing civil actions and instituting criminal prosecutions, was
passed December 28, 1788.   "This law," says Chase, "was disapproved by Congress, May 8, 1792."   Another law on the same
subject was adopted in 1795, which was repealed by the territorial legislature as unconstitutional.   No law on this subject
was afterward enacted until 1803, when the state legislature
passed an act of limitation.

An act of special interest to the legal profession of the
present day regulated the fees of the officers of the court, including attorneys.   It allowed a judge in the general court, for
allowing a writ of error, sixty-two and one-half cents; for every
supersedeas, thirty-seven and one-half cents; the same for taking
bail; for taking an affidavit, twelve and one-half cents; admit-
ting a counselor-at-law, or attorney, one dollar and twenty-five
cents; licensing a counselor-at-law, or attorney, three dollars and
seventy-five cents.

The following were some of the fees allowed the Attorney-
General: Entering every *cessal processus* or *nolle prosequi* for

each defendant, sixty-two and one-half cents; every indictment per sheet, eighteen cents; fee on trial, three dollars; for trial of every capital cause where life was concerned, eight dollars.

To attorneys in a general court, it allowed for a retainer fee, three dollars and fifty cents, but where several suits were brought upon one note or bond, no more than one retainer fee was allowed; drawing warrant of attorney, twenty-eight cents; drawing of *processus* and returns, twelve and one-half cents; for argument on special motion, one dollar and twenty-five cents, · while to attorneys in the Court of Common Pleas, it allowed the following: Drawing warrant of attorney, twelve and one-half cents; every motion, twenty-five cents; drawing a declaration and other pleadings, per sheet, containing seventy-two words, twelve and one-half cents, and every copy thereof, six cents per sheet.

This act distinguished between counselors-at-law and attorneys-at-law, and between the practitioner at the General Court and the Common Pleas Court. By the year 1790, the business of the courts had grown to such an extent that an act was passed increasing the number of terms of the Common Pleas Court in each year from two to four, and the number of Common Pleas judges to not less than three or more than seven.

Other important acts were adopted, such as the act regulating marriage, a law for the partition of lands, a law respecting divorce, a law authorizing the judges to subdivide the counties into townships; and here we find for the first time in our judicial history a recognition of those small political subdivisions.

The ordinance of 1787 provided, that as soon as it was proven that there were five thousand free male inhabitants of lawful age in the district, they should be authorized to elect representatives to the general assembly. How the proof was to be made does not appear, but in 1798, Governor St. Clair issued his proclamation that the territory contained the requisite number of free male inhabitants, and called upon the people to elect representatives, the proportion of representatives being one to every five hundred voters; but no one could be a representative unless he had been a citizen of the United States for three years and a resident of the district, or unless he had resided in the district for three years, and in either case he must own in fee simple two hundred acres of land within his district.

The general assembly consisted of the Governor, a legislative council, and a House of Representatives. The council consisted of five members, who held their office for five years, unless sooner removed. They were selected in the following manner: The representatives who were elected by the people met at the time and place designated by the Governor, and nominated ten persons, each of whom were required to be a resident of the district and possess a freehold estate in five hundred acres of land, and the names of these ten persons were sent by the representatives to Congress, and Congress selected five out of the ten and appointed them to serve as members of the council. The members of the council and house of representatives met at Cincinnati on the 16th of September, 1799, and organized the first general assembly of the Northwest territory, at which time the authority of the Governor and judges to adopt and promulgate laws ceased, and the territory was thereafter governed by laws passed by the territorial general assembly. Edwin Tiffin was elected Speaker of the House of Representatives and Henry Vanderberg was elected President of the Council.

In commenting upon the character, ability and general worth of the men who constituted this general assembly, Judge Burnett, in his notes on the Northwest Territory, says: ''In choosing members to the first territorial legislature, the people in almost every instance selected the strongest and best men in their respective counties. Party influence was scarcely felt, and it may be said with confidence, that no legislature has been chosen under the State government which contained a larger proportion of aged intelligent men, than were found in that body. Many of them, it is true, were acquainted with the forms and practical duties of legislation, but they were strong-minded, sensible men, acquainted with the condition and want of the country, and could form correct opinions of the operation of any measure proposed for their consideration.

One of the most important duties which devolved upon the assembly was to elect a representative of the territory to the National Congress. William Henry Harrison and Arthur St.

Clair, junior, were the candidates. The former received twelve
votes, while the latter received ten. Mr. Harrison was accordingly declared elected.

The first act passed at this session of the general assembly,
was one approving and declaring to be in force, certain acts
which had previously been adopted by the Judges and the Governor.

The second act passed—which was on the 29th of October,
1799—was one regulating the admission and practice of attorneys and counselors-at-law, the first section of which provided
for the applicant obtaining a license to practice, from the Governor of the territory, which admitted him to practice as an
attorney-at-law according to the laws and customs of said territory, during his good behavior, and authorized him to receive
such fees as might be established; and required all judges, justices, and others concerned to respect him accordingly; but he
could not receive such license from the Governor until he had
obtained a certificate signed by two or more of the judges of the
general court, setting forth that he had been regularly examined;
but before he could be examined, he was required to produce a
certificate that he had regularly and attentively studied law
under the direction of a practicing attorney, residing within the
territory for the period of four years. This act, like the one
adopted by the Governor and Judges, retained the distinction
between counselor and attorney-at-law, and their admission to
practice at the general term and Court of Common Pleas. It
gave the judges of the General court, and of the several Common Pleas courts, power to punish in a summary way, according
to the rules of law and the usages of the courts, any and every
attorney or counselor-at-law who should be guilty of any contempt in the execution of his office, and every attorney or counselor-at-law who received money for the use of his client and refused to pay the same when demanded, could be proceeded
against in a summary way, on motion.

On November 3, 1800, the second session of the first general assembly met at Chillicothe and adjourned on the 9th of December following.

The second general assembly held its first session at Chillicothe, commencing on the 23rd of November, 1801, and ending on the 23rd of January, 1802. Edward Tiffin was again elected Speaker of the House of Representatives, and Robert Oliver was elected President of the Council. Notwithstanding the assembly adjourned to meet in November following, a second session was never held, for the reason that soon after the adjournment of the first session, a census was taken of the population of the Eastern Division of the territory, and it was found that it exceeded forty-five thousand persons. Thereupon, an appeal was made to Congress, that the inhabitants of the Eastern Division be authorized to call a convention and form a constitution with the view of establishing a State government. Congress passed an act authorizing the convention to be held, and as the result, a constitution was adopted and a State formed, and admitted into the Federal Union.

The convention which framed the first Constitution of our State met at Chillicothe on the first Monday of November, 1802. It was expeditious in its work, for on the 29th of the same month it adjourned, having adopted a Constitution without submitting it to the people for ratification. Concerning the judiciary it contained the following clause: "The judicial power of the State, both as to matters of law and equity, shall be vested in a Supreme Court, Court of Common Pleas for each county, in Justices of the Peace, and in such other courts as the Legislature may, from time to time, establish.

It further provided, that the Supreme Court should consist of three judges, any two of whom should be a quorum; that they should be appointed by a joint ballot of both Houses of the General Assembly, and should hold their office for the term of seven years, if so long they behaved well.

The first General Assembly of the State of Ohio convened at Chillicothe on Tuesday, March 1st, 1803. On the 15th of April following, it passed a general act providing for the organization of "Judicial Courts," and abolished all courts which had been established during the existence of the Territorial Government. During the session, the convention elected the following State officers: William Creighton, jr., Secretary of State; Thomas Gibson, Auditor; William McFarland, Treasurer, while

Return Jonathan Meigs, jr., Samuel Huntington and William Sprigg were elected Judges of the Supreme Court, and Francis Dunlavey, Wyllys Sillman and Calvin Pease, Judges of the District Courts.

The second General Assembly met on December 5th, 1803. On February 18, 1804, it amended the act of the first General Assembly providing for the organization of the courts. On the same day it passed an act "regulating the duties of Justices of the Peace and Constables, in criminal and civil cases," making their jurisdiction co-extensive with their counties in criminal matters, and with their townships in civil causes, which is still the provision of our statutes. It also prescribed the forms which should be used by the Justices in their practice, and with little, if any change, they are still used.

The third General Assembly began its session on December 3, 1804. The first act which it passed related to crimes and punishments. On the 12th of February, 1805, a general act was passed defining the duties of Justices of the Peace and Constables, and repealing all former laws in force on that subject. Among other things, this act provided that Justices should have jurisdiction in civil cases to the amount of fifty dollars without the right of jury trial. Subsequently, Judges Huntington and Todd of the Supreme Court, and Pease of the Common Pleas Court, who afterward was on the Supreme Bench, held this provision of the law to be in conflict with that section of the Federal Constitution, which provides that "in suits at common law when the value in controversy shall exceed twenty dollars, the right of trial by jury shall be preserved." The court also held the act to be in conflict with that clause of the State Constitution providing that "the right of trial by jury shall be inviolate." Out of this decision arose a most interesting and exciting proceeding. The indignation of the public toward the Judges who rendered the decision, was violent and almost unrestrained. It was asserted that the judicial branch of the government was invading the domain of the legislature, and assuming legislative powers, and such conduct was not to be tolerated even from the Supreme Court. In consequence of the bitter feeling among the members of the General Assembly, that body undertook to impeach the Judges who had rendered the decision. The records of the proceedings show that on December 24, 1808, the following message was sent from the House of Representatives:

"The House of Representatives having instructed the managers appointed to conduct the impeachment against Calvin Pease, Esquire, President of the Third Circuit of the Court of Common Pleas of this State, to proceed to the bar of the Senate with the articles of impeachment against the said Calvin Pease, Esquire, and there demanded that the said Calvin Pease, Esquire, be put to answer the said articles of impeachment exhibited against him." Committees were then appointed to prepare and report the method of proceeding in the conduct of the trial. On December 27, the Managers on the part of the House, took seats assigned them within the bar, and the Sergeant-at-Arms made proclamation of the trial in the following words: "O, yes! O, yes! O, yes! all persons are commanded to keep silence under pain of imprisonment, while the grand inquest of the State is exhibiting to the Senate of Ohio, articles of impeachment against Calvin Pease, President of the Courts of Common Pleas of the Third Circuit." The articles were then read. In the course of the trial, the Sergeant-at-Arms was directed by the Speaker to call Calvin Pease, Esquire, three several times in the following manner, to appear and answer: "Hear ye, Hear ye, Hear ye, Calvin Pease, President of the Court of Common Pleas of the Third Circuit, come forward and answer the articles of impeachment exhibited against you by the House of Representatives." Articles were drawn up against each of the Judges. The one against Pease contained three distinct charges, while that against Todd contained but one. Judge Harrington in the meantime had been elected Governor, and for that reason the charges against him were not pressed. The accused were each furnished copies of the charges and then filed their answers. Several days were spent in the trial. In the Senate Journal of 1808–9 appears this short, but interesting record: "High Court of Impeachment, Monday, February 6th. The State of Ohio vs. Calvin Pease." The court was opened by proclamation. Ordered, that the Clerk notify the House of Representatives that the Senate is in their public chamber and ready to proceed farther with the trial of impeachment of Calvin Pease, President of the Courts of Common Pleas of the Third Circuit of this State. The Managers accompanied by the House of Representatives, attended. The respondent with his counsel also attended on the first article of impeachment. The clerk took the opinion of the members of the court, respectively, in the form following: Mr. ——, how say you, is the respondent, Calvin Pease, guilty or not guilty, of the high crime or misdemeanor as charged in the first article of impeachment?" The respondent was unanimously acquitted on the first charge. The Clerk then took the opinion in the same way of each member on the second article of impeachment. Fifteen members voted "guilty" and nine "not guilty". Whereupon, the Speaker declared that "Calvin Pease, President of the Courts of Common Pleas of the Third Circuit of this State, is acquitted of all the charges contained in the articles of impeachment exhibited against him by the House of Representatives," and the court adjourned without day. The proceedings against Judge Tod were then commenced and lasted several days, the vote standing as it did in the case of Judge Pease.

The business of the courts kept pace with the rapid commercial developments of the new State and the increase in its population. The members of the Supreme Court were required to travel the circuit, and as there were no carriages or railroads, they were compelled to go on horseback, and in the absence of the modern turn-pike or even the old corduroy road, the journey was undesirable and frequently hazardous.

For many years the annual salary of a Supreme Judge was only eight hundred dollars, but neither the corduroy roads nor the small salary were permitted to stifle the social side of the court, and there is abundant evidence that the good nature of the dignified judges sometimes manifested itself in ways that were calculated to develop social amenities at the expense of judicial gravity. I am indebted to Senator Sherman for the following incident, who recently related it to me and authorized its use in this connection. Judge Hitchcock had often said that circumstantial evidence was stronger than direct evidence, for the rea-

son that "witnesses will lie and you can not prevent it, but circumstantial evidence never lies." It was one of the Judge's
peculiarities that he was greatly averse to card playing. Once
when the Judges were holding court in Columbus, they all occupied one room at the hotel. One evening after Judge Hitchcock
had retired, several members of the bar called, and "old sledge"
and "whiskey poker" were indulged in until a late hour. When
the callers had departed, one of the judges opened Judge Hitchcock's valise, and taking out a soiled garment wrapped it around
a well-worn pack of cards, and then replaced it in the valise.
The next day the judges went to their homes, when Mrs. Hitchcock (as the Judge afterward told the other members of the
court) opened his valise for the purpose of getting his wash, and
was horrified at discovering the pack. She was convinced that
the Judge had learned to "play," and in great distress went to
him and said: "Peter, Peter, what have you been doing? It is
too bad, and I never would have thought it of you; see what I
have found in your shirt!" At the same time exhibiting the
cards. Judge Hitchcock told it to the other judges as a joke,
when one of them remarked that it might have been a joke, but
the *circumstantial evidence* seemed complete. The judge saw
the point and thereafter had less to say about the weight of such
testimony.

In the preface to Wright's Reports is the following statement made by that excellent judge, relative to the labors of the
Supreme Court at that time: "The Supreme Court of Ohio is
now composed of four judges, the largest number the Constitution permits. The Constitution requires a court to be holden
once a year in each county, and makes any two of the judges a
quorum. A legislative act imposes upon the judges the duty of
holding every year a court in banc at the seat of government.
* * * The principal result of this organization of the court
is, that the Supreme Court is generally held in the several counties by two judges only. The judges relieve one another to suit
their own convenience, so dividing their labor that each may perform one-half of the circuit duty. The duties imposed on this
Court are so great as to make this relief necessary, for it would
be difficult to find men of sufficient physical ability to partici-

pate in all of them. These judges now hold court in seventy-two counties each year, requiring 2250 miles travel. The number of cases on their trial dockets in 1834 was 1459. The judges are occupied in banc from three to four weeks annually. If that time and Sundays are deducted from the year and the usual allowance is made for travel, the Court, to clear its docket, would be under the necessity of deciding on an average, about seven cases a day for each remaining day of the year."

To relieve the pressure upon the courts it became necessary to increase the number of Supreme Judges and to create new Courts of Common Pleas. There were thirty Judges of the Supreme Court under the old Constitution, which covered a period of forty-nine years. The decisions of the Court were not published by legislative authority and in permanent form until 1823, when the first volume of the Ohio Reports was issued.

The earlier judges who graced our Supreme bench were Huntington, Meigs, Sprigg, Todd, Symmes, Scott, Morris, Irwin, Brown and Pease, two of whom, Huntington and Meigs, were afterward Governor of the State. Following these were McLean, afterward a Cabinet officer and a Justice of the Supreme Court of the United States; then Couch, and Burnett, who was afterward a United States Senator; and Hitchcock, who occupied the position for twenty-eight years—longer than any man before or since his time. Then came Sherman, the father of the General and Senator, who died while on the bench, at the early age of forty-one. Then Gustavus Swan, the uncle of Joseph R. Swan, who was on the same bench under the new Constitution; then Hayward, Goodenow, Brush, Wood and Wright. They were followed by Collet, Lane, Grimke, Birchard, Read, Avery, Spalding, Caldwell and Ranney. These were all able judges, but some of them were especially eminent, and their opinions made the Court distinguished throughout the entire country. But the reputation of the bar was equal to that of the bench, and many of the greatest lawyers of our State practiced under the old Constitution. Among the earlier names which became illustrious was that of William Creighton, of Chillicothe. He was educated at Dickinson College, where he was a fellow-student of the great Tanney, afterward Chief Justice of the

United States. He was especially distinguished as a jury lawyer. He served many years in Congress, and was an intimate friend of Daniel Webster. I have heard it said that if Mr. Webster had reached the Presidency, Mr. Creighton would have been a member of his Cabinet.

Another great member of the Chillicothe bar was Benjamin F. Leonard. He was a man of profound learning in the law and all kindred subjects. Then came a cluster of names which will forever remain unsurpassed for their learning, eloquence and wit, every element, in fact, which enters into consideration in the make-up of a great lawyer. Among them was Samuel F. Vinton. Like others who helped to make our State illustrious, he was born in New England. He graduated at Williams College and settled in Gallipolis in 1816. He was elected a Representative in Congress in 1823 and served for fourteen years. He was again elected in 1843 and served eight years, in all a period of twenty-two years. His greatest legal effort was his argument in the case of the commonwealth against Garner and others, before the Supreme Court of Virginia, in 1845. Peter M. Garner, Mordecai Thomas and Graydon J. Loraine were citizens of the State of Ohio, while John H. Harwood resided in Wood county, Virginia, and was the owner of slaves. On the 9th of July, 1845, some slaves, intending to escape from Harwood, crossed over the Ohio River in a canoe to the Ohio shore, where said Garner, Thomas and Loraine met them and were in the act of assisting them from the canoe and up the river bank, when they were all arrested, taken to Virginia, imprisoned, and subsequently indicted. As the arrest was made on the Ohio side of the river, the only question in the case was, what was the extent of Virginia's jurisdiction over the rivers. The case attracted national attention. Mr. Vinton, in his argument, claimed that the jurisdiction of Virginia did not extend on the north side of the river beyond low water mark. He asserted that Virginia never had an ownership in the Northwest Territory, first, because the charter which King James granted in 1609, and which was claimed as the source of Virginia's title, did not include land which lay beyond the Ohio, or west of the Allegheny Mountains; and, second, if the grant was originally

broad enough to embrace the land lying within the Northwest
Territory, the charter which the King granted to Virginia had
been revoked by the Court of King's Bench in 1824, "when a
judgment was rendered against the corporation, canceling the
patent and ordering the franchises of the charter resumed by
the crown."

The argument of Mr. Vinton in this case will always be
classed among the greatest arguments of the greatest American
lawyers. As an historical production it was overwhelming, and
absolutely unanswerable. It was delivered to twelve judges,
and by a majority of one, the decision was in his favor. Simeon
Nash of Gallipolis was also a distinguished lawyer and judge,
but his reputation chiefly rests upon being the author of Nash's
Pleadings. William Allen of Chillicothe was another man who
won his way to distinction at the bar. He afterward was United
States Senator and Governor of Ohio.

Greatest, perhaps, of all, were Ewing, Stanbury and Corwin.
Whether their fame rests wholly upon their distinction at the bar
or not, it is certain they fill the largest horizon and occupy the
greatest places in history of any lawyers which our State has
produced. Each rose from humble birth to a place in the Nation's cabinet; and great as they all were, each was without a
peer in his especial field.

Ewing's intellect was strong and rugged. He would have
been a great natural lawyer had he never seen a law book, a
great logician had he never seen a work on logic. Nature made
him to be an expounder of the law. If his arguments were
somewhat devoid of ornament, it was because they needed no
ornament; they were too great to be ornate.

Mr. Stanbury was a broader scholar than Mr. Ewing. Mr.
Ewing was master of the rough logic of nature, while Mr. Stanbury was always equipped in the armor of the books. He was
a thorough student of the law, and always knew the decisions
of the courts. Strong as he was in this particular, another element of his strength was his unrivaled eloquence and the purity
of his diction.

Mr. Corwin was not the equal of either Mr. Ewing or Mr.
Stanbury as a lawyer in the strict sense of that word. Neither

were either of them his equal in his special adaptation. It is questionable if he ever had a superior as an advocate before a jury. The burning eloquence and impassioned oratory with which he swayed a popular audience — at one time making his hearers weep, in the next convulsing them with laughter, and then in an instant filling them with awe at the grandeur and sublimity of his rhetoric — was always at his command in the trial of a jury cause.

Among the many members of the legal profession who came in an early day to our young State and made it their future home and afterward became famous lawyers, Salmon P. Chase was the most conspicuous. His edition of the Revised Statutes of Ohio was an invaluable compilation, and could not have been prepared by any but the most careful and thorough lawyer. It contains a preliminary history of Ohio which is the best ever written. The career of this great man fully sustained the promise of his early life. He was a member of President Lincoln's Cabinet, and for many years was a conspicuous figure in the Republic, and died as the Chief Justice of its Supreme Court, the peer of his illustrious predecessors.

It would be interesting to mention the great judges who have adorned our Supreme Bench under the present Constitution, among whom Ranney and Thurman would be entitled to special notice; and also interesting to dwell at length on the many lawyers who have risen to eminence and fame since the adoption of that instrument; among whom are Stanton, Waite, Swayne, Matthews, Groesbeck, Perry, Hoadly, Pugh, Hunter, Taft, Harrison, Boynton, Shellebarger, Hutchins, West, Ambler and others; but my theme relates to our *early* judiciary and *early* bar, and precludes me from coming beyond the adoption of the present Constitution. Much as Ohio has to be proud of, and great as her position is in the National Union, nothing has contributed more to her greatness and the permanency of her institutions, than her early judiciary and early bar.

DAVID K. WATSON.

Following Mr. Watson's address, several short speeches were made, after which Mr. Graham repeated somewhat briefly his illustrated address on the "French Discoveries and Claims in America." This done, a reception was held, and the exercises for the day closed. The next day, the Sabbath, the Centennial day, was properly and fittingly observed in all the churches. In the afternoon, in the opera house, Rev. Washington Gladden preached the anniversary sermon. This sermon, as well as abstracts of those preached in the pulpits of the city churches, conclude this part of the volume.

REMARKS OF GOVERNOR JAMES E. CAMPBELL.

It was a long-deferred pleasure one year ago, on the 19th of October, to make my first visit here. I learned after arriving that it was an auspicious day, being the ninety-ninth anniversary of the landing upon the banks of yonder river of the little band of French settlers who founded this handsome and flourishing city. During an address to the people, who gathered on that occasion to hear the political discussion of the then existing campaign, I said, in a half-jocular way, that I would return in a year as Governor of the State to celebrate the city's centennial. In response to that promise, and your subsequent courteous invitation, my military staff and myself have come to participate in these interesting ceremonies. We are here rather to be seen than heard.

The programme announces that I am to deliver an address, but the unexpected and overwhelming labors of the last fortnight have absorbed my time to the exclusion of anything but official work, and I am, therefore, obliged to confess that I have no address—that the little I am to say must be without preparation. I am simply a gleaner in the field that has been harvested so well by those who have preceded me.

The French settlers who came here a century ago were, as we all know, not the first French settlers in the Ohio valley, for the lilies of France had floated to the breeze, both on the Ohio and the Mississippi, a hundred years before. They were found north of the great lakes, and around the southern bayous. Parkham has happily described it by saying that "French America had two heads; one among the snows of Canada, the other among the cane-brakes of Louisiana!" Northern Ohio was occupied by French fur traders as early as 1680. They were scattered along the lake from the Maumee to the Cuyahoga.

Forty years before the settlement of Gallipolis the English settlers were warned out of Ohio by the French commander, and formal possession taken in the name of Louis Fifteenth by burying leaden plates along the Ohio river, engraved with appropriate inscriptions. The bloody and picturesque drama of

frontier settlement was participated in by French officers of various dates.

But the French who came here a century ago, did not come
under the auspices of the French Government. They expatrat-
ed themselves, and left their allegiance and friends behind them.
They came not for conquest, nor for glory, but were in a sense
refugees from the bloody wars then raging in their own country.
They sought quiet homes, peaceful pleasures, and frugal but
contented lives. They and their careers have been accurately
and graphically depicted by your fellow townsman who addressed himself to that part of the subject yesterday. He has
told in elaborate detail of the fraudulent titles and false pictures
of pioneer life that brought them here; of their departure full
of the enthusiasm that characterizes the mercurial and versatile
Gaul; their shipwreck at sea; their landing at Alexandria, then
one of the most important points of the infant republic; of
their troubles after landing; their correspondence with Washington about the titles to their lands; of their western trip, and
their landing here in the beautiful autumn season; of their in-
aptitude, by reason of their former habits and customs, for the
hardships and struggles of their new home. All this has been
recited, and to repeat it now would be but a work of supereroga-
tion.

The history of Gallipolis and the surrounding country from
that day to this has doubtless been well told here under the title
of "A Century and its Lesson," by a distinguished citizen of
the oldest city in Ohio. The history of your people for the century is the history of all the people of Ohio. In the beginning
there were the dangers from savages; from fever and ague, and
the climatic diseases of a new country. They lived in the same
log huts, with the same puncheon floors; were clothed in the
same deer-skin garments; used the same hewn furniture; ate the
same hoe-cake, fish and game; indulged in the same shooting
matches, bear-hunts and militia musters, as all the other pioneers
in the other counties of the State. The men were of sturdy
stock, and the women were fit mothers for the generations that
were to follow.

As they lived here upon the banks of the river they saw

many changes. They saw the first steamboat, the "Orleans," pass down in 1811. Some thought it was a comet, and some that the British had come; and to all it was a wonder, a marvel. In 1812 (a year later), they went with McArthur's regiment to fight the British. From that day to this the citizens of Galli-polis have done their part as Americans and Buckeyes, adding to the glory and greatness of their State and country in peace and in war. Some of them went to Mexico and helped to bring the "Lone Star" and the "Golden Gate" into the sisterhood of the republic. Hundreds of them, during the last war, did their full share in restoring their country to its integrity, and were a glorious part of the three hundred and twenty thousand names which Ohio wrote upon the muster roll of the Union. Your people have taken their part in the field of statesmanship and letters. They have been guided by lofty patriotism and high in-telligence; and as they gather here to-day by the thousands, with all the evidences of culture and wealth—the product of American school houses and churches—they fitly represent the free institutions which have arisen from the hopes, ambitions, and successes of the pioneers who gathered here one hundred years ago.

RIO GRANDE COLLEGE—REV. J. M. DAVIS, PRESIDENT.

When asked but a few hours ago to take part in the exercises of this forenoon, I gladly consented; for, in my opinion, no interest that has been developed in Gallia county in the first century of its settlement is more worthy of being brought to remembrance and notice than its educational interests, and my connection for a number of years with Rio Grande college enables me to set forth briefly its history and present condition. Other gentlemen, who have given much time and research to the task, have given an account of the public and other schools of this city and of the county in general. I will confine my remarks to the institution just named.

Shortly after the war of 1812, Nehemiah Atwood, a native of Shenandoah county, Virginia, a man who had done honorable service as an officer in the American army, settled in this county. In 1819 he was married to Permelia Ridgeway, daughter of David Ridgeway, who had come to Gallia county from South Carolina in 1803. Mr. Atwood and his wife settled upon a farm near where the present village of Rio Grande stands, and the remainder of their long and active lives was spent in the same neighborhood. Without children, with good health, industry, economy, and more than ordinary business qualifications, they accumulated in about thirty years an estate of one hundred thousand dollars.

About 1850 a new personal force began to make itself felt in the vicinity of their home, and we are called to notice a man who afterward became one of the most useful and honored citizens that this county has ever had. Rev. I. Z. Haning, a native of Athens county, and a student of the Ohio University, came as an evangelist into Huntington and Raccoon townships, and under his divinely blessed labors a profound and extended religious reformation took place, the good results of which are yet visible in many forms.

Mr. and Mrs. Atwood listened to his teaching, were converted to Christ, and from that day forth lived a new life. They became studious and constant workers in their church and

RIO GRANDE COLLEGE.

Sunday-school. They contributed largely to the building of a meeting house near their home, and gave two thousand dollars as an endowment fund to aid in the support of regular preaching at this church for all time. They gave financial assistance to the organized charities of the church to which they belonged, and to a school at Albany, Ohio, called after that the Atwood Institute.

As a result of their growing conceptions of Christian benevolence, and influenced by the advice of Mr. Haning, they finally decided to give their estate for the founding and endowment of a college in the place where they had spent the most of their lives and accumulated their fortune. Mr. Atwood died in 1869, before any steps had been taken toward carrying out this plan. At the invitation of his widow, Mr. Haning soon afterward removed to Rio Grande, and action was taken toward the erection and opening of the college. The college building costing, $17,000, and the boarding hall, costing $13,000, were erected, and the college opened in September, 1876.

A few weeks before its opening, the founder executed her will, bequeathing her entire estate for its endowment. This estate, which came into the possession of the college trustees upon her death in 1885, now amounts to about $66,000.

The college has been in continued and successful operation since its opening; and at the present, with its fine buildings and grounds, its income equal to the economical but vigorous manner in which it is carried on, its established character for thorough work and for the inculcation of those principles which are the prime essentials in all the true manhood and womanhood, and with a warm place in a large and growing portion of our people, is one of the things that, as citizens of Gallia county, we can look upon with the deepest gratification as we recount the progress of a century and take account of the things that make the coming years bright and hopeful.

It is our privilege to rejoice in the fact that our city and county are sharing richly in all the elements of welfare to be found in a highly developed social condition. We have left the pioneer days behind us.

The clearing of the forest, the opening of roads, the bridging of streams, the building of comfortable places for residence, business, instruction, and worship have been accomplished.

Already, we are not only in the possession of schools and churches, but have entered upon the day of orphanages, hospitals and asylums.

All that a complex Christian society can do for the pleasure and improvement of adults, for the culture of the young, for the relief of the suffering and for the care of the unfortunate, has its foundation already laid in this county. In matters pertaining to higher education, we have not been entirely outside the great movements of thought and beneficence that have done so much for the advancement of learning in our country in the last thirty years.

What great and happy things of this kind we can recount. The wise and munificent benefactions of George Peabody have shed a lustre on his name that is only surpassed by the richness of the benefits they have produced. The John F. Slater fund, in the management and disbursement of which one of the best citizens of our State, ex-president Hayes, is doing himself additional honor and his fellow-citizens additional service, is one of the greatest and best gifts of this kind. A citizen of New York, in the building of Cornell University, has reared a noble monument to his name.

The Johns Hopkins University, at Baltimore, has leaped into vigorous being and is doing a great work toward that which its own president has pointed out as the true office of all higher institutions, the work of "bestowing upon society continual accessions of highly-trained and liberally-educated young people, capable of contributing to human welfare not only in the traditional professions but in all the complex affairs of modern life which require the application of intellectual force to difficult and often unexpected problems."

On our Pacific coast a United States Senator now has it in mind and hand to establish, upon a financial basis of twenty million dollars, an institution in which any person may pursue any line of profitable study possible to the human mind.

To these larger and more noticeable gifts are to be added the numerous smaller but not less praiseworthy and useful gifts all over the country that of late years have enlarged the resources of existing institutions and founded a multitude of new ones, thus bringing the facilities for learning to almost every door in the land.

I repeat, it is something that may well move our gratitude to-day, that among all its other elements of progress and prosperity, Gallia county has also had a share in those gifts and works that look toward the highest intellectual and moral possibilities of its sons and daughters. We may well rejoice that among our many worthy citizens in the past there have been some who labored and planned for these things; that out of the abundant wealth created by honorable toil from the material resources of this county, every acre of which except the little spot where these meetings are held was an undeveloped wilderness a century ago, one goodly portion of one hundred thousand dollars has been sacredly set apart for the work of higher Christian education. Looking at this fact, taking into consideration the history and work of the other schools of the county, to be presented to you by others, and firmly believing that these institutions will be fostered and enlarged by the wisdom and benevolence of our citizens in all coming days, the only feelings possible to my mind as I join with you in this centennial celebration are gratitude for the past and high hopes and purposes for the future.

"THE EDUCATIONAL LESSONS OF THIS HOUR."
REV. H. A. THOMPSON.

I appreciate the high honor done me by your Chairman in
the invitation which he has extended me to speak for a few
moments. I must tell you in advance that I am not on the pro-
gram for the day; that I have no speech prepared for your listening ears. I am here as a member of the Ohio Historical
Society, whose members are the guests of your committee. I
am here for the first time in your beautiful little city to rejoice
with you in the good fortune which has come to it, and to you,
in being able this day to celebrate its one hundreth anniversary.
Such occasions are fraught with interest and profit to us all. In
the olden time the Jews were annually required to go to Jerusalem, the capital city, to keep the feast of the passover. As the
children of the household saw the preparation made for this remarkable feast they would naturally inquire what it all meant.
The sacred historian instructed the master of the household how
to answer: "When thy son asketh thee in time to come saying
what mean the testimonies, the statutes, and the judgments
which the Lord, our God, hath commanded you, then shalt thou
say unto thy son, we were Pharaoh's bondmen in Egypt; and
the Lord brought us out of Egypt with a mighty hand; and the
Lord showed signs and wonders great and sore upon Egypt,
upon Pharaoh and upon all his house before our eyes; and he
brought us from thence that he might bring us in to give us the
land which he swear unto our fathers; and the Lord commanded
us to do all these statutes, to fear the Lord, our God, for our
good always, that he might preserve us alive, as it is this day.
And it shall be righteousness unto us if we observe to do all
this commandment before the Lord, our God, as he hath commanded us."—Deut. VI., 20.

So as your children sit with you to-day on these seats, listening to the addresses made and witnessing the parades and
displays, they shall want to know what it all means; and then
you can interest them in the history of the nation as they have
never been interested before. It will be your work to recount

to them the deeds of your ancestors, the sufferings endured, the privations undergone, to help build up this glorious republic, where every man can work out his own destiny untrammeled by the customs and traditions of the old world; a land in which above all other lands we recognize the truth uttered by Scotland's humble, though illustrious singer:

> "What though on hamely faer we dine,
>   Wear hoddin, gray and a' that;
> Gye fools their silks and knaves their wine
>   A man's a man for a' that."

And not only will the young people thus be taught to love their country, and to make themselves more worthy of the heritage which it is theirs to enjoy, but those of us who are older and who can better appreciate our advantages, may well in this sacred spot, made sacred not only by the presence of those who came here one hundred years ago, but later still by those noble patriots who fought to save this nation from dismemberment, consecrate ourselves anew to our country's good, and to be citizens worthy of such illustrious ancestors.

I have listened, as you no doubt have also, with intense pleasure to the distinguished gentleman who has discoursed to us so eloquently of the " Lessons of the Century," as well as to the gentleman who followed him in his interesting sketch of the college you have planted in your midst. I think it is Cotton Mather, the New England historian, who says that one of 'the first things our Puritan fathers thought of after their settlement in the American wilderness was the founding of a college, that their children might not grow up in ignorance, nor their churches be without pastors, and that the cause of religion and education might be advanced among them. Your ancestors looked to your welfare in planting a college in your county and you will prove yourselves degenerate sons of worthy sires if you do not rally about it and make it a place whither your sons and daughters may go to receive that training which shall fit them for the duties and responsibilities of this life and the enjoyments of the life to come. By the help which you can give it, it will revolu-

tionize your county and give you a citizenship excelled by none
in the land.

As I listened to the lessons of the century I tried to look
forward to see what they taught us as to the destiny of our own
fair land.   Surely the reign of bloodshed and of cruel war in
which the nations of the olden time indulged must now be over.
The sword must no longer be the arbitrament of nations, since
the "Prince of Peace" has come proclaiming peace on earth
and good will to all men.   We have outgrown our infancy and
are now marching forward to a grander and richer civilization.
We have made such a conquest of matter as men never saw before; the forces of nature have been harnessed as in no other
age to do our bidding.   The masses have broken through the
debris that has kept them down; they have burst asunder the
trammels that bound them and the reign of the common people
has commenced.   Never have the possibilities of manhood been
greater and never has there been such a field for the manifesta-
tion of man's noblest powers as in this land whose citizenship
we honor to-day.   Never before has it meant so much to live.
The very air is thick with questions that teem with interest, and
that demand a solution at our hands.   While men never lived
with greater possibilities they never rested under greater responsibilities.   We cannot rest satisfied with the fact that we are
growing in wealth; that our forests have been subdued; our
lands tilled and our population enlarged.   To whom much is
given of these shall much be required.   The problems of civil
government have not all been solved.   We are to show the
nations of the earth such an example of enlightened citizenship
as they have not yet seen.   We are to be a beacon light to those
that sit in darkness showing them the way out of their disabili-
ties into the coming light.   We are to show them that a government of the people, for the people, and by the people is to be
the most permanent as it is the freest form of civil government.
Let us see to it that we make of this people a nation whose God
is the Lord.   Not only our own destiny but the destiny of other
peoples is in our hands.   Let us see to it that we are worthy of
the high trust which God and our fathers have committed to us.
When our descendants shall come one hundred years hence to

celebrate this anniversary may they find a great nation without a peer; whose rulers rule in righteousness, a terror to evil doers and a praise to them that do well; a people true to their highest convictions of duty and yielding rightful homage to Him who is the King of kings and the source of all human government.

REMARKS OF R. D. MARSHALL, ESQ.

Your presiding officer has called on me, owing to some delay in the arrival of trains, which has delayed the forming and moving of the procession, to address you for a few minutes, and has charged me with being a speaker of some note, and as he has placed me on trial before you on that charge, I feel pretty certain that when you have heard me, you will promptly acquit me of the charge, as it was not my expectation to address the people here, for I came to see and hear, and not to talk.

This is my first visit to your city, and those of you who know the place so well, with its beautiful surroundings, no doubt think that my traveling in this respect has been sadly neglected.

One hundred years ago! What a change! When the 600 pioneers, or thereabouts, landed here one hundred years ago, if this city as it is now could have then met their gaze as they floated down the Ohio river, how different would have been their feelings from what they were under the circumstamces at that time? In place of the log cabins, uninhabited, that then met their gaze on their first visit to this place, I, on my first visit, look upon a beautiful city of more than 12,000 inhabitants.

We are now, I am told, holding this meeting on the grounds where stood the log cabins that met the gaze of your ancestors when they arrived here, but instead of log cabins, you now have this beautiful park; the Ohio river sweeps on the south side of it just as it did one hundred years ago, but, on the bosom of that river now float the magnificent steamers that we see at your wharfs, instead of an occasional flat-boat; and in place of the thick forest that then covered these grounds, you now have this fine park, your level streets, miles in length, built up on either side with fine business blocks, or beautiful residences. What a change! But all this had a beginning, and that beginning was one hundred years ago to-day, and under circumstances that would have appalled a less heroic people.

Among the pioneers that landed here, most, if not all of them, knew but little about such hardships, as were to stare them in the face, and had but little idea how to contend with, or overcome the same. Again, they had been deceived as well as defrauded. But, among these, your pioneers, there were heroes and heroines, there were brave men and brave women, and they have left their footprints here which we are looking at now, admiring and honoring, for

> " Lives of great men all remind us,
> We can make our lives sublime,
> And, departing, leave behind us,
> Footprints on the sands of time."

You men will pardon me, if I should give even more credit to the women than to the men, for whilst under trying circumstances men are frequently so courageous as to make them great, women under similar circumstances become not only great, but almost reach sublimity with their greatness.

Said a great thinker, '' The greatest and grandest words known to anyone, are mother, home, and heaven.'' This is a sentiment that I fully endorse, and may farther add, the one you all have, or have had, and it would be better that a mill stone were tied to your neck, and that you were planted in the bottom of the Ohio river, than that you should at any time, by any act or word, bring shame or dishonor upon that name. The second, every one should strive to have and secure, if he can honorably do so. And the third, we are assured by Him, who makes no promise that He can not and will not fulfill, that we can finally reach if we are worthy of it.

Your respected townsman, Colonel Vance, has requested me to speak of the Miami Valley, and its early history. Such a task ought not to be attempted without a preparation commensurate with the subject. And again it seems to me that there is but one person that I know of in Ohio, who can do the Miami Valley and its early pioneers justice, and that person is Judge Joseph Cox, of Cincinnati; he knows its history, and knows it as fully and correctly as if he had grown up with its every movement since its first discovery by the white man, and its history, growth and progress should be written by him, and not by a novice like myself. It is true that there are some things that I

know about that great valley. A wag once said of it: "It is
God's country, for if it were otherwise, he never would have
made it so rich, so beautiful and so productive."

Will it be considered too facetious for me at this time to say
that this valley produces larger corn, and a greater abundance
thereof, than did Egypt at the time Joseph garnered it there in
anticipation of the many years of famine; and in its early history it had its pioneers, its heroes and heroines, and yet at this
day it is not without its noted men. As you are aware, the Governor of this great State of Ohio, who is with us to-day, was
born and reared in this valley, and his ancestors lived there long
prior to his birth. And the Lieutenant Governor, who is also
with us, comes from Logan County; the head-waters of the
river from which the valley takes its name, are located in this
county. To this county my maternal ancestors moved at an
early date, and endured the trials and hardships of pioneer life.
In this county my grandmother, with gun in hand, took command of the fort and stockade built near the Miami river, about
eight miles west of Bellefontaine, and in which fort were placed
the pioneer women and children of that day, whilst her husband,
with other men along that valley, rushed to the front, after
Hull's surrender; and it is said of her, being surrounded by Indians as they were, that her courage, coolness and heroism under
these trying circumstances were so noted, that she was afterward
spoken of as "Heroic Betsy." But it is not my purpose to
speak of anything that would come so near personal, and I only
refer to this as one of the matters that is spoken of by one of
the pioneer writers of Ohio.

But I notice that the Governor of Ohio, with his staff, and
the Governor of West Virginia, with his staff, are already
mounted, and the band begins to play, and the procession is beginning to move, and you, like myself, will want to witness the
grand display of the moving thousands in this procession.

REMARKS OF J. V. JONES, ESQ.

LADIES AND GENTLEMEN:— It would hardly be proper for me to say "fellow-citizens," for the reason of having been absent from your county for nearly fifty-eight years. During that time many changes have been wrought in the city of Gallipolis and Gallia county. Eighty-one years ago a young married couple might have been seen slowly wending their way on horseback down the slopes of the Blue Ridge and foot-hills of the Allegheny Mountains of Virginia toward the beautiful Ohio River as it swept majestically past the town of Gallipolis, or the "City of the French." These young people brought all their worldly goods with them on horseback and settled north of this city, somewhere near what is now known as "Kerr Station," on the river division of the Columbus, Hocking Valley and Toledo Railroad. The names of these young adventurers were James Jones and Priscilla Jones, *nee* Blagg. After remaining in old Gallia county for about twenty-three years they, with a family of nine children, of whom your speaker was one, removed northward to the great valley lying between the Sandusky and Maumee Rivers, and bounded on the north by the beautiful Lake Erie. This great forest valley was the hunting grounds of Indian tribes, known as the "Senecas" and "Wyandotts." Our evening serenades in the grand old forests were not the handsomely-uniformed bands of music you have here on this Centennial occasion, but were the whooping of the hunting bands of Indians, the hooting of the night owl and the howling of the wolves. There we lived in the rude log cabin, and lived on corn bread and the wild game of the grand old forests. It was there that we received a common school education in round log school houses, daubed with mud and with greased paper for window lights and rude benches made from split logs. But your speaker, one of the descendants of that family, has lived to see the wilderness and the solitary places be made glad and the desert places to rejoice and blossom as the rose.

The Indians have gone to their happy hunting grounds, the bear and the wild-cat have fled from advancing civilization, the forests have given way to countless thousands of beautiful and productive farms, the log cabins have disappeared and their places filled with beautiful farm houses. And in place of the log school houses and churches we now have beautiful wood, brick and stone structures with their spires pointing heavenward. Then the Sandusky and Maumee rivers and the beautiful Lake Erie were dotted only by the Indian's canoe and the trader's small craft. Now they carry the commerce of the great Northwest, assisted by the railroads, to the markets of the East — the cities of New York, Baltimore, Boston, and from there to the markets of the old world. In the great valley of the Northwest we slumbered for more than fifty years over mines of wealth in what was once known as the great "Black Swamp." Natural gas and pools of oil lay buried beneath us in vast quantities, which have lately been developed into sources of luxury and great wealth. Natural gas is now used as fuel in thousands and millions of homes and manufactories, bringing wealth and prosperity to many persons who were formerly in poverty and moderate circumstances.

And now, my friends, after an absence of nearly fifty-eight years, I have returned to join with you in celebrating the one hundredth anniversary of the first settlement of the city of Gallipolis in 1790. My return, after an absence of so many years, is almost like coming back from the grave. In that period time has wrought wonderful changes, and I see but one old landmark in this large audience that I recognize, and that one is the venerable old pioneer and patriot, William Waddell, who in the early days of his manhood was a dear friend of my departed father, and who will soon join him in a more beautiful land than this in the country far away.

In returning to the grand old county of Gallia and the historic city of Gallipolis to participate in this grand and beautiful display and celebration, I feel like one treading the streets of an historic city, as a stranger in a strange land. Yet I am mindful of the fact that behind me rolls the majestic Ohio River, its waters bathing the shores of Ohio and West Virginia; before me are the grand old hills of Gallia, my native heath; under this pavillion is assembled youth, beauty and old age, while I am like one who stands alone in some banquet hall deserted, and, like the soldier on the hill, I turn to take a last fond look at the scenes of my childhood, the beautiful Ohio River, the grand old hills, the valley and the country church, and the remains of the old cottage by the brook.

Joy and sadness are strangely mingled on this occasion. Here I recall the sweet reminiscences of the child-life, which illumined the past, and touched the hours with golden light. Memory lingers upon the solemn bridge beyond which in my childhood I played, and in which I still see little faces flushed with laughter and childish sports; their little voices prattling in melodious heavenly music. I thank you, my friends, for inviting me to address you on this occasion, and for your attentive listening. I will remember it as one of the pleasant scenes of my life, and in memory of which I will often think of the good people of this city and surrounding country and the beautiful hills of Gallia, the place of my childhood.

Thanking you again, my friends, for this compliment and your close attention, I bid you good-bye.

MIGRATIONS AND THEIR LESSONS.

SERMON PREACHED IN THE OPERA HOUSE, SUNDAY, BY WASHINGTON GLADDEN, OF COLUMBUS.

By faith, Abraham, when he was called, obeyed to go out unto a place which he was to receive for an inheritance; and he went out, not knowing whither he went.—Heb. ix, 8.

This is the first notice in ancient records of that great movement westward which occupies so many chapters of the history of the human race. From that unknown country named Ur of the Chaldees, Terah, the father of Abraham, had already journeyed westward, bringing his household to Haran; here they tarried for a little, and here it was that Abraham heard the divine call and went forth to the land of Canaan. A mighty river, the Euphrates, rolled between him and his destination; two days' journey brought him to its banks. Nothing daunted, he made his way across, perhaps at that point where the great river is still forded; and when he had gained the other shore he had won his cognomen of "Hebrew"—the man who had crossed. Weary days of desert journeying were yet before him, but the divine voice was still calling him, and he pushed steadily forward, halting for a little in the bright valley of Damascus, but resting not till his tent was pitched at Bethel, and he looked abroad from the hill tops upon the fertile plains and smiling valleys of the land that was to be his inheritance, and where that great nation which should spring from his loins was to have its seat.

Abraham's migration was undertaken for a different reason and with a higher purpose than that of many of his contemporaries and successors; nevertheless he was moved with the current. Where that Semitic race to which he belonged had its origin may not be clearly known. We find it first in the lower valleys of the Euphrates and the Tigris, whence, moving northwestward and southwestward, it populated Babylonia, Syria, Phœnicia and the rest of Canaan. Even the ancient Egyptians were not an autochthonic race. Their features, their languages link them with Asia rather than with Africa. They, too, were a people who had come in the early dawn of prehistoric times from the East.

Those successive migrations of our own Aryan tribes from their nest in Asia westward over Europe I need only stop to mention. From the remotest antiquity we see these people moving in vast masses toward the setting sun, one column following another at intervals of time which no monuments or memorials seem to mark; the Hellenic and the Latin groups flooding the Mediterranean peninsulas, and pausing before the mighty barrier of the Alps; the Kelts, the Teutons, the Slavs, moving northwestward in their order, expelling the Aborigines, and, in time, subjugating one another. It would seem that the configuration of the northern temperate zone of the Eastern Continent was favorable to such movements; for the vast central plains of Eastern Asia are prolonged westward through Russia, Northern Germany and Holland; and a man can walk, says one authority, from the Pacific to the Atlantic Ocean, across Asia and Europe, without encountering any elevation of more than a few hundred feet, or any stream which it is difficult to ford. But when these Aryan peoples had poured their floods for uncounted centuries over Europe, which was their Promised Land; when they had overspread its plains and possessed themselves of its substance, they found themselves standing on the shores of a trackless ocean, whose billows, breaking at their feet in endless mockery, flung back to the rushing tide of humanity their challenge: "Thus far shalt *thou* come and no farther, and here shall *thy* proud waves be stayed."

For many centuries this watery barrier restrained them. From the Cantabrian mountain tops, from the low-lying shores of Brittany, from the rocky coast of Cornwall, or the green hills of Ireland, they looked away to the westward wondering and longing. What lands might lie beneath that misty horizon? Was it true, indeed, that

> "Sweet fields beyond *this* swelling flood
> [Stood] drest in living green?"

Who should dare to sail forth unto that No Man's Land and ravish its secret from the unchartered ocean? It was well that

they waited. Art had time to germinate and fructify, civilization
had room to expand and ripen; in all these European lands,
races were in training for the task of subduing another continent.
In the fullness of time, the word that Abraham heard was
spoken again, and the brave Genoese sailor turned the prows of
his little ships toward the setting sun, and sailed away, not
knowing whither he went, but greatly hoping to find beyond the
sea a land which he should receive for an inheritance. How
steadily, during the four centuries that have elapsed since Columbus landed on our western coast, the tide of migration has
flowed hitherward, I need not spend any time in showing. There
may be, at this time, one hundred of millions of people upon
this Western Continent, in North and South America; of these,
probably not more than ten millions are natives of the soil; ninety
millions are the dsscendants of men who came across the sea.
Of these ninety millions, eight or nine millions are the offspring
of those who came, much against their will, in the holds of
slave ships, victims of the cruelty and cupidity of the stronger
race; and there are a few hundred thousand Semites, the
descendants of Abraham whose Promised Land, far away in the
heart of the other continent, was the first stage of this secular
progress; but the great mass of these inhabitants of the New
World belong to that Aryan race, whose teeming millions have
been hurrying westward ever since the dawn of time. From
the mountain slopes and broad plateaus of Central Asia—from
the cradle of the human race—these eager, adventurous throngs
have come. Past the snowy heights of the Himalayas, over the
ridge of the Ural Mountains, across the steppes of Tartary, and
along the shores of the Caspian and the Black Seas, they have
thronged into Germany and France and Spain and England and
Scandinavia; here, dividing into tribes, each with a tongue of
its own (though all these tongues are kindred), here tilling fields,
sinking mines, building cities, and hence, on the wings of the
wind and the vapor, flying over the sea to this Western Continent, to rear on this fresh soil, as we hope and trust, a nobler
fabric of social order than any they have left behind.

And here, too, the power that brought them still compels
them. The Pilgrims were scarcely landed on the New England

coast when they began to push their way out westward into the interior. Within twenty years after the Mayflower anchored in Plymouth harbor, there were several prosperous settlements on the Connecticut river, a hundred miles inland, though the savages resisted the advance at every step, and every town was stockaded for defense against the midnight foe. And ever since that day the tide of emigration has been flowing steadily westward—westward—over the Appalachian range, down the valley of the Ohio, along the borders of the Great Lakes, across the teeming prairies, over the Rockies and the Sierras to the western shore. That mighty movement of the people westward, westward, which began long before Abraham took up his journey from Haran toward Canaan, has been going on ever since; all the greatest nations of the earth have taken part in it; in the path of this movement have arisen all the splendid monuments of civilization; our own highways are trembling yet with the tread of its triumphant host.

Is not this phenomenon worth looking at, soberly, for a little while this afternoon? May we not safely infer that a process of this nature, stretching through untold centuries, covering two continents, spanning one stormy ocean, enlisting more or less directly all the great nations of modern history, is a process with which Providence has something to do? One need not be a very strong Calvinist to believe that such vast on-goings as these are provided for in the plans of an omniscient Ruler.

What are the causes of this great movement of the peoples? They are many and various. The forces which impel families and tribes to go forth from their country and their kindred unto lands more or less dimly shown them in prophetic vision are of many kinds, and operate in diverse ways. Not seldom the great law of population operates to produce these movements of the people. Population, according to the Malthusian statement, always tends to increase more rapidly than subsistence; hunger drives forth hordes of men to seek a livelihood in fresh fields and pastures new. This law operates even where the population is sparse and the resources of nature not at all developed. The southward movements of the Gothic tribes upon the cultivated lands of Southern Europe may have been due in part to this cause. The lands they left behind were by no means exhausted by cultivation, but they depended mainly on pasturage, and therefore needed far more land than modern agricultural people. Many of the movements of the Aborigines upon our own soil may have been produced by this cause. When the game had disappeared from its territory the tribe must move on to unoccupied lands. Indeed, the less civilized the people, the greater the need of frequent migration. Two or three acres will support a skillful farmer or gardener; the primeval hunter and fisherman cannot live on less than two or three thousand acres. And we may well suppose that the population on the central steppes of Asia, growing faster than their subsistence grew, were thrust out of their nests, in larger and smaller numbers, and started on their westward journeyings. The pressure of population upon subsistence being relieved by each exodus, the tribes left behind multiplied faster than ever, and soon a new swarm was ready to go forth from the hive.

In our own time, great movements of population have been due to the failure of the means of subsistence. The Irish famine of 1846–7 started a tidal wave of emigration to this country, and the current thus set in motion has been kept flowing by other causes. And while the great emigrations of modern years toward this hemisphere have not generally been due to famine or starvation in the old countries, they have resulted in considerable part from the over-crowdings of those countries, and from the expectation, on the part of the emigrants, of finding larger wages, ampler opportunities and better prospects for themselves and their children in this land than in the homeland.

Other causes have constantly been operating. Wars of conquest and ambition, and the burdens caused by war, drive many of the sons of peace forth from their homes to seek residence in more pacific countries. The militarism of Germany explains the presence on our soil of hundreds of thousands of the German people. Political oppression, the domination of privileged classes, the tyranny of priests and hierarchs hasten the departure from lands that they love of those to whom liberty is dear. The Pilgrims of Plymouth, the Roman Catholics of Baltimore were fugitives from ecclesiastical persecutions. Sometimes these emigrants have been social or political idealists with plans for the reorganization of society to which their native land was not hospitable; and they have sought upon virgin soil a free area for the development of their ideas. Cabet and his Icarians, Owen and his New Harmonists, were the leaders of colonies in the interest of new social schemes.

To all these forces of propulsion by which men have been driven from their ancestral seats must be added those forces of attraction by which they have been drawn toward the new countries. Discoveries of mines of the precious metals, of soils of phenomenal fertility, of climates serene and delectable, have been reported to them, and they have been tempted by the prospects of unwonted gains and enjoyments to separate themselves from kindred and companions to set up their habitations in distant lands.

Nor will the external motives—whether of propulsion or of attraction—account for all these movements. There are powers within their own breasts that start men upon these journeys. A native restlessness, a love of novelty, a passion for adventure, account for many of them. There are men who never could be quiet long in Paradise; it would take a battalion of angels with flaming swords to keep them within its bright enclosures. There are men to whom the order and restraint of civilized society are irksome; they would rather rove through forests than travel in highways; they prefer the freedom of the woods which is the barrenest and poorest sort of freedom, to the freedom of the city, which, when its laws are most firmly enforced, is the completest and most perfect liberty. Such unbridled spirits are always found in the frontier lines of emigration.

Thus we see how many and varied are the ascertained forces by which these great tides of population are controlled, but I think we must add to these another and far more subtle force—that divine impulse by which all the greater movements of history must be explained. For while it is true that hunger and fear, and the love of life, and the love of liberty, and the love of change, and the impatience of restraint and the greed of gold, and the ambition to found new empires, and a thousand other motives have acted upon the minds of men urging them

into these currents of emigration, yet all over these conflicting
motives, harmonizing them all and bringing order out of them,
is the plan of the all-wise Ruler of the world, who makes the
wrath and the folly and the greed of man to praise him, and
restrains the remainder thereof.

The greatest fact in all these world movements is that they
are fulfilling a design that is more comprehensive and farther-
reaching than wisdom of man could conceive. Those Aryan
peoples, when they started on their journeys from Eastern
Asia, had no more conception of the splendid European and
American civilizations which they were going forth to build,
than the iron ore in the mountain has of the mighty genie
of fire and steam, fashioned from its substance, which will soon
be ploughing the Atlantic main; any more than the spring at the
farthest sources of the Amazon has of the majestic river into
which its tiny fount will grow. This movement westward, ever
westward, was all unconscious. They had some small and dim
purpose of their own, but the great purpose of God they knew
nothing about. There was an instinct, partly human, that
impelled them; but of the divine leadings they were wholly
oblivious. They went forth, not knowing very well whither
they went, not knowing at all why they went. It would have
been very difficult for any careful student of human welfare,
contemplating the whole problem with such light as he could
get, to justify their going. In these later years the case is
greatly altered; a large share of the immigrants who cross from
the old world to the new speedily better their condition; but in
the earlier years this was not the rule. Most of those who then
went forth in search of new homes received, during their lifetime, no adequate reward for their risks and their labors. If you
had measured what they lost and what they suffered against
what they gained and what they enjoyed, the balance, so far as
worldly comfort is concerned, would have been on the wrong
side. They sought, no doubt, to escape from penury and dis-
comfort, and restraint; but they encountered hardships, labors,
miseries, worse than those from which they fled. Half of the
Pilgrims who landed on Plymouth Rock in December were in
their graves before the violets ever bloomed again upon that

sterile coast. The case with the majority of our early emigrants and pioneers was not much better. Of one hundred and five colonists in Virginia in June, 1607, sixty-seven had died before the next year was ten days old. The winter of 1609 began with four hundred and ninety persons in that colony and ended with sixty. Surely this was not a profitable speculation, from the point of view of individual interest. If it is the highest wisdom of a man to look out for his own individual interest, these men were not wise. If they acted upon a calculation of personal gains and losses, it was a bad calculation. Europe and America would have been peopled and developed by the Aryan races far less slowly than they were, if these movements of population had been guided by prudential and economical considerations.

No! these movements of population were very largely instinctive rather than rational; spontaneous rather than deliberate; prophetic more than economic. Sometimes, no doubt, the chances were calculated and miscalculated owing to defective knowledge of the facts. The reports which reached the old countries were not always accurate. Travelers were sometimes enthusiastic; land speculators were sometimes unscrupulous; men were beguiled into enterprises which they would never have undertaken if they had known what perils and what toils were before them. But most often they were only too eager to believe the glowing tales that were told them; they were more than half to blame for the deceit which was practiced on them; they took but little pains to find out the facts before they set out. The movement was not rational. It was instinctive. It was the fruit of that world-compelling plan by which nations and tribes and peoples are driven forward in the ways of destiny.

Do we mean, then, to say that Providence decreed all the sufferings and losses and discomforts of these westward-moving hosts? That Providence impelled them to enter paths that led to hardship and famine and disaster? No, I do not dogmatize about the designs of Providence; how much suffering He has decreed I will not undertake to say; but it is evident that He has appointed for men a destiny from which suffering is never absent, and that the paths which conduct to His most glorious gifts are paths which lead through toil and trial. The Captain

of our salvation was made perfect through suffering, and where
the Captain leads His followers must go. And I think that we
can discover, as we study these world-movements, some of those
deep things of God concerning whose meaning it is not wise to
be too confident, but whose manifestations, so far as they come
within the range of our own understanding, are full of stimu-
lating suggestion.

It is evident, to begin with, that these migrations of the
nations furnish a field for the culture of all the more robust virtues. I do not mean to assert that pioneers and emigrants, as a
class, are in these days, or ever were, in all respects exemplary.
They are often persons of coarse fiber and reckless temper; they
are for a time, in the earlier period, beyond the restraint of laws
and social conventions; sometimes they become lawless and
vicious in the extreme. Nevertheless it is certain that many of
those groups who came to America in the last two centuries
brought their moral standards and their social conscience with
them, and established upon these shores a purer type of society
than they had left behind. But all these, whether they be stiff
Puritans or free-living Cavaliers, have need of cultivating and
manifesting the great virtues of courage, of endurance, of self-
sacrifice; to face danger calmly, to bear hardships quietly, to
meet death serenely — these are indispensable qualities in the
pioneer. No such opportunities of heroism come to us. There
are chances enough even for us to be heroic, but they are not
like these. These hand-to-hand encounters with savages and
wild beasts; these fights with frost and flood and pale-faced
famine; these measurings and weighings of the hoarded ears of
maize to make them last till harvest; these lonely marches and
bivouacs in the primeval forest; these persistent struggles with
the fierce wilderness to subjugate its soil — all these are the very
alphabet of heroism for future generations.

Close akin to the pioneer's courage is his faith in the future.
It takes a high order of faith to discern the beauty and bounty of
the ages to come and to be willing to live for them and die without seeing them. I do not mean to assert that all these pioneers have possessed this heroic faith, but that it has lived in the
breasts of many of them their own words bear witness. In the

ancient records of the Plymouth Pilgrims we read that one reason, and not the least reason, of their removal to America was
"a great hope and inward zeal they had of laying some good
foundation, or at least to make some way thereunto, for the
propagating and advancement of the Gospel of the Kingdom of
Christ in those remote parts of the world, yea, although they
should be but as stepping stones unto others for the performance
of so great a work." Very few, indeed, of the great army of
pioneers have had any reasonable expectation of enjoying in
their own lifetime the fruits of their own labors. Abraham went
out from Haran to Canaan in hope that the land would some day
belong to his descendants; yet, as Stephen in his speech before the
Sanhedrim so strongly said, "God gave *him* none inheritance in it;
no, not so much as to set his foot on, and He promised to give it
to him in possession, and to his seed after him, when as yet he
had no child; but God spake on this wise, that his seed should
sojourn in a strange land, and that they should bring them unto
bondage and entreat them evil four hundred years; but the nation to which they shall be in bondage will I judge, saith God;
after that shall they come forth and serve me in this place."
After the call to Abraham, in Haran, and the migration of Abraham to Canaan, there were to be hundreds of weary years —
years of nomadic life in Palestine, years of famine, of bondage,
of wandering in the wilderness — before his descendants should
gain full possession of the promised land; but there was the
promise, and Abraham believed the promise and imparted his
own great faith to his children and his children's children, and
this faith never failed them; it upheld them under all the hardships of the Egyptian slavery, and it brought them back, centuries later, to the land which had been promised to their father,
Abraham. This is, no doubt, the most striking instance in history of the faith of a pioneer and of its influence upon the life
of generations following; but something not unlike it is witnessed in the conduct of many of those who have laid the foundations of great States in toil and tears, hoping that those who
should come after them would reap the fruit of their sowing,
and through their sacrifices enter into security and peace.

And this brings us to one more great motive which the

migration of nations emphasizes and reveals—the motive which springs from the solidarity of races; which leads a man to feel that he is a partner, not only with his coevals, but with his forebears and his posterity; that much of the best part of his gains and his joys comes from the labors of those who have gone before him, and much of his most fruitful work must be done for the benefit of those who shall come after him.·

It is when man rises to this height of vision, and sees the generations all linked together for weal or woe, helpers of one another's welfare, sharers of one another's misfortune, that he becomes worthy of that word which defines him as a being of large discourse, looking before and after. All the greater motives of our work spring from the realization of these sublime facts; from our sense of gratitude to those who have gone before us, and our sense of obligation to those who are coming after us. These are the truths which are brought home with power to our minds as we look back upon the lives of our forerunners, and which, beyond a doubt, were present in the minds of many of them as they laid the foundations whereon to-day we build.

Such, then, are some of the gains that spring from these great migrations; they furnish a field for the development of the robust virtues, they provide a discipline for faith, they strengthen the bond that binds together the generation.

The connection of these thoughts with this occasion is not, I trust, obscure. I have not thought it any part of my duty at this time to undertake the recital of the annals of the colony that landed on this spot one hundred years ago. That task has been entrusted to other and more capable hands. It seemed more fitting that I should rather attempt to connect the founding of this colony with the great historic movement of which it was a part, that we might discern something of the sweep and significance of that movement. With how many of these great purposes of Providence which we have been studying these colonists consciously connected themselves I do not know; certain it is that they had a great opportunity of illustrating upon this soil the robust virtues; and I doubt not their faith and courage are living here in the lines of their descendants. It was a stormy time in history when they took their departure from their native land. On July 14, 1789, the Bastile had fallen, the first resounding success of the French revolution, the signal of the destruction of feudal France, and of the coming of a new regime.

This was more than a political upheaval; it was a social and economic crisis. France had been cursed and impoverished for centuries by the most burdensome tyranny; the people were loaded with debt; agriculture was crushed, trade was crippled, all industries were paralyzed. The people were striking about them madly and blindly, caring little who was smitten or what went down before their wrath, resolute only to make an end of the existing order. The Bastile was the object of their fury, but dramatic as its downfall was, it brought no relief from the present misery. Still the dead hand lay on all the industries of the nation; still work was scarce and bread was dear though harvests were abundant, and famine in the midst of plenty stared the multitude in the face.

"Fair prophesies are spoken," writes Carlyle, "but they are not fulfilled. There have been Notables, Assemblages, turnings-out and comings-in. Intriguing and maneuvering, Parlimentary eloquence and arguing, Greek meeting Greek, in high places, has long gone on, yet still bread comes not. The harvest is reaped and garnered, yet still we have no bread. Urged by despair and by hope, what can Drudgery do but rise as predicted, and produce the General Overturn. Fancy, then, some Five full-grown millions of such gaunt figures with their haggard faces, in woollen jupes, with copper-studded, leather girths, and high sabots, starting out to ask, after long unreviewed centuries, virtually this question: How have ye treated us? How have ye taught us, fed us, and led us, while we toiled for you? The answer can be read in flames over the nightly summer sky. *This* is the feeding and leading we have had of you; EMPTINESS of pocket, of stomach, of head and of heart. Behold there is *nothing in us;* nothing but what Nature gives her wild children of the desert; Ferocity and Appetite; Strength grounded on Hunger. Did ye mark among your rights of men that man was not to die of starvation while there was bread reaped by him? It is among the Mights of man."

All over the land, castles are flaming, bands of smugglers wander unrestrained; "the barriers of towns are burnt, toll gatherers, tax gatherers, official persons put to flight." And from all over France hordes of these half-civilized, half-starved, half-infuriated people are pouring into Paris. Such is the situation during the Summer and early Autumn of 1789. The foundations of the great deep of Feudalism are broken up; the Deluge is at hand. As for the king there is no help for him; he is too weak a man to deal with such an insurrection. He dallies with the revolution, tries to ride upon the crest of its advancing wave, but it skills not; his queen and his court are sullen and revengeful; there is a banquet at Versailles one night, while thousands in the great city are starving; and the king's officers trample under their feet the national cockade, while the queen looks on applauding, and the people see that the court despises them and plots to treat their newly gained liberties as it has treated their emblem. And now the strangest, the most hysterical of all historic episodes takes place: ten thousand women lead a howling mob to Versailles, a dozen miles away, followed by the national guard, with Lafayette at its head, and they capture the king and queen and bring them to Paris, making them prisoners in fact, in their own royal palace of the Tuilleries, and stamping out the counter revolution with two hundred thousand hob-nailed shoes. It was an anxious day for Paris; who could tell what might be coming next? Obviously the reign of the mob was well begun; those who had everything to lose might as well convert it into portable securities and silently steal away. It was on the 6th of October that the king was escorted to Paris by the shrieking Amazons; before this month had ended tens of thousands of Frenchmen had bidden good-bye to France. This was the time of what is known as the second migration—"most extensive," says Carlyle, "among commons, deputies, noblesse, clergy, so that to Switzerland alone there go sixty thousand. One emigration follows another, grounded on reasonable fear, unreasonable hope, largely, also, on childish pet. The high-flyers have gone first, now the lower flyers, and even the lower will go, down to the crawlers."

What has all this to do with our colonists of Gallipolis? I

hardly know how much it has to do with them; but putting this and that together, it might signify something. For it was right in the midst of all this panic and terror that there appeared upon the scene the agents of the Scioto Company, the Yankee, Joel Barlow, and the Englishman, William Playfair—with their maps and their prospectuses, and their glowing promises, telling of a country where the climate was semi-tropical, where the rivers abound with enormous fish, and the forests with venison; where the trees exuded sweetmeats, and candles grew on trees; where there were no taxes to pay and no conscriptions to dread. Is it any wonder that such a manifesto strongly appealed to the excited and apprehensive Parisians? Less than a month after Louis was brought to Paris, and while the alarmed citizens were flying from France by thousands, Barlow formed his company of the Scioto, and the emigrants came flocking to his headquarters; five thousand of them were ready to set forth in the early spring in quest of their Utopia.

It is a pitiful and painful story; I will not dwell upon it. We can see how several of the motives which we have traced in our study may have operated to set in motion this migration; how pinching want, and political oppression, and the horrors of civil war and social strife made these Frenchmen willing to leave their native land: and we can see, also, how grievously they were deceived by the representations made to them, and how great was their need of courage and faith and patience, and all the heroic qualities of the pioneer, when they landed on the bluff and took possession of the log huts that awaited their occupation.

I will not undertake to tell how bravely they met the perils that surrounded them, nor with how much steadfastness and fortitude they wrought out their difficult problem. I know that our hearts go out to them to-day in compassion for their sufferings, and in gratitude for their toils and self-denials; for it is to them, and to all the noble army of pioneers in whose rank they marched, and in whose battle with the wilderness they fought and fell, that we owe the fertile fields, the beautiful homes, the teeming cities, the wealth and the culture and the power of our great commonwealth, of our Native Land.

And now, fellow citizens, there remains but one question

more: What admonition, what incitement comes to us from
this glance across the centuries? We have seen this mighty
march of the peaceful armies of industry around the world,
from east to west; we have counted, as they could not, the cost
of their enterprises; we have learned how much we owe to
them. Can they teach us any thing that we need to know? Do
they summon us to any work which we are prone to neglect?

We honor and applaud their heroism; have we any call to
imitate it? For the physical courage which they displayed there
is not much demand in these piping times of peace; but of the
courage which fears not to confront the enemies of the State,
and the destroyers of our youth, this generation still has need.
It is not with wolves and painted savages that we are called to
fight; but with foes far more dangerous: with robbers of revenues; with pilferers of public funds; with men who make a
trade of politics and are ready always to subordinate the public
welfare to their own ambition; with banditti whose dens are in
the lobbies, and sometimes in the offices of court houses and
city halls, and capitols; yea, with all the purveyors of vice and
crime, with hyenas in human form who get their living by helping their fellow-men on the road to ruin, and whose property increases just in proportion as their neighbors are impoverished
and degraded. To confront such foes takes a different kind of
courage from that which the pioneers exhibited; a courage less
dramatic, less spectacular, less impressive to crude minds; but no
less genuine, or less noble. And there is always room for self-
sacrifice in our encounters with these foes. It generally costs
something, in this world, to secure good government; it costs
something to establish it; it costs something to maintain it.
Hardships, losses, privations untold were endured by those who
laid the foundations of the State, and the State will not be kept
from overthrow unless we are ready to suffer some hardships
and losses in its defense. To challenge and resist the enemies
of the State—to keep its councils pure and its honor stainless—
will require of you and me some sacrifices. We must be willing to face opposition, contempt, contumely; to be called all
manner of hard names; to be stigmatized as cranks, feather-
heads, doctrinaries, dudes; nay, we must even be willing to lose

customers, to see our income reduced, and our prospect of pro-
motion cut off; to suffer the loss of many things rather than be
false to our convictions of duty. Unless this spirit abides in us,
we are unworthy of the liberties which were purchased for us at
so great a cost, and we shall not long retain them.

The faith of the pioneers must also animate our souls.
Unless we believe as they did, that there are better days to
come, our heartless labor will be utterly in vain. If they did
not despair of the future nation, when they held the forlorn
hope here in the wilderness; when half and more than half
their number perished in a single winter; when trackless forests
encircled them, and stubborn soils defied them, and bloody foes
lurked everywhere in ambush for them, surely we should not
despair of the Republic now, when so many fields have been
won, and the forces of intelligence and virtue are so many and
so mighty.

> "Amid the storms they sang,
>   And the stars heard, and the sea,
> And the sounding aisles of the dim **woods rang**
>   With the anthems of the free."

Unless we, their children, in the midst of the foes that be-
league us, can lift up our voices in the same triumphant strain,
we are recreant to the charge they have given us to keep.

Above all, there is need that we should grasp with new conviction the great truth of the solidarity of the generations; that
while we confess our obligations to those who lived before us,
we should feel, as we never yet have felt, our duty to those who
will live after us. This is the one clear and strong impression
which such an occasion as this should stamp upon our thought.
To see to it that the treasures of just law and large liberty which
we have inherited shall receive no detriment at our hands, but
shall be handed on unimpaired, unpolluted, undiminished to our
children, this is our supreme obligation. With a great sum have
we obtained this freedom; but the price was not paid by us; we
are the beneficiaries of past generations. We have no right to
waste our patrimony. What cost our fathers such an outlay of
pain and privation we ought to cherish with reverent devotion.

It is worth all it cost, all and infinitely more, and it must be transmitted without loss to our successors.

Every thoughtful man admits that the people of one generation have no right to exhaust the soil from which their sustenance is derived, passing it on to their posterity poorer than it was when they received it. Such wasteful or careless use of natural resources is criminal. The land, the forests, the mines, the fish of the streams, all the bounty of nature, are here not for us alone, but for our children and our children's children for ages to come. In all our use of these things we must keep them in mind. Their numbers will increase; the productive energies of the earth must not be reduced, but reinforced and reinvigorated for their benefit. It is a stupid crime, it is treason against humanity to impoverish by our greed the soil on which millions must dwell after we are gone.

If such is our responsibility for the careful and productive use of natural resources, what shall we say respecting those higher and more precious portions of our inheritance—the muniments of law, the safeguards of liberty, the wholesome customs, the sound sentiments, the reverence for God, the respect for man, the true equality, the genuine fraternity—without which government is anarchy and society is pandemonium? Must not these be preserved in their integrity, and transmitted to those who come after us? These are the talents which the Lord of the earth entrusts to the people of each generation, and which they are to deliver up to their successors multiplied and improved by God's own law of increase. The world that we resign to those who come after us must be a better world than that which we received from our fathers—a more productive world, a healthier, happier, safer, purer, freer, nobler world; if we fail in this, our material gains will only hasten our national decay; the mighty forces of nature that we have harnessed will but drag us to destruction; the swift-flying steeds of fire and lightning coursing over our land and churning our seas to foam will speed us to our doom.

Fellow countrymen, fellow Christians, those great currents of migration from east to west, whose course across the continent we have followed, are stayed upon our western shore and can no farther go. For numberless centuries they have been flowing westward; and the slow tides of time have brought them to the final barrier. At the Golden Gate, on the snowy summits of the Cascade Mountains, the pilgrims stand and gaze afar to that Asian continent from which in the dim twilight of history their father set forth—to countries crowded with a decadent civilization. The circuit of the earth is completed; migration has come to its term; here, upon these plains, the problems of history are to be solved; here, if anywhere, is to rise that city of God, the New Jerusalem, whose glories are to fill the earth. O, let us not forget what foundations we are laying, what empires are to stand upon them; and in the fear of God and the love of man let us build here a city in whose light the nations of the earth shall walk; whereinto kings may bring their glory and honor; into which there shall enter nothing that worketh abomination or maketh a lie.

The following is an abstract of the discourse delivered to
the Methodists of Gallipolis by the Rev. David H. Moore, D. D.,
of Cincinnati, Editor of the *Western Christian Advocate:*

THEME — PHILOSOPHY OF METHODIST SUCCESS; WITH SPECIAL
    REFERENCE TO THE NORTHWEST TERRITORY.

'Thou shalt remember all the way which the Lord thy God hath led
thee.—*Deut.* viii. *2.*

It is worthy of note that the successful peopling of North
America was providentially delayed until the Pilgrim Fathers
were ready to plant Christianity in the colonies settling the new
world.   But the Pilgrim Fathers were only one remove from
bitter persecutions, and schooled in enforced obedience naturally
became themselves dogmatic and arbitrary.   A freer polity and a
more genial faith were needed for the expanding populations of
the colonies;   one whose reactions upon the various forms
of Puritanism should be liberalizing and quickening.   This new
religious factor — coeval with the political birth of the United
States and ordained to far reaching influence upon its development and destiny — was that form of belief and life known as
Methodism.   It was unique in its absolu'e separation from the
arm of flesh, its constant dependence upon the Holy Spirit, and
its single aim of spreading Scriptural holiness throughout the
lands.   It was little thoughtful of numbers, no stickler for form;
it feared God, honored the King, and believed in the equal par-
ticipation of all men in the benefits of the atonement through
Christ.   It was conceived in Epworth rectory, born in Oxford
University, and reached the strength and beauty of maturity in
free America.

We who sometimes despair of the cause of God amid the
Sabbath-breaking, drunkenness, sensuality, worldliness and infidelity of the day, need only look at the origin of Methodism
to be assured that our fears are idle.   The reign of George II
seems to have had swept down into it from the corrupt court of
Charles the accumulated frivolity, coarseness, libertinism, and
unbelief of all the past.   True, some lights were unquenched,
but they were rush-lights disputing with midnight gloom.   Overwhelming wickedness rolled over the land.

Says Tyerman: "Never has a century risen on Christian England so void of soul and faith as that which opened with Queen Anne, and which reached its misty noon beneath the second George — a dewless night, succeeded by a sunless dawn. There was no freshness in the past and no promise in the future. The Puritans were buried and the Methodists were not born. The philosopher of the age was Bolingbroke; the moralist was Addison; the minstrel was Pope; and the preacher was Atterbury. The world had the idle, discontented look of the morning after some mad holiday, and, like rocket-sticks and the singed paper from last night's squibs, the spent jokes of Charles and Rochester lay all about, and people yawned to look at them. The reign of buffoonery was past, but the reign of faith and earnestness had not commenced."

In 1756, every sixth house in London was a licensed grog-shop; and sign-boards advertised to make a man drunk and furnish him straw to lie on to sleep off his drunken stupor — for a penny. High and low were corrupt. Dissenters lamented the worldliness of their ministers, and of the candidates for orders in the established church, Bishop Burnet — 1713 said: "The much greater part are ignorant to a degree not to be apprehended by those who are not obliged to know it."

Toplady declares that "a converted minister was as great a wonder as a comet." Even in the University, such was the prevalence of aggressive infidelity that the Vice Chancellor was constrained to issue an edict pointing out this deplorable condition, and directing the tutors to use diligence in counteracting it. But the Dean of Christ College, where Wesley was preparing for his mission, was so maddened by infidelity that he forbade the posting of the edict in his hall.

Existing forces were inadequate. The crisis was extreme. It was indeed man's extremity become God's opportunity; and He led Charles and John Wesley, Robert Kirkham and Wm. Morgan, to form the "Holy Club" and lay the foundation of world-wide Methodism. .

The persecution they suffered, the self-denial they practiced, the emergencies they met, the experiences they gained, were providential preparations for the perils in the wilderness of

the New World. Mind you, Wesley and his co-laborers were
not adventurers, seeking cheap notoriety in this enterprise because excluded by their inferior genius from the more attractive
fields open to talent and learning. Lord Macaulay thus estimates
Wesley's ability: "He was a man whose eloquence and logical
acuteness might have rendered him eminent in literature; whose
genius for government was not inferior to that of Richelieu; and
who devoted all his powers in defiance of obloquy and derision,
to what he sincerely considered the highest good of his species."

Yet their name was cast out as evil. All manner of contempt was heaped upon them. *Fogg's Journal,* one of the most
literary and respectable papers, held them up to scorn. "Among
their own party," says the writer, "they pass for religious persons and men of extraordinary parts; but they have the misfortune to be taken by all who have ever been in their company for
madmen and fools." They were forbidden the churches and
prosecuted for preaching in the open air. They were dragged
before magistrates, hooted by mobs, pelted with filth and bruised
with stones, tumbled into lime-pits and then into water. But in
the midst of this burning furnace of trial, the Spirit taught
Wesley to sing:

> "Ye mountains and vales, in praises abound;
> Ye hills and ye dales, continue the sound;
> Break forth into singing, ye trees of the wood,
> For Jesus is bringing lost sinners to God!"

Every moment was precious, for some perishing soul might
be saved. So he calculated for every minute. Lying awake in
the middle of the night, he set his alarm for seven, but his wake-
fulness continued; then for six, with the same result; then for
five, and no change; then for four, and there was no more wake-
fulness; and thereafter he arose at that early hour.

So of money. God needed it for His poor and for His work.
And so Wesley practiced and preached that it was the duty of
each one to give away every year all he had after providing for
his own necessities. Thus when he received £30 a year, he
lived on £28 and gave away 40 shillings; when he received £60,
he lived on £28 and gave away £32; £90, still £28 sufficient for

his living, and he gave away £62; when he received £120, he still lived on £28 and gave away all the rest.

Consider the character of his preaching. Like the great French evangelist he knew but three things—a ruined world, a mighty Savior, brought together by an earnest ministry. Every sermon brings out—man's damning guilt, his almighty Savior, and a witnessed salvation.

And with this thrilling Gospel he went where sinners most abounded. A prelate of the Established Church sneeringly called the first Roman Catholic Archbishop of Westminster "Archbishop of the slums." "Exactly," was the noble reply, "that is just what I am. I am an archbishop of the slums; that is my business; that is what I desire to be. My ministry is among the hordes and the garrets and the slums; yours, I admit, is something very different."

Such was Wesley's spirit. This high-bred gentleman, this profound scholar, this man "whose eloquence and logical acuteness might have rendered him eminent in literature; whose genius for government was not inferior to that of Richelieu;" whose earlier devotion to the establishment was such that he would have thought the saving of a soul "a sin almost if it had not been done in a church"—turned from all his past and from all his churchly future, with quenchless zeal for souls, counting all things loss that stood between him and their salvation through his instrumentality.

"His frame of adamant and soul of fire" were taxed to the utmost. Says a biographer: "He exposed himself with the utmost indifference to every change of season and inclemency of weather; snow and hail, storm and tempest, had no effect on his iron body. He frequently lay down on the ground and slept all night with his hair frozen to the earth; he would swim over rivers with his clothes on and travel till they were dry, and all this without any apparent injury to his health."

Even a Catholic historian is constrained to say of him and his co-laborers: "They taught moral doctrines which we all accept in common, but they did not teach them after the old and barren way of the plodding, mechanical instructor. They thundered them into the opening ears of thousands who had never been roused to moral sentiment before. They inspired the souls of poor and common-place creatures with all the zealot's fire and all the martyr's endurance. They brought tears to penitent eyes which had never been moistened before by any but the selfish sense of personal pain or grief. They pierced through the dull, vulgar, contaminated hideousness of low and vicious life, and sent streaming in upon it the light of a higher world and a better law."

Wesley had but one aim — to save men — and counted every man called of God to do what he could to this end. Hence, pressed by the teeming work and sadly needing workmen, he called into service lay preachers, applying only the simple test of "gifts, grace and usefulness." Thus he advanced with every arm of the gospel service against the foe; and his line of battle resting its right on the schools and its left on "the slums," with Christ in the center, leaped forward unto victory.

Beloved, little need were there to rehearse things you know so well, if history were all we sought. It is not history, but the philosophy of history we seek — the philosophy of our wonderful Methodist history. I seek to show you in these things why Methodism has triumphed so gloriously. Sprung from Wesley's loins it could not be otherwise. He projected himself upon America. His ministers here caught his courage, zeal, enerey, self-denial. He multiplied himself by every preacher who bore the double standard of Christ and Methodism over the mountains, through the savannahs and into the forests of North America.

So, I repeat, Wesley was God's providence for America. For consider — here were wildernesses, infested by savages, and thinly settled by desperate men; here was a new world, with men's thoughts absorbed in its conquest; here were colonies, drunk with the first long draught of civil liberty, the plains yet soaking with the blood of the Revolution. Here were no funds to be drawn upon for church extension or domestic missions; no meeting houses; no salaries; nothing in sight but trials, losses, dangers, suffering, death. Only men of the most heroic mould could be equal to tasks like these. Such men were the product of the great Wesleyan movement, this the second Reformation that sprang from Luther's first. Time will not allow us many examples to show that the Wesley spirit is the secret of our success. One suffices: Asbury was the American Wesley, and his signature attested the appointment of the noble men who first broke the solitude of the Northwestern Territory with the songs and words of life.

Asbury! name heroic and inspiring,

> "He would not flatter Neptune for his trident,
> Or Jove for his power to thunder."

Facing maddened mobs, traveling trackless forests, braving hostile savages, enduring want and weariness and poverty extreme, he reflected at once the strength and gentleness of Christ. His salary was $30 a year! Yet he murmured not. "What matters it where I go or what comes upon me if God is with me," he writes in his Journal, "or where I live or where I die, if holy and ready."

Again he writes: "My present mode of conduct is as follows: to read about one hundred pages a day; usually to pray in public five times a day; to preach in the open air every other day, and to lecture in prayer meeting every evening. And if it were in my power, I would do a thousand times as much for such a gracious and blessed Master. But in the midst of all my little employments, I feel myself as nothing and Christ to me is all in all."

This was our FRANCIS ASBURY, who spent forty-five years in the American ministry, traveled 270,000 miles—6,000 a year; preached 16,500 sermons, at least one a day; presided at not less than 224 annual conferences and ordained more than 4,000 preachers.

Bascom, and Finley, and Cartwright, and Young, and Morris, followed by Trimble, and Moody, and Ferree, and Dillon, and Brown, and they by those now in our midst; these constitute our unbroken apostolic succession. Gallipolis traces its descent from pastor Baker back through this magnificent ancestry to Asbury and Wesley.*

So does every other church in Methodism. And only the reflection which these centennial occasions promote is needed to make us give thanks that the lines have fallen to us in such pleasant places and that ours is so goodly a heritage.

You ask me to glance at the development of our church in the Northwest Territory, and a glance is all my time will admit.

More than fifty volumes, chiefly biographical, have been written upon it. The same adventurous spirit that led our fathers into Kentucky and into the Ohio wilderness, led them also into Indiana and Illinois, into Michigan and Wisconsin; and substantially the same hardships and dangers were encountered and the same prejudices met and overcome. Each conference has its heroes; and no legacy is so precious as the memory of its pioneers. Such hero worship is inspiring and ennobling.

Says Carlyle: "We cannot look, however imperfectly, upon a great man without gaining something by him. He is the living light-fountain, which it is good and pleasant to be near; the light which enlightens, which has enlighted, the darkness of the world; and this not as a kindled lamp only, but rather as a natural luminary shining by the gift of Heaven, a flowing light-fountain, as I say, of native original insight, of manhood and heroic nobleness, in whose radiance all souls feel that it is well with them."

An unpublished Mss. by Prof. S. W. Williams, book editor of the Western Methodist Book Concern, and probably unsurpassed in Methodist antiquities, gives valuable facts concerning "the introduction of Methodism into Southwestern Ohio." [Copious extracts were read, which are necessarily omitted here.] Up to the organization of the Northwestern Territory in 1787, the only white residents on this side of the Ohio were a few transient traders, perhaps a half-dozen Moravian missionaries, and a score or two of straggling squatters.

When this was opened to settlement the emigrants began to

---

* The history of Gallipolis M. E. Church, prepared by Rev. P. A. Baker, is appended, as an essential part of this Centennial Record.— D. H. M.

push in, braving the hostility of the cruel and treacherous red men. In 1788-89 they settled at Marietta, at the mouth of the Little Miami, and where Cincinnati now stands, and when Wayne's victorious campaign in 1794 brought peace the settlers crowded into the interior and founded Hamilton, Franklin, Dayton and Chillicothe. Before 1800 there was a chain of settlements in Southern Ohio up the Miami valleys as far north as Dayton and Xenia and up the Scioto to Franklinton.

As nearly as I can determine, the first Methodist preacher who visited this section of Ohio was Wm. Burke, a remarkable man of the Asbury-Wesley stamp. He was appointed by Bishop Asbury, October 2, 1803, to cross the Ohio and form a new district in the wilderness. He says: "I entered upon my work about the last of October, 1803. * * The Miami circuit included all the settlements between the Miamis and as far north, including the settlements of Mad river, as high up as the neighborhood where Urbana now stands, and east of the Little Miami as high up as the settlements on Bullskin, and all the settlements on the East Fork of the Little Miami and a few settlements in Campbell county, Ky." This was a six weeks' circuit. "The most easterly appointment was at Brother Boggs's, on the Little Miami, a few miles from the Yellow Springs. From that point we generally started at daylight for the settlements on the Scioto, having between 40 and 50 miles, without a house, to the first inhabitants at old Chillicothe.

"Scioto circuit included all that tract of country inhabited on Paint creek out to New Market, Brush creek, Eagle creek, and Ohio Brush creek, and up the Ohio to the mouth of the Scioto, and then up the Scioto to the Pickaway Plains, including Chillicothe and the settlements on White's creek, a four weeks' circuit.

"From thence one day's ride to the settlements in the Hocking Valley, which was called Hocking circuit, which laid principally on that river and its tributaries, and a few settlements on Walnut creek. From Lancaster we generally took two days and a half to reach the bounds of West Wheeling circuit, near where St. Clairsville is now located. This was a four weeks' circuit, including the settlements on the Ohio river and extending back to the frontier settlements on the West Wheeling and Short creeks, etc.

"From this point we returned by the same route to New Lancaster, and then down the Hocking to Sunday creek and Monday creek, and then over to Marietta circuit.

"This circuit was up and down the Ohio from Marietta, as low down as the settlements were formed, and up the Muskingum as far as Clover Bottom and Wolf Creek, and so down to the neighborhood of Marietta, and over to Virginia on the waters of Little Kanawha. This was called the Muskingum and Little Kanawha circuits. It was but a three weeks' circuit and had one preacher.

"From the neighborhood of Marietta we started down the Ohio, by way of Graham's Station, to the mouth of the Great Kanawha and down to Green Bottom — Brother Spurdock's — which was the first appointment on Guyandotte circuit.

"This circuit contained all the territory south and west of the Great Kanawha, and down to the mouth of Big Sandy and the settlements back from the Ohio river. This field required about eleven weeks and many privations. The Methodists were, in those days, like angels' visits, few and far between, and we were half our time obliged to put up at taverns and places of entertainment, subject to the disorder and abuse of the unprincipled and half-civilized inmates, suffering with hunger and cold, and sleeping in open cabins on the floor sometimes without bed or covering, and but little prospect of any support from the people among whom we labored, and none from any other source; for there was no provision in those days for missionaries. But, notwithstanding all the privations and sufferings that we endured, we had the consolation that our labor was not in vain in the Lord. We were gratified in having souls for our hire, and rejoiced to see the wilderness blossom as the rose. New societies sprang up, circuits were enlarged, immigration increased, the forest was subdued, and comforts multiplied."
—Finley's Sketches of Western Methodism.

In 1798, John Kobler was the only Methodist preacher in the Northwest Territory and the total membership numbered ninety-nine. Now there are in

	Con-ferences	Preachers	Members	S. S. Scholars	Church Property.
Ohio	5	1,063	231,492	214,889	$8,865,481
Indiana	4	659	148,904	124,725	4,014,318
Illinois	4	991	146,344	143,868	8,010,891
Michigan	2	670	79,553	94,418	3,756,245
Wisconsin	2	337	32,599	28,849	1,794,829
N. W. Territory ...	17	3,120	638,892	606,749	$26,441,764

In 1790, John Dickins, on $600 borrowed capital, was beginning the Methodist Book Concern, the secret of our marvelous doctrinal unity; a concern that in its New York and Cincinnati branches represents a *net* capital above all liabilities of $2,957,331.47; has published 3000 various books and 1300 different tracts and Sunday-school requisites; and has a yearly circulation of 3,133,666 periodicals. The Cincinnati house, the Western Methodist Book Concern, beginning in 1820, in a room 15 x 20, corner Fifth and Elm, has now a net capital of $1,020,515.52, spacious buildings in Cincinnati, Chicago, and St. Louis, with every appliance for a great publishing house. In the Northwest Territory it publishes four great newspapers, the *Western Christian Advocate*, the *Christian Apologist*, the *Northwestern Christian Advocate*, and the *Central Christian Advocate*. "From the three centers, Cincinnati, Chicago and St. Louis (the two last as depositories), trains loaded with solid Methodist literature are sent forth every week into every part of the West and Northwest."

The Ohio Wesleyan University, the DePauw University, the Northwestern University, the Garrett Biblical Institute, and a score of other institutions in the same boundaries illustrate Methodism's devotion to higher learning.

What it is in the Northwest Territory it is throughout the United States and Canada.

And no marvel; for its inception in England and its expansion in newest America has proven its adaptation alike to the ripest and to the crudest civilization; that is to say, to all conditions and to all times. Other denominations have caught its spirit and adopted its methods. Hoary creeds have been modified so as to conform more nearly to its standards; and the pulpits of Christendom have kindled with its evangelical fervor.

But still its mission is to the regions beyond; its position in the advancing columns is on the front line. Its business is to find and drive the enemy, leaving to the slower-moving forces the work of fortifying and garrisoning the conquered provinces. Its muster roll begins with those of Cæsar's household and ends not until it includes the faithful Onesimus. Quenchless zeal for souls is and must forever be its characteristic; a simple and full salvation its message; and its reward not human applause, but the well-done of its Lord.

METHODISM IN GALLIPOLIS.

The Rev. Henry Baker preached the first Methodist sermon in Gallipolis sometime during the year 1817, at the residence of Ahaz S. Morehouse, a log house located at the mouth of Mill creek. The Methodist itinerant was not then received with as cordial a welcome as others have been since. "The rowdies were so troublesome," the minister stated, "that Mr. Morehouse could not have services there any longer, and unless someone else would open a house he would not come again." Calvin Shepard, who may justly be entitled the "father of Gallipolis Methodism," was present, though not then a member, and cheerfully offered his house as a place of worship, and from that time they continued to hold regular services. Shortly afterward, Brother Shepard, while on a visit to some friends near Cincinnati, sought and found the Savior. A class was then formed consisting of the following persons: Calvin Shepard, Mahala Shepard, his wife, John Knapp and wife, Christopher Randall and wife, Stephen Sisson, Mary Varian and her two daughters, Abigail and Matilda. The society was soon strengthened by the addition of James Hanson, Sarah Dranillard and David Smithers, and many others. In 1820, under the labors of John P. and William Kent, there was a very successful revival in which about thirty more were added to the society. About this time, says the Rev. T. J. N. Simmons, in Calvin Shepard's obituary, written October 10th, 1856, "They met with much opposition, and from a source that would dispose us now to throw over it the mantle of charity. Having been denied the court house and school house for public worship, they continued to meet in father Shepard's house and barn until able to erect a church for themselves." Says a later writer in speaking of these persecutions: "The perpetrators were not all rowdies; Satan himself seemed to control public sentiment from those high in religious, as well as in civil authority, down to the lowest in society against the despised Methodists. It was considered fatal to every good person to become a Methodist, and these opinions were enforced by stones and eggs and filth. Vehicles were thrown over the river bank, harness and saddles were cut and smeared, and persons passing to and from the meetings were subjected to every annoyance." The circuit, of which this was but one appointment, extended from Letart Falls, thirty-six miles above us, to Wheelersburg, eighty miles below, embracing large territory on both sides of the river. The first Methodist church was built in Gallipolis in 1821, and stood where the parsonage now stands. The deed for the lot dates from May 7th, 1793, from George Washington (by Thos. Jefferson), to Rufus Putnam, Rev. Manasseh Cutler, Robt. Oliver and Griffin Green, for Ohio company. Rufus Putnam and others to Return Jonathan Meigs, in trust for French inhabitants. December 26, 1796, Fearing and Meigs to Lewis LeClercq. July 30, 1811, Lewis LeClercq and wife to Anthony Maguet. June 2, 1821, Anthony Maguet and wife to trustees of M. E. church, viz.: Calvin Shepard, Daniel Combs, Christopher Randall, Moses Brown and John Knapp, for which was paid the sum of $150 in specie."

This church built in 1821, was 44x50 feet—one story brick, and ceiling twelve feet high. This served as a place of worship until 1849, when a new church was built at a cost of about $1,675.00. This building was of brick, 40x60 feet, two stories high; basement nine feet high; upper story sixteen feet, vestibule 8 feet wide; four class rooms twelve feet square; lecture room 23x40 feet. The pastor was Rev. W. T. Hand. The society worshiped and prospered here for twenty-six years, when it became necessary to "tear down and build greater." Accordingly in the year 1875, under the pastorate of the Rev. C. D. Battelle, the present beautiful and commodious building was erected, at a cost of $20,000. This church is 70x86 feet, with a lecture room 45x50 feet. There are six class rooms and a vestibule below. The upper room is equal to about seventy feet square, a comfortable seating capacity for 700, with a gallery seating 150. The building committee was D. Y. Smithers, John T. Holliday.and J. W. Gardener; architect, T. S. Ford. The church was dedicated June 25, 1876, by Bishop R. S. Foster.

The vine that was planted here,.though under much persecution, early in the century, has been a very prosperous one. The secret of its prosperity here, as it is of Methodism everywhere, is in her revivals, and as long as she clings to her revival methods, no weapon that is formed against her will prosper. The first record, made by the first legally constituted Board of Trustoes, contains a list of all the members and adherents of the Methodist church, January 18, 1821. The list contains fifty-one names. There are now on the church record 612 names of members in good standing. The Sunday-school enrolls over 400 scholars and has a library containing 600 volumes.

*The following is a list of the ministers that have served the charge from 1817 to 1890.

LETART FALLS CIRCUIT.

1817 — William Cunningham.   (To January, 1818.)
1818 — Abner Bowman.
1819 — Henry Baker and John P. Kent.
1820 — William Kent and James Gilruth.
1821 — Ebenezer Webster.
1822 — Edward Taylor.
1823 — James Gilruth.
1824 — John P. Kent.
1825–26 — Francis Wilson.
1827 — Henry and Stephen Rathburn.

---

*In 1885, a mission chapel, known as "*Domron Chapel*," was built in the upper end of the city, with a seating capacity for two hundred. Sunday-school, class and prayer-meetings are held there weekly.

1828—Jacob Delay.

(Gallipolis circuit was then formed.)

1829—Jacob Delay and Ebenezer Webster.

1830—John Ulen and James Callahan.

1831—William Herr.

1832—James Armstrong.

1832—David Whitcomb. (From February to June.)

1833—Elijah Field and Adam Miller, Benj. Ellis and Abraham Miller.

1834—Charles R. Baldwin.

1835—Jas. Parcells an Benj. D. Jefferson.

1836—Wm. P. Stricklen and Jacob Martin.

1837—Jacob Delay and Elijah Pilcher.

(In March, 1837, Gallipolis city became a station.)

1837—Elijah Pilcher.

1838-39—W. P. Strickland.

1840—A. M. Alexander.

1841-42—E. V. Bing.

1843-44—E. M. Baring.

1844—A. I. Lida.

1846—C. C. Lybrand.

1847-48—W. T. Hand.

1849-50—Samuel Baleman.

1851-52—Andrew Correll.

1853-54—E. V. Bing.

1855-56—T. J. N. Simmons.

1857-58—H. Z. Adams.

1859-60—E. P. Hall.

1861-62—J. T. Miller.

1863-64-65—Joseph F. Williams, under whose pastorate the present parsonage was built, valued at $2,500.

1866-67—Levi Cunningham.

1868—Wm. Glenn.

1869-70—F. S. Davis.

1871-72-73—J. E. Moore.

1874-75—C. D. Battelle.

1876—E. H. Heglar.

1877-78—J. W. Dillon.

1879—T. M. Leslie.
1880–81–82—C. F. Creighton.
1883–84–85—W. H. Lewis.
1886–87—Benj. A. Stubbins.
1888—M. V. B. Evans.
1889–90—P. A. Baker.

NAMES OF PRESIDING ELDERS FROM 1816 TO 1890:

1816 to 1822—Jacob Young.
1822 to 1824—John Witterman.
1824 to 1829—Zachariah Connell.
1829 to 1833—Isaac C. Hunter.
1833 to 1835—Robt. O. Spencer.
1835 to 1837—John Ferree.
1837 to 1841—Samuel Hamilton.
1841 to 1842—Isaac C. Hunter.   (Died June 18, 1842.)
1842 to 1845—John Ferree.   (Died 1845.)
1845 to 1846—J. M. Jamison.
1846 to 1850—John Stewart.
1850 to 1853—Robt. O. Spencer.
1853 to 1854—Andrew Correll.
1854 to 1856—N. Westerman.
1856 to 1860—John Stewart.
1860 to 1864—A. M. Alexander.
1864 to 1868—H. Z. Adams.
1868 to 1871—J. T. Miller.
1871 to 1875—John Dillon.
1875 to 1877—John W. Dillon.
1877 to 1881—T. H. Monroe.
1881 to 1885—Z. W. Fagan.
1885 to 1889—J. C. Arbuckle.
1889—M. V. B. Evans.

I have been greatly aided in preparing the above by a historical memoir of the society, prepared by the Rev. C. F. Creighton, J. G. Domron, J. W. Gardener and M. Malahan.

Gallipolis, O., Dec. 4, 1890.   P. A. BAKER.

ABSTRACT OF THE SERMON ON "THE PRESBY-TERIANS OF OHIO."

BY REV. SYLVESTER F. SCOVEL, PRESIDENT OF WOOSTER UNIVERSITY, WOOSTER, OHIO, PREACHED IN THE FIRST PRESBYTERIAN CHURCH.

The Christian is a cosmopolitan. Every land is his father-land since God is his father. So every Christian is brother to all other Christians. Yet we may have a just concern which shall be special for our country and our church.

We have a century of Presbyterian experience behind us, and each one of the Centennial occasions which have been oc-curring since 1776 (and all have been useful in many ways), in-vites us to consider the facts and lessons of that experience.

The Centennial record of any religious body cannot be repre-sented by processions and pageantry however elaborate. Not to the eye but to the heart must we appeal. We go deeper even than the references to ancient places of worship or their for-gotten customs. We must find the teacher and the truth, the communicant and his conduct, the home life and the school of the Sabbath and of the week day. We must linger beside the couch of the sick and beside the open tomb and the shadowed homes. We must go out from these centers to the sure but often silent influences which have told upon manners, and standard of conduct and social life, and upon law and order, and even upon legislation and administration. We must trace footfalls that are not heard primarily on the hurried streets, and search out the hidden causes in thought and feeling of much that we admire externally.

The motives for Centennial review are potent and dignified. The present reaps the fruit of the past, and is the product of the past to be understood fully only in its procuring causes. The noble men of other days were the friends of many, the kindred of some. The heritage of Christian life and character which any long record brings to view is the Church's true glory, the proof of the presence and power of Christ, her divine head, and of the spirit her divine heart. Moreover, the complex elements of our life of to-day need to look steadily at the simpler life of the past, the condition of its heroic virtues.   In such records we honor God by noting what he has wrought.

And while we concentrate for a little our attention upon our predecessors in this commonwealth, we must remember what and who preceded them.   Away in the dim distance and across the seas we discover names whose influence lived in our pioneers and still survives.   These may be names not often mentioned, but they came bringing the principles we revere into the life of their own age, disturbing the apparently external uniformity of the Papacy.

Then well known conflicts show us the head of the emerging column, compacted and partly created by these conflicts themselves.   At and in and after the Reformation we hear stronger voices and see more guiding rods in the hands of leaders. Presently the column crosses to our own shores and buries itself in the din and battle of our own Revolution, and then is seen later in the nearer coasts of our neighboring States, and finally reaches our own streams and forests.

We cannot possibly isolate any band of Presbyterians.   Our church in our locality is surrounded by concentric circles and becomes our church in our commonwealth, in our country, in the world, and in the church universal and militant, which is itself encircled again by the white-robed throngs of the church invisible and triumphant.   It is a blessed thing that we cannot localize too much.   The vista and outlook must be kept clear. This is what *intensifies* and *expands* at the same time.   It enlarges both *intent* and *content*, contrary to the rules of formal logic.   The genesis of each Christian goes back to the forces which build and sustain the universal church.   All the way down the chain is vital in its continuity.   If we put a finger upon any one link of the chain for some special purpose, we are never to detach it.   Looking upon our church in our commonwealth we stand half way between our universal and our local attachments.   Such distinction for thought or study will not put us out of touch with any others who love our common Master, but the contrary.   Other churches and other countries shall become dearer to us by the privileges of our own.

If we ask for the influences which prepared the Presby-

terians who came to Ohio, we must turn our faces to the past.
We must hover over the advancing column and mark its constitution and character. It is a long column and a noble one. Its
ranks are starred with heroes. Truth floats from all its banners.
Its inscriptions are condensed principles of almost Omnipotent
force. Its uniform is often dyed like His from Bozrah, for with
Him and for Him they suffered. It is grand review even for a
glance of the eye. Mark the Bible, held up aloft as Beza's
statue bears it up over the borders of the lovely Lake Neuchatel.
See the broken fetters lifted ready to strike tyrants! See the
compact organization which proves that an integument is necessary to a vigorous body, from the enclosure of a blood-corpuscle
to the retaining walls of a vast civilization! See the step they
keep in the witness against a false individualism, and even
against an independent and disintegrating ecclesiasticism! See
the rugged faces and the fair ones — Coligny side by side awhile
with Margaret d'Angouleme. Break up the picture, study any
of its divisions, and each will be found to have contributed
something of permanent value to the whole Presbyterian tone
and temper, and something important to our common Christianity
and our advancing civilization. As we pass from Continental to
Scotch Presbyterianism the truth becomes clearer, the tread
firmer, and the struggles terminate more decisively in victory.
As we pass over into the New World little seems to remain but
the legitimate sequences of (1) dissolution of the bond between
Church and State; (2) the office of securing American liberties;
(3) the consolidation and organization of the scattered churches,
and (4) the great revivals. These came in their turn, and the
church of our fathers was fully ready for the newer and yet
larger work on our frontiers and beyond, until the advancing influence reached the western limit of this great land. And there
it was ready again to make a league with the modern giant,
steam, and pass onward with the Gospel into the far East just in
time to reach its hitherto immobile masses as they began to be
stirred with the breath of a new life.

[After this introduction the speaker traced some of the lines
by which Presbyterians came into Ohio.]

Like other immigrants they came rather drawn than either

drifting or driven. The Ohio Land Company, formed by King in 1750–51, proved attractive. The codfish brought many a Puritan to our shores, and good soil brought many a Presbyterian to Ohio. The movement into Ohio was part of the greater Western movement. Some went farther North and some away to the South. The centre of population began soon to go West, and certainly it grew up with the country. Great trade - winds blew over the lands with steadiness, and any vessel could go by them from a shallop to a frigate. So Presbyterians came into Ohio. Nor had they far to be blown. The drift into western Pennsylvania had been equally mercenary, but equally moral in its outcome. Those who came were just in time to settle the question as to France and Roman Catholicism, or England and Protestanism. The drift into Virginia thought about tobacco lands probably; but its constituents were just in time to help settle the question of State and Church, and that of freedom to preach the gospel and build churches unmolested. It was now time that the Pilgrims should move on into our borders, in order to help in settling the northwest for liberty, and to carry out the true spirit of the Declaration, that "morality, religion and knowledge being necessary to good government, schools and the means for education shall forever be encouraged." Here, too, they came just in time.

The immigration had a moral end as well as a material impulse; and it surely had a magnificent opportunity. The question *whence* they came who entered Ohio as Presbyterians a number of years ago, must bring our glass down to the distant horizon half around the circle of the compass. Waldensian bravery, Huguenot skill, Holland simplicity and heroic patience, Scotch valor and stubborness, all mingled with German fervor and conviction. Some of these stumbling one over the other in Pennsylvania, reached Ohio; but most of all there and here the mark of the Scotch - Irish immigrant is most plainly discerned. Some of their best and noblest leaders set sail in 1636 to form a colony in New England. Driven back by the sea, they returned and fought in Scotland. Two-thirds of a century later, after 1720, the emigrants left in swarms, penetrating New England, New York, Pennsylvania, Virginia and the Carolinas. Lord Montjoy said: "America was lost by Irish emigration." What mark they left on the Revolutionary time, I need not indicate; nor that they came from John Calvin, so cordially hated by the Romanists, or from John Knox, the rush of whose impetuous speech for the crown-rights of Jesus brought tears and trembling to the scheming Queen. Rugged was he as his own mountain, but fair as the shining of an eternal, because supernal, light upon the summit of his fame. There were great men all along the line: Makemie in Maryland, Davies in Virginia, McMillen and his coadjutors in Western Pennsylvania, Rice in Kentucky, and hundreds of others.

Presbyterians came from New England, and our heritage in Puritan blood must not be forgotten. They came from Eastern Pennsylvania, they came from Kentucky. Kentucky's churches are daughters of Virginia; but Virginia had been largely peopled by Scotch-Irish. "In obscurity and neglect Presbyterianism, in spite of Virginia laws, planted itself unmolested west of the Blue Ridge. Frederick county was leavened, Augusta county was nearly filled; McDowells, Alexanders, Lyles, Stuarts, and even the Campbells kept coming, and Moore came and Brown, and the list closes with the Makemie as it began." (Gillett, Vol. I.) As late as 1794 the Synod of Virginia included the Presbyteries of Red Stone and Ohio; and as early as 1791, the General Assembly approved and commended the plans of the Synod of Virginia "for the multitudes who are ready to perish on the frontiers."

Currents drew into Ohio from all around the horizon. Maryland had been singularly prepared to feed Ohio. But most came, of course, from Western Pennsylvania. In 1831 the Synod of Pittsburgh calls for appreciation of the task "now opening in the great Western Valley." Pittsburg is pronounced "the commercial center of more than eight thousand miles of steamboat navigation." God in His providence, says the Synod, "seems almost to have annihilated distance. The member of this Synod is still living who first sounded the silver trumpet of the gospel and broke the first loaf of the Bread of Life (with a handful convened in a log barn) *west of the Ohio*. Population has more than doubled every ten years; at this rate there will be a population west of the Alleghany Mountains in twenty-five years of twenty millions. Can we close our eyes? Brethren, keep the sacred fire ever burning upon our altars, and send down this immense valley *one thousand torch-bearers.*"

But I cannot stay for further particulars. Though many of the world's people misunderstood, or doubted, or denied, the work went steadily forward. The most intimate sympathy has always existed between the Presbyterianism of Ohio and that of Western Pennsylvania. The larger religious movements made visible in the Pittsburgh conventions of 1842 and 1857, were shared alike. And many of the baptisms and gracious revivals were alike pervasive. The movement was of the kind to produce this. It was not *en masse* nor by colonies; it was by families and by ministers. It was by transfusion rather than deportation and immigration.

Enough has been said to show what mingling of currents from the far Northeast, the East and South, came in upon Ohio. Conflicts of jurisdiction were brought to a close. Those who were entering saw eye to eye, and flowed together. Everything seemed favorable to the inclusion of the best possible elements in the stimulative immigration.

Moreover, it was a singularly important time—a blossoming for which there were long preparations. Yet we must remember the discouragements and difficulties through which they must yet pass; the stubborn character of the many foes they met and the exacting conditions under which they labored. The work was only begun, though well begun. We may turn from any study of its details to ask for the main influences by which these who came from so many of the four winds of heaven had been trained for all they were to do and suffer.

I.   The first influence was, definiteness of conviction. This appeared in their estimate of the Bible as the only rule of faith and practice, in accurate expressions of their faith by formulæ, and in their developed and systematic schemes of church order. In all these things, they were staunch and firm. They, like Francis Makemie, when arraigned by the High Church government in New York in 1707, were able to say: "As to our doctrines, we have our Confession of Faith, which is known to the

Christian world." No one can over-estimate the values of the positiveness of Presbyterianism in shaping the religious life of our State. " Presbyterianism did not come into the New World passive and plastic, to be determined in its character and history by force of circumstances or by the accident of its environment, but came with positive opinion, deep and strong convictions of truth and duty, with clear conceptions of its mission to mold and determine the character of the New World. An acorn planted at the foot of the Alleghanies, is not in doubt as to the form it is to assume. In Druidical groves and in American forests, oaks grow according to inner life. The seed of Presbyterianism here was the same as in Geneva and Edinburg. Indefiniteness is reduced to a minimum in Presbyterianism. The indefinite man is evasive and deliquescing and evaporative. The definite man will be a rallying point in the community. Such was the first influence, and this became characteristic. Presbyterians came to be known in Ohio as being able to say not only, "I know *whom* I have believed," but also to add, " I know *what* I believe, and can give a Scriptural reason why."

II. The second characteristic discloses independence of man and love of liberty. This especially fitted Ohio Presbyterians to live under and carry out the spirit of the great Ordinance of 1787. Nothing could be finer than the exact adjustment of that ordinance, which recognized nothing but free men, and the inner spirit of Presbyterianism as it had come to be developed by the Assembly, 1788–9.

Presbyterian love of liberty is founded on an appreciation of man as man. Upon that recognition of the *soul* in man which makes a "Common," a great middle class, self-respecting and attracting the respect of others. Presbyterian love of liberty grows out of the Kingship, the Priesthood, and the Prophetic commission of all believers.

III. But an equally strong influence was exerted upon the Presbyterians who settled Ohio, and through them, in the conservative direction. They always believed in good and strong government, and were ready to say with Washington, "Influence, sir, is not government." They strongly held government to be *from* God, and therefore held the Government *to*

God. Conscience was for them the source of power in securing obedience to law. Law and order and the limitations of liberty were their household words. They were inclined to this direction both by doctrine and order. Publicists, like Gladstone, discerned this trait. Our faith has some very persevering saints. It can stand by the difficult and the old, and even the inexplicable (when that is divine), with only a patient smile for all gain-sayers; and after awhile the gain-saying ceases, and the admiration of what the world calls "*Staying qualities*" begins. This conservatism it was which fitted them for the following change of correspondence with the father of his country. "We shall consider ourselves doing an acceptable service to God in our profession, when we contribute to render men sober, honest, and industrious citizens and the obedient subjects of a lawful government." To which, George Washington replied that, "The general prevalence of philanthrophy, honesty, industry and economy, seems in the ordinary course of human affairs particularly necessary for advancing and confirming the happiness of our country." Calvinism's sense of accountability is a friend to st.ong government. Presbyterianism gives a rational conservatism. It is not fatalistic. Presbyterians went about arranging for government as naturally as they began felling trees and planting crops. They had no hesitation and no squeamishness, either in theory or practice. They had little use either for vigilance committees or white caps.

The speaker then simply enumerated other characteristics of which time forbade the discussion:

    IV.   The Intellectual.
    V.   The Ethical.
    VI.   The Evangelical.
    VII.   The Catholic.
    VIII.   The Disciplinary.

Some of the closing words were as follows:

Here, then, we rest the case. The decision and convincing and definite element fulfilled the first condition and adaption to the work before them.

The liberating element brought freedom for movement, with all the sacred passion of patriotism and all its honorable record, growing more distinguished as the years go on.

The conservative element established as other work progressed.

The intellectual element quickened all the faculties of all with whom they came in contact, and by press and school and fireside and pulpit they kindled such general ardor for mental power and furniture as has made Ohio a new mother of Presidents.

The ethical element aided to break the dominion of border savagism, and cleft the way for sound morals in law and practice, in society and business.

The evangelical and spiritual element kept descending the dews of the Holy Spirit's presence, and kept ever visible the radiant face of the Savior of men, and kept ever open the shining way to the celestial city — how many thousands have already trod it?

The Catholic element came on, in its own time, like the color on perfect and mellow fruit.

And ever and always to awaken and help us stands the disciplinary element in this great preparation.

What a series of marvelous combinations might be here enlarged upon. Stability and freedom; adaptation to common people, yet demanding the highest intelligence; doctrinal strictness, and yet liberality in the matter of non-official membership and in co-operation with other churches; devotional fervor, yet joined with marked ethical force; independence of the state, yet demand for state allegiance to God, intense conservatism and rapid progress.

But I forbear. I will not even attempt to voice the appeal which so noble an ancestry awakens; nor will I ask whether we who have known and enjoyed will prove as heroic in transmitting the sacred content of our blessings to those who come after us. It is certainly our duty to maintain, to restrain, to educate, to evangelize. When the churches had "*rest*" at the beginning, then they were "edified." Then also they walked "in the fear

·of the Lord and in the comfort of the Holy Ghost, and were
multiplied."

What better can we do with our exemptions and advantages
than to imitate them by growth in grace, and unsparing efforts
to multiply the number of the saved? What deep gratitude
should characterize the tone and temper of the Presbyterian
hosts at every review of the century. In His name who gave
us such a cloud of witnesses, we set up our banners. Let confi-
·dence, born of our past, and willingness, born of our gratitude,
and hope, born of the promises, and energy, born of love and
loyalty, be enough to compact us and drive us forward, as the
:sandblast drives its granite atoms into the hard, crystal surface.

SERMON BY REV. JOHN MONCURE, RECTOR OF ST. PETER'S CHURCH.

TEXT —"Remember the days of old, consider the years of many generations."— Deuteronomy 32, 7.

A hundred years in the history of a place affords a fruitful subject for study. When we gaze through the vistas of past events, and consider the whys and the wherefores, and when we thus are brought into realization of the fact that the things which once appeared to men as "through a glass, darkly," by the light of a century, are brought "face to face" with us, we are more than impressed, particularly if our meditations are of that devotional nature which enables us to glean the "truth, as it is in Jesus," from the passing years Matters once considered comparatively unimportant, when viewed in their places as links in the great chain of events, which unites our time with past ages, are not only important as eras in history, but as stages of development of the plan which our Father devised for our good and His glory.

To-day we stand at the finishing point of a century in the history of Gallipolis. The words of Moses to the children of Israel, when the work of journeying from Egypt to Canaan was nearing completion, and a new life was opening before them, will form the basis of our thoughts in this sermon. He enjoined them to "remember the days of old," and to "consider the years of many generations," in order that they might be convinced of God's wisdom and mercy. We view the history of His dealings with our forefathers, and with us, in the same spirit. The happenings of a hundred years, considered from a national and local standpoint, have been impressed upon your minds by the exercises of the past few days, and we need not dwell upon them here. * * * The subject which we would emphasize in connection with the history of our nation, state and city, is that which is so dear to every true heart, the Church of God. When we say that its growth has been great, we express God's favor and loving kindness in no slight degree. The church was the comforting medium in America one hundred years ago, as it has been in all others of the world's ages, and as it will be until "time shall be no more." The good and the true became better and stronger at the foot of the Cross, and the "weary and heavy laden" there found rest with Him who died for them, as they do now.   One point not to be lost sight of in this connection is that the cause of true religion has kept pace with the march of progress; indeed, men cannot but realize that it has been the cause of all enlightenment of the ages.   While our country has extended her field of active operations, she has also assisted in the extension of the Church of the Living God, for which fact, 'tis needless to say, that the good and true are devoutly thankful.   Our interest is centered upon the progress of that branch of the church to which we belong, the Protestant Episcopal Church.   The history of this body in the United States during the hundred years has been a history of triumph. Our separation from the mother church of England, and the establishment as a separate organization in this land dates back to but a very few years previous to the founding of this town.

In the "Handbook of the General Convention of the United States," by Bishop Perry, of Iowa, appears these words concerning the first meeting for organization of the church in America, which occurred May 11, 1784: "A single sheet of foolscap, faded and yellow with age, contains the records of the preliminary gathering of clergy and laity, out of which grew the independent organization of the American Church."   The work before the then very small body of workers was no easy one, for in addition to the efforts necessary to push forward the organization, there was a deep-set prejudice in the minds of the people against the English Church, growing out of the animosities incident to the revolution, and which it was necessary to overcome. God was with the noble band, however, and as His cause could not fail, our numbers gathered in strength.

He indeed raised up His power and came among us, and with great might succored us, and the efforts of the faithful for His glory were fruitful.   Our grand and comforting Book of Common Prayer, modified from the English book by our "fathers in God," and which was put into the hands of the people, has been an inestimable comfort in matters of worship,

and has rendered valuable assistance in our devotions, thus adding one to the many proofs that God's word, in whatever form it
may be presented, is not bound. As a result of the work of a
hundred years, our church presents a record of which we are not
only proud and grateful, but which will serve to inspire us to
even mightier efforts under the leadership of God. The
days of old, and the years of past generations are thus the
mediums of assurance of God's favor and protection, and
hence of strengthening the faith of the workers in the gospel
field. Our influence as a church is making itself felt all over
this mighty country, and beyond the seas men " take knowledge
of us, that we have been with Jesus." As the preached gospel
carries its comfort to the weak and needy, we thank God that
our church is among the foremost of its workers, and of the
thousands who yearly seek refuge from the storms of life in the
ark of safety, our numbers are great, and our prayers fervent,
that it may please God to defend these, His children, with His
Heavenly grace, that they may be His forever, and daily increase
in His Holy Spirit more and more, until they come to His everlasting kingdom.

We refrain from detailed statistics in regard to our growth,
but will say that only a few thousand communicants of a hundred years ago have grown into nearly half a million, and probably a hundred clergy to nearly four thousand, and from no one
in the Episcopate, to sixty-six Bishops, actively at work in a corresponding number of dioceses and missionary jurisdictions. In
the State of Ohio, the progress of the church has been very
gratifying. The Diocese of Ohio was not organized until some
time in 1819, when that great and good man, Rev. Philander
Chase, was consecrated its first Bishop.

As the population of the State increased and cities and
towns multiplied, the church became stronger, being presided
over by the holy man just named, and his successors, Rt. Rev.
Charles P. McIlvaine, D. D.; Rt. Rev. Gregory T. Bedell, D. D.,
and Rt. Rev. Wm. Leonard, D. D., the present incumbent. In
1875, the diocese having grown to great strength, a division became necessary, and the Diocese of Southern Ohio was organized, with Rt. Rev. Thomas A. Jaggar, D. D., as its Bishop. In

this part of the field our lot is cast, and, under God's blessing,
we have received strength and consolation. Our Bishop having
been incapacitated from work by very bad health, in October,
1888, an Assistant Bishop was elected in the person of Rev.
Boyd Vincent, whose efficient work among us is greatly redound-
ing to God's glory. Lastly, but particularly, we turn our eyes
to the church in Gallipolis. Our meditations, while savoring of
humility here, are not unmingled with a sense of gratitude.
Work in the interest of the Episcopal Church was begun in our
town in the year 1840, when occasional services were held by
Rev. James B. Goodwin, a clergyman engaged in mission work
in the Diocese of Virginia. There being no church building,
these were held in the court house. The parish organization
was completed in December, 1841, when a vestry, composed of
leading citizens, was chosen. The first minister engaged was
Mr. Goodwin, and his work among the people is even now gratefully remembered. January 13, 1843, a committee appointed by
the vestry to secure a lot for a church building, obtained one on
lower Second street, on which a church was begun but never
completed, owing to a defective title to the property. Business
complications having arisen in consequence of this, a compromise was effected and the building surrendered. In May, 1858,
the vestry purchased of the board of education the lot on which
the church now stands, and subsequently the present building
was erected and opened for divine service the first time on the
19th of December, 1858, the Rev. G. B. Sturgess being rector at
the time. On the 12th of April, 1859, the church was consecrated with the name of St. Peter's, Rt. Rev. Charles P. McIlvaine, D. D., officiating. During the years which have inter-
vened since that time, the parish has been served by eleven rec-
tors, whose efforts for the glory of God and the salvation of
souls we feel have not been in vain. There have been periods
of clouds as well as of sunshine; at times the condition of affairs
was very promising, and again, there have been discouragements
which required the strongest faith to face bravely. Looking
over our records, however, we find sufficient testimony as to the
fidelity of the workers in St. Peter's Parish, to encourage us,
and cause us to devoutly thank God. The names of some of

the most honored citizens of our town appear on our communion list, and the numbers who have confessed God by baptism and confirmation assures us that the love of souls has not been lacking among the churchmen of Gallipolis. Many of them have gone to their reward, and hence the memory of what has been done among us is doubly sacred, in that we have our representatives in that land where all is righteous.

To recall by name the ministers who have served our people here would be but to emphasize what has been said in regard to the work. This building should be held in sacred memory by our people. At this chancel rail have your children been given to God in baptism. Here the vows of God have been taken by which many of you have enlisted in the armies of righteousness. Up these aisles have swept the bridal trains, and from this sacred place have fair and loving brides and happy bridegrooms gone forth to fight together life's great battle. Before this chancel have reposed for the last time the forms of those we loved, who have answered the summons of death's angel, and from that door been called home to their last resting places. Hallowed, indeed, is the place, being the "House of God;" to many it has been the "gate of Heaven." The effect of these meditations should be of a strengthening character. We should, by the light of past blessings see the glories of future success. Remembering the days of old, and considering the years of past generations, we gladly believe that St. Peter's Parish is recorded in the Everlasting Book as one of the mediums by which men have learned the truth which has made them free. May this parish continue its work of usefulness even unto the far distant future, and by it may every year bring into the fold of safety many such as shall be saved. God is true to His people, and is a "rewarder of those who diligently seek Him," and the blessings of the life which is gone are indications of that which is to come to "the faithful in Christ Jesus," for He "will never leave us nor forsake us."

"The flood of years," which has borne our city so far upon the stream of time, is bearing us onward. As we assemble here to-day to consider the lives of those of the past, whose places we now fill, others will, ere long, have our lives to think of, when we shall have gone hence to join the unnumbered hosts "of that other living, called run with patience life's race, or will we be as warnings of the dead." Will our example be such as to inspire them to the consequences of unfaithful lives? These are thoughts which suggest themselves in connection with what has been said, and their consideration rests with each individual, for "'all must stand before the judgment seat of Christ."

REJOICING IN DIVINE WORKMANSHIP.

Abstract of a sermon preached by the Rev. George W. Lasher, D. D., editor of the *Journal and Messenger*, Cincinnati, Ohio, in the First Baptist Church. Text: Psalm CXLIX, 2. "Let Israel rejoice in Him that made him; let the children of Zion be joyful in their King."

There are two ways of writing history; the one to refer every event to some over-ruling power superior to man and to human agency; the other to find the spring of every event in some other antecedent event. Israel was taught to understand that, whatever the instrumentalities used, it is God who works in and through and by means of the instrument, so that, in the last analysis, it is Jehovah who casts down or raises up, creates or destroys. This was the idea in the mind of the author of the psalm and of the text. And the principle which underlies the history of the ancient Israel also underlies the history of the modern "Israel," the people of God, to-day.

In attempting to direct the thought of the Baptists of Gallipolis, on this centenary occasion, this principle must not be forgotten nor overlooked. We must take into account the divine guidance, the evidence of a divine purpose, the development from small beginnings, the evolutions and the retrogressions, the renewed impulses and the recurring relapses which have characterized the history of the Baptists; we should mark well, and with peculiar joy, the onward march, the increasing influence and the present dominance of the great principles which give occasion to cite the language of the psalmist.

Let us try to answer three questions:

1. Who are the Baptists?
2. Whence are the Baptists?
3. Whose workmanship are the Baptists?

1. Who are the Baptists? We answer, *They are a peculiar people.* They stand before the world as exponents and advocates of truths and principles which it is liable to forget; which, indeed, have been overlooked again and again, and which would now be lost sight of but for those who are called by our name.

Baptists stand for what is known as "*a converted* (regenerated) *church membership.*" With all their faults and with all their failures to conform their practice to their theory, Baptists have never forgotten the fundamental principle of their historic faith, viz.: that the visible Church of Christ should be made up of those, and those only, who give evidence of having been born of God, whose hope of eternal life rests upon the atonement of Christ, in which the professor of religion has come to have a personal interest. We do not deny that some of our neighbors seem to themselves to be doing the same things. But the difference between them and us is in this—that they sprinkle water, in the name of the Trinity, upon the faces of their children, and call them members of the church, "members of the body of Christ;" or they tell us that, having been born of parents who are church members, the infants are church members, and are, therefore, entitled to receive recognition as such; or, they tell us that baptism is intended and appointed of God to be the means or instrument for the perfecting of the work of the word in the heart, so that, while repentance and faith may be present, it is needful that baptism be received, in order that sin may be remitted. It is readily seen, therefore, that Baptists are a peculiar people. They stand for the great principle which they find inwrought in the word of God, and which was the foundation of the Apostolic church. For its vindication they point to the New Testament and to the history of the Apostolic age.

2. *Baptists stand for an entire separation between Church and State.* Jealous as they are for the gospel; anxious as they are that all the nations may come to a knowledge of the truth; untiring as they are in efforts to carry the gospel to the ends of the earth: pioneers in modern missions, they yet ask nothing of the State. They delight in quoting that saying of the Master, "Render unto Cæsar the things that are Cæsar's, and unto God the things that are God's." They are not willing that those who have no interest in the God of the Bible, who profess no allegiance to the Christ of Calvary, shall be taxed to maintain the institutions of Christianity. They do not believe that Christianity can be best and permanently promoted by legal enactments, nor that human governments have anything to do with the religious

life of the people. They ask simply that they be free to exercise their own faith, and to practice according to their own convictions; that they have opportunity to make known their views and exemplify their practice before the world, with none to interfere, either to aid or hinder. Baptists are not politicians. They say to legislators, "Gentlemen, hands off. Let religion alone. We ask nothing of you, except that you unbind and loose." The first amendment to the constitution of the United States was secured by Baptists—that section which says: "Congress shall make no law respecting an establishment of religion, or prohibiting the free exercise thereof." Baptists have labored, and others have entered into their labors, not knowing whence came the blessings in which they often rejoice.

3. *Baptists stand for a faithful obedience to the commands of the Lord Jesus Christ.* They do not profess to be above criticism. They are too painfully aware that they do not, in all things, come up to the divine requirements. They often quote to themselves that caution of their Lord against straining out the gnat and swallowing the camel. But they do not wilfully minimize, nor obscure, nor change a commandment of their Master. They understand that the Lord Jesus gave a commandment to "disciple" the nations and to baptize the believing—the discipled—and no others, in the name of the Father, the Son, and the Holy Ghost. They dare not alter the terms of that commandment. They believe that baptism is given to be an emblematic testimony to faith in the Christ, because of His death as an atonement for sin and His resurrection to a new and glorified life. They believe that, in order to show forth these great ideas and to perpetuate them before the world, it is requisite that the believer be buried with Christ, "in the likeness of his death," and be raised again "in the likeness of his resurrection." They therefore repudiate all else that is called by the name of baptism, and practice only that which they have received from the Lord by example and precept.

For these reasons Baptists do not shrink from the penalty of being called "a peculiar people."

2. Whence are the Baptists? Their own answer is, Of Christ and his Apostles.

1. They refuse to regard as authoritative anything that originated this side of the New Testament. It matters little to them what "the Fathers" of the second century taught, or what the Church of that century practiced. Those things may be of historical importance and interest; but whatever the Church of the second century taught, as distinguished from the teachings of the Church of the first century, that is to be distrusted and rejected. They find that views cherished by them were held by individuals and small communities, during all the ages by John Wycklif, John Huss, and others; but they care little for these, except so far as they bore witness to the truth.

2. They find that, at the time of the great religious awakening in Europe, in the sixteenth century, not only Martin Luther, Staupitz, Cajetan, Bullinger, Melancthon and their associates were thinking and reading the word of God, but that others, a mighty host, were thinking and searching the scriptures, "whether those things were so." They find that among these were such men as Simon Stumpf, Conrad Grebel, Felix Mantz, Balthazar Hubmeier, George Blaurock, and a host of others, men of learning, priests of the Church of Rome, who had come to doubt the correctness of her teaching and practice; earnest students of the Bible, both in the Hebrew and the Greek; and that these men, with their associates, became convinced of the error of infant baptism, requiring of each member of their order a personal profession of faith in the Lord Jesus Christ, and baptism on the ground of such profession. They find that these men refused to have their children sprinkled, and for this reason many of them suffered death by fire and water, or by the sword. These were the Swiss "Anabaptists," from whom we date the rise of the Baptists of England and America.

As to the sword, these men said: "It is not to be used to defend either the gospel or those who receive it." As to baptism, they said: "From the scriptures we learn that baptism signifies that by faith in the blood of Christ our sins have been washed away and we have died to sin and walk in newness of life." Concerning infant baptism, they said: "We believe the Scriptures teach that all children who have not arrived at the knowledge of good and evil are saved by the sufferings of Christ."

The doctrines of these men passed down the Rhine to Holland, and thence across the Channel to England, where, in the next century (the seventeenth), they were cherished by such men as William Kiffin, Benjamin Keach, John Bunyan, and others. The Westminster Assembly met in 1642, and it was not till 1647 that the Confession was adopted and published; but in 1643, "seven congregations" of Baptists in the city of London, agreed upon a Confession which challenges admiration to-day, and which there has been but little occasion to alter.

In 1631 (twelve years before the formulation of the Confession above named) Roger Williams, a graduate of Pembroke College, Oxford, and a minister of the Church of England, arrived in Massachusetts. He was an inquirer after truth, little regardful what others might think or do. He became pastor of a Congregational Church in Salem, Massachusetts, but soon began to put forth ideas for which the colonists around him were not prepared. In 1635, he was banished from the colony, and in January, 1636, he landed at Wheet Cheer rock, in Rhode Island. In March, 1639, he was baptized by Ezekiel Holliman, and having in turn baptized Holliman and ten others, formed a Church which is held to still exist and to be the oldest Baptist Church on the American Continent—the first Baptist Church of Providence, Rhode Island. In 1638 (three years after the arrival of Williams and one year before his baptism), Hanserd Knollys, likewise a minister of the Church of England, who had become dissatisfied with the practices of that Church, arrived in Massachusetts, having come to escape the persecution to which he was subjected in his own country. He became pastor of a Congregational, or Puritan Church, in Dover, New Hampshire, and in the course of three years, had made such progress in the direction of the truth that, with a portion of his congregation, he became a Baptist. Soon after, he was recalled to England by his enfeebled father and there became one of the leading Baptists of his age; but the portion of his Dover Church which accepted his teachings removed, first to Long Island, New York, and and thence to New Jersey, where they formed the Baptist Church Piscataway, which still exists. About the same time other men of similar views arrived in the country from England,

and settled, some in Rhode Island, others in Pennsylvania, and others in Delaware. They all came to hold the same views of Bible doctrine and to practice according to the same rule.

3. Whose workmanship are the Baptists? They are frank to say that they *did not make themselves*. They have, at all times, regarded the Omnipotent God as both the author and the finisher of their faith. No people has more frequently or more sincerely quoted that scripture, "Not by might nor by power, but by my Spirit, saith the Lord." They have not been a worldly-wise people. They have never depended upon kings and governors for the advancement of their principles. For, though they have been among the most loyal and patriotic of citizens, their rulers have regarded their lives as of but little account, and have been willing to see them exterminated. Such were the pains and penalties imposed upon them during the first two hundred years of their history that their growth in numbers was very slow, and they came to almost regard it a crime (as the State regarded it, and as it is now regarded in Russia) for one to proselyte, or put forth efforts to win others to a knowledge of the truth. In Switzerland, Zwingle (who looked with favor upon the views of Grebel and Blaurock, until he saw that they involved the principles of a pure church) became their most bitter enemy. Hubmeier was burned; Mantz was drowned; Blaurock was whipped and banished; Hetzer was beheaded; Grebel, Hottinger and innumerable others were imprisoned, while the rest of them fled the country. In England, the Dutch and Flemish "anabaptists" were the peculiar horror of Henry VIII, when he was wresting his subjects out of the hands of the Pope. When the wilderness of the New World began to attract attention as an asylum for the oppressed—especially for those whose religious convictions rendered them obnoxious to home laws—it was found that not only Puritans of the Cotton Mather stripe, but those of more radical convictions, were ready to brave the sea and the land of the savage that they might enjoy what they could not have in their native land.

And here again the growth of the Baptists was slow, at first, and their churches were sporadic. But when the revolution of 1776 had been accomplished, and the first amendment of the Constitution had been adopted (in 1789), immediately they began to increase in numbers and to put on the strength of their Maker, God. At the time of the adoption of the amendment to the Constitution (that which placed them upon an equality with any other religious denominations) the Baptists of the United States numbered less than 65,000, or about one to every 56 of the population. In 1812, less than twenty years after, they were as one to thirty-eight; in 1832, as one to thirty-three; in 1852, as one to thirty; in 1872, as one to twenty-five, and in 1889, as one to twenty-one. And all this has been achieved without a hierarchy, without a bishropic, with no great court to which difficulties can be referred, and notwithstanding it is required of every person proposing to unite with the Baptist Church that he give to the brotherhood "a reason for the hope that is within him," and that he receive the unpopular rite, a baptism beneath the surface of the water in the name of the Father, the Son and the Holy Spirit. These things are marvelous in our eyes. For the growth of the past century we can give no adequate reason, except that *God is in it.*

PROGEEDINGS, REPORTS, ETC.

OF THE

FIFTH AND SIXTH

ANNUAL MEETINGS

OF THE SOCIETY

AND

ACCOMPANYING PAPERS.

MINUTES

OF THE

Fifth Annual Meeting of the Society,

HELD IN

COLUMBUS, MARCH 6 AND 7, 1890.

The Society convened in the hall of the House of Representatives at 7:30 p. m., and was called to order by the President, F. C. Sessions, Esq. The usual annual address of the President was omitted, as the reports of the committees and officers would cover all essential points. Dr. Edmund Cone Brush, of Zanesville, was introduced and read an address upon "The Pioneer Physicians of the Muskingum Valley." The address is printed elsewhere in this volume.

At the conclusion of the address the President introduced Prof. George Frederick Wright, of Oberlin College, who gave an interesting and instructive address on "The Ice Age in North America," illustrated by stereopticon views. It was hence of a nature precluding its publication. At its conclusion the thanks of the society were voted both Dr. Brush and Prof. Wright, after which a recess was taken until 2 p. m., the next day.

Friday, March 7th. The Society met in the committee rooms of the Senate. The Secretary presented a summary of the year's work, and outlined the policy of the society for the coming year. The annual reports of the Secretary and Treasurer were presented and referred to the Executive Committee. The consolidation of the society and State Library were discussed. The unwillingness of many members of the General

Assembly to such a plan was presented, and it was decided to postpone the matter. A plan to raise a publication fund was brought forward by the Secretary. The plan was to permit all active members to pay at one time such a sum of money necessary in addition to what each had paid as an active member, to make the amount $50. The plan was favorably received, and was referred to the Executive Committee with power to act.

The minutes of the previous annual meeting having been printed as approved by the Executive Committee, were approved by the Society.

The president appointed a committee to nominate five trustees for the term of three years. The secretary made a statement of the valuable collections and publications in charge of the society, and the necessity for better arrangements for their care and preservation, and that under existing conditions the society was obliged to refuse to accept valuable specimens that had been offered to them. The passage of some measures by the legislature would provide such means and place these collections under the charge of the State.

Professor G. F. Wright made a few pointed remarks on the necessity of some steps being taken for the preservation of the ancient earth works in Ohio, and offered the following resolution, which was adopted:

Resolved, That the members of the Archæological and Historical society are heartily in favor of the objects aimed at in Senator Oren's Senate joint resolution looking to the preservation of Fort Ancient, and that we do all in our power to aid said committee and the legislature in devising some plan whereby this great prehistoric work may be preserved.

The proposed purchase by the State of 1200 copies of Mr. Henry Howe's work on Ohio was discussed, and the following resolution was adopted:

Resolved, That this society heartily approves of the purchase by the State of Ohio of 1200 copies of Mr. Henry Howe's Historical Collections of Ohio as not only valuable for the purpose of securing exchanges for the State library, but as a means of extending the circulation of the work and as an act of needed justice to Mr. Howe to help him to complete publication.

That we also recommend a liberal subscription to the Historical Collections by the members of this society and all other citizens of Ohio to create and sustain an intelligent sentiment of State pride in the present and coming generations.

The committee to nominate five trustees reported the following names: Dr. N. S. Townshend, Columbus; Rev. Wm. E. Moore, Columbus; E. C. Dawes, Cincinnati; Israel H. Harris, Waynesville; Prof. G. F. Wright, Oberlin. The report was approved and the foregoing named gentlemen elected.

The society then adjourned.

F. C. SESSIONS, President.

A. A. GRAHAM, Secretary.

MEETING OF THE TRUSTEES.

Friday, March 7, 1890, the trustees met in the senate committee room and elected the following officers: President, F. C. Sessions; Secretary, A. A. Graham; Treasurer, S. S. Rickly.

The following members were elected to serve as Executive Committee: F. C. Sessions, S. S. Rickly, H. A. Thompson, Daniel J. Ryan, Rev. W. E. Moore, Dr. N. S. Townshend, Prof. S. C. Derby.

The Executive Committee was authorized to appoint such standing committees as might be found necessary, and also to examine and approve the reports of the officers, and to publish the same in the society's publication. The committee was further authorized to transact such business as might be necessary.

The Board of Trustees then adjourned.

F. C. SESSIONS, President.

A. A. GRAHAM, Secretary.

THE SOCIETY'S ANNUAL DINNER.

At this meeting the holding of a dinner in connection with the annual meeting was inaugurated. The practice has long been successfully maintained in older societies and it was determined to try the feature in Ohio. The dinner was a most enjoyable event, and it was decided to continue this feature. The dinner was held at the American House, and at the conclusion the following toasts were offered and responded to: "The Ohio Man in History," Governor James E. Campbell; "Ohio's Sons and Daughters of the American Revolution," Col. W. A. Taylor; "The Yankee and the Buckeye," Judge M. D. Follett; "The Western Reserve and New England," Hon. O. J. Hodge; "The Maumee Valley," Hon. Chas. P. Griffin; "The Old Schoolmaster," Dr. John Hancock; "The American College in American History," Dr. W. H. Scott; "Ohio's First Governor —Edward Tiffin," Hon. Dan'l J. Ryan; "Our Forefathers,"* Hon. M. T. Corcoran; "Our Foremothers," Mrs. Delia A. Williams.

At the conclusion of the addresses the Society adjourned.

---

* Senator Corcoran being called away this toast was omitted.

THE PIONEER PHYSICIANS OF THE MUSKINGUM VALLEY.

BY EDMUND CONE BRUSH, A. M., M. D.

A Paper Read at the Fifth Annual Meeting of the Society, in the Hall of the House of Representatives, at Columbus, March 6, 1890.

Generation after generation of pioneers have gradually carried the star of empire westward, until it would seem as if the work of the pioneer was nearly done. As these hardy and adventurous men and women have gradually opened up the new world to civilization, they have been closely followed or accompanied by members of the medical profession. These physicians have shared the hardships and privations of the early settlers, joined them in their joys and sorrows, helped them to build their rude homes and to defend them against the natives of the forest. To the loyal Buckeye, and especially to the descendants of the Ohio pioneers, Marietta is a hallowed spot. Branching out from Marietta, the pioneers followed the two great water courses uniting there, and dotted their banks with settlements. In these early settlements the members of the medical profession took a modest but important part. Forty years ago the late Dr. Samuel Hildreth, of Marietta, wrote a series of biographical sketches of the early physicians of that place. These sketches have a short preface, in which occurs the following:

"As a class, no order of men have done more to promote the good of mankind and develop the resources and natural history of our country than the physicians, and wherever the well-educated in that profession are found, they are uniformly seen on the side of order, morality, science and religion."

What is here given in regard to the Marietta physicians is obtained almost entirely from Dr. Hildreth's sketches and from his "Pioneer History."

Doctor Thomas Farley, the son of a revolutionary officer, emigrated to Marietta in 1788 from Ipswich, Massachusetts. He went with the little colony in the spring (April 20) of 1789 to make the settlement some twenty miles up the river, where Bev-

erly and Waterford now stand.   In 1790 he was back in Marietta, helping Doctor True attend smallpox cases.   Six died of
the disease "who took it by infection," and out of over one
hundred inoculated by the doctors, two died.   In 1791 he was
back at Waterford and one of the inmates of Fort Frye.   Col.
Joseph L. Barker, one of the early settlers, said of him: "He
was a modest, amiable young man, always ready to obey the
calls of humanity, and had the good will and confidence of all
who knew him."   Dr. Hildreth says: "The country being
new, and but a few people in the settlements, he became dis-
couraged, and returned to his former home in the autumn of
1790."   This date must be a mistake or a misprint, as Dr. Hildreth in his history, and Horace Nye in his "Reminiscences,"
both speak of Dr. Farley as being in Fort Frye, and Fort
Frye was built in 1791.   He probably went back in that year.
During his short stay he nobly fought one of the most loathsome
of diseases, and shared the hardships of an Indian war.   The
date of his birth and death is not known.

Dr. Solomon Drown was a native of Rhode Island and came
out to Marietta in the summer of 1788 as one of the proprietors
and agents of the Ohio Land Company.   It does not appear that
he intended to settle in the place as a physician, although he
attended General Varnum as consulting physician in the sickness
(consumption) of which he died in January, 1789.   Dr. Drown
was educated at Brown University, Rhode Island, and was a
man "of literature and classic elegance as a writer."   The
directors of the Ohio Company selected him to pronounce the
eulogy at the funeral of General Varnum.   He also delivered
the first anniversary (April 7, 1789) address commemorative of
the landing of the pioneers.   At the breaking out of the Indian
war, Dr. Drown returned to Rhode Island, and was appointed
professor of botany and natural history in Brown University.

Dr. Jabez True, the first physician to make the territory his
life-long home, was born in Hampstead, New Hampshire, in
1760.   His father was a minister, and in the French war served
as chaplain of a colonial regiment.   He was the father of ten
children, and in addition to his pastoral duties prepared young
men for college.   Among his students was his son Jabez.   The

latter received his medical education under the preceptorship of Dr. Flagg, of Hampstead, and having completed his course in medicine before the end of the revolutionary war, at once entered the service of his country as surgeon on a privateer. The ship was wrecked on the coast of Holland and the crew was taken in and kindly cared for by the Hollanders. Dr. True remained in Holland until the close of the war, when he returned and settled in Gilmantown, New Hampshire. Staying in that place but a few years, he came to the then far western country, and early in the summer of 1788 landed at Marietta. The settlement was only a few months old, very small, and the country was one vast forest. Dr. True seems to have been of the same sturdy stuff as those who came before him. He built himself a log cabin to be used as an office and settled himself to business.

When the Indian war broke out in 1791, Dr. True was appointed surgeon's mate to the troops employed by the Ohio Company's directors, with a salary of $22.00 per month. Dr. Hildreth says: "This salary was a welcome and timely aid during the years of privation which attended the war, and sorely tried the resources of the most able among the inhabitants." This appointment was held until the close of the war. "During the most gloomy and disheartening periods schools were kept up by the inhabitants." Dr. True taught school a part of the time in a large lower room of one of the block houses in the garrison at "the point."

In 1790 smallpox broke out in the settlement at Marietta. In 1793 this same disease invaded the Farmers' Castle at Belpre, twelve miles below Marietta, on the Ohio. "A meeting of the inhabitants was at once called, and it was voted (as there was no chance of escaping it, cooped up as they were in the narrow walls of a garrison), to send to Marietta for Dr. True to come down and inoculate them in their own dwellings. The doctor accepted the invitation, and Farmers' Castle became one great hospital, containing beneath each roof more or less persons sick with this loathsome disease. The treatment of Dr. True was very successful and, out of nearly a hundred cases, not one died. There being no roads or bridges at this time, Dr. True's visits to the different settlements were made in a canoe. In making trips down the Ohio, by keeping in the middle of the stream there was comparative safety, but when returning it was necessary to keep near the shore and take the chances of a bullet from an Indian rifle. Dr. True made several narrow escapes, but a kind providence seemed to have protected him and saved him to administer to the relief of his fellow men. After the war was over Dr. True took a step up in the world, and built himself a frame house and office, and began clearing and cultivating a small farm on the Ohio, a short distance above Marietta. In 1796 he united with the Congregational Church and for many years was a deacon. In 1806 he married Mrs. Sarah Mills, widow of Captain Charles Mills. " She was a cheerful, humble and sincere Christian, with a lively, benevolent temperament, ever ready to aid the doctor in his works of charity." They had no children, but the children of Mrs. True were treated with all the love and tenderness he could have bestowed upon his own."

By this time the settlers had increased in numbers and spread out over the country. Dr. True, being the leading physician, his visits extended twenty or thirty miles through the forest. He followed the Indian trails marked by " blazes " on the trees, and swam his horse across the streams.

One of Dr. True's strongest characteristics was charity ; and these long, lonesome rides were made to the poor with the same willingness as to those who were able to pay. He gave freely of what he had, often depriving himself. During the last year of his life he was county treasurer. This office gave him additional means with which to help on charitable and religious work. His house was the stopping place for Congregational and Presbyterian ministers who visited the town. Samuel J. Mills, the projector of foreign missions, spent two weeks with Dr. True during the year 1812, and instituted the Washington County Bible Society, which is still in existence. Dr. True was tall and spare, with simple, but not ungraceful manners. His eyes were gray and small, one being destroyed by a disease of the optic nerve; with full, projecting brows; nose large and acquiline; forehead rather low, but face mild and expressive of benevolence. He was a man of whom no enemy could say hard things, and whom everybody loved and respected. He died in

1823, of the prevailing epidemic fever, aged sixty-three years. "His memory is still cherished by the descendants of the early pioneers for his universal charity, simplicity of manners and sincere piety." The man's name seems to have been emblematic of the man, and his life seems to have been one of steadfast duty to those around him and to his God. Although occupying an humble position in the settlement of the great Northwest territory, Dr. True filled that position to the best of his physical and mental strength. He fell with his face to the foe, and while trying to alleviate the sufferings of others. What man can do more?

The late Dr. S. P. Hildreth, began the practice of medicine in Hempstead, New Hampshire, and boarded in the family of John True, a brother of the doctor. Through Mr. True, Dr. Hildreth learned that there was a good opening for a young physician in Marietta and came to that place in 1806. Drs. True and Hart were the only physicians in practice when Dr. Hildreth arrived. Thus it was that the man who has done more than any other to make us acquainted with pioneer history came to Ohio.

Drs. Farley, Drown and True all came to Marietta during the summer of 1788. It is not known which one arrived first.

Dr. Nathan McIntosh was born in Needham, Massachusetts, in 1768. He was educated at Cambridge and came to Marietta in 1789. His journey west was prolonged by an attack of smallpox that laid him up at Meadville, Pennsylvania. In 1791, Dr. McIntosh was appointed surgeon's mate to Fort Frye at Waterford. At first he was employed by the Ohio Company and afterward by the government. He remained at Fort Frye about two years, and during this time—May 23, 1792—he was married to Rhoda, the daughter of Deacon Enoch Shepherd, of Marietta. In July, 1793, the people of Clarksburg, Virginia, were in need of a physician and sent to Marietta for Dr. McIntosh. The request was accompanied by a company of soldiers to escort the doctor to that place. Mrs. McIntosh, with a baby six weeks old and a sister, went with the doctor. There were no roads or public houses on the way, so that when night came they camped out. In order to keep the baby from crying and thus attract the Indians, it was dosed with paregoric and a handkerchief used to suppress its cries. This baby grew to be Colonel Enoch Shepherd McIntosh, one of the most respected and best known citizens of the Muskingum valley. He died not long since in his ninety-sixth year. Think of the bravery of that young mother and her sister! Imagine if you can a journey on horseback eighty miles through the forests, in constant danger from Indians! Imagine camping out at night with the sky for a covering and a six-weeks-old baby to care for! No truer, nobler, or more heroic women ever lived than those who helped to settle the great Northwest territory. Their many good qualities are reflected in the younger generations of Buckeye women.

Dr. McIntosh came back to Marietta in two years and remained there until he died, September 5, 1823. He was among the victims of the fever epidemic of that year. When first married the doctor and his wife were members of the Presbyterian church. Afterward he joined the "Methodist Society;" finally, he came to believe in the universal salvation and held that belief until the end. He lectured and wrote a great deal on religious subjects, and published a book on "Scripture Correspondencies." He was violently opposed to secret societies and slavery. Dr. McIntosh was socially inclined and fond of society. His rich and fashionable dress and gentlemanly manners greatly promoted his favor with the community. He excelled in surgery and made quite a reputation in that line. During the latter years of his life Dr. McIntosh devoted himself to brick-making and contracting. One of the doctor's last acts was to ride to Macksburg to be at the death-bed of his oldest daughter. Three weeks more and the doctor, too, had gone to his reward.

Dr. William Pitt Putnam, a grand-son of General Israel Putnam, was born in Brooklyne, Connecticut, December 11, 1770, and came to Marietta in 1792. He spent part of his time with a brother in Belpre, and in 1794 went back to his eastern home. In 1795 he married Bertha Glyssan and came back to the new territory during that year. In 1799 he purchased a tract of land eight miles above Marietta, on the Ohio river, and turned his attention to clearing and cultivating it. In 1800 he died of bilious fever.

"In person, Dr. Putnam was tall and commanding, with a cheerful, lively countenance and genteel address."

Dr. Josiah Hart was born in Berlin, Connecticut, about 1738, and graduated at Yale in 1762. He had entertained the idea of studying for the ministry, but gave it up and studied medicine under Dr. Potter, of Wallingford, Connecticut. "In 1765 he married Miss Abigail Sherman, of Stonington, and commenced the practice of medicine in Wethersfield." He served as a regimental surgeon during the revolution. In 1778, his first wife having died, he married Mrs. Abigail Harris. This made his second Abigail. The doctor "represented his town in the legislature, and often filled the more important town offices, as well as that of deacon in the church." In 1796 his second wife died and he came to Marietta. Here he married Anna Moulton. He was one of the first deacons of the Congregational church at Marietta. "In 1811, having become too aged to practice, he moved to a farm ten miles from Marietta. He died in August, 1812, of spotted fever, aged seventy-four years. His wife died a few hours after, and they were both buried the same day. In person, Dr. Hart was below the medium size, but well formed; countenance mild, pleasing and intelligent. In manners very gentlemanly, and kind, exhibiting a true Christian spirit in his intercourse with his fellow men."

Dr. William B. Leonard was born in London in the year 1737. "When in the prime of life he served as a surgeon in the British navy. About the year 1794, having lost his wife, he decided on removing to the United States to be concerned in a woolen factory. For this purpose he secretly packed up the machinery and put it on board the vessel in which he had engaged his passage. Before he sailed it was discovered by the officers of the customs, and being a contraband article prohibited by the laws of England to be transported out of the realm, he was arrested and confined for some time in prison. Being finally discharged he came to America about the year 1797."

The following year he was practicing his profession in Newburyport, Massachusetts, where he again married, but his wife dying soon after, he moved to Marietta in 1801, and boarded in the family of Mr. William Moulton. Here he again renewed the practice of medicine, and in 1802 married Lydia Moulton, the maiden daughter of his landlord and sister to the wife of Dr. Hart. He appears to have been a skilled surgeon, but was rough and coarse in his manners and language, retaining the habits acquired in his naval service. He retained and kept up the fashion of the showy dress, such as prevailed in the days of Queen Elizabeth, which in the backwoods of Ohio excited the curiosity of a people accustomed to the most simple attire. His favorite costume was a blue broadcloth coat, trimmed in gold lace, and enormous gilt buttons, a waistcoat of crimson velvet, with large pocket flaps, and small clothes of the same material, a pair of silk or worsted stockings drawn over his slender legs, with large silver buckles at the knees and in his shoes. On his head he wore a full flowing periwig (of which he had six or eight varieties), crowned with a three-cornered or cocked beaver hat. Over the whole, when he appeared on the street, unless the weather was very hot, he wore a large scarlet colored cloak. This dress, with his gold-headed cane, always called forth the admiration and wonder of the boys, who followed close in his train, and were often threatened with his displeasure in not very civil language. When traveling on horseback to visit his patients, he road a coal black steed with long flowing mane and tail, the saddle and trappings of which were as antiquated and showy as his own dress." He died of consumption in 1806, aged sixty-nine years.

On a copper plate prepared before his death, he had the following engraved:

"Friend: for Jesus' sake forbear
To touch the dust enclosed here;
Blest is the man that spares this urn,
And he's a knave that moves my bones."

Which epitaph will be recognized as the one Shakespeare wrote for his own tomb, but slightly changed by Dr. Leonard.

Dr. John Baptiste Regnier was born in Paris in the year 1769. He received a good education, but studied chiefly architecture and drawing. He also attended a course of lectures on scientific subjects, including medicine. His father was a loyalist, and when his sons were called upon to enroll themselves in the ranks of the reformers, he collected all the money he could and sent them out of the country. The doctor was in his twentieth year, and with his brother, Modeste, aged fourteen years, joined a company of emigrants and embarked for the United States. In May, 1790, these brothers landed at Alexandria, and finally reached Marietta in October following, with a number of their companions. In a few days they all started down the Ohio river to settle on a tract of land purchased before leaving France. Landing at what they supposed to be their purchase, they at once erected houses. The next summer they spent in clearing land, only to find their title was not good and they were in a wilderness without a home. About this time the Indian war broke out, and the emigrants abandoned their homes and moved to other towns. Little Modeste had imbibed such a dread of the Indians, that he did not cease to importune his older brother, whom he looked upon as a father, until he decided on leaving the place and going to New York. Toward the last of February, 1792, they embarked in a large perogue, with a small party who had joined them, and proceeded up stream for Pittsburg. Near the head of Buffington's island, in passing around a fallen tree top, their vessel upset. They lost all their provisions and clothing, while they barely escaped with their lives to the shore. Among the other effects of the unfortunate Regnier then lost in the Ohio, was a curiously wrought octagonal cylinder of black marble, made with mathematical accuracy, eight or ten inches long and one in diameter. Several years after this curious stone was found on the head of a sand bar some distance below, and presented to an eastern museum as a relic of that singular but unknown race who built the mounds and earth-works in the valley of the Ohio. The spot where they were wrecked was many miles from any settlement, and the rest of their journey was made on foot. They suffered much for food and were made sick by eating the seeds of decayed pawpaws. They finally reached Pittsburg, and after resting a few days proceeded on to New York. Not finding employment here, the young Regniers went to Newfoundland, where there was a French settlement. In 1794 they returned to New York. For three years, in a land of strangers, with an imperfect knowledge of their language, destitute of all things but his head and his hands wherewith to procure a support for himself and brother, he was many times tempted to give up in despair and cease any further struggle for existence. But his buoyant French heart enabled him to resist such thoughts and kept him afloat in the wide sea of life.

After returning to New York he seems to have prospered and in 1796 he married Miss Content Chamberlain, the daughter of a tavern keeper in Unadilla, New York. Regnier had met her on his journeys. In 1800, unfortunate investments made him again a bankrupt and left him as destitute as when upset in the Ohio, eight years before. He now had a wife and two children to provide for and must make one more effort for a living. A lingering desire to see once more the beautiful shores of the Ohio, on which he had labored and suffered so much, still continued to haunt his imagination; and most especially his brother Modeste, now arriving at manhood, never ceased to importune him to return. Finally, determining to perfect himself to the healing art, he left his family with his wife's people and went to Washington, Pennsylvania, to be under Dr. Lamoine. After a year's study he went back for his family, and they started for the Ohio. In November, 1803, they landed at Marietta. A Frenchman living there offered the doctor 100 acres of land situated on Duck creek, nine miles from town. This the doctor bought on credit. By the aid of neighbors, the Regniers soon had a log cabin built and were settled on their farm. It was soon spread through the country that the new settler was "a French doctor," and as there was no one of his calling within a circuit of twenty or thirty miles, except in Marietta, he was soon employed by the sick in every direction. For several months he visited his patients, who were within six or eight miles distance, on foot. He did this until able to purchase a horse. There was a good deal of sickness during the early years of the settlement on the creek, and also many cases of surgery, such as fractured limbs and wounds from axes. These he dressed in the neatest and most rapid manner. One singular case is worth reporting here. A man was thought to be mortally wounded by being injured from a fallen tree, which caught him under its extreme branches, bruising the flesh all over his body as if whipped with a thousand rods. So many blows paralyzed the heart and rendered him as cold as if dead. The doctor immediately ordered a large sheep to be killed and the skin stripped hastily off, wrapping the naked body of the man in the hot, moist covering of the animal. The effect was like a charm on the patient, removing all the bruises and the soreness in a few hours. In 1807, his brother Francis came out to Ohio and proposed to enter into partnership with him in a store at Marietta, Ohio. In order to afford educational advantages to his children, he decided to accept the proposition, and in February, 1808, left the farm. Before moving he went to Wheeling to select goods for the store. While away, Modeste was taken with fever and died a few days after the doctor returned. The shock of his death quite overwhelmed the doctor, especially as he thought that had he been home he could have saved him. No telegraph or fast trains in those days to bring him home in a few days. His brother Francis becoming dissatisfied moved away, taking the store with him. Soon after this the doctor purchased a drug store. Success now attended all his endeavors, and his wealth increased in full ratio with his family, which consisted of six sons and one daughter. About 1814 he enlarged his town possession by buying a square, which he improved by planting fruit trees and laying out a large flower garden ornamented with arbors and walks. It was a model for others and ultimately implanted a permanent taste for this refining art among the citizens of Marietta. He was an original member of the first incorporated medical society of Ohio in 1812. In 1818 he was elected county commissioner and assisted in drafting the model for the court house now remodeled. In May, 1819, he sold his property in town to Dr. Cotton and purchased three hundred and twenty acres of land on Duck creek, twenty-two miles from Marietta. Here he removed with his family having in view the establishing of his sons as farmers.

Dr. Regnier died in 1821, aged 52 years. His death was a severe loss to the community. Two of his sons became physicians.

Dr. Increase Mathews was born in New Braintree, Massa-

chusetts, December 22, 1772. He was the son of General Rufus
Putnam's older sister, Hulda, and Daniel Mathews. John
Mathews, who came out to Ohio with the original forty-eight,
was a brother. In 1798, Dr. Mathews came to Marietta on a
prospecting tour, and to visit relatives. His diary of this journey is in the possession of his descendants, and is a very interesting document. Under date of August 13, 1798, 1 P. M., is
found the following note: "Went with Mr. Edward Tupper to
call on Mr. Blennerhasset and his lady, by whom we were
politely received. Met Miss Sallie Loudon there on a visit. She
is on the whole an amiable girl, and possessed of many of those
qualities which make a good companion; kind, obliging, ever in
good spirits and free from affectation." The young doctor seems
to have been impressed, and human nature seems to have been
the same then as now. Under date of August 31, 1798, is the
following: "Attended a ball at Colonel Putnam's in Belpre.
We had a large collection of ladies, some from Marietta and the
Island, who made a brilliant appearance. Spent the evening
very agreeably." The ladies from the Island were, no doubt,
Mrs. Blennerhasset and her guest, Miss Loudon. After a pleasant visit, Dr. Mathews went back east and married (April 25,
1799) Abigail Willis, of Oakham, Massachusetts. In the fall of
1800, with his wife and baby, he again came to Marietta, arriving there October 4. The winter was spent in Marietta, and the
other half of the house in which they lived, was occupied by the
father of the late Governor Brough. In the spring of 1801 the
Mathews family moved to Zanesville, Ohio. This same year
General Rufus Putnam, his nephew, Dr. Mathews and Levi
Whipple purchased the land now composing the Seventh and
Ninth wards in that city, and laid it out into a town, which they
called Springfield, afterward Putnam. Dr. Mathews, after about
one year's stay in Zanesville, moved across the river to the newly
laid out town, and lived there the remainder of his life. He
was the first physician to permanently settle on the Muskingum
river above Marietta. In 1802 (June 14) the doctor's wife died,
and in 1803 (March 23) he married for his second wife Betsy,
daughter of Captain John Leavems. They were married in
Marietta at Major Lincoln's, who had married Betsy's sister,

Fannie. Possessing large landed interests, and having a taste for agriculture, Dr. Mathews retired from practice as other physians settled around him. He was a man of many accomplishments, with more than the usual amount of energy and push so characteristic of the pioneers. He established the first drug store and was one of the five original members of the first church organized in Muskingum county. Dr. Mathews sent to Spain for the first full-blooded Merino sheep brought to Ohio. These sheep were delivered in Washington, D. C., and hauled in a wagon through to Putnam, Ohio, by a man sent to Washington for that purpose.

In 1801, when Dr. Mathews went to Marietta to buy the land above mentioned, he had part of the way as his companion, John McIntire. These young men rode together, camped together the night out on the road, but neither mentioned his business. When they arrived at Marietta, Dr. Mathews turned up Washington street to go to his uncle (General Putnam's) office, whilst John McIntire went on to the tavern. The next day the two men found themselves bidding against each other on the same tract of land. John McIntire already owned a large tract where Zanesville proper now stands, but Dr. Mathews bid in the tract in question at four dollars and five cents an acre. Many years after it became blended with McIntire's tract in the City of Natural Advantages. The doctor enjoyed telling his grandchildren that the earliest distinct recollection of his childhood - was the ringing of the bells to celebrate the declaration of independence. He was a cultivated gentleman of the old school and a man whose energy and character were felt in his day, and are still exemplified in his descendants. He was an accomplished performer on the violincello, an entertaining and instructive conversationalist. His life was characterized by its simplicity and purity. He died June 6, 1856, full of years and with the high esteem of all his fellow townsmen, in the eighty-fourth year of his age, and is buried in Woodlawn Cemetery, which was part of his original purchase from the government in 1801.

In 1796, Dr. Jenner's great discovery of vaccination was announced to the medical world. When smallpox broke out in

Putnam in the fall of 1809. Dr. Mathews procured vaccine virus
and vaccinated himself and family. People in general had no
confidence in it and would not consent to it. In order to prove
its efficacy Dr. Mathews took his two little daughters, Abigail
and Sarah, aged six and seven years, who had been vaccinated,
into a house and up to the bedside of a patient very ill with vir-
ulent smallpox. The children did not take the disease and the
doctor triumphantly proclaimed the protecting powers of vaccination. The rest of the villagers were inoculated, but Dr.
Mathews' family was the only one that depended upon vaccination. So far as can be learned the doctor's family was among
the first, if not the first in Ohio, to be vaccinated.

Dr. Jesse Chandler was the second physician to settle in
Putnam. He was born in Vermont in 1764, and studied medicine in his native state. After practicing a few years he came
with his family to Ohio and located in the village of Putnam,
across the river from Zanesville, and now, as has been stated, a
part of that city. At that time there was but little difference in
the population of the two rival villages, both being quite small.
But in the year 1814 Zanesville was made the permanent county
seat with a fair prospect of being made the state capital, and
took the lead. In order to look after his land, Doctor Mathews
gladly relinquished his practice upon the arrival of Dr. Chandler. No other physician settled in Putnam while Dr. Chandler
lived. His practice, like Dr. Mathews', extended over all the
western part of the county and into the adjoining counties.
Traveling was, of course, done on horseback, and in the earlier
years without roads. Trails, or bridle-paths, led from house to
house, or from neighborhood to neighborhood. Dr. Chandler
spent a large part of his time in the saddle, but possessing an
unusually robust constitution, he was always ready to respond
to calls. The fees in those days were very much out of proportion to the time and labor expended. There being no pharmacists, every physician furnished his own medicines. The doctor's books were a curiosity. He would often ride a dozen miles,
furnish the medicine needed, and charge one dollar. Visits in
the village were fifty cents. When many of his people came to
settle, the credit side would read, by so much corn, or oats, or

potatoes, or cash, as the case might be, and by discount for the balance. Frequently the "by discount" was the larger part of the credit. Dr. Chandler did not become wealthy.

In the fall of 1809 a bad case of smallpox developed in the town. As might be expected there was a scare. Vaccination was not yet relied upon, and the doctor had not seen it sufficiently tried to be entirely satisfied with its protecting qualities. Some of the older people had been inoculated with smallpox, but the children, and many of the adults, had no protection. So all were made ready by the perscribed dieting, and a general inoculation took place. The inoculated cases all got along nicely, no deaths and no disfigurements. There were in the town a dozen or more transient persons, mostly young men, without friends. The doctor turned his house into a hospital, took these young men in, "without money or price," and carried them safely through. In the winter of 1813–14 an heretofore unknown epidemic broke out in Putnam, which for the want of a better name, was called "the cold plague." The attack came on with a congestive chill, unconsciousness soon followed, and death resulted in two or three days. Some recovered, but among the victims was Dr. Jesse Chandler. A true, self-sacrificing physician and man, he was ready for the summons and faced death as he had disease, without a tremor. His age was fifty years.

Dr. Daniel Bliss, son of Deacon Isaac Bliss, was born in Warren, Mass., April 10, 1761. He was educated in medicine in Springfield, Mass., and June 6, 1789, married Prudence, a sister of Dr. Jesse Chandler. They came out to Ohio in 1804 with (or about the same time as) Doctor Chandler. Doctor Bliss settled in Waterford (on the side of the river where Beverly now stands) but continued sickness led him to seek another location, and he removed to Chandler's salt works (now Chandlersville) a place twelve miles east of Zanesville. Settling on a farm the doctor intended retiring from practice, but there being no other physician in that section, the inhabitants kept him busy. For over twenty years he was the first and only physician in the settlement and his practice extended into what are now Guernsey, Noble and Morgan counties. The doctor kept his farm well stocked with good horses. He always rode horseback, and traveled fast. It was a good horse and rider that could keep up with him on his rounds. As a physician, Doctor Bliss was successful and popular. He was a man of strong opinions, and fearless in expressing them. He dared to do right, and take the consequences. In religious belief he was a Congregationalist. Doctor Bliss died March 17, 1842, age eighty-one years. At a ripe age he surrendered to a great reaper, and with a heavy credit on the Lamb's book of life he went to his reward.

Doctor Robert Mitchell was born in Westmoreland county, Pennsylvania, in 1778. He studied medicine there, and in 1808 married Catharine McCulloch. For a wedding trip the young couple came to Zanesville, Ohio, on horseback. When they settled in that place there were but twelve shingle roofed houses in it. The Indians were still there, but friendly, and would come to the doctor's house to see the white papooses. Dr. Mitchell served in the war 1812, and was afterward a general in the Ohio militia. In 1833 he was elected to Congress, but in 1835 was defeated for re-election by his Whig opponent. It is said that the rejoicing of the Whigs over their success, caused more drunkenness in Zanesville than ever was known there in one night. Doctor Mitchell died November 13, 1848.

Doctor Ziba Adams was, so far as can be learned, the first physician to settle in what is now Morgan county. Doctor Daniel Rusk, of Malta, made an earnest effort to find something of this physician. Just when Doctor Adams arrived, and just when he left, could not be ascertained. That he first settled some four miles above Malta, on the river, and afterward in Malta, is known. Taking the dates of other events as a criterion, the probabilities are that Doctor Adams came to the Muskingum Valley about 1815 or 1816 and left three or four years after. What little is known of him is to his credit; and he, no doubt, was of the same character as his colleagues in the valley.

Dr. Samuel Augustus Barker was probably the second physician to settle in Morgan county, and was certainly the first one to make it his permanent home. He settled in McConnelsville in 1818, one year after the place was laid out. Dr. Barker was born in Dutchess, County, N. Y. He received a thorough education, and graduated in medicine in time to serve in the war of 1812. Coming west soon after the war, the doctor first stopped at Williamsport, W. Va., a town across the Ohio from Marietta, where he taught school until he removed to McConnelsville. In the latter place he also taught school until his professional duties demanded all of his attention. In 1822 he was married to Eliza B. Shugert. Dr. Barker was the first county auditor and the first clerk of the court of Morgan county. He was the first postmaster in McConnelsville. He was sheriff four years and represented his county in the legislature for two terms. He ran for congress in 1843, but was defeated by his Whig opponent. Dr. Barker was an honest, upright gentlemen, and filled many positions of trust without a blemish on his character. His many social qualities made him universally popular. He died May 12, 1852.

Dr. Samuel Martin was born in Trowbridge, England, in 1796, and died in Zanesville, Ohio, May 25, 1873. When a young man, Dr. Martin attended school at Bath, and, living twenty miles from that place, he walked home every Saturday night. Sunday nights he would walk back in order to be on hand for school on Monday. He was apprenticed to a physician for a term of seven years, and received his medical education in London. He was a fellow of the Royal College of Surgeons, and an accomplished Latin, Greek and French scholar. In 1819 Dr. Martin came to McConnelsville, Ohio, and went into partnership with Dr. Barker. This partnership was soon dissolved by Dr. Martin moving into Bloom township. (He was the first physician in it.) He married Sarah Montgomery, a daughter of one of the early settlers. Dr. Martin would not send his children to school, but educated them himself, not only in the common school branches, but in Latin, Greek and French. He retired from practice early in life, and moved to Zanesville in 1856. He and many of his family were Deists. The doctor's belief was characterized by its sincerity, and he had his feelings sorely wounded once while serving on a jury. The judge took occasion in delivering a charge to say "that a man who did not believe in the Revelations was not fit to be a juror." Dr. Martin was a scholarly gentleman, a man of fine instincts and refined sensibilities.

Dr. Martin, in his younger days, was quite a pedestrian. Upon arriving in this country he landed at Philadelphia. From there he walked across the State of Pennsylvania to Olean, in western New York. Here he and his companion took a canoe and journeyed down the Allegheny and Ohio rivers to Louisville, Kentucky. Leaving the canoe here, Dr. Martin walked to Nashville, Tennessee. From this place he tramped through Kentucky to the Wabash river, opposite Shawneetown, Illinois; then on to East St. Louis, and from there through Illinois and Indiana to Zanesville, Ohio. Hearing of the newly developed salt industry down the Muskingum, Dr. Martin walked to Bloom township, Morgan county, and stopped at "Squire" Montgomery's, where he met his future wife. He soon moved into Mc-Connelsville and began the practice of medicine.

That journey on foot covered many hundreds of miles and part of it was made alone. Many nights were spent by the road side, as in parts of the country gone over settlements in those days were far between. Probably the first castor oil mill established west of the Allegheny mountains was built at Dresden by Drs. Nathan Webb, senior and junior. They came to the shores of the Waukatomiky in 1821 and cultivated the castor oil bean. Their mill was located on the "Little Prairie." Two lodges of Shawanese Indians were still there and interested spectators of this symptom of civilization. The doctors were not learned in their profession, but were the pioneer physicians of Dresden and evidently had confidence in castor oil. From whence they came or where they went I am not able to state.

It is impossible for us to fully appreciate the primitive manner in which these men practiced medicine. They had to be, in a degree, pharmacists and practical botanists. Roots and herbs were an important part of their armamentarium. Infusions and decoctions were the order of the day. The sugar-coated pill was then unknown. In fact the life of the modern physician is sugar-coated when compared with that of the pioneers. These men were obliged to be fertile in resources, apt in expedients, and ingenious in improvising. Compare, if you can, the log cabin office of one hundred years ago with the physician's office of to-day. Think of the progress made in medical science since the days of these men. Chloroform, cocaine, the hypodermic syringe, the fever thermometer, and hundreds of other things were unknown to them. Notwithstanding all the new ideas and inventions the rate of mortality, from the ordinary aches and ills of life, was about the same then as now.

In looking over the lives of these men we find general characteristics that are worthy of thought. They were interested and active in educational and religious matters. They were energetic and progressive beyond their times. They took an active part in politics and questions of State. If they were alive now they would probably let politics alone. They were brave men, for on their lonely travels in the earlier years they had to face the treachery of the Indian and the hunger of the wolves. The more the lives of these men are held up to view, the more sterling qualities we find to admire.

There were one or two more of the very early physicians about Marietta, Waterford and Zanesville of whom the writer could learn nothing, only that they had once lived in these places. Their descendants either could not be found, or when found could give no information.

MINUTES

OF THE

Sixth Annual Meeting of the Society,

HELD IN

COLUMBUS, FEBRUARY 18 AND 19, 1891.

Thursday, February 19th the society came to order in the State Library. There being present the following members: Wm. E. Moore, of Columbus; A. A. Graham, of Columbus; N. S. Townshend, of Columbus; H. A. Thompson, of Westerville; J. A. Anderson, of Columbus; L. B. Wing, of Newark; Geo. F. Bareis, of Canal Winchester; A. R. McIntire, of Mt. Vernon; D. J. Ryan, of Portsmouth; J. J. Janney, of Columbus; S. S. Rickly, of Columbus; Thos. E Van Horne, of Columbus; J. A. Shawan, of Columbus; J. C. Reeve, of Dayton; Cyrus Falconer, of Hamilton; B. D. Hills, of Columbus; Mrs. N. E. Lovejoy, of Columbus; Edw. Orton, of Columbus; R. Brinkerhoff, of Mansfield; John G. Doren, of Dayton; Thos. F. Moses Urbana; Rev. J. A. Snodgrass, of Columbus; A. H. Smythe, of Coumbus; Isaac Kagy, of Tiffin; Frank H. Leib, of Millersport; W. H. Morton, of Cincinnati; John T. Gale, of Columbus; Charles Parrett, of Columbus; Henry Howe, of Columbus; James Poindexter, of Columbus; Chas. P. Griffin, of Toledo; R. W. McFarland, of Oxford; Ralph Reamer, of Colnmbus.

In the absence of the President of the Society, F. C. Sessions, Rev. Wm. E. Moore, First Vice Presidsnt, presided. The Secretary, A. A. Graham, presented and read his annual report, which, upon motion, was accepted and ordered filed.

On motion of Mr. Doren, a committee was appointed to nominate to the society the names of five members to serve as trustees for three years. The chair appointed as such committee, Messrs. Doren, Anderson and Janney.

The report of the Treasurer, S. S. Rickly, was then read, and on motion approved, and on his request a committee was appointed to examine the books at a time suitable to its convenience. The chair appointed Messrs. Hancock and Townshend as such committee.

The Secretary made report of the circular issued to the members concerning proposed changes in the act of incorporation and by-laws regarding change of name, and increasing number of trustees. The circular had been sent to all of the members. Out of 54 replies, 52 voted for both changes and two against change of name. After discussion of the matter, involving the legality of such change, it was decided to refer the matter to the trustees with authority to take the necessary steps looking to a change of name.

The committee appointed to nominate five trustees for three years reported the following names: F. C. Sessions, of Columbus; Calvin S. Brice, of Lima; Robert W. Steele, of Dayton; A. R. McIntyre, of Mt. Vernon.

The report of the committee was accepted, and on motion the rules were suspended and the Secretary was instructed to cast the vote of the members in favor of the names proposed.

John S. Rhodes and George R. McDaniels, of Fort Recovery, presented the matter of the anniversary of the Centennial of Gen. St. Clair's defeat by the Indians in the site of that town in November, 1791, and asked that some action be taken by the society looking to the proper observance of this Centennial. After discussion of the matter, it was on motion referred to the Executive Committee with power to act.

A committee of the citizens of Newark came before the society, asking its aid and co-operation to secure the purchase and preservation of that part of the extensive system of earthworks near the city, known as the "octagon and circle." The design being that when purchased the State could use the land for the erection thereon of such institution as might be best.

After a full discussion, in which it was stated the society could not be engaged to secure for any distinct institution, the following resolution was, on motion of Mr. Wing, adopted:

Resolved, That the members of the Ohio State Archæological and Historical Society are heartily in favor of the passage of the bill introduced in the Senate by Senator Gaumer, for the purchase by the State of the pre-historic earthworks at Newark, and that the Executive Committee of this society be instructed to use all proper effort to aid the passage of the bill.

This done, after discussion of various miscellaneous matters, the society on motion adjourned to meet the following evening at the American Hotel, at 8 p. m., for the annual dinner.

Friday evening, 8 p. m., the society met in the parlors of the American House, and after a short time spent in a social way, met around the tables in the dining room. Rev. W. E. Moore, the First Vice President presiding. After the dinner, which was greatly enjoyed, the members were called to order by the chairman, Dr. Moore, and the following toasts were presented: "The Miami Valley," Governor James E. Campbell; "The Old School Mistress," Miss Margaret Sutherland; "Gen. Arthur St. Clair and the Indian Campaign of 1791," Gen. E. B. Finley; "The Maumee Valley in History," Hon. Chas. P. Griffin, "The Old Moravian Missions in Ohio," Hon. Wm. Farrar, "Ohio at the Columbian Exposition," Gen. R. Brinkerhoff.

In the absence of the Governor, to whom had been assigned the place as toastmaster, Mr. Claude Meeker, his private secretary, was called to the chair, and in that capacity filled the place most acceptably.

At the conclusion of the responses to the toasts, the following resolution, offered by Dr. H. A. Thompson, was unanimously adopted:

Whereas, Having listened with pleasure to the interesting remarks of General Brinkerhoff as to the part Ohio should take in the Columbian Exposition in 1893, and believing with him the State we represent, occupying as she does so conspicuous a position among the Mississippi Valley States, should be represented in a manner in keeping with her position and history; therefore, be it

Resolved, That we most heartily commend the effort being made by Representative McMakin to secure from the General Assembly such an appropriation as will enable the State to make a creditable representation of her material and educational interests in said exposition. In the event of an adequate appropriation for such purpose by the General Assembly, we believe that no small place should be given to the work of the Ohio Archæological and Historical Society, and do hereby pledge ourselves to make such an exhibit as shall do honor to the State.

The society, through Prof. John Hancock, expressed its thanks to the proprietors of the hotel for the excellent manner in which the dinner was served, and upon motion the sixth annual meeting adjourned.

WM. E. MOORE,

A. A. GRAHAM,   *First Vice President.*

Secretary.

MEETING OF THE TRUSTEES, THURSDAY, FEBRUARY 19, 1891, FIVE P. M.

The Trustees met in the State Library. Dr. Townshend in the chair. The selecting of officers was considered. On motion of Dr. H. A. Thompson, Mr. F. C. Sessions was elected President.

On motion, Rev. W. E. Moore was elected First Vice President, and R. Brinkerhoff Second Vice President.

On motion, Mr. S. S. Rickly was elected Treasurer, and A. A Graham elected Secretary.

The following were elected as an Executive Committee: F. C. Sessions, Wm. E. Moore, S. S. Rickly, D. J. Ryan, John Hancock, H. A. Thompson, N. S. Townshend. The committee was authorized to fill vacancies and to appoint such standing committees as should be deemed necessary. There being a vacancy in the Board of Trustees, Mr. George F. Baries, of Canal Winchester, was appointed to the place to serve three years, from February 19, 1891.

The Executive Committee was instructed to meet the next day, Friday, at 10:00 A. M., to consult further with the committee from Fort Recovery, relating to the centennial exercises to be held at that place in November, 1891.

The question of the contemplated change in the society's name was then considered. The Secretary presented the circular which had been sent to the members, and after discussion, it was, on motion of Mr. A. R. McIntyre,

Resolved, That the Board of Trustees of this Society deem it desirable that the articles of incorporation of this Society be amended by striking out the first, or naming clause, and inserting in lieu thereof the following: The name of this corporation shall be "The Ohio Historical Society," and the proper steps be at once taken to submit the question of making the amendment to a meeting of the members called for that purpose.

After which, upon motion, the Board of Trustees adjourned.

N. S. TOWNSHEND,

A. A. GRAHAM, *Chairman pro tem.*

Secretary.

Meeting of the Board of Trustees May 7th, 1891, in the State Library. Present, Messrs. Sessions, Brinkerhoff, Rickly, Thompson, Read, Griffin, Gilmore, Bareis, McIntyre, Hancock, and Lockwood.

Minutes of the last annual meeting of the Society and of the Board of Trustees, February 19th and 20th, were read and approved. The memorial regarding the work of the Society in the Ohio exhibit at the Columbian Exposition, was read, discussed and approved. The Secretary was instructed to arrange for a conference with the Ohio Commissioners, in session in the office of the State Board of Agriculture, and it was resolved that the sum of $2,500 be requested for this year's work.

On motion of Dr. Thompson, the Secretary was authorized to draw an order upon the Treasurer for the expenses of the Trustees in attendance at this meeting. A conference having been arranged, the Board met the Ohio Commissioners and through Messrs. Brinkerhoff and Read, presented the memorial of the Trustees regarding the Department of Archæology and History in the Ohio exhibit at the World's Fair.

After the conference, the Board renewed deliberations. On motion, a committee consisting of Messrs. Brinkerhoff, Wright, Baldwin, Read and the Secretary was appointed to appear before the Ohio Commissioners at their meeting in Cleveland, June 4th, the Committee to present a plan of the proposed department, and to report the same to the Executive Committee. The Secretary was instructed to send each member of the Board the names of the Ohio Commissioners to the World's Fair.

The Board then adjourned to meet at Fort Ancient the next day, Friday, May 8th.

Fort Ancient, Friday, 2 P. M. Present, Messrs. Brinkerhoff, Read, Lockwood, Bareis, Williams, Gilmore, Harris, McIntyre and Thompson, and by invitation, Senator Jesse N. Oren. Second Vice President Brinkerhoff in the chair. The minutes of the previous day were read and approved. The "Care and control of Fort Ancient" was considered. After discussion, the the appointment by the Executive Committee of Messrs. Oren, Harris and Williams, as a special committee in charge of Fort Ancient, was confirmed; this committee to enter upon its duties as soon as the transfer of the property is made. This committee was authorized to appoint a custodian for the property, and to establish such rules and regulations for its care and control as may be necessary, the action of the committee in these matters to be submitted to the Board of Trustees for approval. After an informal discussion of matters connected with the Fort, the board adjourned.

R. BRINKERHOFF, Chairman.

A. A. GRAHAM, *Secretary.*

———

SECRETARY'S REPORT.

To the Executive Committee:

The year closed has been marked by steady progress. Little in detail need be said. The publication of the Quarterly to the end of Volume II was completed. Owing to the expense of fitting the Society's room with the necessary cases and furniture, an expense of near $300, sufficient money did not remain to continue the Quarterly last year. Another item which entered into this matter was the fact that the Society had been for some time engaged in gathering the material on the question of the boundary between Ohio and Virginia with a view to publication, in connection with the reprint of the notable and strong argument on that question by Mr. Samuel F. Vinton, before the Virginia Supreme Court in the Garber Slave case, the intention being to issue the argument and accompanying papers in a single bound volume, as Volume III. An examination of the matter developed the fact that some time would be necessary to secure and prepare, as it should be done, such an important matter, and the publication was therefore deferred for the present. In the meantime, the Centennial of the settlement of Gallipolis by the French, October, 19, 1790, was brought before the Society, and it was decided to assist in that event, as the Society had done at Marietta in the centennial of April 7, 1888. The present volume will be the result, and will speak for itself.

The Society not finding sufficient encouragement in the effort to unite the Society and the State Library upon the plan followed in Wisconsin, Kansas and several other states, turned its attention elsewhere, upon the request and suggestion of several members, a publication fund was started. Each active member who desired to pay an amount of money in addition to what each had paid as active members to equal a life member's fee, $50, was given the opportunity. The treasurer's report shows the present condition of the fund.

The necessary care of the rooms, the work of the Society in its various branches, required all the secretary's time, which could not be given gratuitously. No fixed amount until this year was paid, only such as could be spared, and without which I could not have continued, and no one capable of carrying it forward could be found to do the work free.

During the last term of the General Assembly an appeal was made to that body to aid the Society. This was cheerfully done, the Society being required to place all its library collections in the State Library. A grant of $2.000 was made, and

the Society placed in the State Library some 900 bound volumes
and pamphlets.

It is expected that this policy will be continued, and a closer
union between the State Library and the Society be maintained.
A safe receptacle will be provided for the library accommodations of the Society, where they can be consulted by any who
may want them.

The coming World's Fair at Chicago will afford the Society
an opportunity to extend its usefulness, and its aid in making a
proper display of articles illustrating the history of the State.
The General Assembly has already taken steps to assure an exhibit of Ohio's industries and Ohio's history, and the Society
should be not only recognized, but required to aid in the exhibit.
At the close of the exposition, the Society can assume full care
of such articles as may be secured from the exhibit there. By
such means, at the centennial expositions held in Ohio in 1888,
a large and valuable collection illustrating our archæology and
history was secured. These collections can now be seen in the
rooms of the Society, which now contains some four thousand
articles of archaeology. A large number of maps, charts, carts,
photographs and other articles illustrating the archæology and
history of Ohio. The room is now crowded, and the question
of larger and more convenient quarters confronts us.

The interest in the approaching centennials of many settlements and many important events in our history is apparent.
All turn to this society to see that these are properly celebrated.
They tend to stimulate historical enquiry and interest, and their
proper observance is a part of our work and should receive the
attention each demands. The year closed emphasizes the fact
that the growth of the society, its usefulness, and its utility depends on unremitting steady efforts. This we shall try to do as
long as strength and support continues.

A. A. GRAHAM, *Secretary.*

REPORT OF THE TRUSTEES TO THE GOVERNOR FOR THE YEAR ENDING FEBRUARY 19, 1891.

To His Excellency, JAMES E. CAMPBELL,
Governor of Ohio:

The following report of this Society for the current year is herewith presented:

The fiscal year of the Society ends February 19th, at which time a full and detailed report of our proceedings, receipts, and expenditures is annually made.

At the last sesion of the General Assembly an appropriation of two thousand ($2,000) dollars was made to this Society "for books, manuscripts, etc., to be placed in the State Library." Under this authority the Society has catalogued to date, and placed in the State Library, about four hundred (400) bound volumes, about six hundred (600) pamphlets, not including files of magazines, many manuscripts, etc. This enumeration does not include duplicates nor remaining parts of the Society's publication, which will be used for exchange purposes, and the works so received be placed in the Library. It also has twenty-nine framed charts, illustrating the archæology of Ohio, costing originally about ten dollars each, which were donated to the Society; and several paintings, drawings, and charts, which the Library, owing to lack of wall-space, cannot receive, and which will therefore be left for the present in the Society's room. The Society has increased its permanent fund to seven hundred ($700) dollars, the intention being to secure eventually twenty-five thousand ($25,000) dollars, this fund to be known as the "Publication Fund," the income derived therefrom to be devoted to publications. The experience of all historical societies shows a very slow growth, and years must elapse before the fund will reach the desired limit. In other States more than half a century elapses before such a fund is secured. Several subscriptions not yet due have been made, and as time progresses more will be secured. The report of the Treasurer is as follows, and exhibits in detail the financial transactions of the year:

Balance on hand from 1889	$ 527 13
From active membership fees	470 00
Subscriptions to publication fund	580 00
From appropriations	2,000 00
From interest on permanent fund	27 33
	$ 3,604 46

DISBURSEMENTS.

For postage	$ 175 00
Railway fares of Secretary	22 00
Janitor and clerk hire	163 15
Office desk	25 00
Repairs in room	14 50
Sundry expenses, chiefly in connection with Gallipolis Centennial	162 34
Secretary's salary for February, March and April, 1890	300 00
Expenses, same period	22 11
Salary Secretary, May 1, 1890, to March 1, 1891	1,000 00
Job Printing	298 50
Balance printing of Volume II	96 29
Money expended for books	5 40
Transferred to publication fund	500 00
Total	$ 2,815 67
Balance on hand	788 79
	$ 3,604 46

From the balance on hand will be paid the printing of Volume III, now in press, about $ 400, a copy of which will be placed on the desk of each member of the Senate and House, and the necessary expenses, including the Secretary's salary, until May 15th.

VALUE OF PUBLICATIONS AND STOCK ON HAND, FEBRUARY 19, 1891.

Plates of Volume I cost	$ 182 10
Matrices of Volume II cost	73 22
Single copies of Quarterlies, value	72 00
Eight bound copies Volume II	40 00
Total value publications, etc., on hand	$ 367 32

The supply of volumes *one* and *two*, bound and unbound, and of single numbers of the Quarterly, is constantly being depleted by calls for them from all parts of the country. As soon as the funds of the Society permit, these volumes will be reprinted from the plates.

The permanent fund is now $700, invested and drawing annual interest.

The Society will now issue Volume III of its publications. This will embody the Centennial exercises, addresses, etc., at Gallipolis, October 16–19 last, and also several valuable papers relating to the important historical questions.

Arrangements have been made to exchange the publications of this Society with all other societies of a similar nature, not only in Ohio and the United States, but also in many foreign countries. The publications of all scientific, historical and kindred societies are exceedingly valuable. They do not contain, as a rule, reading that interests every citizen, but they do contain monographs, carefully prepared, of great value to students of history, government, science, political economy, and to those whose vocations necessitate the use of such material. The publications of such societies are not, as a rule, on sale, hence no commercial value can be placed on them. They are, like the issues of this Society, given to those who support the organization, and to those who give in return the results of their labors.

Under the appropriations given the Society, we are required to place in the Library not only our present collection, but also the accumulations received during the year, whether by gift, purchase or exchange. It also places an injunction on the Society to be diligent in acquiring documents, publications, etc., of a governmental, scientific, historical and economic nature, and by a system of exchange to secure as many as it can. This it has labored faithfully to do. The issues of its first two volumes are entirely exhausted, and as calls for them are constantly being made, the Society will, as soon as its funds permit, republish them. It will also, as has already been said, issue its third volume soon, and through it receive a large number of exchanges.

These, with all other accumulations, will be placed in the State Library.

The Society desires to commend the efforts to secure and build up pamphlet and manuscript departments in the State Library. The move is most excellent. So careful a student of history as ex-President Hayes, when Governor of Ohio, saw the value of such departments, and did what he could to establish and maintain them.

Such material is of inestimable value. Pamphlet publications are the cream of economical literature. The great libraries of this country are exceedingly careful to secure such collections. A system of exchange can and should be systematically arranged with all other libraries, and, through this Society, with societies issuing such publications. The Legislator, the man of business, and the student of government should have them at ready command. We are well aware this entails additional labor on the Librarian, who now, with a Library of some sixty thousand (60,000) volumes, has the same assistance as the Librarian of twenty-five years ago with less than half the number of volumes and not one-fourth the applicants to examine them. If this Society can be of any aid in this matter it will be glad to do so. In view of the labor which these collections with its own will impose, and the necessary work of caring for the sections of pamphlets and manuscripts, the Society will assist, by its Secretary, in such manner as the Library Commissioners and its Trustees may decide. It is the earnest desire of the membership, which comprises the intelligent citizens of the State, to co-operate with the Library Commissioners to secure in our Capitol a State Library of reference works such as Ohio should have and such as the State can have if the proper efforts be encouraged.

In regard to future publications, the Society desires to call your attention to unpublished manuscripts and documents in the archives of the State House. Many are valuable and are giving way to the "tooth of time," which will ere long destroy them. We wish to collect them and publish such as are valuable. We can do so should the small aid hitherto given be continued.

As far back as the year 1814, the Historical Society of New

York sent to the Legislature of that State, through their distinguished Vice President, Dewitt Clinton, Esq., a memorial drawn by his own hand, in behalf of the perishing records of that Commonwealth. This document presented in strong terms the urgency and importance of the measure suggested. It appealed to the patriotism of the people, whose State pride should prompt them at once to rescue their history from threatened oblivion. The eloquent author called upon the State to assist the Society he represented, "in drawing from their dark abodes documents that would illume the obscure, explain the doubtful, and embalm the memories of the good and great." This effort was not in vain—funds sufficient to carry out the purpose suggested, were at once appropriated; competent persons were employed to translate the earlier records of the Colony while under the Dutch, and agents were sent abroad to collect in England, Holland and France, original documents and copies of everything relating to the history of the Empire State of America.

At a subsequent period, and after the materials had been collected, a proper person was appointed "to compile the Documentary History of New York," which work is now to be found in an imposing array of folio volumes upon the shelves of our State Library, secured through this Society.

Other American Commonwealths, in the meantime, have not been idle. The Historical Society of Massachusetts has rescued from loss most of the records of that ancient colony and influential State. They have been collected, printed and bound in series, each one of which consists of numerous volumes. The Historical Society and other agencies of that State were stimulated to this action by occurrences, such as the burning of the old State House at Boston; the destruction of part of old Cambridge College, and of certain private residences which involved the loss of many valuable documents. Convinced by such disasters that no depository at that time was free from danger, it was wisely determined to multiply copies of their records through the printing press.

In the year 1851, the Executive of Pennsylvania, by special message to the Legislature of that State, set forth the great importance of preserving the perishing records of the Common-

wealth. A committee was at once appointed to consider the subject, and now the "Documentary History of Pennsylvania" appears in more than a dozen large volumes, beginning at the year
1664 and coming down to the latest dates.

Further south Maryland has accomplished much, and the
States of Georgia and Louisiana have not been idle. The records
of the latter have been preserved, in part, from the time when
the royal standard of Spain was first set up in the Floridas, until
the period of the American Revolution.

Even some of the newer States, Wisconsin and Michigan in
particular, have already taken steps to preserve their early
records. In Wisconsin, Minnesota, and Kansas, the State Historical Societies are entrusted with this work. The annual volumes of these Societies, and their various publications, attest the
fidelity with which it is done.

Dr. Palmer, of the Virginia Historical Society, speaking of
manuscripts, says:

"The real value of manuscripts is not always at once appreciated. A paper cannot be without interest, for instance, should
it but preserve the peculiarities of style, the quaint phraseology
and antique orthography in use when it was written. In the
earliest papers before us these are prominent characteristics.
They appear as much in the private correspondence as in official
documents, in which latter, however, as may be expected, a
more stately, and often-times pompous, diction prevails.

"It should be remembered that the best educated of our
fore-fathers were compelled to employ the only vocabulary
known to them. They had inherited the style transmitted from
a more primitive age in letters, than that even in which they
lived, and which did not begin its approach to the smoother diction of the present day until about the beginning of the second
century after the founding of the colonies.

"Another merit of these documents consists in their perpet-
uating certain phrases and expressions, the only vehicles of a
class of ideas purely technical in their signification. In many of
the oldest may be recognized also much of the ruggedness of the
ancient Saxon tongue, as it appeared before the Norman dialect
had added its softer elements, whereby what may be termed the

stone-age of our language began to pass away. The papers of this description are common until about the time of Spotswood when their style begins sensibly to change. A little latter a taste for the ornate becomes more apparent; quaintness and simplicity gives way to decoration, and as we pass on to times nearer our own day, the measured sentences and rounded periods of the more modern diction come into frequent use.

"Still another value attaches to these fading manuscripts which may not, at first view, be recognized. In the letters and other communications interchanged by people of every class of society, one is impressed with the courteous regard for the amenities of social life exhibited in them, although often couched in awkward and commonplace language."

The foregoing presents cogent reasons why such materials should be preserved, and should have attention from those who possess the power to do for Ohio what has been done in New York, Pennsylvania, Massachusetts, Virginia, Wisconsin and in other American states, not to speak of what has been done by the National Government through such men as Peter Force, the compiler of the "Annals of Congress," and by the publication of such documents as the "American State Papers."

Ohio has many valuable official letters, orders, correspondence, etc., etc., some of official nature, much unofficial, yet all of such a nature not at the time it was issued best to print; yet of such a nature that it should now be preserved, and which would go far toward correcting many matters of history.

A little encouragement granted to the Society will secure the publication of all such a competent committee would deem of value. We trust some attention will be given this matter, and other volumes, like the "St. Clair Papers," be issued, e'er the material for them is irretrievably lost.

We also wish to call attention to the coming World's Fair. Ohio should not be behind. Already the Society possesses many valuable articles, charts, maps, etc., of a historical nature that should be there, and it will cheerfully do all it can for this work.

The appropriation for our general work could include this, and thus no little expense be spared to the State. The appropriation for publication purposes can also be included. This,

with its annual receipts from members' dues, interest, sale of
publications, etc., will keep it on a plane with the best societies
in the country and enable it to do its full share of usefulness.

The General Assembly has provided for the purchase and
preservation of that remarkable earth-work—Fort Ancient—in
the Little Miami valley. It is the largest and most extensive
prehistoric remains now in Ohio. The move was most com-
mendable, and will result in its preservation, whatever may be
the use of the grounds enclosed by the embankments. The
Society was invited by the Legislative Committee to visit the
place with them, and many members did so. The Society will
assume the care of the "Fort," and place it under such use as
the General Assembly may direct. We would also say that by
resolution of the members, such legislation is requested as will
represent the state on the Board of Trustees of the Society.

FRANCIS C. SESSIONS, *President.*
S. S. RICKLEY, *Treasurer.*
A. A. GRAHAM, *Secretary.*

By order of the Board of Trustees.

THE MORAVIAN MASSACRE.

[A paper read at the Sixth Annual Meeting of the Society at Columbus,
by William M. Farrar.]

It is now more than a century since what is known to history
as "The Moravian Massacre," occurred at Gnadenhutten, on
the Tuscarawas branch of the Muskingum river; so long ago
that all those concerned in that affair have long since passed to
their graves and been forgotton. This sad affair was unique in
character, from any thing of the kind recorded in ancient
or modern history, and has been more persistently misrepre-
sented than any other event relating to the early history of the
country, many of those misrepresentations have passed into
history and been accepted as true.

It is the duty of this society to vindicate the truth of history
and place upon record any facts that time may have developed

Indian Monument, Gnadenhutten.

tending to explain, or throw light upon, what has always been a subject of much controversy.

This expedition which originated in the western townships of Washington, County, Pennsylvania, during the fall and winter of 1781, has been represented as a military one, authorized by the lawfully constituted military authority of that county, commanded by a regularly commissioned militia officer, and called out in the regular way. And yet no such order has ever been found, nor is there any muster roll* in existence giving the list of names of the officers and privates composing the expedition, showing to what companies or battalion of the enrolled militia of the country they belonged, nor has any claim for services rendered, damages sustained, provisions furnished, arms provided, or property lost, ever been presented either against the State or general government, by any person claiming to have been a member of the expedition. Neither is there any official report of the expedition extant, made by either Col. Williamson the officer in command, by James Marshel the lieutenant of the county who was responsible for it, if any such expedition was ordered out, or by Brigadier General Irvine the commandant at Fort Pitt in whose department it occurred.

It is true that so accurate and careful a historian as Mr. Butterfield has pronounced otherwise, but a review of the authority upon which he relies does not seem to justify his conclusions, based as they are upon a single statement made by Gen. Irvine in a letter written from Fort Pitt, May 3, 1782, to President Moore of the executive council of Pennsylvania.†

Brigadier Gen. Wm. Irvine was appointed to the command of the Western Military Department, October 11th, 1781. At that day the Ohio river marked the dividing line between barbarism and civilization, east of it, the hardy pioneers, after making their way across the Alleghany mountains with Fort Pitt as their objective point, had extended their settlements north and south along the rich valleys of the rivers forming the Ohio, and pushed them westward until the smoke of their cabins

---

* See Crumrine's History, Washington County, Pennsylvania, page 110.
† See W. & I. cor. 239 and 245.

could be seen, and the sounds of their rifles and axes heard by the red men who dwelt among the deep forests beyond. To guard this frontier line and protect the settlements against Indian raids, was the work assigned to the commanding officer of the Western Department, and for that purpose small garrisons of regular troops were stationed at the several forts built along this frontier line, and companies of militia drawn from the counties of Westmoreland and Washington kept constantly ranging along the border, to give timely notice of the approach of hostile bands of savages.

To assist the commandant at Fort Pitt in this work, an officer with the rank of Lieutenant Colonel, and known as the County Lieutenant, was appointed by the Supreme Executive Council of the State of Pennsylvania, for each of the several counties embraced in the Department, whose duty it was to attend to the enrollment and equipment of the militia of the county, and provide for their subsistence when called into actual service; also to make return of the number and names of those subject to military duty, together with the names and rank of the officers commanding the different companies composing the several Battalions to the commanding officer at Fort Pitt, upon whose requisitions they were called into active service as necessity required, whether by battalions, companies, or in smaller details, the officer in each and every case being required to wait upon the commandent at Fort Pitt for instructions as to the kind of service required and his own duty in the premises.*

The orders of Congress and the Executive Council, which were the law in the case, together with the explicit instructions

---

* See History Washington County, Pennsylvania, by Crumrine, page 136.

See Res. of Congress assigning General Irvine to command of Fort Pitt and his instructions dated September 24, 1781.

See order Supreme Executive Council, Pennsylvania, October 11, 1781.

See Letters Marshel to Irvine, November 20, 26 and 28, 1781.

See Requisition of Irvine to Marshel, January 10, 1782.

See Letter of Irvine to Cook, January, 1782.

See instructions to Lieutenant Hay, November 28, 1781, and January, 1782.

See Instructions to Major Scott, April, 1782.

See Letter, Marshel to Irvine, Washington County, April 2, 1782.

given to the general and subordinate officers employed in this frontier service, and the uniform manner of calling out the militia, are so plain and so consistent with good military sense, that it seems strange that any person could be misled as to the true character of the Moravian Expedition, and yet Mr. Butterfield has taken a single expression used by General Irvine in his letter of May 3, 1782, to President Moore, of the Executive Council, as "unequivocal" evidence that the militia who went to the Muskingum were *"ordered out"* by Colonel James Marshel, the Lieutenant of Washington County, Pennsylvania. The letter reads as follows:

FORT PITT, May 3, 1782.

Sir: Immediately on receipt of your excellency's letter of the 13th of April, I wrote to Colonel James Marshel, who ordered out the militia to go to Muskingum (to that branch known as the Tuscarawas) for his and Colonel Williamson's report of the matter, Colonel Williamson commanded the party. Inclosed you have their letters to me on the subject, by way of report. I have inquiries making in other quarters; when any well authenticated accounts come to my knowledge, they shall be transmitted.   WM. IRVINE, *B. Gen'l.*

It is somewhat difficult to reconcile the statements contained in the foregoing letter with the facts and circumstances of the case, for, if true, Marshel, as County Lieutenant, had been guilty of a palpable violation of law, in calling out the militia of the county without authority, and sending them upon an unauthorized expedition beyond the limits of the state, without the proper instructions, where they had committed excesses unheard of in civilized warfare, excesses that were being very generally condemned as a lasting reproach to the good name of the state, and yet he was never court-martialed, investigated, or even called upon by the Executive Council of the state from whom he held his appointment for an explanation of his conduct.

That General Irvine wrote to Marshel and Williamson for their reports of the matter, and transmitted the letters received from them in reply to the President of the Council, *"by way of report,"* as stated, is no doubt correct. But to assume that these were the official reports of the transaction is not warranted.

The President of the Council, in acknowledging their receipt, speaks of them as not reports, but as "the *representations* made by Colonel Williamson and Colonel Marshel."

It is greatly to be regretted that these letters cannot be found, as they would no doubt settle the question whether Marshel had anything to do with calling out the militia that went to the Muskingum, and would show to what extent, if any, he was responsible for the movement.

James Marshel survived the massacre forty-seven years, and for almost twenty years thereafter was continuously in public office; Lieutenant of Washington county in 1781–2–3; Register in 1781; Recorder in 1791; Coroner from 1794 to 1799; and

Sheriff from 1786 to 1787, when he was succeeded by Col. Williamson, whose election was opposed because of his connection with the massacre, while no such objection was ever made against Marshel, who was certainly more to blame for ordering out the expedition, if he did so. But no such charge was made during his lifetime, nor until more than fifty years after his death, when the letter of May 3, 1782, was found among the Pennsylvania Archives and given to the public by Mr. Butterfield. (W and I cor. p. 239).

About 1799, Col. Marshel removed to Wellsburgh, Virginia, where he died in 1829. For many years he was the neighbor and friend of Doddridge, the historian, and during the time his history was being written and published (in 1824) they were intimate personal friends, and it is at least reasonable to suppose that if Marshel had ordered out the militia that went to the Muskingum it would have been known to the historian and so stated. Had it been a military expedition, acting in pursuance of any competent authority, would Doddridge have stated (after detailing the events that led to it, as he does on page 248) "accordingly between eighty and ninety men were *hastily* collected together for the fatal enterprise?" That "each man furnished

himself with his own arms, ammunition and provisions." * * *
That "many of them had horses;" that "the murder of the
Moravians was intended;" that "no resistance from them was
anticipated" (page 253); that "in the latter end of the year
1781, the militia of the frontier came to a determination to break
up the Moravian villages on the Muskingum" (page 259); and
that "it (the massacre) was one of those convulsions of the
moral state of society, in which the voice of the justice and
humanity of a majority, is silenced by the clamor and violence
of a lawless minority." (Page 261.)

His son, John Marshel, who died in 186–, was for many years
a well known resident of Washington, Pennsylvania, cashier of
the old Franklin Bank, a man of much intelligence and integrity
of character, with whom the writer often conversed about the
Moravian Massacre, and he repeatedly said that his father always
spoke of it as the outgrowth of a mistaken belief that prevailed
at the time; as a matter of course his father's connection with it
was not spoken of, because he was not implicated.

It may, and does seem strange, that an officer like Gen.
Irvine should write such a letter unless there was some foundation for it, and yet to take the statement as correct, shows a dis-
regard of the instructions contained in his letter of January 10,
1782, so gross and inexcusable, that it would not have been
passed over with so much indifference. By that letter the Lieutenants were notified of his intended absence, that Colonel Gibson would be left in command, that he would be the best judge
of the necessity for calling out the militia if one should arise,
and that they should *"on his requisition,"* order out such members of the militia *as he will call for.*

These orders Colonel Gibson exercised during his absence,
by making a requisition upon the Lieutenant of Westmoreland
county for militia to protect the frontier, and to presume upon
no better authority than the statement contained in the letter of
May 3, 1782, that a much larger and more important expedition
to extend beyond the borders of the State, was ordered out by
the Lieutenant of Washington county, upon his own motion and
without even consulting Colonel Gibson, would be very unreasonable, and yet, Colonel Gibson's letter of May 9, 1782,

written to the Rev. Nathanial Seidel at Bethlehem, Pennsylvania, shows that he had no knowledge of such an expedition,
and that if he had, ''he should have prevented it by informing
the poor sufferers of it.''

Gen. Irvine left Fort Pitt on the 16th day of January, 1782,
on a visit to his family at Carlile, and did not return until the
25th day of March following, and it was during his absence on
the 8th day of March that the massacre occurred. Nineteen
days after his return, on the 12th day of April, he wrote his wife
a letter, showing that he then knew all that could be learned of
the massacre, as he details all the terrible features of the affair,
including the fact that *'' Many children were killed in their
wretched mothers' arms.''* And then adds, *'' Whether this was
right or wrong, I do not pretend to determine.''* But the key to
such inexcusable indifference on the part of General Irvine is
found further along in the same letter, as follows: *'' Whatever
your private opinion of these matters may be, I conjure you by all
the ties of affection, and as you value my reputation, that you will
keep your mind to yourself, and that you will not express any
sentiment for or against these deeds; as it may be alleged the
sentiments you express may come from me or be mine. No man
knows whether I approve of killing the Moravians.''*

It is evident from this correspondence that General Irvine
was much alarmed about his own reputation; that he withheld
from the council the information written to his wife on the 12th
of April; that in his reply to Pres. Moore, of May 2d, he sought
to give the impression that he was in possession of no news
upon the subject, and on the 9th of May, after due consultation,
he joined with Pentecost in advising against an investigation.

The first news the people residing to the east of the Allegheny mountains received of the massacre, was from a notice
published in the Pennsylvania Packet, of April 9th, 1782, one
month after it had occurred, and which came through Moravian
sources by way of Bethlehem, Pennsylvania, and read as follows:

'' A very important advantage has lately been gained over
our savage enemies on the frontiers of this State, by a party of
back-country militia; we hope to give particulars in our next.''

But before the next issue of the Packet came to hand, fuller information received through the same sources, showed a very different state of affairs; the killing was confirmed, but instead of the victims being "savage enemies," they were found to have been Christian Indians, reclaimed from savage life by the Moravian missionaries, who ten years before had planted their missions in the deep wilderness, and succeeded in christianizing several hundred of the rude and warring savage tribes, who had become converts, abandoned savage life, and made considerable progress in civilization. It was these converts who had been killed, their villages destroyed, and the missions broken up, and what was worse, even the women and children, the old and infirm, had been cruelly slaughtered in a manner that was shocking to humanity, and a lasting disgrace to civilization. And as the details of the massacre became more fully known east of the mountains, a strong public sentiment developed in condemnation of an outrage so manifestly in violation of the rules and usages of civilized warfare. Whereupon, Dorsey Pentecost, a member of the executive council from Washington county, left his post of duty and hastened home, to stay, if possible, the tide of popular indignation that seemed to be setting in so strong against his constituents. He reached Pittsburg on the 2d of May. and on the 8th wrote his chief as follows:

"PITTSBURGH, May 8th, 1782.

"*Dear Sir:*—I arrived at home last Thursday without any particular accident. Yesterday I came to this place; have had a long conference with General Irvine and Colonel Gibson on the subject of public matters, particularly respecting the late excursion to Kushocton. * * That affair * is a subject of great speculation here—some condemning, others applauding the measure; but the accounts are so various that it is not only difficult, but almost, indeed, entirely impossible to ascertain the real truth. No person can give intelligence but those that were along; and notwithstanding there seems to have been some difference amongst themselves about that business, yet they will say nothing; but this far I believe may be depended on, that they killed rather deliberately the innocent with the guilty, and it is likely the majority was the former. I have heard it insinuated that about thirty or forty only of the party gave their consent or assisted in the catastrophe. It is said here, and I believe with truth, that sundry articles were found amongst the Indians that were taken from the inhabitants of Washington county.

DORSEY PENTECOST.

Before this letter had been forwarded, and on the next day, he wrote again as follows:

" PITTSBURGH, May 9, 1782.

"*Dear Sir:*—Since writing the letter that accompanies this, I have had another and more particular conversation with General Irvine on the subject of the late excursion to Kushocton, and upon the whole, I find that it will be impossible to get an impartial and fair account of that affair; for although sundry persons that were in the company may disapprove of the whole or every part of the conduct (of those engaged in the killing), yet from their connection they will not be willing, nor can they be forced to give testimony, as it affects themselves. And the people here are greatly divided in sentiment about it; and on investigation may produce serious effects, and at least leave us as ignorant as when we began, and instead of rendering a service may produce a confusion and ill-will amongst the people. Yet I think it necessary that the council should take some cognizance or notice of the matter, and in such a time as may demonstrate their disapprobation of such parts of their conduct as are censurable; otherwise it may be alleged that the government, tacitly at least, have encouraged the killing of women and children; and in a proclamation of this kind, it might be well not only to recommend but to forbid, that in future excursions that women and children and infirm persons should not be killed—so contrary to the law of arms as well as christianity. I hope a mode of proceeding something like this would produce some good effects, and perhaps soften the minds of the people, for it is really no wonder that those who have lost all that is near and dear to them go out with determined revenge and extirpation of all Indians.   DORSEY PENTECOST."

By way of contrast to these apologetic letters of Mr. Pentecost, we have that of Col. Edward Cook, Lieutenant of Westmoreland county, who was called upon during General Irvine's absence from his post of duty for a detail of men for frontier service, by Colonel Gibson, and furnished the same, the officer in command waiting upon Colonel Gibson for instructions. It bears date September 2, 1782, and addressed to President Moore of the Executive Council, as follows:

" I am informed that you have it Reported that the Massacre of the Moravian Indians obtains the approbation of Every man on this side of the Mountains, which I assure your Excellency is false; that the better part of the community are of Opinion the Perpetrators of that wicked Deed ought to be brought to Condein Punishment; that without something is Done by Government in the Matter, it will disgrace the Annuls of the United States, and be an Everlasting Plea and cover for British cruelty."*

These letters of Pentecost serve to show the difference in public sentiment that then prevailed east and west of the Allegheny Mountains in regard to the massacre. Pentecost was a politician, and therefore anxious to avoid a public investigation of the matter, and Irvine, in great alarm for his own reputation, readily joined him in advising against one.

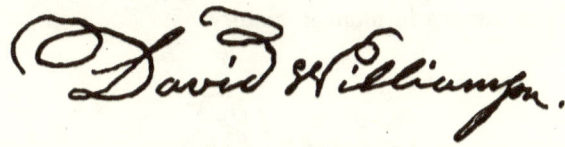

Colonel David Williamson, who commanded the expedition, has probably received a great deal more than his share of public censure, because of the prominent part he acted in the affair. Whether he held a commission at the time as a militia officer is uncertian; he certainly did soon after, and if so, that was about all the military character the expedition had. The fact that Williamson was chosen commander after they had assembled at Mingo, goes to show that he commanded by virtue of that authority, whatever it was, rather than because of any he exercised as a militia officer.

The expedition was neither infantry nor cavalry, mounted nor dismounted, but a mixed crowd made up from that reckless and irresponsible element usually found along the borders of civilization, boys from eighteen to twenty years of age, who joined the expedition from love of adventure, and partly of such well-known characters as Captain Sam Brady, of West Liberty, Virginia,

---

* See Crumrine's History Washington County, Pennsylvania, page 110.

and at least one of the Wetzels from near Wheeling, who, from
their experience and well-known bravery as frontiersmen, are
said to have exercised very great influence in deciding the fate
of the Indians.

It has always been a matter of some surprise that the
brothers, Andrew Poe and Adam Poe, were not members of the
expedition. They were well known as stout, hardy, fearless
backwoodsmen, experienced leaders in Indian warfare, and on
hand wherever courage and endurance were required. But for
some reason, now unknown, they were not along, and, so far as
known, do not appear to have been advised of the movement.

Their absence is all the more unaccountable as they had, in
the September previous, greatly distinguished themselves by a
vigorous pursuit of a Bigfoot party, which was overtaken at the
Ohio River and dispatched, after a struggle that has made the
name of Poe famous in pioneer history.

Andw Poe

Adam Poe (by Andw

The greater portion of the crowd were mounted, the others
on foot; each man provided his own horse, arms and provisions,
and it was noisy, turbulent and disorderly from the start,[1] and
the authority exercised by Williamson over it, about equivalent
to that usually conceded to the leader of an ordinary mob.

Who suggested that the question, whether the Indians
should be killed or taken prisoners to Fort Pitt be submitted to
a vote, is not known, but the fact that he did so only serves to
show the extent of Williamson's authority. It has never been
claimed, however, that he cast his own vote or participated in
the slaughter. He is represented by those who knew him per-

Note 1.— Statement of a member of the expedition.

sonally as a man of naturally pleasant and agreeable disposition, six feet in height, rather fleshy in his make-up, of florid complexion, and of "too easy a compliance with public opinion," as Doddridge says.

In the Sandusky expedition that followed closely upon the Moravian massacre, Williamson was in command, and it was largely to his unremitting activity, courage and judgment, that any considerable number of the men were kept together after the defeat and brought back in even tolerable order. He afterward filled a number of important and responsible offices in Washington County, Pennsylvania, and in 1787 was elected sheriff of the county after a warm canvass, during which his connection with the Moravian expedition was strongly urged against him. He was born in Carlile, Pennsylvania, in 1752, was thirty years of age in 1782, and died at Washington, Pennsylvania, in 1814, aged sixty-two years, and is buried in the old graveyard on North Main street, but no stone or other monument marks his last resting place. He married Polly Urie, the daughter of Thomas Urie, a well-known family of Washington County, Pennsylvania, and left a family of four sons and four daughters. Two of his daughters married into the well-known McNulty family, of West Middletown, Pennsylvania, and Caleb J. McNulty, of Mt. Vernon, Ohio, who died on his way to Mexico during the war with that country, was his grandson. He was the one member of the expedition who, by reason of the position he filled, could not hide from public censure, and hence his undue share of it. During a large part of his lifetime he resided on Buffalo creek, near to the Virginia line, where he was personally acquainted with the historian, Doddridge, whose statements concerning his character and disposition may be safely taken as correct.

John Carpenter has always been quoted as an authority whose statements go to extenuate the massacre. The story is that about the time of the Wallace tragedy, or very soon afterward, he was captured on the waters of Buffalo creek by six Indians, two of whom spoke good Dutch, and called themselves Moravians; that he was carried a prisoner to the middle Moravian town, where, among other things, he saw the bloody dress of Mrs. Wallace.

This was accepted as proof positive that the Moravians were in the habit of raiding the settlements, or of harboring and trading with those who did, and therefore should be exterminated.

The value of this evidence, however, depends upon the date of Carpenter's capture. If it occurred prior to the Wallace tragedy, the conclusion is inevitable that he did not see the bloody clothing of Mrs. Wallace at the Moravian town, as stated.

John Carpenter was among the first, if not the very first, white man to settle on the west side of the Ohio river. He lived for some years on Buffalo creek, ten or twelve miles east of the river, and in his hunting excursions often crossed to the west side, where game was more plentiful, and believing, as many settlers did, that the Indian titles would, ere long, be extinguished and the rich lands on that side of the river come into possession of the government, and be opened to settlement, he determined to secure a claim by making an improvement in advance, and therefore in the summer and fall of 1781, he proceeded to clear a piece of ground and build a cabin near the mouth of Rush Run, the same that was afterward strengthened and became Carpenter's Fort. It was this work he was engaged upon in the month of September, 1781, when the second Indian attack upon Fort Henry (at Wheeling) took place, and barely received warning of their approach in time to escape to the east side of the river and remove his family to a place of safety.

After the raid was over and all again quiet, Carpenter returned and continued his work, which he finished late in the fall, when he removed the game he had killed across the river, where it was loaded upon horses and carried to his home on Buffalo.

Having done this, he took a pair of horses and started to Fort Pitt in order to secure a supply of salt, and while on his way was captured, taken to the Moravian town, and started from there in charge of two of his captors, from whom he escaped and made his way back to Fort Pitt as has been related, but all this took place two months or more prior to the 17th day of

February, 1782, when the Wallace cabin was destroyed and his wife and children carried into captivity.

In 1801, Edward Carpenter, the oldest son of this John Carpenter, took a government contract to open a road from Steubenville to the Wills creek crossing on the Zane Trace, and while so engaged entered a quarter of land in section 26 of township 11 of the 6th range, where he continued to reside until his death, January 12, 1828. And upon the same quarter section of land his son, Edward, lived until March 22d, 1882, when he died at the age of 80 years, and it is from him that the facts stated concerning the capture of his grandfather were obtained. He was a gentleman of much intelligence, served for many years as a justice of the peace, took much pride in the history of his ancestry, and had learned many of the incidents relating to his grandfather from the pioneer himself, and many more from his own father, both of whom were very reliable men, whose statements are much more likely to be correct than the indefinite rumors published in the Pennsylvania Packet at that time, based as they necessarily were upon the most meagre information concerning a transaction that occurred several hundred miles distant, the true character of which it was the interest and purpose of those implicated to conceal.

Another misrepresentation that has passed into history and been often repeated, even as late as 1882 in Crumrine's history of Washington county, Pennsylvania,[1] is, that the massacre was an after-thought, the result of frenzied feelings, provoked by finding the dead body of Mrs. Wallace impaled on the wayside, directly leading from Mingo bottom to the villages on the Muskingum, and also by finding in possession of the Indians, property stolen from the plundered cabins of the settlers, trinkets and clothing of murdered relatives, at the sight of which they became exasperated and forgot themselves. In all such statements, which have times without number been urged in excuse of the massacre, there is no truth whatever.

The site of the Wallace cabin was a short distance north of

NOTE 1. See Crumrine's History, Washington county, Pennsylvania, page 104.

what was long known in the early settlement of the country as
Briceland's cross-roads, and the Indians that committed the outrage reached it by crossing the Ohio river at the mouth of
Yellow creek and thence following the well known trail along
the dividing ridge between the waters of King's creek on
the south, and those of Travis creek on the north, until the
advanced settlements were reached, when having killed the
stock and plundered the cabin they set it on fire and retreated by
the same route, carrying with them as prisoners, Mrs. Wallace
and her three children, one being an infant. This soon became
too much of an incumbrance for the mother to carry and keep up
with the party as they feared pursuit and were anxious to reach
the river and cross to the west side, but when they attempted to
take it from her, or dispatch it in her arms, she resisted so vigorously that the Indian having her in charge became enraged and
struck his tomahawk into her own skull. The bodies of mother
and child were then carefully hidden, that they might not aid the
pursuit, and remained concealed until found years afterward.

The Indian trail followed by this party, and within a few
rods of which the remains of Mrs. Wallace* were afterward
found, was as much as twenty-five or thirty miles further north
than the one followed by the Moravian expedition through
Mingo, hence the absurdity of finding the body of either mother
or child impaled by the wayside.

At the date of the massacre, Robert Wallace did not know
that his wife was dead, but supposed her to be a prisoner among
the Indians, nor did he learn otherwise until nearly three years
afterward, when an Indian trader who had been among the
Wyandots at Sandusky, learned that his younger son (Robert)
was still living, but that the elder one was dead, and that the
mother and youngest child had been killed before reaching the
Ohio River, as has been stated. In a letter written by the Lieutenant of Washington county, Pennsylvania, addressed to Gen-

---

*NOTE—Her maiden name was Jane McKay, and Mr. Wallace always
insisted that she could easily have kept up with the party and carried her
babe, had it not been that an old pair of shoes she happened to have on
that day impeded her, as she was a strong, hearty woman. (Statement of
her surviving son, Robert.)

eral Irvine, and dated October 21st, 1782, it appears that at that time, more than eight months after the capture, Wallace believed his wife to be living, and was making efforts, through General Washington, to find out where she was and effect her recovery. He finally secured possession of the younger boy, and ascertained about the locality where the mother and child had been killed, when he made search and found the remains, which he gathered up carefully, carried back to his home and buried in the graveyard at Cross Creek, Pennsylvania.

In 1792 he married Mary Walker, by whom he had five children, and died in 1808 at the age of seventy-three years. He is buried in the old cross-roads burying ground at Florence, Pennsylvania.

Robert Wallace

The son Robert, redeemed from the Wyandotts, lived to be seventy-seven years of age, and died in 1855. He had a large scar on his right ear, given him while a prisoner, made by a squaw who became offended and swore she would kill him, but was prevented by another Indian from doing so.

Whoever follows the affair carefully from beginning to end, will be convinced that the massacre was no accident or after-thought, but the result of a fixed and predetermined purpose, of which there is conclusive evidence, traditional, to be sure, but of the most reliable character.

The Lyles removed from Northampton county, Pennsylvania, to the headwaters of Cross Creek, in 1784, two years after the Moravian massacre took place. East of the mountains the affair was almost universally condemned as being an inhuman outrage, and Robert Lyle so continued to speak of it after his removal west, but was soon given to understand that he must not so express himself, as public opinion would not permit it.

In 1792, Robert Lyle and Joseph Vance, the proprietor of Vance's Fort, who had become brother church members and

fast friends, were riding together in advance of the funeral procession of David Hays, when Lyle asked his friend if the deceased had not been a member of the Moravian expedition, to

Joseph Vance

which Vance replied, "No, he was not," and after a few minutes' silence said, "Did you ever know how that affair happened?" and then went on to say that it originated in Vance's
Fort in the fall of 1781, at a time when some twenty-five or
thirty families were forting from the Indians. The opinion
had long prevailed among the frontier settlers that the half-
way houses, as they characterized the villages on the Muskingum, were simply resting places for the Sandusky warriors on their plundering raids into the settlements, and that
the settlers would get no permanent relief until those villages·
were broken up and destroyed. The military authorities at
Fort Pitt knew better, knew that the Moravian missions
were not only what they pretended to be, but that they
had frequently received information from them of Indian
expeditions into the settlements that enabled them to counter-
act and defeat them. But they dared not communicate the
same to the settlers, as it would have exposed the Missions to
sure destruction by the Sandusky warriors, as eventually happened. Driven from their homes and shut up within the fort,
the men became very impatient and frequently discussed the
situation with much earnestness. Prayer meetings were held
daily, and often in the Vance cabin, which stood outside of but
near to the stockade. After one of these meetings, Vance and
two of his neighbors remained after the others had returned into
the fort, and while talking over their troubles one of them said,
"There is no use in talking, this thing will never be better until
the half-way towns are destroyed." "Yes," replied another,
"and I will be one of a company to go and wipe them out," to
which the others assented, and that then and there the Moravian
Massacre originated. The proposition was thereupon stated to

those in the fort, who approved it and pledged their assistance to carry it into execution, but what steps were taken to communicate with the other frontier settlements and secure their co-operation is not known. The organization was, however, complete, and the intention to move promptly on the half-way towns about to be carried out, when the movement was frustrated for the time being by two companies sent out by the commandant of the Western Department, under Colonel Williamson, for the purpose of taking the Indians at the Muskingum towns back to Fort Pitt. The Pennsylvania Archives, page 753, contains what is believed to be a complete roll of these companies, including the names of two captains, two lieutenants, one sergeant and fifty-one privates, but it bears no date and only contains the names of four persons known to have been present at the massacre in March following. But Williamson found himself anticipated by an expedition from Detroit that had already removed the Missionaries and their converts to Sandusky, and finding but half a dozen Indians there, who had either strayed into the place or found their way back after the removal, they were taken back and delivered to the authorities at Fort Pitt, who soon after released them, thereby giving great offense to the settlers, who thought they should have been killed. The authorities were denounced, Williamson severely censured, and the frontier filled with exaggerated rumors of Indian depredations and plots that were really without foundation.

The expedition to the Muskingum was not abandoned, only in abeyance, when the Wallace tragedy set the frontier in a blaze of excitement, the word was passed around, and on Monday, the 4th of March, men in couples, squads and singly, on horseback and on foot, appeared suddenly on the east bank of the river at Mingo, crossed over to the west side, where, when all had assembled, they chose officers, and on the next morning disappeared, going west along the old Moravian trail up Cross Creek. Doddridge says,[1] "They chose their own officers, furnished their own means, and conducted the war in their own way." On Wednesday evening they encamped within one mile

---

NOTE 1. — See Doddridge's Revised History, p. 256.

of the middle Moravian village, but carefully concealed their approach until the next morning, when, having discovered that some of the Indians were at work on the west side of the river, they divided their force, part of which crossed the river, when they approached the town from different directions. To show the purpose with which they went there to be murder, and murder only, the party that crossed to the west side killed and scalped the first Indian they saw, while he was pleading with them not to kill him, that he was the son of John Schebosh, a well-known Christian convert. Others were shot and killed before the town was entered, proving that it was not the sight of what was found in the town that induced the killing.

They deliberated all day of the 7th while waiting for the return of the parties sent out to bring in the Indians from Salem and Schoenbrun, and it was during this delay that some of the better element among them began to relent, to realize that they had misjudged the Moravians, and that it would not do to kill them.

Among others who had joined the expedition burning with revenge, was a young preacher whose affianced bride had been carried off a prisoner by Indians, but the prayers and songs of the poor creatures softened his heart and turned aside his wrath, until he not only voted to take them prisoners to Fort Pitt, but remonstrated against the killing; all in vain; the demon had been roused, and only blood could stay his hand. Whether Colonel Williamson witnessed the slaughter or retired from the scene with those who voted against it, we are not told, but to those who have visited the place and are familiar with the locality, that excuse is valueless.

The river on the west side of the village runs deep in the earth, and it was under the bank where the eighteen retired, distant by measurement not more than seventy-five yards from the church out of which the victims were dragged to the slaughter houses. Standing there, they could not see, but could distinctly hear all that was going on above. And one of those who stood there and lived to be the last survivor of the eighteen, has told persons yet living, that while so waiting, a young Indian escaped from his murderers, and all covered with blood, came running to the river, plunged in and swam to the other side and was already clambering up the bank, when one of the party raised his gun and shot him through the body.

Of the details of the massacre little is known. The survivor of the eighteen referred to, who died in 1839 at the age of ninety-six years, said that after all was over, Robert Wallace came to where several of the company, including himself, were standing, and bursting into a flood of tears, said: "You know I couldn't help it!" His clothing was soiled and bloody, and he was laboring under great excitement and exhaustion.

Gathering together the plunder found at the village, and fastening it upon the backs of their horses, they set fire to the houses and set out upon their return. They must have traveled nearly all night, for they reached Mingo late in the afternoon of Saturday, where they halted only long enough to readjust the packages of plunder to their horses, when they recrossed the river and disappeared from the public notice almost as completely as if they had perished in crossing the stream.

Whether they had agreed among themselves to say nothing is not known, but it is more than likely that on the way back to the river they had begun to realize what they had done, that they would be called to account for it by the military authorities at Fort Pitt, and therefore the less said about it the better. And no expedition of equal importance, military or civil, so suddenly and so entirely disappeared from public notice. Even the families of many of the members being entirely ignorant of their connection with the affair.

One example may be given; a colored man (the slave of one of the parties) who died in 1812, was wont to tell that upon going to the stable one Monday morning, he discovered that the horse his master usually rode when absent on hunting or scouting expeditions, was missing from his accustomed place, but as such things were not uncommon, nothing was thought of it, nor did any member of the family speak of it. But on the next Sunday morning, upon going to the same place, the horse was found in his stall, bearing marks of hard usage, and his sides and flanks streaked with blood; that nothing was seen of his master until the following morning, when he shaved, washed and dressed himself carefully and ate his breakfast, after which all the family were called in to prayers, and that during the day his master busied himself in stretching a couple of scalps upon a hoop, which was then hung up in the great wooden chimney to dry.

Although born and raised in the community from which the expedition was mostly raised, the writer, in a peried of forty years, has only been able to collect the names of about thirty persons that he has reason to believe were members of the ex- pedition, and as to only a few of those is there absolute certainty.

A gentleman born in 1796 said that he was present at Bur- gettstown, Pennsylvania, in August, 1812, upon the day when volunteers were raised to march to Detroit to repel the British and Indians reported to be marching upon the frontiers in con- sequence of Hull's surrender of the post at Detroit. It was a day of great excitement, and called together a large crowd of people from the surrounding country. That among other sights that drew the attention of a boy of sixteen years, he came across a crowd being entertained by an old man much the worse for liquor, who was singing maudlin songs, when some person said, "Now, Uncle Sol, show us how they killed the Indians." That at once the old fellow's whole manner changed from the gay to the grave, and he began crying and cursing the cowards who killed women and children. Presently he ran forward, making motions as if throwing a rope over the heads of those in front of him, and then running backwards as if dragging an object after him, seized the large stick held in his hands, and be- gan beating an imaginary object, all the time howling and curs- ing like a demon, when somebody pulled him away, saying it was a shame. That having but imperfectly comprehended what he saw, my informant made inquiry, and learned that Uncle Sol had been at the Moravian Massacre, and when in his cups, as he had seen him, would show how they killed the Indians, but when sober could not be induced to open his mouth upon the subject.

But little more remains to be said. None of the excuses urged in extenuation of the affair are tenable. No murder was ever so well kept. The early historians were meagre and indefinite in their accounts of it, because there was nothing known to tell, and it was only after half a century that a few details leaked out and became known, as already stated.

The Sandusky expedition followed so soon after, with Colonel Williamson second in command, that many of the same persons joined it and took part in the disastrous defeat at Sandusky, resulting in the terrible death of the commanding officer, who was burned at the stake in retaliation for the Moravian Massacre, and in the shocking details of his sufferings and death the Moravian affair was lost sight of and forgotten.

The men concerned in the affair returned to their homes, where many of them lived to a good old age and spent exemplary lives, a number having become ruling elders and leading members in the churches at Cross Creek, Upper Buffalo, and other places. And it is a curious fact that in the great religious movement that swept over Western Pennsylvania during the latter part of the eighteenth and beginning of the nineteenth centuries, many of these same men were active and leading participants; and that the great religious movement had its origin at Vance's Fort* and among the same men with whom the Moravian Massacre originated. But time has drawn the veil of oblivion over their names and nothing could now be gained by removing it.

Ninety years after the occurrence of this sad event the Moravian brethren met at Gnadenhutten, and with appropriate ceremonies dedicated a monument to the memory of the poor Indian converts who perished there with a heroism worthy of all praise.

This monument stands upon the site of the old Mission Church, and the shaft, which rises 25 feet above the base, was unveiled by four Moravian Indians, one of whom was the great-grandson of Joseph Schebosh, the first victim of the Massacre. On its western face the shaft bears this inscription:

---

* See historical discourse of Rev. John Stockton, D. D., on fortieth anniversary of his ministry at Cross Creek, Pa., page 7.

HERE

TRIUMPHED IN DEATH,

NINETY

CHRISTIAN INDIANS,

MARCH 8, 1782.

In the address of Bishop DeSchweinitz, delivered on that occasion, the names of the victims were given and are herein copied that they may go upon record and never be forgotten.

NAMES OF THE VICTIMS OF THE MASSACRE.

Members of the Gnadenhutten Mission.

1. JOSEPH SCHEBOSH, a half-breed, son of John Joseph Schebosh or John Bull (which was his real name), a white man and assistant Missionary.

2. CHRISTIANA, his wife, a Sopus Indian from New England.

3. JOHN MARTIN, a distinguished national assistant.

4 and 5. LUKE, and his wife, LUCIA.

6, 7 and 8. PHILIP and his wife, LOVEL, and their little daughter, SARAH.

9. ABRAHAM, surnamed the Mohican.

10 and 11. PAUL and ANTHONY, John Martin's sons.

12. CHRISTIANA, a widow, educated in the Moravian schools at Bethlehem, a refined and cultured woman.

13 and 14. MARY, another widow, and her little daughter, HANNAH.

15, 16 and 17. REBECCA, RACHEL and MARIA ELIZABETH, a young daughter of Mark.

18 and 19. GOTTLIEB and BENJAMIN, two little sons of Joanna.

20 and 21. ANTHONY and JOHN THOMAS, two other little boys.

Members of the Salem Mission.

1. ISAAC GLIKKIKAN, one of the most illustrious of Moravian Indians, formerly a great warrior, and after his conversion a faithful assistant of the Missionaries, baptized on Christmas eve, 1779, by Zeisberger, at Friedenstadt.

2. ANNA BENIGNA, his wife, who took the pony of one of the Sandusky warriors and rode all night in order to notify the garrison at Fort McIntosh of the Indian movement upon Fort Henry.

3 and 4. JONAH, another assistant, and his wife AMELIA.

5 and 6. CHRISTIAN and his wife, AUGUSTINA.

7. SAMUEL MORE, a Jersey Indian.

8. TOBIA, a venerable sire.

9. ISRAEL, a celebrated Delaware chief, known as Captain Johnny.

10. MARK, surnamed the Delaware.

11 and 12. ADAM, and his wife CORNELIA.

13 and 14. HENRY, and his wife, JOANNA.

15, 16, 17, 18, 19 and 20. SALOME, PAUL, MICHAEL, PETER, GOTLEIB, DAVID.

21 and 22. LEWIS, and his wife, RUTH.

23 and 24. JOHN, and another John, a young man who was shot after swimming the river.

25. HANNAH, Joseph Peepis' wife.

26. JUDITH, an aged gray-haired widow, the first killed among the women.

27, 28, 29, 30, 31, 32, 33. CATHARINE, MARIA SUSANNA, JULIANA, ELIZABETH, MARTHA, ANNA ROSINA, SALOME, together with the following little boys and girls:

34, 35, 36, 37, 38, 39, 40, 41, 42, 43, 44, 45, 46, 47, 48, 49, 50. CHRISTIAN, JOSEPH, MARK, JONATHAN, CHRISTIAN, GOTT-LIEB, TIMOTHY, JONAH, CHRISTIANA, LEAH, BENIGNA, GER-

TRUDE, CHRISTINA, ANNA CHRISTINA, ANNA, SALOME, and
ANNA ELIZABETH.

Besides these there were five adults, one man, SCHAPPIHIL-
LEN, the husband of Helen, together with four women and thirteen babes not yet baptized, and the following members of the
Mission at Schoenbrun, who happened to be at Gnadenhutten,
to-wit: NICHOLAS and his wife, JOANNA SABINA, ABEL, HEN-
RY, ANNA, and BATHSHEBA, the last two daughters of Joshua,
the founder of Gnadenhutten; in all, twenty-eight men, twenty-
nine women, and thirty-three children. Two boys, Thomas and
Jacob, escaped.

I cannot better close this paper than by quoting the words
of Charles McKnight, who, in his centennial work entitled,
"Our Western Border One Hundred Years Ago," says:

"The whole massacre leaves a stain of deepest dye on the
page of American history. It was simply atrocious and execra-
ble—a blistering disgrace to all concerned, utterly without excuse, and incapable of defense. It damns the memory of each
participator to the last syllable of recorded time. All down the
ages the Massacre of the Innocents will be its only parallel."

WM. M. FARRAR.

THE MILITARY POSTS, FORTS AND BATTLEFIELDS WITHIN THE STATE OF OHIO.

The centennial is approaching of the greatest battle fought
on the soil of Ohio, the battle between the Indians and the army
under General Arthur St. Clair, November 4, 1791. It is well
to note in detail the important military posts in our State. An
examination of the map accompanying this article will show
that not many northwestern states have such a military record.

The accompanying sketches are compiled from so many
sources that it is impossible to give credit to all, and hence none
will be mentioned. The description of each is brief, and confined to the important facts connected with each. On each of
these places pages could be written, but the object of this
article, however, is to place in compact form the salient points

only. The narrative will, as far as possible, follow the chronological order.

FORT MIAMI, the oldest fortification in Ohio, was built by an expedition sent by Frontenac, Governor of Canada, in 1680, as a military trading post, about fifteen miles up the Maumee from its mouth. It stood on the left bank of the river, in what is now Maumee City. It was used but a short time, the trading of the French being moved farther into the Indian country. In 1785 the abandoned fort was rebuilt and occupied by the British, who remained in possession until the treaty of peace with the Indians in 1795. They again occupied the fort during the war of 1812. After its close, the post came into use as a trading place, being such when the Maumee valley was settled by Americans.

FORT SANDUSKY, a small stockade trading place of the French, was built about 1750, on the left bank of the Sandusky River, not far from the site of Sandusky City. It was a trading post only, and was abandoned soon after the Peace of 1763.

LORAMIE'S FORT, as it was called, was originally a trading post, occupied by the English as early as 1750 or 1751 as a trading station. It was then known as Pickawillany. In 1752 the place was attacked by an Indian and French force sent from Canada, the station being considered an encroachment on French territory. Not long after a Candian Frenchman named Loramie, established a store and trading post here, and the place became a hostile center against the American settlements. In 1782, Gen. George Rogers Clarke and a body of Kentucky troops invaded the Miami country and destroyed this post. In 1794, Gen. Wayne built a fort here called "Fort Loramie." The fort became a prominent point on the Greenville Treaty line, and soon afterward was abandoned as a military post.

FORT JUNANDAT. A trading station on the right bank of the Sandusky river, was built about 1754 by French traders. It was occupied but a short time, and with other French posts, was abandoned soon after the close of the French and Indian war.

FORT GOWER—named for Earl Gower—a small stockade, was built by Lord Dunmore, at the mouth of the Hocking river in 1774, when on his march against the Indians in the Northwest Territory. From this place he marched his troops up the river to an encampment—Camp Charlotte—in what is now called Ross county, on the Scioto river, about seven miles south of the present city of Circleville. Here a treaty of peace was concluded with the Indians, and the army returned to Fort Gower, and then to Virginia.

FORT LAURENS—named in honor of the first President of Congress, was erected in the fall of 1778, by a detachment of one thousand men under command of General McIntosh, commander at Fort Pitt, to act as a check on the Indians who were at that time hostile to the Americans, and who gave the western settlements no little cause for alarm. After its completion a garrison of one hundred and fifty men was placed therein, under charge of Col. John Gibson. The Indians attacked the fort in the winter following and gave the garrison much trouble, killing some of the soldiers who ventured outside the walls of the stockade. The Indian siege lasted until late in February, reducing the garrison to close straits. Couriers were sent to General McIntosh, who brought provisions and aid. The fort was evacuated in August, 1779, being untenable at a such a distance on the frontier.

The fort stood "a little below the mouth of Sandy Creek," on the west bank of the Tuscarawas river, half a mile south of the present village Bolivar. The walls were octagonal in shape, enclosing about an acre of ground. The palisades were split tree trunks, inside of which were the soldiers' quarters. Col. Charles Whittlesy visited the spot about the time the canal was made and traced the old embankment now almost obliterated.

FORT HARMAR was built by Maj. John Doughty in the autumn of 1785 at the mouth (right bank) of the Muskingum river. The detachment of United States troops under command of Maj. Doughty, were part of Josiah Harmar's regiment, and hence the fort was named in his honor. The outlines of the fort formed a regular pentagon, including about three quarters of an acre. Its walls were formed of large horizontal timbers, the bastions being about fourteen feet high, set firmly in the earth. In the rear of the fort, Maj. Doughty laid out fine gardens, in which were many peach trees, originating the familiar "Doughty peach." The fort was occupied by a United States garrison until September 1790, when they were ordered to Fort Washington (Cincinnati). A company under Capt. Haskell continued to make the fort headquarters during the Indian war of 1790–95. From the date of the settlement at Marietta across the Muskingum in the spring of 1778, the fort was constantly occupied by settlers, then rapidly filling the country.

FORT STEUBEN was built in 1789, on the site of the present city of Steubenville. It was built of block houses connected by a row of palisades and was one of the early American out-posts in the Northwest Territory. It was garrisoned by a detachment of United States troops under command of Col. Beatty. The post was abandoned soon after Wayne's victory in 1794.

FORT WASHINGTON was built by Maj. John Doughty, who was sent with a detachment of troops from Fort Harmar in September, 1789, to build a fort for the protection of the settlers in the "Symmes Purchase," between the Miami rivers. It was completed during the winter following, and under date of January 14, 1790, Gen. Josiah Harmar wrote that "It is built of hewn timber, a perfect square, two stories high, with four block houses at the angles. The plan is Maj. Doughty's and on account of its superior excellence I have thought proper to honor it with the name *Fort Washington*." This was an important post during the Indian war of 1790–1795, being headquarters for all military operations.

FORT HAMILTON, built in September, 1791, by Gen. Arthur St. Clair, governor of the Northwest Territory and commander of the troops raised to pursue and punish the Indians who the year before broke out in open hostility to the young American settlements. The army under St. Clair had rendezvoused at Fort Washington, and after being divided into three military organizations had started northward into the Indian country. Fort Hamilton, built principally as a depot for supplies, stood

on the east bank of the Great Miami river, on the site of the
present city of Hamilton, Ohio, at the east end of the bridge
connecting Hamilton and Rossville. The fort was a stockade,
somewhat triangular in shape, with four good bastions and plat-
forms for cannon. The officers' quarters were near the river.
Eastward stood the soldiers' barracks and southward was the
magazine. The next summer an addition to the north was
erected by General Williamson, commander of the army. The
fort was occupied until the close of hostilities and was almost
the equal of Fort Washington in importance.

FORT JEFFERSON. This post was erected in 1791 by General St. Clair, forty-four miles north of Fort Hamilton. It
stood in a rich tract of country about six miles south and a little
west of the present city of Greenville. It was used chiefly as a
depot of supplies, and hence was not a fortification nor a place
to harbor troops. No plan of this fort is known to exist, but
examinations have shown it was probably erected somewhat
square within, with projecting corners, these being protected by
block house defenses.

FORT ST. CLAIR was built about a mile north of the site of
the present town of Eaton, in Preble county, in the winter of
1791–92, by a detachment of Gen. Wilkenson's troops under
command of Major John S. Gano. Gen. William Harrison,
then an ensign, commanded the guards each alternate night.
During its building no fires could be built, hence the soldiers
suffered greatly from the cold. The fort was a stockade, used
for storage and supply purposes. On the 6th of November,
1792, a severe battle was fought near the fort between a corps
of riflemen and a body of Indians under command of Little
Turtle, the latter attacking the former about runrise. After
severe fighting the Indians were defeated and driven away, having suffered disastrously in the action.

FORT GREENVILLE, on the site of Greenville, Ohio, was
built in December, 1793, by Gen. Anthony Wayne, while on his
march to the Indian country on the Maumee river. The fort
occupied a large part of the town site, and was an irregular
fortification. It was occupied as a storage place for supplies

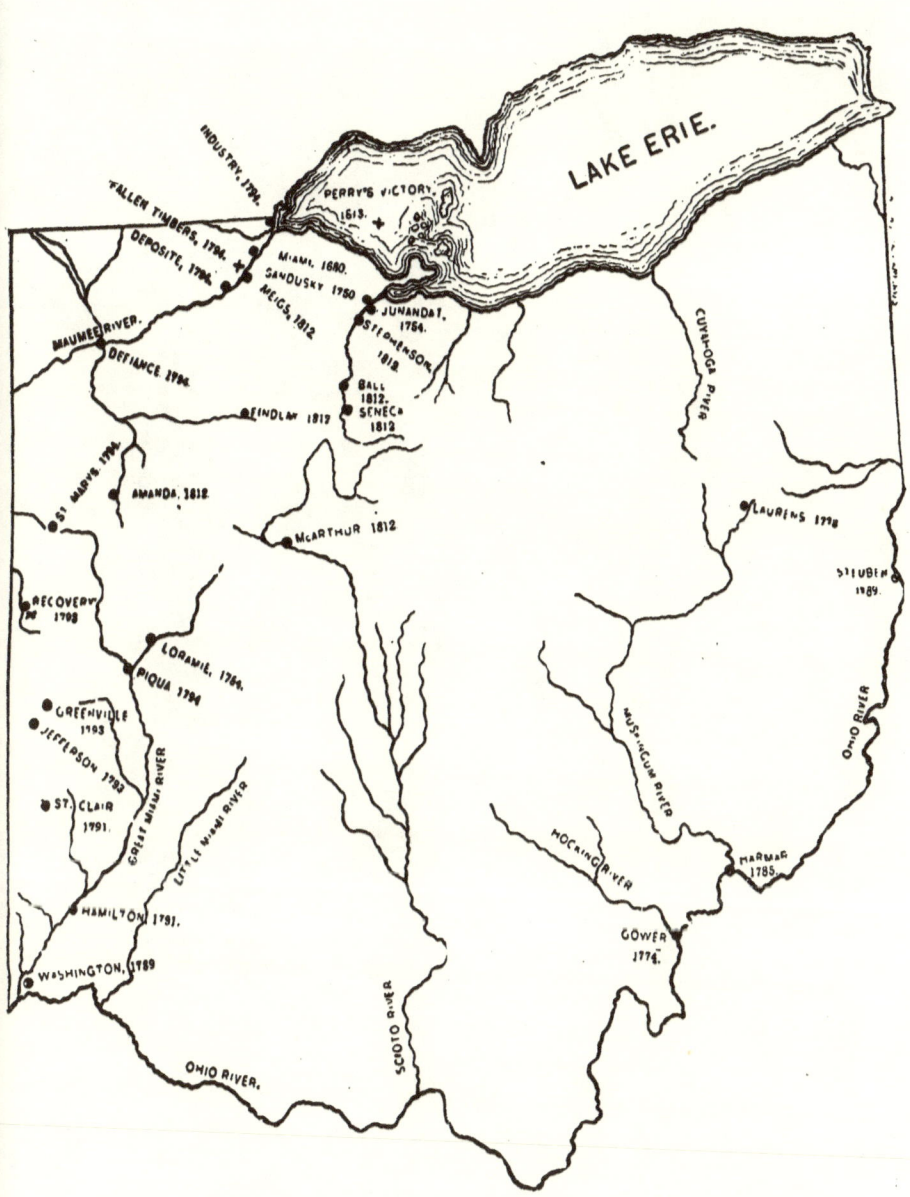

MAP SHOWING MILITARY POSTS, FORTS AND BATTLEFIELDS IN OHIO.

until after the Indians were conquered in the summer of 1794, when General Wayne and his army returned, increased its defenses, and improved its quarters. Rows of log houses were built for the soldiers, and comfortable quarters for the officers. At this fort, in August, 1795, General Wayne concluded a treaty of peace with the following tribes of Indians: Wyandots, Delawares, Shawnees, Ottawas, Chippewa, Pattawatamies, Miamis, Weas, Kickapoos, Piankeshaws and Kaskaskias. In all, about thirteen hundred persons. The geographical limits of these tribes included the country north of the Ohio river, westward to the Mississippi. The Indian boundary line established at this time began at "the mouth of the Cuyahoga river, thence up the same to the Portage between that and the Tuscarawas branch of the Muskingum; thence down that branch to the crossing place above Fort Lawrence; thence southwesterly to a fork of that branch of the Great Miami river running into the Ohio, at or near which fort stood Loramie's store, and where commenced the portage between the Miami and the Ohio and St. Mary's river, which is a branch of the Miami (Maumee) which runs into Lake Erie; thence northwest to Fort Recovery, which stands on a branch of the Wabash; thence southwesterly in a direct line to the Ohio so as to intersect that river opposite the mouth of the Kentucke or Cuttawa river."

No plan of the fort other than that of the survey made by James McBride of Hamilton, can be found. The embankments could plainly be seen in many places as late as 1840. It was a large irregular work, not only a fortification, but a depot of supplies and a rendezvous for the army. After the Treaty of 1795 it was soon abandoned.

FORT RECOVERY was erected in December, 1793, by a detachment of troops from Gen. Wayne's army. The troops arrived Christmas day, and built at once a stockade on the site of the disastrous defeat of Gen. Arthur St. Clair by the Indians, November 4th of 1791. No plan of this stockade has been preserved, and but little regarding its construction is known. It stood on the left bank of the river (the Wabash) and was, no doubt, somewhat octagonal in shape, the corners protected by

block houses.   The palisades forming its walks were firmly set
in a small embankment made by digging a trench about the circumference.   On June 30, 1794, while the main army was still at
Fort Greenville, the detachment at Fort Recovery was subjected
to a short but severe siege by the Indians, whose actions showed
them to be under superior leadership, probably British.   The
fort was used but little after 1794, being simply a "way station"
for supplies for the army.

Fort Recovery occupied the site of the greatest and most
disastrous defeat of Americans by the Indians in western history.
Gen. St. Clair, with his army, gathered hastily in Pennsylvania,
Maryland and Virginia, had left, after an imperfect organization,
Fort Washington in August, 1791; moved forward Ludlow's station six miles distant, remaining there until September 17th.
From there the army moved farther up the Great Miami, erecting first Fort Hamilton (already noticed), thence to Fort Jefferson, which they left October 24th, and began their march farther
northward, expecting to find the Indians in the country about
the head waters of the Maumee.   On the 3rd of November the
army reached the banks of a small river, supposed to be the St.
Mary's, but really the head waters of the Wabash river.   That
afternoon the army camped in a commanding rise of ground, the
river in the front.   The militia had gone about a mile farther,
crossing the river, and a low wooded meadow half a mile wide,
and camped in the forest on the high land beyond.   It was the
intention of Gen. St. Clair to fortify this position and await the
arrival of the first regiment sent back at Fort Jefferson for provisions.   Weary with their march the soldiers lay down to rest.
About daylight the next morning, just after the parade, and as
the soldiers were preparing their breakfast, the militia were suddenly and vigorously attacked by an unseen foe, and becoming
frightened, ran back toward the camp of the regular troops.
The onslaught was checked by the first line of troops, but soon
a heavy and constant firing came from all quarters, and, concen-
trating upon the artillery stationed in the center, soon silenced it
by killing the gunners and wounding and killing the horses.
The artillery being useless, several vicious onslaughts were
made, and though repulsed again and again, the wary foe steadily

gained ground. A retreat was necessary and was ordered. A panic seized the soldiers and the retreat became a disorderly and unmanageable rout. The soldiers and camp followers fled in great confusion, despite all attempts of the officers, many of whom were slain while in their efforts to restore order. The fire of the savages had been fearfully destructive; fully 600 persons perished, and of those wounded none were spared the horrible tortures of Indian warfare. The army fled precipitately to Fort Jefferson, where, meeting the first regiment, they were stayed, and where an account was taken of their awful losses. From this place they retreated to Forts Hamilton and Washington, and further attempts to conquer the Indians were, for a time, abandoned.

FORT PIQUA was a small 'stockade built for storage purposes by General Wayne's army in 1794, in what is now Miami county, about three miles north of Piqua. It was in the portage between Fort Loramie and St. Mary's. The garrison was under command of Captain J. N. Vischer. After the treaty of peace in 1795, the place was abandoned.

FORT ST. MARYS was built by a detachment of General Wayne's army in 1794 on the site of the town of St. Marys in Mercer county. It stood on the west bank of the St. Marys river. It was erected as a supply depot, and was under command of Captain John Whistler, during what time the garrison was kept within its palisades.

FORT DEFIANCE was built by General Wayne's army in August, 1794, when on their march against the Indians. It stood in the angle formed by the junction of the Auglaize and Maumee rivers. The fort was built in the form of a square, at each corner of which were block houses projecting beyond the sides of the fort, thus protecting the external sides. These block houses were connected by a line of strong pickets. Outside of these, and also of the block houses, was a wall of earth eight feet thick, a ditch fifteen feet wide and eight feet deep surrounding the whole except the side next the Auglaize river. The stockade was well built, characteristic of the General's actions, affording the garrison which might occupy it a safe retreat. It was little used after the treaty of peace in 1795.

FORT DEPOSIT was built by General Wayne in August, 1794, as a depot for supplies. It stood on the left (north) bank of the Maumee. No plan of the fort exists. It was simply a palisaded stockade, built for storage and not for defensive purposes. Leaving this place, General Wayne marched toward the Indian encampment, about two miles south of the present town of Maumee City, and about four miles from Fort Miami, erected and occupied by British troops. The Indians were met and a decisive battle fought, a complete victory being gained by the Americans.

THE BATTLE OF FALLEN TIMBERS. This famous battle decided the fate of the Indians in the Northwest. Their power was broken, and after the treaty at Fort Greenville the next summer, their claims to Ohio's territory were practically ended. The battle occurred August 20, 1794. That morning, General Wayne having decided his plan of operations, moved from Fort Deposit down the left bank of the Maumee toward the Indians, who had refused all overtures of peace, and who were arranged in camps on the river bluffs. The army had marched about five miles when the advance guard was suddenly attacked by a vigorous fire from an unseen foe, and was compelled to fall back. The army was at once formed in two lines in a dense wood on the borders of a swampy prairie, where a tornado had at some preceding time blown down many trees. This fallen timber gave the name to the battle-ground. This timber afforded good shelter to the foe, who were aided by many Canadians, all under superior discipline. General Wayne's troops fell upon them with relentless fury, and in a short time put them to flight toward the guns of Fort Miami, a few miles down the river, and then garrisoned by a British force under command of Major Campbell. Wayne's army pursued the Indians under the very walls of the fort, despite the protests of the British commander and the British trader, Colonel McKee, whose property was destroyed, General Wayne maintaining the attitude that the fort stood upon American soil. For three days and nights this warfare was continued until the Indians were thoroughly subdued, and promised, through their chiefs, to treat for peace the next year at Fort Greenville. At this battle the celebrated chief, Turkey Foot, was slain, whose rock, marked by prints resembling turkeys' feet, perpetuates his memory and his death.

FORT WAYNE. Though not in the confines of Ohio, it should be mentioned here. At the junction of the St. Joseph and St. Marys rivers, the head of the Miami of the lakes—the Maumee—it appears in French history, first as a trading post and station. After the defeat of the battle of Fallen Timbers, General Wayne's army went first to Fort Defiance, and soon after, in September, to the head of the Maumee, and there built a strong fortification, calling it Fort Wayne. It was completed by the 22d of October, and garrisoned with infantry and artillery, under command of Colonel John Francis Hamtranck. Soon after the treaty at Greenville, in 1795, the fort was practically abandoned, though the place was always well noticed as a great outpost. In the war of 1812 the fort was built new, became a conspicuous place, and withstood several sieges. It was an excellent fortification, and after peace was declared in this war, became a peaceful trading village, and is now a prosperous city.

FORT INDUSTRY was built by a detachment of Wayne's troops soon after his victory over the Indians. It stood on a bluff on the left bank of the Maumee, a few miles above its mouth, in what is now the city of Toledo. It seems to have been used but a short time.

FORT FINDLAY, a small stockade about fifty yards square, was built on the south side of Blanchard's Fork, in what is now Hancock county, during the war of 1812. At each corner was a block House, the soldiers' quarters and the palisades protecting the other portions. It was, like many others of its nature, erected as a supply depot, and was little used for defensive purposes. It was abandoned at the close of the war.

FORT AMANDA, a small stockade, was built during the war of 1812, in what is now Allen county, on the west bank of the

Auglaize River, near the west line of the county, on the site of an old Ottawa town.   It was used but a short time as a supply depot and a halting place for the troops.

FORT MCARTHUR was built during the war of 1812, on the Scioto River, in what is now Hardin county.   It was a stockade enclosing about half an acre.   A block house in the northwest and southeast angles, a row of log cribs covered with "shed" roofs sloping inward, and palisades completed its defenses.   The soldiers' huts were just inside the palisades.   It was in a dangerous locality and more than once was attacked by Indians.   The garrison was commanded by Captain Robert McClelland.   After the war the post was abandoned.

FORT BALL was built during the war of 1812 by a detachment of General Harrison's army, on the west bank of the Sandusky River, in what is now the city of Tiffin.   It was a small stockade, enclosing perhaps one-third of an acre, and was used as a supply depot.

FORT SENECA was built during the war of 1812, by a detachment of Gen. Harrison's army, as a depot for supplies.   It was a stockade, including several acres, and stood on the right bank of the Sandusky, a few miles above Fort Stevenson.   It was used only during the war.

FORT STEVENSON was built during the war of 1812 at the head of navigation on the Sandusky river, on the site of the present city of Fremont.   The fort was a well built structure, enclosing an acre of ground.   Col. George Croghan, the commander, with a small body of troops, on the 2d of August, 1813, successfully defended the fort against a vigorous attack of the British and Indians.   Commanded by Gen. Proctor, the British force consisted of some five hundred regulars and eight hundred Indians, their gun boats from the river carrying five six-pound guns, and their howitzer on shore, bombarded the fort all night of the first.   The next day the enemy massed his troops at one angle of the fort and attempted to capture it by assault.   The one six-pound gun of the garrison, loaded with small missiles, was discharged into their ranks when they neared the fort, with such fearful destruction, that with the effective fire of the soldiers they were repulsed, and retreated. Soon after, fearing an attack by General Harrison, whose troops had so valiantly defended Fort Meigs but a few days before against the same foe, they suddenly retreated, leaving the gallant Croghan and his handful of men in victorious possession of the fort. After the war the post was abandoned.

FORT MEIGS was built by Gen. William Henry Harrison, in the winter of 1812–13, on the right bank of the Maumee, opposite the rapids. It was a large palisaded ground, occupying about ten acres in all, protected by block houses, soldiers' barracks, and a strong line of palisades. Early in the summer of 1813 the fort was attacked by a large force of British and Indians under Gen. Proctor, who formed artillery encampments on both sides of the river. Reinforcements came, and the British were repulsed in July. It became an important frontier post, and after peace came was abandoned.

PERRY'S VICTORY.— This remarkable victory occurred on the waters of Lake Erie, September 10, 1813. At ten o'clock on that day Commodore Oliver H. Perry, in command of the United States lake squadron, consisting of two ships, the Lawrence and the Niagara, and four small vessels, formed in line and advanced to attack the British squadron. The action was sharp and decisive, and lasted only three hours, resulting in the capture of the enemy. The losses of both combatants on the leading ships were heavy. Commodore Perry's memorable dispatch reporting the victory to General Harrison is well known in American annals: "We have met the enemy and they are ours; two ships, two brigs, one schooner and one sloop."

A large painting in the rotunda of Ohio's capitol represents the conflict at the time Commodore Perry is leaving the Lawrence, almost disabled, for the Niagara.

A. A. GRAHAM.

FORT ANCIENT.

The General Assembly at the last session passed an act to purchase this remarkable earth-work on the bluffs on the left bank of the Little Miami river in Warren county. By some oversight, the number of acres authorized to be purchased did not include the entire fortification, and there still remains a portion of the south or "old" fort and little of the north end unpurchased. A bill was afterward introduced by Senator Jesse N. Oren, through whom the first bill was introduced, to buy the remainder; but by an oversight it was omitted in report of the House Committee, after having passed the Senate. The measure will be again introduced at the coming session, and it is confidently believed the next General Assembly will complete the work. The "care and control of Fort Ancient was," by another act of the Assembly, "vested in the Trustees of the Ohio Archæological and Historical Society." The trustees have accepted the trust, and placed the Fort in charge of a committee, consisting of Jesse N. Oren of Wilmington, Israel Harris of Waynesville, and Israel Williams of Hamilton. A competent custodian has been placed in charge of the grounds, and will proceed at once to put the same in proper keeping. In time, it is hoped to have a fine park here, such as is now the "Serpent Mound Park" in Adams county, enclosing the famous effigy of the serpent.

Mr. Warren K. Moorehead, of Xenia, has spent almost a year measuring, surveying, and exploring Fort Ancient. He has written a very creditable work of 130 pages on the subject, and at my request has furnished the following brief description of the fort. The following map used to illustrate this article is a reduced copy of the large map in his work.

A. A. GRAHAM.

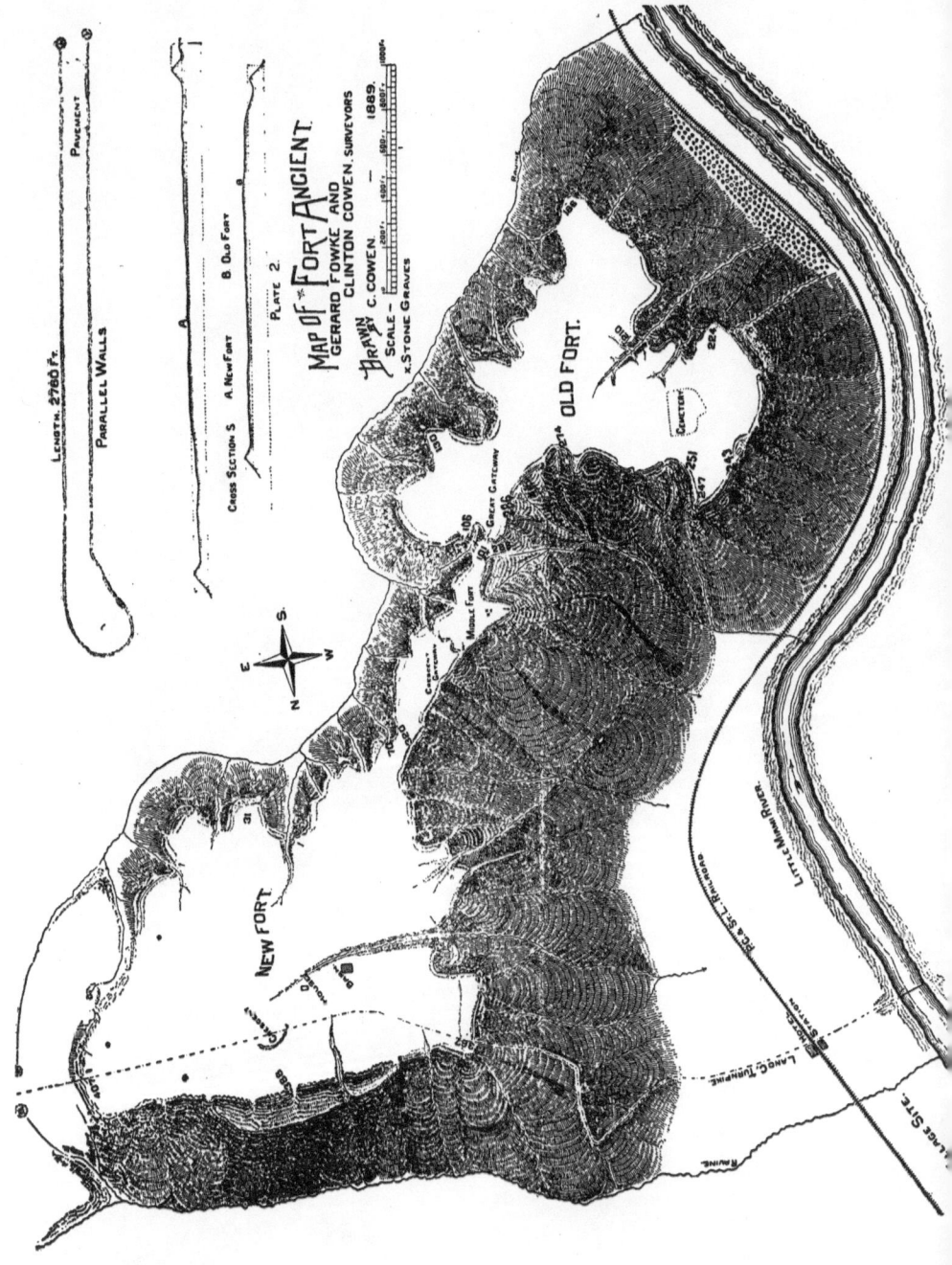

MAP OF FORT ANCIENT.
GERARD FOWKE AND
CLINTON COWEN, SURVEYORS.

DRAWN C. COWEN ——— 1889.
SCALE —

PLATE 2.

CROSS SECTION S   A. NEW FORT   B. OLD FORT

PARALLEL WALLS

LENGTH. 2760 FT.

PAVEMENT

× STONE GRAVES

OLD FORT.

CEMETERY.

MIDDLE FORT.

GREAT GATEWAY

CROSSING

NEW FORT

LITTLE MIAMI RIVER.

LANGE C. TURNPIKE

STATION

P.C. & ST.L. RAILWAY

RAVINE

LANGE SITE.

FORT ANCIENT, AN OUTLINE DESCRIPTION.

The accompanying map from the survey made under my direction by Messrs. Fowke and Cowen will acquaint the reader with the hillsides and the embankments. The walls run in very crooked lines, always following the brink of deep ravines, twisting and turning in the directions which would afford best protection. The following briefly narrated facts regarding the embankments should be carefully noted.

The composition is tough, glacial clay. A stone wall is frequently found within the earth embankment. The stones average in size 14x20 to 9x14 inches and in places remain standing to a height of eight feet. The earth from the top of the embankment washes down and covers them, hence the wall cannot be witnessed save by excavation.

Height and breadth. The embankments average $13\frac{1}{2}$ feet in height. The average $43\frac{1}{2}$ feet wide at base, 4 feet at summit. Maximum height $33\frac{1}{2}$ feet. Minimum, $4\frac{1}{3}$ feet.

Number of gateways 74.

Number of natural washes, occasionally mistaken for gateways 9.

Average length of walls between gateways, $239\frac{1}{2}$ feet. Height above Atlantic Ocean level, 941 feet.

Divisions. The portion north of the Isthmus is called upon the map New Fort. A better name is South Fort. The central part, Middle Fort; the portion south of Great Gateway has been called Old Fort. A better and not so confusing a name would be South Fort.

Terraces, bastions, etc. There are artificial "roads" or terraces extending around the hillsides on the river side of the fortification. One or two short ones follow the foot of the wall just east ot the Great Gateway for a few hundred yards. These terraces are covered with stone graves. Many spurs or bastions run out for varying distances from each gateway, and overlook or command the ravine. This is particularly true of the great hollow east of the structure, against which the builders seem to have protected themselves with the greatest of care.

Washes and erosion. The fort walls do not easily erode, being composed of very tough clay. They are covered with shrubs and large trees, the roots of the latter, together with grass and moss, forming a considerable protection against storms and wearing paths such as the thousands of visitors to the enclosure would undoubtedly make.

"Some ravines were probably small when the fortification was built, and others were large and deep. The wall was carried across the smaller ones, but stopped on the edge of the bank of the larger ones. Many of these have since washed out, and the washes in some of them are very old. A good idea of the age of this fortification can be obtained by studying these washes.

Length of Embankment. Total length 18,712.2 feet or 3⅔ miles.

Two races fought for position and supremacy at Fort Ancient. The one had a skull of Brachycephalic type, the cranium of the other was Solichocephalic. One buried in hollowed vaults or stone graves, the other underneath small mounds rudely thrown up upon the terraces. Both were savages, the "stone-grave people," being but a degree removed from their enemies in that they were able to construct the fortification.

The proofs of the two races are:

(a)   Two types of crania.
(b)   Two modes of burial.
(c)   Two classes of implements and pottery.
(d)   Two kinds of lodge or house circles.

That neither of these peoples were "civilized" is set forth in the manner employed in the construction of the embankments; in the cemeteries, in the village site debris. Dark patches of earth of the size of peck measure, several of which still retain the *imprint*, the *laced work* of a basket around them, have been found in the walls. In the village sites twenty-seven birds, animals, fish and reptiles in ashes and cooking places have been found, together with a multitude of bone shell, stone and clay objects used by the woman, the man and the child of the fort-construction-period.

We have found a complete chain of testimony regarding the purpose for which the fort was erected, we now know *how* it was built, the characteristics of the builders and their enemies; in short, old Fort Ancient is no longer a mystery. In the near future, the writer hopes to be able to give to the public a lengthy and comprehensive account of the discoveries made this summer.

WARREN K. MOOREHEAD.

THE OHIO

Archæological and Historical Society.

ORGANIZED MARCH 13, 1885.

Articles of Incorporation, Synopsis of By-Laws
and List of Members,

FROM DATE OF ORGANIZATION UNTIL FEBRUARY 19, 1891.

ARTICLES OF INCORPORATION.

The undersigned, citizens of Ohio, having associated themselves together, and desiring to form a corporation, not for profit, under the laws of said State of Ohio, do hereby subscribe and acknowledge the following articles of incorporation:

1. The name of this Society shall be THE OHIO STATE ARCHÆOLOGICAL AND HISTORICAL SOCIETY.

2. Said corporation shall be located and its principal business transacted in the City of Columbus, County of Franklin, and State of Ohio.

3. Said Society is formed for the purpose of promoting a knowledge of Archæology and History, especially in Ohio, by establishing and maintaining a library of books, charts, manuscripts, maps, etc., properly pertaining thereto; a museum of prehistoric relics and natural or other curiosities or specimens of art or nature promotive of the objects of the association — said library and museum to be open to the public on reasonable terms—and by courses of lectures, and publication of books, papers and documents, touching the subjects so specified, with power to receive and hold gifts and devices of real and personal estate for the benefit of such Society, and generally to exercise all the powers legally and properly pertaining thereto.

4. Said Society has no capital stock.

The articles of incorporation were signed by the following

CHARTER MEMBERS.

Allen G. Thurman, Columbus.
John W. Andrews, Columbus.
Hylas Sabine, Richwood.
Charles J. Wetmore, Columbus.
Wm. P. Cutler, Marietta.
John J. Janney, Columbus.
John B. Peaslee, Cincinnati.

Douglas Putnam, Marietta.
Samuel S. Rickly, Columbus.
E. B. Finley, Bucyrus.
Wm. E. Moore, Columbus.
A. W. Jones, Youngstown.
Israel W. Andrews,* Marietta.
N. S. Townshend, Columbus.

* Now deceased.

SYNOPSIS OF THE BY-LAWS.

The members are divided into four classes, *i. e.*: Active Members, Life Members, Corresponding Members and Honorary Members.

Active members pay annually a fee of five dollars, or its equivalent, in donations acceptable to the Society, and are exempt from all dues.

The government of the Society is vested in a board of twenty-one (21) trustees, divided into three classes of seven members each, each serving three years, one class being elected annually. The Society elects five of each class annually; the State, through the Governor, appoints two. Fifteen of the trustees are therefore elective, six appointive. The trustees have entire control of the Society, of its property, and all its interests, and appoint annually all standing committees, elect all officers, etc.

The present Board of Trustees is composed of the following persons:

BOARD OF TRUSTEES.

Elective for three years, terms expire in 1894:

F. C. Sessions, Columbus.

Geo. F. Bareis, Canal Winchester.

A. R. McIntyre, Mt. Vernon.

Calvin S. Brice, Lima.

Robert W. Steele, Dayton.

Appointive:

Charles P. Griffin, Toledo.

Andrew Robeson, Greenville.

Elective, for two years, terms expire in 1893:

N. S. Townshend, Columbus.

E. C. Dawes, Cincinnati.

Geo. F. Wright, Oberlin.

Wm. E. Moore, Columbus.

I. H. Harris, Waynesville.

Appointive :

Israel Williams, Hamilton.   E. B. Lockwood, Batavia.

Elective, for one year, term expires in 1892 :

C. C. Baldwin, Cleveland.   D. J. Ryan, Portsmouth.
M. D. Follett, Marietta.   R. Brinkerhoff, Mansfield.
H. A. Thompson, Westerville.

Appointive:

N. C. Reed, Hudson.   W. J. Gilmore, Columbus.

EXECUTIVE COMMITTEE.

F. C. Sessions,   D. J. Ryan,
W. J. Gilmore,   Wm. E. Moore.
N. S. Townshend,   H. A. Thompson.
S. S. Rickly.

The officers of the Society are elected annually by the Trustees. They are: President, F. C. Sessions; First Vice President, R. Brinkerhoff; Second Vice President, Wm. E. Moore; Secretary, A. A. Graham; Treasurer, S. S. Rickly.

All correspondence and communications regarding the Society and its work should be addressed to the secretary,

A. A. GRAHAM,
Columbus, Ohio.

By authority of the General Assembly the library of the Society is made part of the State Library. A separate room is set appart in the State House for the Museum.

LIST OF MEMBERS OF THE SOCIETY, FROM DATE OF ORGANIZATION, MAY 15 1885, UNTIL FEBRUARY 19, 1891.

HONORARY MEMBERS.

*Baird, Prof. S. F., Washington, D. C.
Bancroft, Hon. Hubert Howe, San Francisco, Cala.
DeReune, Mrs. Mary, Augusta, Ga.
Force, M. F., Sandusky.

Howe, Henry, Columbus.
Nicholson, Jno. P., Philadelphia, Pa.
Smucker, Isaac, Newark.
*Whittlesey, Col. Chas., Cleveland.

CORRESPONDING MEMBERS.

Darling, Chas. W., Oneida, N. Y.
Putnam, Prof. F. W., Cambridge, Mass.
Ward, Mrs. Fanny B., Ravenna.

Thomas, Prof. Cyrus, Washington, D. C.
Powell, J. W., Washington, D. C.
Brock, Dr. R. A., Richmond, Va.

Peet, Rev. Stephen D., Mendon, Ill.

LIFE MEMBERS.

Anderson, James H., Columbus.
Andrews, John W., Columbus.
Arnett, Rev. B. W., Wilberforce.
Avery, Elroy M., Cleveland.

Baldwin, C. C. Cleveland.
Bareis, Geo. F. Canal Winchester.
Barney, E. J., Dayton.
Bartholomew, Prof. Geo. K., Cincinnati.
Brice, Calvin S., Lima,
Brinkerhoff, Roeleff, Mansfield
Brown, Benj. S., Columbus.
Burgess, Solon, Cleveland.

Clarke, Robert, Cincinnati.
Conger, A. L., Akron.
Curry, John, San Francisco, Cala.

Curtis, S. H., Cleveland,
Cutler, Rev. Carroll, Charlotte, N. C

Dana, George, Belpre.
Dawes, E. C., Cincinnati.
DePeyster, J. Watts, Tivoli, N. Y.

Falconer, Dr. Cyrus, Hamilton.
Fertis, Aaron A., Cincinnati.
Foster, Charles, Fostoria.

Gard, D. H., Columbus.
Gardner, Geo. W., Cleveland.
Garfield, Mrs. L. R., Mentor.
Gordon, W. J., Cleveland.
Graham, A. A., Columbus.

Handy, Truman. P., Cleveland.

Hart, Dr. B. F., Marietta.
Hart, Dr. Frank O., West Unity.
Harvey, Thomas W., Painesville.
Hay, John, Washington, D. C.
Hayes, Rutherford B., Fremont.

Jewett, H. J., Lansdown, Md.

*King, Rufus, Cincinnati.

*Lindenberg, Henry, Columbus.

McFarland, Robt. W., Oxford.
McIntire, A. R., Mount Vernon.

Macferson, David, Allegheny City, Pa.
Matthews, E. B., Cincinnati.
Miller, T. Ewing, Columbus.
Miles, W. V., Columbus.
Moore, C. H., Clinton, Ill.
Moore, Rev. Wm. E., Columbus.
Morrison, Rev. N. J., Marietta.
Moses, Thos. F., Urbana.

Neil, Robert E., Columbus.
*Noble, Henry C., Columbus.

Ohio University Library, Oxford.
Outhwaite, Jos. H., Columbus.

Parrott, Chas., Columbus.
Patton, A. G., Columbus.
Peters, O. G., Columbus.
Pocock, Dr. Eli D., Shreve.

Poole, Harwood R., New York.
Putnam, Douglas, Marietta.

Randall, O. E., Columbus.
Reeve, Dr. J. C., Dayton.
Rickly, S. S., Columbus.

Sessions, F. C., Columbus.
Shepard, Dr. W., Columbus.
Sherman, John, Mansfield.
Siebert, John, Columbus.
Sinks, George W., Columbus.
Smith Hiram R., Mansfield.
Smythe, A. H., Columbus.
Southworth, G. C. F., Cleveland.
Sturges, Miss Susan M., Mansfield.
Swayne, Wajer, New York.
Swayne, Noah H., Toledo.

Thresher, E. B., Dayton.
Thurman, Allen G., Columbus.
Tiffin, Miss Diathea M., Chillicothe.

Vance, John L., Gallipolis.
Vincent, H. C., Marietta.
Vincent, O. B., Austin, Nev.

Ward, J. Q. A., New York.
Wetmore, P. M., Columbus.
White, Henry C., Cleveland.
Wing, L. B., Newark.
Wooster University Lib., Wooster.

Yorston, John C., Philadelphia.

ACTIVE MEMBERS.

Acheson, E. F., Washington, Pa.
Alderman, E. R., Marietta.
Andrews, Chas. H., Youngstown.
Andrews, Edw. L., Burton.
Andrews, Gwynne, Columbus.
*Andrews, Dr. Israel W., Marietta.

Andrews, Mrs. I. W., Marietta.
Andrews, Prof. Martin R., Marietta.
Andrews, W. C., New York City.
Armstrong, P. B., New York City.
Au, John H., Ontario.
Axline, Gen. H. A., Columbus.

* Deceased.

Babcock, Rev. Chas. E., Columbus.
Backus, A. L., Toledo.
Baldwin, Dr. J. F., Columbus.
Baldwin, Jos. W., Columbus.
Barger, B. F., Dayton.
Barr, Baldwin, Cincinnati.
Barnett, Gen. James, Cleveland.
*Bates, J. M., Columbus.
Becher, C. R., Cincinnati.
Bedell, Rev. G. Thurston, Gambier.
Bennett, S. W., Bucyrus.
Beresford, Dr. A. E., Germano.
*Bliss, Mrs. Ezra P., Columbus.
Bohl, Henry, Marietta.
Bonham, L. N., Oxford.
Bosworth, C. H., Cincinnati.
*Bosworth, Sala, Cincinnati.
Bowers, W. H., Pomeroy.
Brazee, Jno. S., Lancaster.
Bretts, W. H., Cleveland.
Brickell, W. D., Columbus.
Briggs, J. C., Columbus.
Bright, Geo. W., Columbus.
Brister, E. M. P., Newark.
Bromwell, James C., Washington, D. C.
Brooks, J. T., M., D., Salem.
Brown, Abram, Columbus.
Brown, LeRoy D., Los Angeles, Cal.
Brown, Thos. J., Waynesville.
Brown, W. E., Hamilton.
Brown, W. H., New York City.
Bruck, Philip H., Columbus.
Bruhl, Gustave, Cincinnati.
Brush, Dr. Edward C., Zanesville.
*Bryant, Chas. W. Granville.
Buckingham, Jerome, Newark.
Buell, W. H., Marietta.
Burr, Erasmus, D. D., Portsmouth.
Bushnell, Dr. Wm., Mansfield.
Butler, Cyrus, New York City.
Butler, Theo. H., Columbus.
*Byers, Rev. A. G., Columbus.

Cadwallader, C. D., Marietta.
Campbell, James E., Hamilton.
Candy, Robt., Columbus.
Caylor, E. H., Columbus.
Chamberlain, W. I., Ames, Ia.
Chamberlain, W. H., Cincinnati.
Chapin, John W., Columbus.
Chittenden, H. T., Columbus.
Church, S. H., Pittsburg.
Clark, C. F., M. D., Columbus.
Clogston, Wm., Springfield, Mass.
Cochran, T. J., Cincinnati.
College Library, Athens.
Collins, W. A., Toledo.
Cone, Rev. O., Akron.
Cooper, Dr. Albert, Columbus.
Cooper, Hon. W. C., Mt. Vernon.
Cope, Alexis, Columbus.
Cotton, Dr. D. B., Portsmouth.
Cotton, Dr. J. D., Marietta.
Cotton, Dr. J. T., Charleston, West Virginia.
Cowen, B. J., Cinciunati.
*Cowles, Edwin, Cleveland.
Crall, Leander H., New York City,
Curry, Col. W. L., Marysville.
*Curtis, Henry B., Mt. Vernon.
Curtis, W. F., Marietta.
Cutler, F. J., Marietta.
Cutler, Miss Julia P., Marietta.
Cutler, W. P., Marietta.

*Dann, J. W., Columbus.
*Daugherty, M. A. Columbus.
Davie, Oliver, Columbus.
Davis, Theo. F., Marietta.
Davis, Wm. Henry, Cincinnati.
Dawes, R. R., Marietta.
Day, Prof. L. W., Cleveland.
Dean, Prof. B. S. Hiram.
Delano, Columbus, Mt. Vernon.
Dennison, Mrs. Wm., Columbus.
Denver, J. W., Wilmington.

* Deceased.

Derby, Prof. S. C., Columbus.
Derthick, F. A., Mantua.
Deshler, W. G., Columbus.
*Devereaux, J. H., Cleveland.
Dexter, Julius, Cincinnati.
Dodge, Wilson S., Cleveland.
Donaldson, Thos., Philadelphia, Pa.
Doren, Jno. G., Dayton.
Drinkle, C., Lancaster.
Durrett, R. T., Louisville, Ky.
Dutton, A. S., Cheshire.

Eaton, Rev. John, Marietta.
Eels, Dan P., Cleveland.
Egle, Dr. Wm. H., Harrisburg, Pa.
Ellis, John W., New York City.
Ellis, S. H., Springboro.
Ely, Geo. H., Cleveland.
Ely, Herman, Elyria.
Enos, Miss Helen M., Millersburg.
Evans, Dr. E. S., Columbus.
Ewing, Hugh, Lancaster.

Fairbanks, C. W., Indianapolis, Ind.
*Farquhar, Dr. O. C., Zanesville.
Farrar, Wm., Cambridge.
Fearing, Henry, Harmar.
*Fieser, Frederick, Columbus.
Finch, Dr. D. C., Columbus.
Findley, Sam'l, Akron.
Finley, E. B., Bucyrus.
Firestone, C. D., Columbus.
Follett, Martin D., Marietta.
Foraker, J. B., Cincinnati.
Ford, Geo. H., Burton.
Foster, W. S., Urbana.
Fowke, Gerard, Columbus.
Frame, C., Duncan's Falls.
Freed, A., Lancaster.
Freeman, George D., Columbus.

Gano, John A., Cincinnati.
*Gard, Hiram, Vincent.
Garst, Prof. Henry, Westerville.

Gates, Beman, Marietta.
Gates, N. B., Elyria.
Gayman, B. F., Canal Winchester.
Gilmore, W. E., Chillicothe.
Gilmore, W. J., Columbus.
Gladden, Rev. Washington, Columbus.
Glassford, H. A., New York City.
Glazier, A. W. Belpre.
Godfrey, S. J., Celina.
Goodenough, W. S., Brooklyn, N. Y.
Green, Rev. F. M., Kent.
Gregg, H. H., New Lisbon.
Grover, Rev. J. L., Columbus.

Hall, Theo. Parsons, Detroit, Mich.
Hamilton, Dr. J. W., Columbus.
*Hancock, Prof. John, Columbus.
Harris, Israel H., Waynesfield.
*Harter, G. D., Canton.
Harter, M. D., Mansfield.
Hartzler, Prof. J. C., Newark.
Haskins, Chas. F., Columbus.
Hayden, Rev. H. C., Cleveland.
Hayden, W. B., Columbus.
Haydock, Mrs. T. T., Cincinnati.
Haynes, Henry W., Boston, Mass.
Hedges, Henry, Mansfield.
*Henderson, Dr. J. P., Newville.
Herrick, Dr. L. C., Columbus.
Hills, B. D., Columbus.
Hills, Rev. O. A., Wooster.
Hinman, E. L., Columbus.
Hinsdale, Prof. B. A., Ann Arbor, Mich.
Hirsch, Leo, Columbus.
Hite, J. C., Lancaster.
Hoadley, George, New York City.
Holcomb, A. T. Portsmouth.
Holden, L. E., Cleveland.
*Horton, V. B., Pomeroy.
Hott, Harry H., Gallipolis.
Howe, Frank Henry, Columbus.
Hoyt, James M., Cleveland.

---

* Deceased.

Hughes, Phillip, Hamilton.

*Ide, Mrs. H. E., Columbus.
Irons, Rev. Jno. D., New Concord.

Janney, Jno. J., Columbus.
Jennings, W. H., Columbus.
Jewett, H. J., Lansdown, Md.
Johnson, S. L., Columbus.
Johnston, C. W., Elyria.
Jones, A. W., Youngstown.
Jones, E. A., Massillon.
Jones, J. V., Fostoria.

Kagy, Isaac, Tiffin.
Kelley, H. C., Marietta.
Kemmler, Wm. F., Columbus.
Kinney, Chas., Portsmouth.
Kirkley, C. A., M. D., Toledo.
Kirshner, L. M. D. D., Sulphur
　Springs.
Knabenshue, O. D., Columbus.
Knickerbocker, Dr. B., Columbus.
Knight, Ceo. W., Columbus.

Lane, P. P., Norwood.
Lee, A. E., Columbus.
Leggett, M. D., Cleveland.
Levering, Allen, Mt. Gilead.
Lewis, T. H., St. Paul, Minn.
Librarian, Public Library, Boston,
　Massachusetts.
Librarian, State Library, Boston,
　Massachusetts.
Lieb, Frank, H., Millersport.
Linn, D. B., Zanesville, Ohio.
Little, Dr. James, Logan.
Lockwood, C. B., Cleveland.
Love, N. B. C., Upper Sandusky.
Lovejoy, Mrs. N. E., Columbus.
Loving, Dr. Starling, Columbus.
Loy, Rev. M., Columbus.
Lukens, Prof. J. F., Lebanon.
Luse, L. H., M. D., West Mentor.

Lyman, R. H., Cincinnati.

McClymond, J. W. Massillon.
McCord, David A., Oxford.
McCormick, A. W., Cincinnati.
McCullough, H. J., Delaware.
McCurdy, Robt., Youngstown.
McFadden, H. H., Steubenville.
McFadden, Jno. F., Columbus.
McGettigan, John E., Indianapolis.
McIntosh, Mrs. C. J., Beverly.
McIntosh, Mrs. Eliza, Beverly.
*McIntosh, E. S. Beverly.
McKinley, James, Canton.
McKown, G. E., M. D., Mt. Vernon.
McLean, Rev. J. P., Hamilton.
McMahon, J. A., Dayton.
McMillan, R., Canfield.
McMillan, Emerson, Columbus.
McNeil, Jno. B., Lancaster.
McQuigg, Geo., Pomeroy.
MacCown, Townsend, New York.
　City.
Macauley, Dan'l, Columbus.
Manley, Marcellus, Galion.
Markeson, C. E., Columbus.
Marks, E. N., Louisville, Ky.
Martin, Chas. D. Lancaster.
Mather, Sam'l, Cleveland.
Matthews, Alfred, Painesville.
*Mathews, Stanley, Washington,
　D. C.
May, Manuel, Mansfield.
Meredith, Levi, Van Wert.
Metz, Dr. C. T., Madisonville.
Miesse, Dr. B. F., Chillicothe.
Miller, J. W., Cincinnati.
Miller, Charles. C., Columbus.
Millikin, Dr. Dan'l, Hamilton.
Millikin, Thos., Hamilton.
Mills, Jno., Marietta.
Mills, Wm. M., Marietta.
Mills, W. C. Mt. Vernon.
Mikesell, Thos., Wauseon.

* Deceased.

Moore, T. W., Harmar.
Moore, W., Portsmouth.
Moorehead, Warren K., Xenia.
Morey, Henry L., Hamilton.
Morgan, Geo. W., Mt. Vernon.
Morton, W. H., Columbus.
Munsell, Joel, Sons, Albany, N. Y.
Munson, Chas. E., Columbus.

Nash, Hon. Geo. K., Columbus.
Neil, Moses H., Columbus.
Newberry Library, The, Chicago, Ill.
Nissley, J. R., Ada.
Noble, Warren P., Tiffin.
Norris, Chas. H., Marion.
Nye, A. T., Marietta.

*Olds, C. N., Columbus.
Orton, Prof. Edward, Columbus.

Packard, S. S., New York City.
Palmer, Corwin F., Dresden.
Payne, H. B., Cleveland.
Peabody, Jas. R., Zanesville.
Peabody, S. P., Columbus.
*Pearson, H. W., Toledo.
Peaslee, Jno. B., Cincinnati.
Peet, Charles D., New York City.
Peters, Bernard, Brooklyn, N. Y.
Perkins, Douglas, Cleveland.
Perkins, Henry B., Warren.
Peters, Geo. M., Columbus.
Phillips, D. E., Columbus.
Phillips, R. E., Marietta.
Pillars, James, Lima.
Plimpton, H., Columbus.
Poe, E. W., Columbus.
Poland, William, Chillicothe.
Pratt, Amasa, Columbus.
Priest, F. W., Bryan.
Prince, B. F., Springfield.

Read, M. C., Hudson.

*Reinhard, Jacob, Columbus.
Renick, Alex., Chillicothe.
*Renick, Harness, Circleville.
Rice, Harvey, Cleveland.
Robe, W. H., Cherry Fork.
*Robertson, Andrew J., Sidney.
Robinson, Dr. J. D., Wooster.
Robinson, Gen. Jas. L., Kenton.
Robinson, W. F., Harmar.
Ruggles, C. B., Cincinnati.
Rust, H. N., Columbus.
Ryan, Dan'l J., Columbus.

Sabine, Hylas, Richwood.
*Schenck, Robt. C., Washington, D. C.
Schueller, Dr. J. B., Columbus.
Schultz, W. A., Lancaster.
Scott, Rev. W. H., Columbus.
Scovil, Rev. S. F., Wooster.
Sessions, Mrs. Mary, Columbus.
Shawan, J. A., Columbus.
Smalley, Allen, Upper Sandusky.
Smith, Amos, Chillicothe.
Smith, Rev. N. S., Columbus.
Smith, Wm. Henry, New York City
Smith, W. R., M. D., Hillsboro.
Snyder, Jno. Jr., Springfield.
Snyder, P. M., Marietta.
Spofford, Hon. A. R., Washington, D. C.
Squires, Andrew, Cleveland.
State His. Society, Lincoln, Neb.
State Library Pennsylvania, Harrisburg, Pa.
Steele, Robt. W., Dayton.
Stevenson, Job E., Cincinnati.
Stevenson, R. W., Wichita, Kans.
Stimson, R. M., Marietta.
Sturges, Willis M., Mansfield.
Sturgiss, John E., Mansfield.
Sullivan, J. J., Cleveland.
Sullivant, C. S., Columbus.
Super, Dr. Chas. W., Athens.

*Deceased.

*Swearingen, Henry B., Circleville.

Taggart, J. B., Lewis Center.
Taggart, Rush, New York City.
*Tappan, Eli T., Gambier.
Thompson, Dr. H. A., Westerville.
Thompson, Dr. J. C., Rollersville.
Thompson, Peter G., Cincinnati.
Thompson, Ralph, Springfield.
Thresher, E. M., Dayton.
Thresher, J. B., Dayton.
Tod, Henry, Youngstown.
Todd, Dr. Jas. H., Wooster.
Townsend, Amos, Cleveland.
Townsend, Chas., Athens.
Townshend, Dr. N. S., Columbus.
Turner, S. R., Marietta.
Twiss, George E., Columbus.
Tyler, J. H., Napoleon.
Twitchell, Dr. H. E.

Vail, Harry H., Cincinnati.
Van Horne, Rev. Thos. B., Columbus.
Van Metre, S. R., Marietta.
Venable, W. H., Cincinnati.

Waddell, Dr. Wm., Chillicothe.
Waggoner, Dr. Joseph, Ravenna.
*Waite, M. R., Washington, D. C.
Waite, C. C., Columbus.
Wall, Edw., Columbus.

*Ward, Durbin, Cincinnati.
Warner, A. J., Marietta.
Warner, Dr. R. G., Columbus.
Washburn, Geo. G., Elyria.
Waters, Israel R. Marietta.
Watson, D. K., Columbus.
Welch, Agnew, Ada.
Welker, Martin, Wooster.
Wells, C. K., Marietta.
Wells, M. P., Marietta.
Welsh, J. M., Athens.
*Wetmore, C. J., Columbus.
Wheeler, F. A., Marietta.
Whelpley, W. W., Cincinnati.
*White, Dr. C. C., Columbus.
White, E. E., Cincinnati.
Whitely, Wm. N., Springfield.
Wick, Paul, Youngstown.
Wilcox, J. A., Columbus.
Willard, Rev. Geo. W., Tiffin.
Williams, Hon. A. J., Cleveland.
Williams, T. C., Columbus.
Williams, W. W., Cleveland.
Williams, Israel, Hamilton.
Wilson, A. J., Cincinnati.
Wilttheiss, C. T., Piqua.
*Wing, Chas. B., New York City.
Wright, G. Frederick, Oberlin.
Wright, Jos. F., Cincinnati.
*Wright, Silas H., Lancaster.

Young, Jno. H., Urbana.

---

* Deceased.